ADVENTURES To go
Your Home for Multi-Genre Reading Entertainment.

ADVENTURES *To go*

Your Home for Multi-Genre Reading Entertainment.

COVER PHOTO: Thank you to Jürgen Grunau - Bremen - Germany

IMAGE: Detroit Publishing Co., Copyright Claimant, and Publisher Detroit Publishing Co. A Cape Ann fisherman mending his nets. United States Massachusetts Gloucester, None. [Between 1900 and 1906] Photograph. https://www.loc.gov/item/2016804519/.

WWW.OFFBEATREADS.COM

ADVENTURES *To go*

FALL, 2022   ISSUE #5

WHAT

WHERE

EDITOR'S NOTE

A COUPLE MONTHS AGO, THE TEAM HERE AT OFFBEATREADS SAT DOWN IN THE meeting room. We would not let ourselves be distracted. The sole purpose of the meeting was to look at year one of *Adventures on the Go*, which began with the Fall 2021 Issue. Four issues, one for each quarter, came to pass quickly—and there we sat. Under no rush of time with an informal agenda, we each looked at our individual notes, ready to plan, create, and execute. Anything and everything regarding the future of *Adventures* hung in the sunset light glowing red through two windows. It had already been a long Monday.

Light banter soon shifted to an almost melancholy air. Words were tiptoeing as if coming to the edge of a cliff in the dark. "If anyone here thinks the end is nigh for this labor of love, you're wrong. This is supposed to be a positive meeting," I said. Expressions around the table eased at once.

It is true. We are all bibliophiles in the truest sense. Each member of the OffBeat team collects (hoards) books. We always carry a book wherever we go, as if it is a vital inoculation we must have close by. We all love written stories because they give like nothing else can. Doubt scurried away from the awkward start to the meeting and we got to work. (And next time, I will have at least a loose agenda forwarded to them ahead of the meeting.)

During the meeting, we dived deep into the swampy information compiled from the past year, and we made some decisions. First, the suggested retail price of each issue will remain the same. In the current economy, rising costs with book printers and distributors make this difficult, but we understand the need to be consistent for readers.

This brings me to the next two decisions, the results of which can be seen in this issue. The interior layout of *Adventures* is new and more appealing, and the cover design is now classier. Out of four design choices, the one you're holding was unanimously agreed on by twelve people.

The last major decision we made was to rename our multi-genre pulp, *Adventures To Go* (instead of *Adventures on the Go*).

Will *Adventures* ever be monthly or bimonthly? Maybe. No matter what, we will be around to provide a variety of reading entertainment in each issue. We ask for your help by sharing a copy with friends, leaving reviews on Amazon or elsewhere, and writing to me at OffBeatReads@pm.me; *Letter to Editor in subject.*

Thank you for reading,

Robert Kimbrell

ILLUSIONS OF EVIDENCE
ORIGINAL STORY BY KYLE OWENS

"What da ya got, Trapani?"

"White female, thirty-five years old, suicide."

A blond-haired woman was lying on the bed. The covers were wrapped around her waist. A single pillow was on the bed, behind her. A .357 magnum revolver with a six-inch barrel was in her right

hand, her index finger resting on the trigger. A blue substance stained the back of her gun hand. Fragments of her brain were on the lampshade, night table, floor, and far wall. The closet door was open. The window was closed.

"Name?"

"Juanita Perkins."

"Who found her?"

"The husband, Oscar Perkins."

Detective Takata walked to a dark-brown dresser and saw a half-full pill bottle with Juanita's name printed on it.

"Antidepressants?"

"Yeah. Husband said she had been battling depression. A Doctor Renfro is on the bottle."

Detective Takata turned. He saw two sealed, white business-size envelopes on the window sill. "Vonda" was written on one, and "Mom and Dad" on the other. Cursive writing. Black ink.

"What are these envelopes?"

"Suicide notes, presumably. That's for her sister and parents. She also left one for her husband. He opened it and went outside with it. It was her confession about taking her own life and apologizing for taking the coward's way out."

"Was it written on a computer?"

"No. By hand."

"I want a gun residue test on Mrs. Perkins."

"Why? I mean, it seems obvious she shot herself."

"Never believe the evidence, Trapani."

"If you don't believe the evidence, then what do you believe in?"

"The truth. Where's the husband?"

"Outside. Said he couldn't handle being in here right now."

Takata walked out of the bedroom and into the living room. The TV was in the corner. Pictures of family hung on the walls. The front door stood open, but the screen door was closed. A rug sat at the entrance.

Takata walked out the door and onto the porch where moths scrambled around the light. The porch had an empty flower pot on the railing, and a blue swing was anchored to the ceiling.

He made his way toward the garage.

A swoon of stars peppered the night sky. The air was mild, in the upper forties, not bad for Michigan in October. A man sat on the tailgate of his pickup truck facing the open garage doors.

The garage had a 1986 Monte Carlo SS in the other bay. Shelves lined the back wall. Some rat poison sat in the far corner.

"Mr. Perkins, I'm Detective Chen Takata. I'm sorry for your loss."

Perkins was five foot eight. Slight frame. Pale complexion. He had on a white t-shirt, jeans, a baseball cap with the Detroit Tigers logo on it, white socks, and no shoes.

Perkins nodded, though his gaze never left his hands positioned in his lap.

"May I ask you a few questions?"

He nodded again.

Oscar seemed lost. His soul stolen. Too shocked to feel the cool air.

"When did you find your wife?"

"Ten-thirty."

"Were you out tonight?"

"Yeah. I was out with my cousins at the Blue Light cafe. It's about ten minutes from here. She said I could go. I didn't want to, but she encouraged me to—"

"Was your wife going through a difficult period?"

"She had been depressed lately over the loss of our child."

"I see."

"It never came to term. She lost it four months in. It happened almost a year ago, and she never got over it. She became really depressed, but she was seeing a doctor about it and seemed to be getting better. She knew my cousins had asked me to go with them tonight and told me I should go. So I thought I'd go out for a while and play some pool, just me and the guys. At about ten o'clock I called her up just to check on her and let her know that I was going to come home, and she sounded despondent. I excused myself and headed home, and that's when I …"

His voice trailed off. Tears streamed down his cheeks.

"Did she leave you a note?"

"Yes."

He reached down beside him and then gave the note to Detective Takata. The detective looked over it; it did look like a woman's handwriting. And the slant of the writing was the same as it was on the envelopes.

"Did you stop anywhere when you came home after trying to call her?"

"No. I came straight home."

"After you found her, when did you call the police?"

"Right then."

"At ten-thirty?"

"Yes."

Detective Takata walked around the truck and looked into the cab. A large brown paper bag lay on the front passenger floor among fast-food wrappers and empty cups. It was rolled up tight with a clip on it to keep it from unraveling.

"When you found her, did you touch her?"

"No. I saw the wound and immediately knew what happened and went back out of the room. I couldn't handle seeing her like that."

"That's when you called the police?"

"Yes, sir."

"Mr. Perkins, would you object to having a gun residue test performed on you?"

"What?"

"That won't be necessary," said a voice in the dark.

A man walked forward into the garage lights.

"I'm Captain Dillon Adams. I'm sorry for your loss, Mr. Perkins. Detective Takata, may I have a word with you?"

The captain took Takata to the side.

"What are you doing?"

"Trying to solve a crime."

"A crime? It was a suicide."

"No, it wasn't."

"What makes you think that?"

"The scene."

"I've looked at the scene, and it tells me suicide."

"You've been fooled."

"Fooled? How? She left three suicide notes in her own handwriting to her husband, sister, and parents. She has the gun in her hand with her finger still on the trigger. The husband found her. She had been seeing a psychiatrist for depression. How is this not a suicide?"

"You have to find the secrets."

"What?"

"A left-handed person wrote the suicide note. You can tell by the slant of the letters."

"So it's not her handwriting?"

"No, I believe it's her handwriting."

"If it's her handwriting, then it's a suicide. She says in the letters she's sorry for committing the cowardly act, but she sees no way out. That's a suicide."

"Do the gun residue test. That will prove it."

"There's no probable cause for that. Overruled."

The body was taken out on a gurney. The emergency lights flashed about the neighborhood. People gazed out windows. Dogs barked.

The next morning around ten, Takata entered the Blue Light Cafe He walked to the bar and sat down. He looked about the empty room and tried to absorb it all.

Two pool tables stood in the center of the floor. A jukebox sat flush against the east wall. Dust and cigarette smoke stains covered the white blinds.

A heavy-set man walked over to Takata.

"What can I get for you?"

Takata flashed a badge.

"I'm Detective Takata. I'd like to ask you some questions."

"Sure. That seems to be my second job around here. Answering questions for the police."

"What's your name?"

"Everybody calls me Tiny."

"Well, Tiny, do you know an Oscar Perkins?"

"Sure do. He was in here last night."

"Did you know his wife?"

"Only what Oscar told me. She had been depressed and was getting help for it. They lost their baby a while back, and she never got over it. She had gotten real sick when she was pregnant, but no one knew what was wrong with her. When she was in the hospital, she got better, but it was too late for the baby."

"He told you all that?"

"You'd be amazed what people tell a bartender."

"When did Perkins come in last night?"

"Around seven or so. He came in with his cousins. They played pool and drank some beers."

"Did you notice when he left?"

"Which time?"

"He left more than once?"

"Yes, sir. He left at just before nine. He went out the front door, and I saw him outside on his phone. Then he moved out of sight. Later on, I saw him back playing pool with the guys."

"Do you have any idea when that was?"

"It was going on ten. I know the time because the ballgame ended and one of the guys wanted me to check the weather channel. They always give the forecast on the eights. When I turned it, Oscar came over and asked who won the game."

"Did he seem upset or anything?"

"No."

"Was anyone else with him?"

"A woman. He's with a different girl every time he comes in here, you now, kind of a ladies' man."

"Has he been coming in here a lot lately?"

"At least once a week. Sometimes twice."

"Interesting. Do you know the last girl's name?"

"No. Don't really want to either. I think if a man is married, he should stick with her."

"Do you remember what he was wearing?"

"No. But I have security cameras up inside here for insurance reasons. We can go back and look at the footage if you want."

"I want."

The office was small. Cluttered with papers, files, and books. On a shelf was an old dust-drowned TV hooked to a security camera system. It took Tiny some time to find the footage from the previous night.

Oscar was at the pool table at eight forty-nine, then went outside. No one went with him. He didn't come back in until nine thirty-seven. Takata looked at the footage and instantly noticed that Oscar now wore a different shirt than when he left at eight forty-nine. The previous one was dark in color, but this one was white; it was the shirt he was wearing when Takata met him in the back of his truck.

Takata watched more and noted Oscar repeatedly kissed the girl he was with. Then he saw Oscar appeared to be wearing athletic shoes.

"Where are the shoes?" he said to himself out loud.

"What?" asked Tiny.

"You've been a great help. I'm going to need a copy of this footage."

"I can do that."

"By the way, what color is your pool chalk?"

It was noon when Takata walked into his office with a copy of the security footage. He laid it down on his desk, and before he was able to sit down, the phone rang.

"Takata."

"This is Berkley. I did the autopsy on the Perkins woman."

"Anything on the gun residue test?"

"She didn't have any gun residue at all on her hand. All she had on the back of her right hand was some blue chalk."

"Thanks. That clears some things up. I think I need to see a psychiatrist now."

"Me, too."

"Oh, there's something else," added Takata.

"What?"

"I need you to perform an arsenic test on her."

"Are you sure?"

"I am now."

THE EVENING SUNLIGHT PARADED THROUGH A BRAMBLE OF TREES AND ONTO Detective Takata and Doctor Renfro as they stood outside an office building.

"Thank you for meeting me, Doctor Renfro."

"Sure."

"I would like to know about your patient Juanita Perkins."

"I can't give out any private information."

"I understand. All I need to know is if she wrote any suicide notes while under your care?"

The doctor was hesitant to speak.

Takata said, "I don't mean to pry into the doctor-patient relationship, but I need to know this."

"Yes. She did write several suicide notes to members of her family. She had talked about suicide because of her guilt over the loss of her baby. She believed if she hadn't been sick, then the baby would have been okay. She felt like her husband didn't love her anymore and that she should end her life. As an exercise to help her, I told her to write suicide notes and see how that made her feel. She said she felt guilty about it and that it helped to prove to herself that it wasn't the answer to any of her problems."

"Did they ever find out what made her ill?"

"No. But she did start having the symptoms again recently. That made her even more depressed."

"What kind of symptoms?"

"Sick at her stomach. Strident aches and pains. It got so bad that some days she couldn't even get out of bed."

"Thank you, doctor."

"I hope that helped."

"It did."

THE NEXT MORNING BROUGHT DARK CLOUDS AND RAIN. INSIDE THE POLICE interrogation room was Oscar Perkins. He sat in the ten-foot by ten-foot room in a metal folding chair behind a small desk. He wore an orange t-shirt, jeans, and brand-new athletic shoes.

Takata came in with two cups of coffee. Captain Adams was with him.

"Good morning, Oscar," Takata said as he sat down beside the desk, while Adams leaned against that wall.

"Here's your coffee," Takata said.

"Thank you."

Oscar took a sip and sat the cup on the desk.

"I don't understand why I'm here."

"It's about your wife's murder."

"Murder? She committed suicide."

"When you found your wife dead, did you touch her?"

"No. I walked out of the room and called 911. I never went inside."

"You left the Blue Light Cafe at ten?"

"Yeah."

Oscar took another drink of coffee.

"It's ten minutes away?"

"Yeah."

"The nine-one-one call from your home came in at ten forty-five."

"I don't know. I guess. Maybe I got the time wrong. If that's what the record shows, then I believe you."

Oscar took another drink of coffee.

"So when did you place the gun into her hand?"

"What? I didn't do that!"

"Did you play pool at the Blue Light?"

"Yeah."

"Did you use any chalk for the cue stick?"

"Yeah. I mean, I guess."

"Juanita had blue chalk on the back of her hand."

"Well, I … don't—"

"Is that the color of the pool chalk at the Blue Light?"

"I don't—"

"Is your wife right-handed or left-handed?"

"What?"

"Is your wife right-handed or left-handed?"

"Uh, right."

"Your wife is left-handed. You would think that a husband would know that. But I guess when you see a lot of women, you kind of lose track of things like that."

Oscar drank some more coffee.

"You can tell she's left-handed by the lean in the letters of her suicide notes."

"I don't understand your point."

"You left the cafe at eight forty-nine and went home, murdered your wife, made it look like a suicide, changed clothes, and then came back into the pool room at nine thirty-seven. You had to shoot her because the arsenic wasn't working fast enough for you. Although it did kill your baby. Rat poison is quite potent on the unborn."

"This is nonsense! I didn't kill anybody!"

"Hey, you're a young man. You like the ladies. You need your freedom. I understand."

"You don't know what you're talking about! You saw the notes she left. She sealed them into the envelopes and left them for us. She killed herself. I didn't kill anyone."

"She wrote the notes as an exercise under the guidance of her psychiatrist. You found them. I'm guessing that's when you came up with the plan."

Takata took the coffee cup away from Oscar and handed it to Captain Adams, who then left with it.

"Why did he take my coffee?"

"He's going to take the cup to the lab for a DNA test. See, I'm pretty sure you licked those envelopes, and we'll be able to compare the DNA from the cup to the DNA on the envelopes."

Oscar stared down at his hands.

"The truck cab had a paper bag rolled up in the passenger seat. That's where your clothes were, weren't they? Killing someone with a .357 magnum was a little messier than you thought it was going to be, wasn't it? You tried to use a pillow to muffle the sound, but you didn't think about the blood spatter. That's why there was only one pillow on the bed. The shooting was so messy that the blood and brain matter even got on your shoes, and you had to hide them, too."

Oscar said nothing.

"Trapani!"

Officer Trapani walked in.

"Take Mr. Perkins down and book him for murder."

"Yes, sir."

Trapani handcuffed Oscar and took him downstairs to the booking room.

THE FOLLOWING DAY THE SUN BLOOMED SOFTLY INSIDE THE STILL MORN. IN the distance, birds sang until a slammed car door silenced them.

Takata walked into the cemetery and made his way to Juanita Perkins' grave.

"Hello, Juanita, I'm Detective Takata. I was the one in charge of your murder investigation."

He wanted to say something poignant, something reassuring, but his lips didn't move.

Takata knelt and placed a red rose and a pair of white baby shoes on Juanita's grave.

"I got you a rose and a pair of shoes for your baby. It's my way of letting you know that the two of you weren't forgotten by the system."

Strokes of sunlight through the crop of trees softened Takata's hard features. He looked around, taking it all in. A squirrel crested the fence that wrapped the gently sloped manicured grounds before it leaped onto the trunk of an oak tree. The birds regained their courage and called out to one another on the wind.

Takata turned and headed back to his car. He vowed to confront any intruders of the quiet life that shadowed his city.

THE END

KYLE OWENS LIVES IN THE APPALACHIAN HIGHLANDS AND HIS STORIES HAVE appeared in Ahoy Comics, Eastern Iowa Review, Twenty Two Twenty Eight, among others. His novel, *A Mountain Christmas Wedding* was published by Books To Go Now. His cartoon collection, *The New Yorker Hates My Cartoons*, was published by Clash Books.

For more about Kyle visit OffBeatReads.com

ACTRESS ANNE FRANCIS

HISTORICAL EMPORIUM

Est. 2003

Buy at... HISTORICAL EMPORIUM

Whose **REPUTATION** is *celebrated* world-wide as the pre-eminent clothing source for the **ADVENTUROUS** and *Fashionable.*

We are...

REVERED
by our customers

REVILED
by our competitors

RESPECTED
by all who know us

NO LOCAL DEALER CAN COMPETE WITH OUR QUALITY, VARIETY AND INCOMPARIBLE CUSTOMER SERVICE!

ACCEPT NO SUBSTITUTE!
If you require **clothing and supplies** as stylish and **stout-hearted** as you, contact us immediately to be outfitted.

800-997-4311

HistoricalEmporium.com

In 1911, J.R.R. Tolkien and three friends formed the T.C.B.S. (the Tea Club and Barrovian Society). One of these friends, Geoffrey Bache Smith, went to fight in the Battle of the Somme. In December of 1916, Geoffrey died from shrapnel wounds.

A SPRING HARVEST

Geoffrey Bache Smith
Late Lieutenant in the Lancashire Fusiliers

Born
October 18th, 1894

Entered Corpus Christi College, Oxford, as Exhibitioner
October 1913

Received Commission
January 1915

Died of wounds at Warlencourt, France
December 3rd, 1916

First published June 1918

To HIS MOTHER

NOTE

THE POEMS OF THIS BOOK WERE WRITTEN AT VERY VARIOUS TIMES, ONE ("WIND over the Sea") I believe even as early as 1910, but the order in which they are here given is not chronological beyond the fact that the third part contains only poems written after the outbreak of the war. Of these some were written in England (at Oxford in particular), some in Wales and very many during a year in France from November 1915 to December 1916, which was broken by one leave in the middle of May.

"The Burial of Sophocles," which is here placed at the end, was begun before the war and continued at odd times and in various circumstances afterwards; the final version was sent me from the trenches.

Beyond these few facts no prelude and no *envoi* is needed other than those here printed as their author left them.

J. R. R. T.
1918

If there be one among the Muses nine
Loves not so much Completion as the Will,
And less the austere saint than the fond sinner:
Loves scanty ruins, garlanded with years,
Better than lofty palaces entire:
To her I dedicate this spoiled sheaf
Of rime that scarcely came to harvesting.

There is a window here in Magdalen
Composite, methinks, of fragments that stark Mars
Has scattered. Even so my verses be
Composite of memories and half-uttered dreams
Welded together sans due ordinance,
Which might have been far other, but that Mars
Scattered and harried them with his ruthless flail.

A SPRING HARVEST

I. TWO LEGENDS
Glastonbury

Thither through moaning woods came Bedivere,
　　At gloomy breaking of a winter's day,
Weary and travel-stained and sick at heart,
　　With a great wound gotten in that last fray
Ere he stood by, and watched the King depart
　　Down the long, silent reaches of the mere:
And all the earth was sad, and skies were drear,
　　And the wind cried, and chased the relict leaves
Like ships, that the storm-tossed ocean batters and heaves,
　　And they fly before the gale, and the mariners fear.

So he found at the last an hermitage
　　Hard by a little hill, and sheltering trees
That bent gaunt branches in the winter's breeze;
　　And he drew rein, and leant, and struck the door:
Then presently came forth an hermit sage
　　And helped him to dismount with labour sore:
Straight went they in, but Bedivere being lame
　　Stumbled against the open door, and swooned,
And would have fallen, but the hermit caught
　　And laid him gently down; then hurrying brought
From a great chest a cordial, and came
　　That he might drink, and so beheld his wound.

Long time lay Bedivere betwixt life and death,
　　Like a torn traveller on a stormy height
'Twixt one wind and another: till his breath

Came easier, and he prospered. Then did sleep
Bathe him in soothing waters, soft and deep,
    And left him whole, at breaking of the light,
So he beheld the old man, and desired
    That he would tell of whom he was, and whence.

Whereat once more the ancient eyes were fired:
    "I, I was Arthur's bishop, at his court
And in his church I ministered, and thence
    When at the last the whole was overthrown
With wrath and ill designings, straight I sought
    A place where I might die, too feeble grown
To endure a new beginning to my years
    When once the past was lost, and whelmed in tears.
Hither I came, where, in the dawns of time
    Dim peoples, that the very stones forget,
Lived, loved, and fought, and wove the riddling rime
    On a lake island mystically set.
They passed, and after ages manifold
    Came wandering sainted Joseph (even he
That tended God's frail body, and enrolled
    In linen clothes of spiced fragrancy).
He brought the vessel, vanished now from earth
    That wrought destruction to the Table Round,
Since many deemed themselves above their worth
    And sought in vain, and perished ere they found."

Then Bedivere: "Alas the King! I saw
    The unstayed overwhelming tide of war:
And when the opposed standards were unfurled
    Of Arthur and of Mordred, his base son,
Ere yet the noise of battle was begun
    I heard the heralds crying to the world:

"'Ye that have sought out pallid harmonies
    Where never wind blows, save the gentle south:
Ye that have trafficked on the sounding seas
    And fear nor cheerless rains, nor scorching drouth:

"'Ye that have piled the rich, full-ripened crops
    Of word and measure, till the rime, grown proud,

Did straight contemn the leaping mountain tops
    And lose itself in air, and riven cloud:

"'Ye that have lived a dangerous life of war
    Whose speech has been bold words and heady boasts
Gather, for strife and death unknown before,
    Come gather all unto the fronting hosts.'

"I saw the last dim battle in the mist
    There, where a dreary waste of barren sand
Doth mark the ultimate leagues of this fair land;
    Scarce we beheld the foe we struck, or wist
Which party had advantage: like thin wraiths
    Fit to throng Lethe banks the warriors
Struck and o'ercame, or fell, unseen, unwept;
    And alien hopes, lives, peoples, alien faiths
Were all confounded on those desolate shores.
    And ever the mist seethed, and the waves kept
A hollow chanting, as they mourned the end
    Of all mankind, and of created time.
How many fell therein of foe or friend
    I know not, save that when the darkness came
And the mist cleared, I found at last the King,
    His armour and visage fouled with blood and slime,
And fading in his eyes the ancient flame.

"I saw him make on Mordred with his spear,
    And crying 'Tide me death, betide me life,
He shall not live, that wrought the accursed thing,'
    Put a dread ending to the outworn strife.
I saw them fall together, and, drawn near.
    Knew that the King was wounded unto death.

"Then as he drew with growing pain his breath
    I looked, and saw a long, black barge that stole
Across the waters, like a wandering soul
    Returned from the woeful realm, to view
The ancient haunts well-loved that once it knew.
    And when it touched the shallows I did bear
The dying Arthur as he bade, and there
    I placed him 'mid dark forms: I could not tell

Whose they might be; and wept, and breathed farewell."

Then spake the eremite: "Beyond yon door
    There stands a chapel, ancient and weatherworn,
And there did worship in the days of yore
    The sons of kings. The night ere you came hither
I was awakened by the sound of feet.
    And I looked forth, and saw a body borne
By veiled figures straight, as they knew whither,
    In at the chapel gateway. I went down
And found that they had digged a grave, most meet
    For one of saintly life, or king by birth:
They seemed some score, and by blown candles' light
    I saw that each with tears bedewed his gown
Ere sank the corse into the waiting earth,
    Then prayed, and so went out into the night."

Thereon the twain arose, and went straightway
    Toward the old, dim chapel, and beheld
The stone beneath whose length the body lay:
    Kneeling they closely scanned it all, and spelled
Graven in golden character, "Arcturus
    Rex Quondamque Futurus."

Quoth Bedivere:

"Thank God this voice remaineth unto us;
    Now I do mind me of a prophecy
Spoken long since in some emblazoned year,
    How Arthur should escape mortality
And lie beneath the hills, in cavern deep
    Or on some shore, where faery seas do break:
Around him all his warriors shall sleep,
    Who at a great bell's sounding shall awake
What time th' old enemy spreads death and harm
    Thorough his ancient realm, and the last woes
Go over her; his own victorious arm
    Shall rid the stricken land of hate and foes."

So leave we them, each head inaureoled
    With the awakening spring's young sunlight-gold.

Then, on an evening, hurrying footsteps rung
    Without the door, and straight 'twas open flung,
They saw who stood therein, and each one knew
    The face unspared by years and strife and shame,
Pale as the moon is pale on winter nights,
    With deep eyes dreaming like September haze,
Or lit with lust of battle, eyes that few
    Had looked on and forgot; in such wise came
Lancelot, the hero of immortal fights,
    Lancelot, the golden knight of golden days.

"Whence cam'st thou, Lancelot?" "Even from the Queen,
    The Queen that was, whom now a convent's shade
Imprisons, and a dark and tristful veil
    Enwraps those brows, that in old days were seen
Most puissant proud of all that ever made
    The traitor honest, and the valorous frail.

"Yet evermore about her form there clings
    And evermore shall cling, the ancient grace,
Like evening sunlight lingering on the mere:
    And till the end of all created things
There shall be some one found, shall strive to trace
    The immortal loveliness of Guinevere.

"Shall I not mind me of old ecstasies
    In Camelot, beneath the ancient walls,
In shady paths, and marble terraces
    Rose-fragrant, where eternal sunlight falls.
But ah! the last long kiss is ta'en and given,
    And the last look in those unfathomed eyes,
The passionate last embrace is coldly riven,
    And all is grief, beneath the pitiless skies.

"Gods of the burnt-out hearth, the wandered wind,
    Gods of pale dawns that vanished long ago,
Gods of the barren tree, the withered leaf,
    The faded flower, and the ungarnered sheaf,
Gods half-forgot in the wild ages' flow
    Yours, yours am I, that all for nought have sinned."

Spring, summer passed away, and autumn rain
    Swelled the lean brooks, until the gelid year
Shot forth its icy hand, and grasped again.
    Again the hanging clouds were struck and furled
By winds of winter, until skies were clear,
    And there was frost o' nights, and all the world
Lay glistening to the newly risen sun.

Till came that season, wherein solemn days
    Do celebrate the reign on earth begun
Of the most blessed Child, whenas all ways
    Were bound, and all the fields were white with snow.
Then in the chapel at high noon they three
    Offered their quiet orisons and so
Came forth and looked upon the purity,
    And when he saw the fields all stainless-white
Lancelot groaned in spirit, and spake: "How sore
    And no wise joyous to a sinner's sight
Is this dear land, where the snow lies untrod.
    Even so once before the eyes of God
My soul lay all unspotted; now no more."

"Courage, my son, and patience," quoth the sage;
    No sin there is, that shall not lose its stain
Through the great love of God, and His dear Son.
    Repent and be forgiven: know that none
Shall sue before His throne, and sue in vain,
    Nor shall one name be blotted from the page
If he that bears it turn to prayer and tears."

Then Lancelot: "Though through the tale of years
    That still are left before the longed-for earth
Receive my body, I should strive amain
    To slay myself, and gain regenerate birth,
Alas it were all profitless and vain.
    Verily, when I came unto this place
I railed on God, that I had lost my soul
    And nothing gained: until a heavenly grace
Enwrapped me, like some sick man made half whole,
    And now my grief is only for old sin.
But ah, what boots it? Lo, this barren tree

(He touched a shrub that grew beside the door),
This tree, methinks, shall bud and blossom before
    I pass the gates divine, and enter in
To the fair country I must never see."

But even as he spoke, the hand of God
    Worked on the sombre branches, and straightway
They were all green with sap, and bud, and leaf,
    As at the very bidding of the spring,
Burst forth, and soon each tender branch was gay
    With flowers that nodded in the winter's breeze
(So blossomed in old time the prophet's rod),
    And Lancelot stood and saw the wondrous thing.

Then softly spake the hermit, "Now is grief
    Reproved, and sorrow cast out with the lees;
For God beholds the living, not the dead;
    And He that took the semblance of a child
Loves He but penance, and the drooping head,
    Has He not sung for joy, has He not smiled?"

So they grew old together, and the years
    Pressed no more to their lips the cup of tears
(They had drained all, maybe). And ever less
    Seemed all things mortal, as in quietness
They pondered the eternal mysteries
    (The noblest heritage of all men born),
Such as are writ upon the face of dawn,
    Or in the glamour of a moonlit night,
Or in the autumn swallow's southern flight,
    Or in the breaking of the restless seas:
Or dreamed rich, hallowed dreams of aureate days
    While yet the King was young, and sunlight fell
On bower and roof of ancient Camelot:
    Of triumph clarion, and thanksgiving bell,
When all was song, and laughter, and high praise,
    Even when as yet the accursed thing was not.

Then would loom out from the chill mists of time
    The faces and the forms remembered still,
The King and Guinevere, and Galahad,

That rode upon a peerless quest and dire,
Kay, swift and hasty as a flame of fire,
    And gentle Percival, whom to give made glad;
Merlin, contriver of the riddling rime,
    And Gawain, silent harbinger of ill.

So as the day draws ever toward the dark,
    Ever toward peace the great wind's sounding breath,
And ever toward the further shore the bark
    They drew to the dark, silent realm of death.

Far, far away from their old palace-halls
    Where once they lived a splendid life and vain,
That now are scattered stones and crumbled walls
    In some soft vale, or by the echoing main,

Beneath the springing grass, and very deep
    They three do lie, where never mornings rise
To ope the portals of their dazèd eyes,
    Nor ever mortal footstep breaks their sleep,

And near beside lies Arthur, even he
    That was King once, and yet again shall be.

Legend

Grey, ancient abbeys, you may see them yet,
    In that high plain above the western sea:
A broken arch or two, a few worn stones
    Piled one upon another, and for paving
Uneven fragments with tall grass between:
    Grass that is always green, winter and summer,
The grass that grows on long-forgotten graves.

It was a springtime morning long ago,
    A morning of blue skies and whitest clouds,
And singing birds, and singing streams, and woods
    That shone like silver, yet untouched with green:
The brethren of an abbey of the plain
    Whereof what now is ruin yet was whole--
Were labouring as holy brethren must,
    Quietly, and in peace: and elder ones

Paced in the cloister, and some, older still,
     Too old to work or dream, sat in the sunlight,
The sunlight which they soon should see no more.

And there came from the wood upon the hill
     One clothed in the sere habit of a monk,
That passed in at the portal of the abbey:
     Brighter his face than is the face of spring,
And joy was in his tread, as in his soul.

And some that paced the cloister paused to glance
     at him,
And one that went upon an errand stayed,
     And some that laboured left their work, and came
Gathering round him, and he spake, and said:

"Very fair the golden morning
     As in yonder wood I strayed,
And I heard diviner music
     Than the greatest harpers made,

For a sweet bird sang before me
     Songs of laughter, and of tears.
All that I have loved and longed for,
     As I measured out my years.

Sang of blessed shores and golden
     Where the old, dim heroes be,
Distant isles of sunset glory,
     Set beyond the western sea.

Sang of Christ and Mary Mother
     Hearkening unto angels seven
Playing on their golden harp-strings
     In the far courts of high Heaven."

So they stood by, and listened to his speech,
     Rhythmic, for that great joy was in his soul:
But while they wondered whence he was, and who,
     He cast his eyes around, and, shuddering, cried:
"Who are ye, that I thought to be my brothers?

Strangers and sons of strangers! Where are they
I left behind me but an hour ago?"
    Then was there whispering among the throng,
And wonder not a little, and some scorn;
    Till he that spake, with anguish in his eye,
Cried: "Take me to a cell, that I may pray."
    'Twas done, and in the golden afternoon
A brother entered, and found none within,
    Only a sere monk's habit, and much dust,
As of a body crumbled in the grave.

And while they wondered what these things might be,
    At last spake forth the oldest of them all,
Burdened with hundred winters in his soul:
    "I can remember, when my years were young,
Hearing the old monks say, one went from here
    When spring was on the earth, as it is now,
Some five-score years ago, and was not seen
    Again, though search was made in all the land."

And some believed this was the same, and all
    Forgot it in a sennight's silent toil.
Save one, that saw, and seeing understood,
    And for the greater glory of High God
Wrote down the story in a mighty book,
    And limned the old saint hearkening to the bird
With bright hues, and you still may read and see.

II. FIRST POEMS
Rime

O scholar grey, with quiet eyes,
    Reading the charactered pages, bright
With one tall candle's flickering light,
    In a turret chamber under the skies;
O scholar, learned in gramarye,
    Have you seen the manifold things I see?

Have you seen the forms of traced towers
    Whence clamorous voices challenge the hours:
Gaunt tree-branches, pitchy black
    Against the long, wind-driven wrack
Of scurrying, shuddering clouds, that race
    Ever across the pale moon's face?

Have you heard the tramp of hurrying feet.
    There beneath, in the shadowy street,
Have you heard sharp cries, and seen the flame
    Of silvery steel, in a perilous game,
A perilous game for men to play,
    Hid from the searching eyes of day?

Have you heard the great awakening breath,
    Like trump that summons the saints from death,
Of the wild, majestical wind, which blows
    Loud and splendid, that each man knows
Far, O far away is the sea,
    Breaking, murmuring, stark and free?

All these things I hear and see,
    I, a scholar of gramarye:
All are writ in the ancient books
    Clear, exactly, and he that looks
Finds the night and the changing sea,
    The years gone by, and the years to be:
(He that searches, with tireless eyes
    In a turret-chamber under the skies)
Passion and joy, and sorrow and laughter,
    Life and death, and the things thereafter.

To an Elzevir Cicero

Dust-covered book, that very few men know,
    Even as very few men understand
The glory of an ancient, storied land
    In the wild current of the ages' flow,
Have not old scholars, centuries ago
    Caressed you in the hollow of their hand,
The while with quiet, kindly eyes they scanned
    Your pages, yellowed now, then white as snow?

A voice there is, cries through your every word,
    Of him, that after greatest glory came
Down the grey road to darkness and to tears;
    A voice like far seas in still valleys heard,
Crying of love and death and hope and fame
    That change not with the changing of the years.

To a Dürer Drawing of Antwerp Harbour

Figured by Dürer's magic hand wast thou,
    That, lightning-like, traced on the lucid page
Rough, careless lines, with wizardry so sage
    That yet the whole was fair, I know not how:
Ships of gaunt masts, and stark, sea-smitten prow,
    Idle, yet soon again to sweep the main
In the swift service of old merchants' gain,
    Where are ye now, alas, where are ye now?
Gone are ye all, and vanished very long,
    Sunk with great glory in the storied wars,
Or conquered by the leaping breakers wild:
    And yet we love your image, like some song
That tells of ancient days and high, because
    Old Dürer looked upon you once and smiled.

Pure Virginia
York River Returns

Like smoke that vanishes on the morning breeze
    Are passed the first beginnings of the world,
When time was even as a bud still curled,
    And scarce the limit set of lands and seas;
Like smoke, like smoke the composite auguries

Of Hebrew and of Hellene are all furled,
Fulfilled or else forgot, and idly hurled
This way or that way, as the great winds please:
Aye, and like smoke of this delicious herb
Brought by strange ways the curious mind may guess,
From where the parrot and the leopard be,
My thoughts, that should be strong, the years to curb
Go up, and vanish into nothingness
On a blue cloud of exquisite fragrancy.

A Preface for a Tale I have never told

Herein is nought of windy citadels
Where proud kings dwell, that with an iron hand
Deal war or justice: here no history
Of valiant ships upon the wine-dark seas
Passing strange lands and threading channels strait
Between embalmed islands: here no song
That men shall sing in battle and remember
When they are old and grey beside the fire:
Only a story gathered from the hills
And the wind crying of forgotten days,
A story that shall whisper, "All things change--
For friends do grow indifferent, and loves
Die like a dream at morning: bitterness
Is the sure heritage of all men born,
And he alone sees truly, who looks out
From some huge aery peak, considering not
Fast-walled cities, or the works of men,
But turns his gaze unto the mountain-tops
And the unfathomable blue of heaven
That only change not with the changing years"
A tale that shod itself with ancient shoon
And wrapped its cloak, and wandered from the west.

A Sonnet

There is a wind that takes the heart of a man,
A fresh wind in the latter days of spring,
When hate and war and every evil thing
That the wide arches of high Heaven span
Seems dust, and less to be accounted than
The omened touches of a passing wing:

When Destiny, that calls himself a king,
    Goes all forgotten for the song of Pan:
For why? Because the twittering of birds
    Is the best music that was ever sung,
Because the voice of trees finds better words
    Than ever poet from his heartstrings wrung:
Because all wisdom and all gramarye
    Are writ in fields, O very plain to see.

"It was all in the Black Countree"

It was all in the Black Countree,
    What time the sweet o' the year should be,
I saw a tree, all gaunt and grey,
    As mindful of a winter's day:
And that a lonely bird did sit
    Upon the topmost branch of it,
Who to my thought did sweeter sing
    Than any minstrel of a king.

To a Pianist

When others' fingers touch the keys
    Then most doleful threnodies
Chase about the air, and run
    Like Pandæmonium begun.
Rhythm strained and false accord
    In a ceaseless stream are poured;
Then sighs are heard, and men depart
    To seek the sage physician's art,
Or silence, and a little ease,
    When others' fingers touch the keys.

When your fingers touch the keys
    Hark, soft sounds of summer seas
In a melody most fair
    Whisper through the pleasant air,
Or a winding mountain stream
    Glitters to the pale moonbeam,
Or a breeze doth stir the tops
    Of springtime larches in a copse,
Or the winds are loosed and hurled

> About the wonder-stricken world
> With immortal harmonies,
> When your fingers touch the keys.

A Fragment

> And some came down in a great wind
> Under grey scurrying skies
> To where the long wave-beaten shore
> For ever shrieks and cries.
>
> O, fling aside your toil, your care,
> When one cries of the sea,
> And the great waves that foam and toss,
> And the white clouds that flee:
> Let us forget our weariness,
> Forget that we have sinned,
> So we but sail, what matters it
> If Death ride on the wind?
>
> Storm from the sky, storm from the sea
> Beat on them as they stood,
> And a great longing sprang in them
> To cross the roaring flood...

Sea Poppies

> 'Twixt lonely lands and desert beach,
> Where no wind blows and no waves reach,
> A sunken precinct here we keep,
> With woven wiles of endless sleep;
> Our twisted stems of sere-hued green,
> Our pallid blooms what sun has seen?
> And he that tastes our magic breath
> Shall sleep that sleep whose name is death.
>
> Wild clouds are scurrying overhead,
> The wild wind's voice is loud and dread,
> Sounding the knell of the dying day,
> Yet here is silence and gloom alway.
> And a great longing seizes me
> To burst my bondage and be free,
> To look on winds' and waters' strife,

And breathe in my nostrils the breath of life.
Give me not dim and slumbrous ease,
    But sounding storm and labouring seas,
Not peaceful and untroubled years,
    But toil and warfare and passion and tears.
And I would fall in valorous fight,
    And lie on lofty far-seen height.

Yet how to burst these prison-bands,
    Forged by unseen spirit-hands?

O seek not to burst our prison bands
    Forged by unseen spirit-hands.
Clashing battle and labouring sea,
    These be for others, not for thee.
Thou lover of storm and passion and war
    Break'st our charmed circle never more.

"O, sing me a Song of the Wild West Wind"

O, sing me a song of the wild west wind,
    And his great sea-harrying flail,
Of hardy mariners, copper skinned,
    That fly with a bursting sail.
They see the clouds of crisped white
    That shadow the distant hills,
And filled are they with a strange delight
    As shaking away old ills.

O, give me a boat that is sure and stark,
    And swift as a slinger's stone,
With a sail of canvas bronzed dark,
    And I will go out alone:
Nor fear nor sorrow my soul shall keep
    When around me lies the sea,
And I will return with the night, and sleep
    In the wind's wild harmony.

Ære Perennius
Written on Commemoration Sunday, Corpus Christi College, Oxford

We praise, we praise the immortal dead,
    Who strove beneath unheeding skies
For truth that raised the drooping head,
    For light that gladdened weary eyes:

The martyr's cross, the warrior's sword,
    How should they be of lesser worth
Than some unprofitable hoard
    In ancient mines below the earth?

The song that one alone has sung,
    The great uncompromising page,
Are these but glittering baubles, flung
    About the world from age to age?

But ruin'd columns, wondrous tall,
    Built in old time with labour sore,
The mighty deeds done once for all,
    The voice heard once, and heard no more?

Rather they shine as doth the star
    About the close of winter's day,
That cheers the traveller afar
    And draws him on, and points the way.

We praise, we praise the immortal dead.
    Do they not verily wait till we
Of the spoilt years unharvested
    Be also of their company?

The Old Kings

Far away from sunny rills,
    Far away from golden broom,
Far away from any town
    Whither merchants travel down--
In a hollow of the hills
    In impenetrable gloom

Sit the old forgotten kings
        Unto whom no poet sings,
Unto whom none makes bequest,
        Unto whom no kingdoms rest,
Only wayward shreds of dreams,
        And the sound of ancient streams,
And the shock of ancient strife
        On the further shore of life.

When our days are done, shall we
        Enter their pale company?
"O there be Kings whose Treasuries"

O there be kings whose treasuries
        Are rich with pearls and gold
And silks and bales of cramasy
        And spices manifold:
Gardens they have with marble stairs
        And streams than life more fair,
With roses set and lavender
        That do enchant the air.

O there be many ships that sail
        The sea-ways wide and blue,
And there be master-mariners
        To sail them straight and true:
And there be many women fair
        Who watch out anxiously,
And are enamoured of the day
        Their dear ones come from sea:

But riches I can find enow
        All in a barren land,
Where sombre lakes shine wondrously
        With rocks on either hand:
And I can find enow of love
        Up there, alone, alone,
With none beside me save the wind,
        Nor speech except his moan.

For there far up among the hills

The great storms come and go
In a most proud processional
    Of cloud and rain and snow:
There light and darkness only are
    A changing benison
Of the old gods who wrought the world
    And shaped the moon and sun.

A Study

In chamber hung with white,
    Lit by the dawning light,

Upon a slender bed
    She lies, as she were dead:

Most carven-ivory fair,
    And palely gold her hair.

Lo, the sun's yellow ray,
    That, with the rise of day,

Through quartered casement came
    To wake her life's pale flame.

The Eremite

When the world is still in the hush of dawn,
    And yet fast sleeping are hate and scorn,
From my grey lodging under the hill
    I do go out, and wander at will.

Of nights when the riven clouds are hurled,
    And strife and rancour possess the world,
I sit alone, with thoughts that are chill,
    In my grey lodging under the hill.

The House of Eld

Now the old winds are wild about the house,
    And the old ghosts cry to me from the air
Of a far isle set in the western sea,
    And of the evening sunlight lingering there.

Ah! I am bound here, bound and fettered,
    The dark house crumbles, and the woods decay,
I was too fain of life, that bound me here;
    Away, old long-loved ghosts, away, away!

The South-west Wind

The south-west wind has blown his fill,
    And vanished with departing day:
The air is warm, and very still,
    And soft as silks of far Cathay.

This is a night when spirits stray.
    Their wan limbs bear them where they will;
They wring their pallid hands alway,
    Seeing the lights upon the hill.

Schumann: Erstes Verlust

O, dreary fall the leaves,
    The withered leaves;
Among the trees
    Complains the breeze,
That still bereaves.

All silent lies the mere,
    The silver mere,
In saddest wise
    Reflecting skies
Forlorn and sere.

Would autumn had not claimed its own
    And would the swallows had not flown.

Skies overcast!
    Leaves falling fast!
And she has passed
    And left the woodland strown,
The woodland strown,
    The silver mere,
The dying year,
    And me alone.

Skies overcast!
    Leaves falling fast!
Does she that passed
    Dream of the woodland strown,
The woodland strown,
    The silver mere,
The dying year,
    And me alone?

"Dark Boughs against a Golden Sky"

Dark boughs against a golden sky,
    And crying of the winter wind:
And sweet it is, for hope is high,
    And sad it is, for we have sinned.

Perfect is nature's every part
    In sunny rest, or windy strife:
But never yet the perfect heart,
    And never yet the perfect life!

Dark boughs against a golden sky,
    And crying of the winter wind:
And in the cold earth we must lie,
    What matter then if we have sinned?

For evermore and evermore
    Shall the great river onward roll:
And ever winding streams and poor
    Shall lose them in the mighty whole.

"Wind of the Darkness"

Wind of the darkness, breathing round us,
    Wind from the never-resting sea,
Lo, you have loosed the cords that bound us,
    Lo, you have set our spirits free:

Free to take wings, like the sea-bird lonely
    Beating hardily up the wind:
Fixed are his eyes on the waters only,
    Never a glance for the land behind.

Wind of the darkness, breathing round us,
    Wind from the never-resting sea.
Was it the old gods' voice that found us
    Here, where the bars of prison be?

From the far isle that neither knoweth
    Change of season, nor time's increase,
Where is plenty, and no man soweth:
    Calling to strife that shall end in peace.

Creator Spiritus

The wind that scatters dying leaves
    And whirls them from the autumn tree
Is grateful to the ship that cleaves
    With stately prow the scurrying sea.

Heedless about the world we play
    Like children in a garden close:
A postern bars the outward way
    And what's beyond it no man knows:

For careless days, a life at will,
    A little laughter, and some tears,
These are sufficiency to fill
    The early, vain, untroubled years,

Till at the last the wind upheaves
    His unimagined strength, and we
Are scattered far, like autumn leaves,
    Or proudly sail, like ships at sea.

Wind over the Sea

Only a grey sea, and a long grey shore,
    And the grey heavens brooding over them.
Twilight of hopes and purposes forgot,
    Twilight of ceaseless eld, and when was youth?
Is it not lonely here, beyond the years?

Out of the gathering darkness crashes a wind from the
    ocean,

Rushing with league-long paces over the plain of the
    waters,
Driving the clouds and the breakers before it in sudden
    commotion.

Who are these on the wind, riders and riderless horses?
    Riders the great ones that have been and are, and those
to come shall be:
    These are the children of might, life's champions and
history's forces.

Might I but grasp at a bridle, and fear not to be trodden
    under,
Swing myself into a saddle, and ride on greatly, exulting
    On down the long straight road of the wind, a galloping
thunder!

Only a grey sea, and a long grey shore,
    And the grey heavens brooding over them,
Twilight of hopes and purposes forgot,
    Twilight of ceaseless eld, for when was youth?
Is it not lonely here, beyond the years?

Songs on the Downs

1

This is the road the Romans made,
    This track half lost in the green hills,
Or fading in a forest-glade
    'Mid violets and daffodils.

The years have fallen like dead leaves,
    Unwept, uncounted, and unstayed
(Such as the autumn tempest thieves),
    Since first this road the Romans made.

2

A miser lives within this house,
    His patron saint's the gnawing mouse,
And there's no peace upon his brows.

A many ancient trees and thin

Do fold the place their shade within,
And moan, as for remembered sin.

III. LAST POEMS AND "THE BURIAL OF SOPHOCLES"

"We who have bowed ourselves to Time"

We who have bowed ourselves to time
    Now arm an uneventful rime
With panoply of flowers
    Through the long summer hours...

But now our fierce and warlike Muse
    Doth soft companionship refuse,
And we must mount and ride
    Upon a steed untried...

We who have led by gradual ways
    Our placid life to sterner days
And for old quiet things
    Have set the strife of kings,

Who battled have with bloody hands
    Through evil times in barren lands,
To whom the voice of guns
    Speaks and no longer stuns,

Calm, though with death encompassèd,
    That watch the hours go overhead
Knowing too well we must
    With all men come to dust...

Crave of our masters' clemency
    Silence a little space that we
Upon their ear may force
    Tales of our trodden course.

Anglia Valida in Senectute

(On the Declaration of War)

Not like to those who find untrodden ways;
    But down the weary paths we know,
Through every change of sky and change of days
    Silent, processional we go.

Not unto us the soft, unlaboured breath
    Of children's hopes and children's fears:
We are not sworn to battle to the death
    With all the wrongs of all the years:

We are old, we are old, and worn and school'd with ills,
    Maybe our road is almost done,
Maybe we are drawn near unto the hills
    Where rest is and the setting sun:

But yet a pride is ours that will not brook
    The taunts of fools too saucy grown,
He that is rash to prove it, let him look
    He kindle not a fire unknown.

Since first we flung our gauntlet to the skies
    And dared the high Gods' will to bend,
A fire that still may burn deceit and lies
    Burn and consume them to the end.

"Dark is the World our Fathers left us"

Dark is the world our fathers left us,
    Wearily, greyly the long years flow,
Almost the gloom has of hope bereft us,
    Far is the high gods' song and low:

Sombre the crests of the mountains lonely,
    Leafless, wind-ridden, moan the trees:
Down in the valleys is twilight only,
    Twilight over the mourning seas:

Time was when earth was always golden,
    Time was when skies were always clear:
Spirits and souls of the heroes olden,
    Faint are cries from the darkness, hear!

Tear ye the veil of time asunder
    Tear the veil, 'tis the gods' command,
Hear we the sun-stricken breakers thunder
    Over the shore where the heroes stand.

Dark is the world our fathers left us,
    Heavily, greyly the long years flow,
Almost the gloom has of hope bereft us,
    Far is the high gods' song and low.

Awakening

Gold-crested towers against the veiled skies,
    Sere branches of the winter trees beneath,
And a low song, and heavy-lidded eyes;

Is there aught else in all the world beside?
    Is not time stilled and ended in this hour?

Up, and away! the belted squadrons ride!

Ave atque Vale

In Oxford, evermore the same
    Unto the uttermost verge of time,
Though grave-dust choke the sons of men,
    And silence wait upon the rime,

At evening now the skies set forth
    Last glories of the dying year:
The wind gives chase to relict leaves:
    And we, we may not linger here.

A little while, and we are gone:
    God knows if it be ours to see
Again the earliest hoar-frost white
    On the long lawns of Trinity.

In Merton, of the many courts
    And doorways good to wander through,
Gable and spire shall glitter white
    Or tawny gold against the blue:

And still the winter sun shall smile
    At noonday, or at sunset hour
On Magdalen, girt with ancient trees,
    Beneath her bright immortal tower.

Though nevermore we tread the ways
    That our returning feet have known
Past Oriel, and Christ Church gate
    Unto those dearer walls, our own.

Oxford is evermore the same,
    Unto the uttermost verge of time,
Though grave-dust choke the sons of men,
    And silence wait upon the rime.

"O, one came down from Seven Hills"

O, one came down from seven hills
    And crossed seven streams:
All in his hands were thyme and grass
    And in his eyes were dreams:
He passed by a seven fields
    With early dews all grey
And entered in the stricken town
    About the break of day.

"O you old men that stand and talk
    About the market-place,
There is much trouble in your eyes
    And anguish in your face:
O woman in a silent room
    Within a silent house,
There is no pleasure in your voice
    Or peace upon your brows."

"O how should such as we rejoice
    Who weep that others die,
Who quake, and curse ourselves, and watch
    The vengeful hours go by?
O better far to fly the grief
    That wounds, and never kills;
O better far to fly the town
    And seek the seven hills----"

"I will go pray the seven gods
    Who keep the seven hills
That they do grant your city peace,

And easement of her ills."
"Nay, rather pray the seven gods
    To launch the latest pain;
For there be many things to do
    Ere we see peace again."

"Then I'll go praise the seven gods
    With hymns and chauntings seven,
Such as shall split the mountain-tops
    And shrivel up blue heaven:
That there be men who mock at threats
    And wag their heads at strife,
Love home above their own hearts' blood
    And honour more than life."

Sonnet to the British Navy

Lest force aspire to brand an alien name
    Upon the immortal empire of the free:
Lest fire and sword and slaughter strive to tame
    This isle, was ne'er so tamed, and ne'er shall be.
Ye guard the ocean barrier, undismayed
    'Midst hidden perils for a brave man's fears,
In iron craft that many smiths have made
    With peaceful labour in the old, dead years.
In a small vessel, of one Smith ill-wrought
    I must soon venture on another deep,
And dare, with little hope, and little thought
    Of praise and honour and untroubled sleep:
So, as each sails upon his perilous sea,
    I pray High God He strengthen you, and me.

The Last Meeting

We who are young, and have caught the splendour of life,
    Hunting it down the forested ways of the world,
Do we not wear our hearts like a banner unfurled
    (Crowned with a chaplet of love, shod with the sandals
of strife)?

Now not a lustre of pain, nor an ocean of tears
    Nor pangs of death, nor any other thing
That the old tristful gods on our heads may bring

Can rob us of this one hour in the midst of the years.

The New Age and the Old

Like the small source of a smooth-flowing river,
    Like the pale dawn of a wonderful day,
Comes the New Age, from High God, the good giver,
    Comes with the shouts of the children at play:

As an old leaf whirls faster and faster
    From the sere branch that once gave it fair birth,
Into the arms of the devil, its master,
    Be the old age swept away from the earth!

To the Cultured

Sons of culture, God-given,
    First offspring of Heaven,
Athletic and tanned,
    Well-built and not nervous,
With your golf and your tweeds
    And your "noble editions,"
Quiet lives and few needs
    (Say a thousand a year
For your earthly career)
    Who can't understand
Discontent and seditions,
    May Heaven preserve us
From being like you.

What are we, what am I?
    Poor rough creatures, whose life
Is "depressing" and "grey,"
    Is a heart-breaking strife
With death and with shame
    And your polite laughter,
Till the world pass away
    In smoke and in flame,
And some of us die,
    And some live on after
To build it anew.

Afterwards

Afterwards, when
    The old Gods' hate
On the riven earth
    No more is poured:

    When weapons of war
Are all outworn
    What shall become
Of the race of men?

One shall go forth
    In the likeness of a child:
Under sere skies
    Of a grey dawning:

    One shall go forth
In the likeness of a child,
    And desolate places
Shall spring and blossom:

One shall go forth
    In the likeness of a child:
And men shall sing
    And greatly rejoice:

    All men shall sing
For the love that is in them,
    And he shall behold it
And sing also.

Domum redit Poeta

O much desired from far away
    And long, I hold thee once again,
Thou undiminished treasury
    Of small delights, yet nowise vain:

The cat curled on the cosy hearth,
    The thrushes in the garden trees,
The memories of younger years,
    The quiet voices, and the peace.

Memories

Shapes in the mist, it is long since I saw you,
    Pale hands and faces, and quiet eyes,
Crowned with a garland the dead years wrought you
    Out of remembrance that never dies:

One among you is tall and supple
    Good to fight or to love beside,
Only the stain of a deadly quarrel,
    Only that and the years divide:

One there is with a face as honest,
    Heart as true, as the open sea,
One who never betrayed a comrade--
    Death stands now betwixt him and me.

One I loved with a passionate longing
    Born of worship and fierce despair,
Dreamed that Heaven were only happy
    If at length I should find him there.

Shapes in the mist, ye see me lonely,
    Lonely and sad in the dim firelight:
How far now to the last of all battles?
    (Listen, the guns are loud to-night!)

Whatever comes, I will strike once surely,
    Once because of an ancient tryst,
Once for love of your dear dead faces
    Ere I come unto you, Shapes in the mist.

Intercessional

There is a place where voices
    Of great guns do not come,
Where rifle, mine, and mortar
    For evermore are dumb:
Where there is only silence,
    And peace eternal and rest,
Set somewhere in the quiet isles
    Beyond Death's starry West.

O God, the God of battles,
    To us who intercede,
Give only strength to follow
    Until there's no more need,
And grant us at that ending
    Of the unkindly quest
To come unto the quiet isles
    Beyond Death's starry West.

April 1916

Now spring is come upon the hills in France,
    And all the trees are delicately fair,
As heeding not the great guns' voice, by chance
    Brought down the valley on a wandering air:
Now day by day upon the uplands bare
    Do gentle, toiling horses draw the plough,
And birds sing often in the orchards where
    Spring wantons it with blossoms on her brow--
Aye! but there is no peace in England now.

O little isle amid unquiet seas,
    Though grisly messengers knock on many doors,
Though there be many storms among your trees
    And all your banners rent with ancient wars;
Yet such a grace and majesty are yours
    There be still some, whose glad heart suffereth
All hate can bring from her misgotten stores,
    Telling themselves, so England's self draw breath,
That's all the happiness on this side death.

"Over the Hills and Hollows Green"

Over the hills and hollows green
    The springtide air goes valiantly,
Where many sainted singing larks
    And blessed primaveras be:

But bitterly the springtide air
    Over the desert towns doth blow,
About whose torn and shattered streets
    No more shall children's footsteps go.

Sonnet

To-night the world is but a prison house,
    And kindly ways, and all the springing grass
Are dungeon stones to him that may not pass
    Among them, save with anguish on his brows:
And any wretched husbandman that ploughs
    The upland acres in his habit spare
Is king, to those in palaces of glass
    Who sit with grief and weariness for spouse.

O God, who madest first the world that we
    Might happy live, and praise its pleasantness
In such wise as the angels never could,
    Wherefore are hearts, fashioned so wondrously,
All spoiled and changed by human bitterness
    Into the likenesses of stone and wood?

"O Long the Fiends of War shall dance"

O long the fiends of war shall dance
    Upon the stricken fields of France:
And long and long their grisly cry
    Shall echo up and smite the sky:
O long and long the tears of God
    Shall fall upon a barren sod,
Save when, of His great clemency,
    He gives men's hearts in custody
Of grim old kindly Death, who knows
    The mould is better than the rose.

For R. Q. G.
July 1916

O God, whose great inscrutable purposes
    (Seen only of the one all-seeing eye)
Are as unchangeable as the azure sky,
    And as fulfilled of infinite mysteries:
Are like a fast-locked castle without keys
    Whereof the gates are very strong and high,
Impenetrable, and we poor fools die
    Nor even know what thing beyond them is:
O God, by whom men's lives are multiplied,
    Are scattered broadcast in the world like grain,

And after long time reaped again and stored,
    O Thou who only canst be glorified
By man's own passion and the supreme pain,
    Accept this sacrifice of blood outpoured.

"Sun and Shadow and Winds of Spring"

Sun and shadow and winds of spring,
    Love and laughter and hope and fame,
Cloud and storm-light over the hills,
    Tears and passion and sordid shame:

    All, all are but as quenched fire
And vanish'd smoke to him that lies
    Amid the silence of the trees
Under the silence of the skies.

"Let us tell Quiet Stories of Kind Eyes"

Let us tell quiet stories of kind eyes
    And placid brows where peace and learning sate:
Of misty gardens under evening skies
    Where four would walk of old, with steps sedate.

Let's have no word of all the sweat and blood,
    Of all the noise and strife and dust and smoke
(We who have seen Death surging like a flood,
    Wave upon wave, that leaped and raced and broke).

Or let's sit silently, we three together,
    Around a wide hearth-fire that's glowing red,
Giving no thought to all the stormy weather
    That flies above the roof-tree overhead.

And he, the fourth, that lies all silently
    In some far-distant and untended grave,
Under the shadow of a shattered tree,
    Shall leave the company of the hapless brave,

And draw nigh unto us for memory's sake,
    Because a look, a word, a deed, a friend,
Are bound with cords that never a man may break,
    Unto his heart for ever, until the end.

"Save that Poetic Fire"

Save that poetic fire
    Burns in the hidden heart,
Save that the full-voiced choir
    Sings in a place apart,

    Man that's of woman born,
With all his imaginings,
    Were less than the dew of morn,
Less than the least of things.

The Burial of Sophocles
The First Verses

Gather great store of roses, crimson-red
    From ancient gardens under summer skies:
New opened buds, and some that soon must shed
    Their leaves to earth, that all expectant lies;
Some from the paths of poets' wandering,
    Some from the places where young lovers meet,
Some from the seats of dreamers pondering,
    And all most richly red, and honey-sweet.

For in the splendour of the afternoon,
    When sunshine lingers on the glittering town
And glorifies the temples wondrous-hewn
    All set about it like a deathless crown,
We will go mingle with the solemn throng,
    With neither eyes that weep, nor hearts that bleed,
That to his grave with slow, majestic song
    Bears down the latest of the godlike seed.

Many a singer lies on distant isle
    Beneath the canopy of changing sky:
Around them waves innumerable smile,
    And o'er their head the restless seabirds cry:
But we will lay him far from sound of seas,
    Far from the jutting crags' unhopeful gloom,
Where there blows never wind save summer breeze,
    And where the growing rose may clasp his tomb.

And thither in the splendid nights of spring,
    When stars in legions over heaven are flung,
Shall come the ancient gods, all wondering
    Why he sings not that had so richly sung:
There Heracles with peaceful foot shall press
    The springing herbage, and Hephæstus strong,
Hera and Aphrodite's loveliness,
    And the great giver of the choric song.

And thither, after weary pilgrimage,
    From unknown lands beyond the hoary wave,
Shall travellers through every coming age
    Approach to pluck a blossom from his grave:
Some in the flush of youth, or in the prime,
    Whose life is still as heaped gold to spend,
And some who have drunk deep of grief and time,
    And who yet linger half-afraid the end.

The Interlude

It was upon a night of spring,
    Even the time when first do sing
The new-returned nightingales;
    Whenas all hills and woods and dales
Are resonant with melody
    Of songs that die not, but shall be
Unto the latest hour of time
    Beyond the life of word or rime--
Whenas all brooks more softly flow
    Remembering lovers long ago
That stood upon their banks and vowed,
    And love was with them like a cloud:
There came one out of Athens town
    In a spun robe, with sandals brown,
Just when the white ship of the moon
    Had first set sail, and many a rune
Was written in the argent stars;
    His feet were set towards the hills
Because he knew that there the rills
    Ran down like jewels, and fairy cars
Galloped, maybe, among the dells,
    And airy sprites wove fitful spells

Of gossamer and cold moonshine
    Which do most mistily entwine:
And ever the hills called, and a voice
    Cried: "Soon, maybe, comes thy choice
Twixt mortal immortality
    Such as shall never be again,
'Twixt the most passionate-pleasant pain
    And all the quiet, barren joys
That old men prate about to boys."

He wandered many nights and days--
    Whose morns were always crystal clear,
As lay the world in still amaze
    Enchanted of the springing year,
And all the nights with wakeful eyes
    Watched for another dawn to rise--
Till at the last the mountain tops
    Received him, which like giant props
Stand, lest the all-encircling sky
    Fall down, and men be crushed and die.
And so he reached a curved hill
    Whereon the horned moon did seem
Her richest radiance to spill
    In an inestimable stream,
Like jewels rare of countless price,
    Or wizard magic turned to ice.

And as he reached the topmost crest of it,
    Lo! the Olympian majesties did sit
In a most high and passionless conclave:
    They ate ambrosia with their deathless lips,
And ever and anon the golden wave
    Flowed of the drink divine, which only strips
This mortal frame of its mortality.
    And there, and there was Aphrodite, she
That is more lovely than the golden dawn
    And from a ripple of the sea was born:
And there was Hera, the imperious queen,
    And Dian's chastity, that hunts unseen
What time with spring the woodland boughs are green:
    And there was Pan with mirth and pleasantness,

And Eros' self that never knew distress
    Save for the love of the fair Cretan maid;
There Hermes with the wings of speed arrayed,
    And awful Zeus, the king of gods and men,
And ever at his feet Apollo sang
    A measure of changing harmonies that rang
From that high mountain over all the world,
    And all the sails of fighting ships were furled,
And men drew breath, and there was peace again.
    But him that saw, the sight like flame
Or depths of waters overcame:
    He swooned, nor heard how ceased the choir
Of strings upon Apollo's lyre,
    Nor saw he how the sweet god stood
And smiled on him in kindly mood,
    And stooped, and kissed him as he lay;
Then lightly rose and turned away
    To join the bright immortal throng
And make for them another song.

The Last Verses
    O ageless nonpareil of stars
That shinest through a mist of cloud,
    O light beyond the prison bars
Remote, unwavering, and proud;
    Fortunate star and happy light,
Ye benison the gloom of night.

All hail, unfailing eye and hand,
    All hail, all hail, unsilenced voice,
That makest dead men understand,
    The very dead in graves rejoice:
Whose utterance, writ in ancient books,
    Shall always live, for him that looks.

Many as leaves from autumn trees
    The years shall flutter from on high,
And with their multiple decease
    The souls of men shall fall and die,
Yet, while the empires turn to dust,
    You shall live on, because you must.

O seven times happy he that dies
   After the splendid harvest-tide,
When strong barns shield from winter skies
   The grain that's rightly stored inside:
There death shall scatter no more tears
   Than o'er the falling of the years:

Aye, happy seven times is he
   Who enters not the silent doors
Before his time, but tenderly
   Death beckons unto him, because
There's rest within for weary feet
   Now all the journey is complete.

"So we lay down the Pen"

So we lay down the pen,
   So we forbear the building of the rime,
And bid our hearts be steel for times and a time
   Till ends the strife, and then,
When the New Age is verily begun,
   God grant that we may do the things undone.

THE END

MOMENT IN HISTORY

A Cape Ann fisherman mending his nets; between 1900-1906

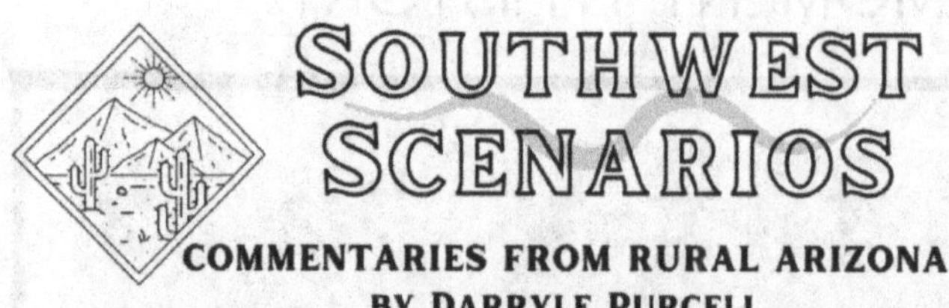

SOUTHWEST SCENARIOS

COMMENTARIES FROM RURAL ARIZONA
BY DARRYLE PURCELL

Because humankind fails to learn from past lessons, we find that many circumstances from yesteryear are repeating themselves yet again. The commentaries that follow here and in future issues were originally published by *The Mohave Valley Daily News* between 1993 & 2013--and in many ways they apply to today.
We are grateful to republish these commentaries written by Darryle Purcell in full and unedited. His own brand of humor and style can deliver insight, provoke thought, and even boil blood.

Tombstone gives scoop on new 'Old West'

From Sept. 22, 1995

THE *MOHAVE VALLEY DAILY NEWS* PRINTED AN ASSOCIATED PRESS STORY Thursday about the Tombstone (Arizona) City Council's vote to force horses that travel on city streets to wear diapers. The council calls them "dung bags." They claim the animal wraps may not do anything for the "Old West" image of the area, but they will help keep the streets clean.

The story went on to say, "Horse owners who fail to equip their animals with dung bags will have to pay a misdemeanor fine ranging from $25 to $300 and face a possible jail term of up to 30 days."

The City of Tombstone should be proud of the progressive thinking of its elected leaders. I am sure western towns would have done the same thing over one hundred years ago if they had thought of it. Perhaps it just took until now for politicians to acquire enough expertise in horse manure.

Whatever the reason, the new policy can become an entrepreneurial boom. Designer horse diapers could be produced for the discriminating cowboy. Think of it: horse diapers with pictures of Phoenix Suns players, city council members, first ladies or rock stars on them; cartoon characters for children's ponies; special designs by Calvin and Ann Klein (which could come with an accessory package including a lace sneeze guard and a happy-trails headband); Marlboro brands for the macho cowboy; and the ever-popular Elizabeth Taylor Black Biscuit design.

Construction companies could jump on the horse wagon by building street corner changing stalls. Mr. Ed, of course, could make a comeback to rival June Allyson as the spokescreature for "Deep Ends" horse diapers. On the other hand, horses that assist Sheriff Joe's chain gangs would have to be issued pink diapers to avoid contraband selling of same.

Retailers would experience an increase in the sales of industrial-sized baby wipes and powder containers.

If the policy had been established in the Old West, the area would have become civilized sooner. Lives might have been saved. Just think. Wild Bill Hickok could have thrown down his poker hand of aces and eights and quietly excused himself to go change his horse. Instead his horse relieved itself in the street and Wild Bill was shot.

Such a waste.

Seriously, this is the kind of thing that makes one appreciate our own (Bullhead City) council. I realize some of them have felt many of my earlier columns were filled with the source of the above topic. And we all have made judgments in the past about some of the Bullhead City issues and actions. But historic Tombstone, Ariz., wins my vote to receive the golden shovel award for silliest political action.

Randolph Scott must be spinning in his grave.

(Arizona has its share of animal activists. And I support the rights of all property owners to follow their dreams even if they value pit bulls over people. But many of those folks didn't find humor in some of my opinion-page blather. In the days when most people still wrote letters, as opposed to today's email and online comments, I would receive about five angry letters for every four that were complimentary. As we used to state, "at least they are reading the paper.")

SEVEN KEYS TO
BALDPATE

CHAPTER I

"WEEP NO MORE, MY LADY"

A young woman was crying bitterly in the waiting-room of the railway station at Upper Asquewan Falls, New York.

A beautiful young woman? That is exactly what Billy Magee wanted to know as, closing the waiting-room door behind him, he stood staring just inside. Were the features against which that frail bit of cambric was agonizingly pressed of a pleasing contour? The girl's neatly tailored corduroy suit and her flippant but charming millinery augured well. Should he step gallantly forward and inquire in sympathetic tones as to the cause of her woe? Should he carry chivalry even to the lengths of Upper Asquewan Falls?

No, Mr. Magee decided he would not. The train that had just roared away into the dusk had not brought him from the region of skyscrapers and derby hats for deeds of knight errantry up state. Anyhow, the girl's tears were none of his business. A railway station was a natural place for grief—a field of many partings, upon whose floor fell often in torrents the tears of those left behind. A friend, mayhap a lover, had been whisked off into the night by the relentless five thirty-four local. Why not a lover? Surely about such a dainty trim figure as this courtiers hovered as moths about a flame. Upon a tender intimate sorrow it was not the place of an unknown Magee to intrude. He put his hand gently upon the latch of the door.

And yet—dim and heartless and cold was the interior of that waiting-room. No place, surely, for a gentleman to leave a lady sorrowful, particularly when the lady was so alluring. Oh, beyond question, she was most alluring. Mr. Magee stepped softly to the ticket window and made low-voiced inquiry of the man inside.

"What's she crying about?" he asked.

A thin sallow face, on the forehead of which a mop of ginger-colored hair lay listlessly, was pressed against the bars.

"Thanks," said the ticket agent. "I get asked the same old questions so often, one like yours sort of breaks the monotony. Sorry I can't help you. She's a woman, and the Lord only knows why women cry. And sometimes I reckon even He must be a little puzzled. Now, my wife—"

"I think I'll ask her," confided Mr. Magee in a hoarse whisper.

"Oh, I wouldn't," advised the man behind the bars. "It's best to let 'em alone. They stop quicker if they ain't noticed."

"But she's in trouble," argued Billy Magee.

"And so'll you be, most likely," responded the cynic, "if you interfere. No, siree! Take my advice. Shoot old Asquewan's rapids in a barrel if you want to, but keep away from crying women."

The heedless Billy Magee, however, was already moving across the unscrubbed floor with chivalrous intention.

The girl's trim shoulders no longer heaved so unhappily. Mr. Magee, approaching, thought himself again in the college yard at dusk, with the great elms sighing overhead, and the fresh young voices of the glee club ringing out from the steps of a century-old building. What were the words they sang so many times?

"Weep no more, my lady, Oh! weep no more to-day."

He regretted that he could not make use of them. They had always seemed to him so sad and beautiful. But troubadours, he knew, went out of fashion long before railway stations came in. So his remark to the young woman was not at all melodious:

"Can I do anything?"

A portion of the handkerchief was removed, and an eye which, Mr. Magee noted, was of an admirable blue, peeped out at him. To the gaze of even a solitary eye, Mr. Magee's aspect was decidedly pleasing. Young Williams, who posed at the club as a wit, had once said that Billy Magee came as near to being a magazine artist's idea of the proper hero of a story as any man could, and at the same time retain the respect and affection of his fellows. Mr. Magee thought he read approval in the lone eye of blue. When the lady spoke, however, he hastily revised his opinion.

"Yes," she said, "you can do something. You can go away—far, far away."

Mr. Magee stiffened. Thus chivalry fared in Upper Asquewan Falls in the year 1911.

"I beg your pardon," he remarked. "You seemed to be in trouble, and I thought I might possibly be of some assistance."

The girl removed the entire handkerchief. The other eye proved to be the same admirable blue—a blue half-way between the shade of her corduroy suit and that of the jacky's costume in the "See the World—Join the Navy" poster that served as background to her woe.

"I don't mean to be rude," she explained more gently, "but—I'm crying, you see, and a girl simply can't look attractive when she cries."

"If I had only been regularly introduced to you, and all that," responded Mr. Magee, "I could make a very flattering reply." And a true one, he added to himself. For even in the faint flickering light of the station he found ample reason for rejoicing that the bit of cambric was no longer agonizingly pressed. As yet he had scarcely looked away from her eyes, but he was dimly aware that up above wisps of golden hair peeped impudently from beneath a saucy black hat. He would look at those wisps shortly, he told himself. As soon as he could look away from the eyes—which was not just yet.

"My grief," said the girl, "is utterly silly and—womanish. I think it would be best to leave me alone with it. Thank you for your interest. And—would you mind asking the gentleman who is pressing his face so feverishly against the bars to kindly close his window?"

"Certainly," replied Mr. Magee. He turned away. As he did so he collided with a rather excessive lady. She gave the impression of solidity and bulk; her mouth was hard and knowing. Mr. Magee felt that she wanted to vote, and that she would say as much from time to time. The lady had a glittering eye; she put it to its time-honored use and fixed Mr. Magee with it.

"I was crying, mamma," the girl explained, "and this gentleman inquired if he could be of any service."

Mamma! Mr. Magee wanted to add his tears to those of the girl. This frail and lovely damsel in distress owning as her maternal parent a heavy unnecessary—person! The older woman also had yellow hair, but it was the sort that suggests the white enamel pallor of a drug store, with the soda-fountain fizzing and the bottles of perfume ranged in an odorous row. Mamma! Thus rolled the world along.

"Well, they ain't no use gettin' all worked up for nothing," advised the unpleasant parent. Mr. Magee was surprised that in her tone there was no hostility to him—thus belying her looks. "Mebbe the gentleman can direct us to a good hotel," she added, with a rather stagy smile.

"I'm a stranger here, too," Mr. Magee replied. "I'll interview the man over there in the cage."

The gentleman referred to was not cheerful in his replies. There was, he said, Baldpate Inn.

"Oh, yes, Baldpate Inn," repeated Billy Magee with interest.

"Yes, that's a pretty swell place," said the ticket agent. "But it ain't open now. It's a summer resort. There ain't no place open now but the Commercial House. And I wouldn't recommend no human being there— especially no lady who was sad before she ever saw it."

Mr. Magee explained to the incongruous family pair waiting on the bench.

"There's only one hotel," he said, "and I'm told it's not exactly the place for any one whose outlook on life is not rosy at the moment. I'm sorry."

"It will do very well," answered the girl, "whatever it is." She smiled at Billy Magee. "My outlook on life in Upper Asquewan Falls," she said, "grows rosier every minute. We must find a cab."

She began to gather up her traveling-bags, and Mr. Magee hastened to assist. The three went out on the station platform, upon which lay a thin carpet of snowflakes. There the older woman, in a harsh rasping voice, found fault with Upper Asquewan Falls,—its geography, its public spirit, its brand of weather. A dejected cab at the end of the platform stood mourning its lonely lot. In it Mr. Magee placed the large lady and the bags. Then, while the driver climbed to his seat, he spoke into the invisible ear of the girl.

"You haven't told me why you cried," he reminded her.

She waved her hand toward the wayside village, the lamps of which shone sorrowfully through the snow.

"Upper Asquewan Falls," she said, "isn't it reason enough?"

Billy Magee looked; saw a row of gloomy buildings that seemed to list as the wind blew, a blurred sign "Liquors and Cigars," a street that staggered away into the dark like a man who had lingered too long at the emporium back of the sign.

"Are you doomed to stay here long?" he asked.

"Come on, Mary," cried a deep voice from the cab. "Get in and shut the door. I'm freezing."

"It all depends," said the girl. "Thank you for being so kind and—good night."

The door closed with a muffled bang, the cab creaked wearily away, and Mr. Magee turned back to the dim waiting-room.

"Well, what was she crying for?" inquired the ticket agent, when Mr. Magee stood again at his cell window.

"She didn't think much of your town," responded Magee; "she intimated that it made her heavy of heart."

"H'm—it ain't much of a place," admitted the man, "though it ain't the general rule with visitors to burst into tears at sight of it. Yes, Upper Asquewan is slow, and no mistake. It gets on my nerves sometimes. Nothing to do but work, work, work, and then lay down and wait for to-morrow. I used to think maybe some day they'd transfer me down to Hooperstown—there's moving pictures and such goings-on down there. But the railroad never notices you—unless you go wrong. Yes, sir, sometimes I want to clear out of this town myself."

"A natural wanderlust," sympathized Mr. Magee. "You said something just now about Baldpate Inn—"

"Yes, it's a little more lively in summer, when that's open," answered the agent; "we get a lot of complaints about trunks not coming, from pretty swell people, too. It sort of cheers things." His eye roamed with interest over Mr. Magee's New York attire. "But Baldpate Inn is shut up tight now.

This is nothing but an annex to a graveyard in winter. You wasn't thinking of stopping off here, was you?"

"Well—I want to see a man named Elijah Quimby," Mr. Magee replied. "Do you know him?"

"Of course," said the yearner for pastures new, "he's caretaker of the inn. His house is about a mile out, on the old Miller Road that leads up Baldpate. Come outside and I'll tell you how to get there."

The two men went out into the whirling snow, and the agent waved a hand indefinitely up at the night.

"If it was clear," he said, "you could see Baldpate Mountain, over yonder, looking down on the Falls, sort of keeping an eye on us to make sure we don't get reckless. And half-way up you'd see Baldpate Inn, black and peaceful and winter-y. Just follow this street to the third corner, and turn to your left. Elijah lives in a little house back among the trees a mile out—there's a gate you'll sure hear creaking on a night like this."

Billy Magee thanked him, and gathering up his two bags, walked up "Main Street." A dreary forbidding building at the first corner bore the sign "Commercial House". Under the white gaslight in the office window three born pessimists slouched low in hotel chairs, gazing sourly out at the storm.

"Weep no more, my lady,Oh! weep no more to-day,"

hummed Mr. Magee cynically under his breath, and glanced up at the solitary up-stairs window that gleamed yellow in the night.

At a corner on which stood a little shop that advertised "Groceries and Provisions" he paused.

"Let me see," he pondered. "The lights will be turned off, of course. Candles. And a little something for the inner man, in case it's the closed season for cooks."

He went inside, where a weary old woman served him.

"What sort of candles?" she inquired, with the air of one who had an infinite variety in stock. Mr. Magee remembered that Christmas was near.

"For a Christmas tree," he explained. He asked for two hundred.

"I've only got forty," the woman said. "What's this tree for—the Orphans' Home?"

With the added burden of a package containing his purchases in the tiny store, Mr. Magee emerged and continued his journey through the stinging snow. Upper Asquewan Falls on its way home for supper flitted past him in the silvery darkness. He saw in the lighted windows of many of the houses the green wreath of Christmas cheer. Finally the houses became infrequent, and he struck out on an uneven road that wound upward. Once he heard a dog's faint bark. Then a carriage lurched by him, and a strong voice cursed the roughness of the road. Mr. Magee half smiled to himself as he strode on.

"Don Quixote, my boy," he muttered, "I know how you felt when you moved on the windmills."

It was not the whir of windmills but the creak of a gate in the storm that brought Mr. Magee at last to a stop. He walked gladly up the path to Elijah Quimby's door.

In answer to Billy Magee's gay knock, a man of about sixty years appeared. Evidently he had just finished supper; at the moment he was engaged in lighting his pipe. He admitted Mr. Magee into the intimacy of the kitchen, and took a number of calm judicious puffs on the pipe before speaking to his visitor. In that interval the visitor cheerily seized his hand, oblivious of the warm burnt match that was in it. The match fell to the floor, whereupon the older man cast an anxious glance at a gray-haired woman who stood beside the kitchen stove.

"My name's Magee," blithely explained that gentleman, dragging in his bags. "And you're Elijah Quimby, of course. How are you? Glad to see you." His air was that of one who had known this Quimby intimately, in many odd corners of the world.

The older man did not reply, but regarded Mr. Magee wonderingly through white puffs of smoke. His face was kindly, gentle, ineffectual; he seemed to lack the final "punch" that send men over the line to success; this was evident in the way his necktie hung, the way his thin hands fluttered.

"Yes," he admitted at last. "Yes, I'm Quimby."

Mr. Magee threw back his coat, and sprayed with snow Mrs. Quimby's immaculate floor.

"I'm Magee," he elucidated again, "William Hallowell Magee, the man Hal Bentley wrote to you about. You got his letter, didn't you?"

Mr. Quimby removed his pipe and forgot to close the aperture as he stared in amazement.

"Good lord!" he cried, "you don't mean—you've really come."

"What better proof could you ask," said Mr. Magee flippantly, "than my presence here?"

"Why," stammered Mr. Quimby, "we—we thought it was all a joke."

"Hal Bentley has his humorous moments," agreed Mr. Magee, "but it isn't his habit to fling his jests into Upper Asquewan Falls."

"And—and you're really going to—" Mr. Quimby could get no further.

"Yes," said Mr. Magee brightly, slipping into a rocking-chair. "Yes, I'm going to spend the next few months at Baldpate Inn."

Mrs. Quimby, who seemed to have settled into a stout little mound of a woman through standing too long in the warm presence of her stove, came forward and inspected Mr. Magee.

"Of all things," she murmured.

"It's closed," expostulated Mr. Quimby; "the inn is closed, young fellow."

"I know it's closed," smiled Magee. "That's the very reason I'm going to honor it with my presence. I'm sorry to take you out on a night like this, but I'll have to ask you to lead me up to Baldpate. I believe those were Hal Bentley's instructions—in the letter."

Mr. Quimby towered above Mr. Magee, a shirt-sleeved statue of honest American manhood. He scowled.

"Excuse a plain question, young man," he said, "but what are you hiding from?"

Mrs. Quimby, in the neighborhood of the stove, paused to hear the reply. Billy Magee laughed.

"I'm not hiding," he said. "Didn't Bentley explain? Well, I'll try to, though I'm not sure you'll understand. Sit down, Mr. Quimby. You are not, I take it, the sort of man to follow closely the light and frivolous literature of the day."

"What's that?" inquired Mr. Quimby.

"You don't read," continued Mr. Magee, "the sort of novels that are sold by the pound in the department stores. Now, if you had a daughter—a fluffy daughter inseparable from a hammock in the summer—she could help me explain. You see—I write those novels. Wild thrilling tales for the tired business man's tired wife—shots in the night, chases after fortunes, Cupid busy with his arrows all over the place! It's good fun, and I like to do it. There's money in it."

"Is there?" asked Mr. Quimby with a show of interest.

"Considerable," replied Mr. Magee. "But now and then I get a longing to do something that will make the critics sit up—the real thing, you know. The other day I picked up a newspaper and found my latest brain-child advertised as 'the best fall novel Magee ever wrote'. It got on my nerves—I felt like a literary dressmaker, and I could see my public laying down my fall novel and sighing for my early spring styles in fiction. I remembered that once upon a time a critic advised me to go away for ten years to some quiet spot, and think. I decided to do it. Baldpate Inn is the quiet spot."

"You don't mean," gasped Mr. Quimby, "that you're going to stay there ten years?"

"Bless you, no," said Mr. Magee. "Critics exaggerate. Two months will do. They say I am a cheap melodramatic ranter. They say I don't go deep. They say my thinking process is a scream. I'm afraid they're right. Now, I'm going to go up to Baldpate Inn, and think. I'm going to get away from melodrama. I'm going to do a novel so fine and literary that Henry Cabot Lodge will come to me with tears in his eyes and ask me to join his bunch of self-made Immortals. I'm going to do all this up there at the inn—sitting on the mountain and looking down on this little old world as Jove looked down from Olympus."

"I don't know who you mean," objected Mr. Quimby.

"He was a god—the god of the fruit-stand men," explained Magee. "Picture me, if you can, depressed by the overwhelming success of my latest brain-child. Picture me meeting Hal Bentley in a Forty-fourth Street club and asking him for the location of the lonesomest spot on earth. Hal thought a minute. 'I've got it', he said, 'the lonesomest spot that's happened to date is a summer resort in mid-winter. It makes Crusoe's island look like Coney on a warm Sunday afternoon in comparison.' The talk flowed on, along with other things. Hal told me his father owned Baldpate Inn, and that you were an old friend of his who would be happy for the entire winter over the chance to serve him. He happened to have a key to the place—the key to the big front door, I guess, from the weight of it—and he gave it to me. He also wrote you to look after me. So here I am."

Mr. Quimby ran his fingers through his white hair.

"Here I am," repeated Billy Magee, "fleeing from the great glitter known as Broadway to do a little rational thinking in the solitudes. It's getting late, and I suggest that we start for Baldpate Inn at once."

"This ain't exactly—regular," Mr. Quimby protested. "No, it ain't what you might call a frequent occurrence. I'm glad to do anything I can for young Mr. Bentley, but I can't help wondering what his father will say. And there's a lot of things you haven't took into consideration."

"There certainly is, young man," remarked Mrs. Quimby, bustling forward. "How are you going to keep warm in that big barn of a place?"

"The suites on the second floor," said Mr. Magee, "are, I hear, equipped with fireplaces. Mr. Quimby will keep me supplied with fuel from the forest primeval, for which service he will receive twenty dollars a week."

"And light?" asked Mrs. Quimby.

"For the present, candles. I have forty in that package. Later, perhaps you can find me an oil lamp. Oh, everything will be provided for."

"Well," remarked Mr. Quimby, looking in a dazed fashion at his wife, "I reckon I'll have to talk it over with ma."

The two retired to the next room, and Mr. Magee fixed his eyes on a "God Bless Our Home" motto while he awaited their return. Presently they reappeared.

"Was you thinking of eating?" inquired Mrs. Quimby sarcastically, "while you stayed up there?"

"I certainly was," smiled Mr. Magee. "For the most part I will prepare my own meals from cans and—er—jars—and such pagan sources. But now and then you, Mrs. Quimby, are going to send me something cooked as no other woman in the county can cook it. I can see it in your eyes. In my poor way I shall try to repay you."

He continued to smile into Mrs. Quimby's broad cheerful face. Mr. Magee had the type of smile that moves men to part with ten until Saturday, and women to close their eyes and dream of Sir Launcelot. Mrs. Quimby could not long resist. She smiled back. Whereupon Billy Magee sprang to his feet.

"It's all fixed," he cried. "We'll get on splendidly. And now—for Baldpate Inn."

"Not just yet," said Mrs. Quimby. "I ain't one to let anybody go up to Baldpate Inn unfed. I 'spose we're sort o' responsible for you, while you're up here. You just set right down and I'll have your supper hot and smoking on the table in no time."

Mr. Magee entered into no dispute on this point, and for half an hour he was the pleased recipient of advice, philosophy, and food. When he had assured Mrs. Quimby that he had eaten enough to last him the entire two months he intended spending at the inn, Mr. Quimby came in, attired in a huge "before the war" ulster, and carrying a lighted lantern.

"So you're going to sit up there and write things," he commented. "Well, I reckon you'll be left to yourself, all right."

"I hope so," responded Mr. Magee. "I want to be so lonesome I'll sob myself to sleep every night. It's the only road to immortality. Good-by, Mrs. Quimby. In my fortress on the mountain I shall expect an occasional culinary message from you." He took her plump hand; this motherly little woman seemed the last link binding him to the world of reality.

"Good-by," smiled Mrs. Quimby. "Be careful of matches."

Mr. Quimby led the way with the lantern, and presently they stepped out upon the road. The storm had ceased, but it was still very dark. Far below, in the valley, twinkled the lights of Upper Asquewan Falls.

"By the way, Quimby," remarked Mr. Magee, "is there a girl in your town who has blue eyes, light hair, and the general air of a queen out shopping?"

"Light hair," repeated Quimby. "There's Sally Perry. She teaches in the Methodist Sunday-school."

"No," said Mr. Magee. "My description was poor, I'm afraid. This one I refer to, when she weeps, gives the general effect of mist on the sea at dawn. The Methodists do not monopolize her."

"I read books, and I read newspapers," said Mr. Quimby, "but a lot of your talk I don't understand."

"The critics," replied Billy Magee, "could explain. My stuff is only for low-brows. Lead on, Mr. Quimby."

Mr. Quimby stood for a moment in dazed silence. Then he turned, and the yellow of his lantern fell on the dazzling snow ahead. Together the two climbed Baldpate Mountain.

CHAPTER II
ENTER A LOVELORN HABERDASHER

Baldpate Inn did not stand tiptoe on the misty mountain-top. Instead it clung with grim determination to the side of Baldpate, about half-way up, much as a city man clings to the running board of an open street-car. This was the comparison Mr. Magee made, and even as he made it he knew that atmospheric conditions rendered it questionable. For an open street-car suggests summer and the ball park; Baldpate Inn, as it shouldered darkly into Mr. Magee's ken, suggested winter at its most wintry.

About the great black shape that was the inn, like arms, stretched broad verandas. Mr. Magee remarked upon them to his companion.

"Those porches and balconies and things," he said, "will come in handy in cooling the fevered brow of genius."

"There ain't much fever in this locality," the practical Quimby assured him, "especially not in winter."

Silenced, Mr. Magee followed the lantern of Quimby over the snow to the broad steps, and up to the great front door. There Magee produced from beneath his coat an impressive key. Mr. Quimby made as though to assist, but was waved aside.

"This is a ceremony," Mr. Magee told him, "some day Sunday newspaper stories will be written about it. Baldpate Inn opening its doors to the great American novel!"

He placed the key in the lock, turned it, and the door swung open. The coldest blast of air Mr. Magee had even encountered swept out from the dark interior. He shuddered, and wrapped his coat closer. He seemed to see the white trail from Dawson City, the sled dogs straggling on with the dwindling provisions, the fat Eskimo guide begging for gum-drops by his side.

"Whew," he cried, "we've discovered another Pole!"

"It's stale air," remarked Quimby.

"You mean the Polar atmosphere," replied Magee. "Yes, it is pretty stale. Jack London and Doctor Cook have worked it to death."

"I mean," said Quimby, "this air has been in here alone too long. It's as stale as last week's newspaper. We couldn't heat it with a million fires. We'll have to let in some warm air from outside first."

"Warm air—humph," remarked Mr. Magee. "Well, live and learn."

The two stood together in a great bare room. The rugs had been removed, and such furniture as remained had huddled together, as if for warmth, in the center of the floor. When they stepped forward, the sound of their shoes on the hard wood seemed the boom that should wake the dead.

"This is the hotel office," explained Mr. Quimby.

At the left of the door was the clerk's desk; behind it loomed a great safe, and a series of pigeon-holes for the mail of the guests. Opposite the front door, a wide stairway led to a landing half-way up, where the stairs were divorced and went to the right and left in search of the floor above. Mr. Magee surveyed the stairway critically.

"A great place," he remarked, "to show off the talents of your dressmaker, eh, Quimby? Can't you just see the stunning gowns coming down that stair in state, and the young men below here agitated in their bosoms?"

"No, I can't," said Mr. Quimby frankly.

"I can't either, to tell the truth," laughed Billy Magee. He turned up his collar. "It's like picturing a summer girl sitting on an iceberg and swinging her open-work hosiery over the edge. I don't suppose it's necessary to register. I'll go right up and select my apartments."

It was upon a suite of rooms that bore the number seven on their door that Mr. Magee's choice fell. A large parlor with a fireplace that a few blazing logs would cheer, a bedroom whose bed was destitute of all save mattress and springs, and a bathroom, comprised his kingdom. Here, too, all the furniture was piled in the center of the rooms. After Quimby had opened the windows, he began straightening the furniture about.

Mr. Magee inspected his apartment. The windows were all of the low French variety, and opened out upon a broad snow-covered balcony which was in reality the roof of the first floor veranda. On this balcony Magee stood a moment, watching the trees on Baldpate wave their black arms in the wind, and the lights of Upper Asquewan Falls wink knowingly up at him. Then he came inside, and his investigations brought him, presently to the tub in the bathroom.

"Fine," he cried, "a cold plunge in the morning before the daily struggle for immortality begins."

He turned the spigot. Nothing happened.

"I reckon," drawled Mr. Quimby from the bedroom, "you'll carry your cold plunge up from the well back of the inn before you plunge into it. The water's turned off. We can't take chances with busted pipes."

"Of course," replied Magee less blithely. His ardor was somewhat dampened—a paradox—by the failure of the spigot to gush forth a response. "There's nothing I'd enjoy more than carrying eight pails of water up-stairs every morning to get up an appetite for—what? Oh, well, the Lord will provide. If we propose to heat up the great American outdoors, Quimby, I think it's time we had a fire."

Mr. Quimby went out without comment, and left Magee to light his first candle in the dark. For a time he occupied himself with lighting a few of the forty, and distributing them about the room. Soon Quimby came back with kindling and logs, and subsequently a noisy fire roared in the grate. Again Quimby retired, and returned with a generous armful of bedding, which he threw upon the brass bed in the inner room. Then he slowly closed and locked the windows, after which he came and looked down with good-natured contempt at Mr. Magee, who sat in a chair before the fire.

"I wouldn't wander round none," he advised. "You might fall down something—or something. I been living in these parts, off and on, for sixty years and more, and nothing like this ever came under my observation before. Howsomever, I guess it's all right if Mr. Bentley says so. I'll come up in the morning and see you down to the train."

"What train?" inquired Mr. Magee.

"Your train back to New York City," replied Mr. Quimby. "Don't try to start back in the night. There ain't no train till morning."

"Ah, Quimby," laughed Mr. Magee, "you taunt me. You think I won't stick it out. But I'll show you. I tell you, I'm hungry for solitude."

"That's all right," Mr. Quimby responded, "you can't make three square meals a day off solitude."

"I'm desperate," said Magee. "Henry Cabot Lodge must come to me, I say, with tears in his eyes. Ever see the senator that way? No? It isn't going to be an easy job. I must put it over. I must go deep into the hearts of men, up here, and write what I find. No more shots in the night. Just the adventure of soul and soul. Do you see? By the way, here's twenty dollars, your first week's pay as caretaker of a New York Quixote."

"What's that?" asked Quimby.

"Quixote," explained Mr. Magee, "was a Spanish lad who was a little confused in his mind, and went about the country putting up at summer resorts in mid-winter."

"I'd expect it of a Spaniard," Quimby said. "Be careful of that fire. I'll be up in the morning." He stowed away the bill Mr. Magee had given him. "I guess nothing will interfere with your lonesomeness. Leastways, I hope it won't. Good night."

Mr. Magee bade the man good night, and listened to the thump of his boots, and the closing of the great front door. From his windows he watched the caretaker move down the road without looking back, to disappear at last in the white night.

Throwing off his great coat, Mr. Magee noisily attacked the fire. The blaze flared red on his strong humorous mouth, in his smiling eyes. Next, in the flickering half-light of suite seven, he distributed the contents of his traveling-bags about. On the table he placed a number of new magazines and a few books.

Then Mr. Magee sat down in the big leather chair before the fire, and caught his breath. Here he was at last. The wild plan he and Hal Bentley had cooked up in that Forty-fourth Street club had actually come to be. "Seclusion," Magee had cried. "Bermuda," Bentley had suggested. "A mixture of sea, hotel clerks, and honeymooners!" the seeker for solitude had sneered. "Some winter place down South,"—from Bentley. "And a flirtation lurking in every corner!"—from Magee. "A country town where you don't know any one." "The easiest place in the world to get acquainted. I must be alone, man! Alone!" "Baldpate Inn," Bentley had cried in his idiom. "Why, Billy—Baldpate Inn at Christmas—it must be old John H. Seclusion himself."

Yes, here he was. And here was the solitude he had come to find. Mr. Magee looked nervously about, and the smile died out of his gray eyes. For the first time misgivings smote him. Might one not have too much of a good thing? A silence like that of the tomb had descended. He recalled stories of men who went mad from loneliness. What place lonelier than this? The wind howled along the balcony. It rattled the windows. Outside his door lay a great black cave—in summer gay with men and maids— now like Crusoe's island before the old man landed.

"Alone, alone, all, all alone," quoted Mr. Magee. "If I can't think here it will be because I'm not equipped with the apparatus. I will. I'll show the gloomy old critics! I wonder what's doing in New York?"

New York! Mr. Magee looked at his watch. Eight o'clock. The great street was ablaze. The crowds were parading from the restaurants to the theaters. The electric signs were pasting lurid legends on a long suffering sky; the taxis were spraying throats with gasoline; the traffic cop at Broadway and Forty-second Street was madly earning his pay. Mr. Magee got up and walked the floor. New York!

Probably the telephone in his rooms was jangling, vainly calling forth to sport with Amaryllis in the shade of the rubber trees Billy Magee—Billy Magee who sat alone in the silence on Baldpate Mountain. Few knew of his departure. This was the night of that stupid attempt at theatricals at the Plaza; stupid in itself but gay, almost giddy, since Helen Faulkner was to be there. This was the night of the dinner to Carey at the club. This was the night—of many diverting things.

Mr. Magee picked up a magazine. He wondered how they read, in the old days, by candlelight. He wondered if they would have found his own stories worth the strain on the eyes. And he also wondered if absolute solitude was quite the thing necessary to the composition of the novel that should forever silence those who sneered at his ability.

Absolute solitude! Only the crackle of the fire, the roar of the wind, and the ticking of his watch bore him company. He strode to the window and looked down at the few dim lights that proclaimed the existence of Upper Asquewan Falls. Somewhere, down there, was the Commercial House. Somewhere the girl who had wept so bitterly in that gloomy little waiting-room. She was only three miles away, and the thought cheered Mr. Magee. After all, he was not on a desert island.

And yet—he was alone, intensely, almost painfully, alone. Alone in a vast moaning house that must be his only home until he could go back to the gay city with his masterpiece. What a masterpiece! As though with a surgeon's knife it would lay bare the hearts of men. No tricks of plot, no—

Mr. Magee paused. For sharply in the silence the bell of his room telephone rang out.

He stood for a moment gazing in wonder, his heart beating swiftly, his eyes upon the instrument on the wall. It was a house phone; he knew that it could only be rung from the switchboard in the hall below. "I'm going mad already," he remarked, and took down the receiver.

A blur of talk, an electric muttering, a click, and all was still.

Mr. Magee opened the door and stepped out into the shadows. He heard a voice below. Noiselessly he crept to the landing, and gazed down into the office. A young man sat at the telephone switchboard; Mr. Magee could see in the dim light of a solitary candle that he was a person of rather hilarious raiment. The candle stood on the top of the safe, and the door of the latter swung open. Sinking down on the steps in the dark, Mr. Magee waited.

"Hello," the young man was saying, "how do you work this thing, anyhow? I've tried every peg but the right one. Hello—hello! I want long distance—Reuton. 2876 West—Mr. Andy Rutter. Will you get him for me, sister?"

Another wait—a long one—ensued. The candle sputtered. The young man fidgeted in his chair. At last he spoke again:

"Hello! Andy? Is that you, Andy? What's the good word? As quiet as the tomb of Napoleon. Shall I close up shop? Sure. What next? Oh, see here, Andy, I'd die up here. Did you ever hit a place like this in winter? I can't—I—oh, well, if he says so. Yes. I could do that. But no longer. I couldn't stand it long. Tell him that. Tell him everything's O. K. Yes. All right. Well, good night, Andy."

He turned away from the switchboard, and as he did so Mr. Magee walked calmly down the stairs toward him. With a cry the young man ran to the safe, threw a package inside, and swung shut the door. He turned the knob of the safe several times; then he faced Mr. Magee. The latter saw something glitter in his hand.

"Good evening," remarked Mr. Magee pleasantly.

"What are you doing here?" cried the youth wildly.

"I live here," Mr. Magee assured him. "Won't you come up to my room—it's right at the head of the stairs. I have a fire, you know."

Back into the young man's lean hawk-like face crept the assurance that belonged with the gay attire he wore. He dropped the revolver into his pocket, and smiled a sneering smile.

"You gave me a turn," he said. "Of course you live here. Are any of the other guests about? And who won the tennis match to-day?"

"You are facetious." Mr. Magee smiled too. "So much the better. A lively companion is the very sort I should have ordered to-night. Come up-stairs."

The young man looked suspiciously about, his thin nose seemingly scenting plots. He nodded, and picked up the candle. "All right," he said. "But I'll have to ask you to go first. You know the way." His right hand sought the pocket into which the revolver had fallen.

"You honor my poor and drafty house," said Mr. Magee. "This way."

He mounted the stairs. After him followed the youth of flashy habiliments, looking fearfully about him as he went. He seemed surprised that they came to Magee's room without incident. Inside, Mr. Magee drew up an easy chair before the fire, and offered his guest a cigar.

"You must be cold," he said. "Sit here. 'A bad night, stranger' as they remark in stories."

"You've said it," replied the young man, accepting the cigar. "Thanks." He walked to the door leading into the hall and opened it about a foot.

"I'm afraid," he explained jocosely, "we'll get to talking, and miss the breakfast bell." He dropped into the chair, and lighted his cigar at a candle end. "Say, you never can tell, can you? Climbing up old Baldpate I thought to myself, that hotel certainly makes the Sahara Desert look like a cozy corner. And here you are, as snug and comfortable and at home as if you were in a Harlem flat. You never can tell. And what now? The story of my life?"

"You might relate," Mr. Magee told him, "that portion of it that has led you trespassing on a gentleman seeking seclusion at Baldpate Inn."

The stranger looked at Mr. Magee. He had an eye that not only looked, but weighed, estimated, and classified. Mr. Magee met it smilingly.

"Trespassing, eh?" said the young man. "Far be it from me to quarrel with a man who smokes as good cigars as you do—but there's something I haven't quite doped out. That is—who's trespassing, me or you?"

"My right here," said Mr. Magee, "is indisputable."

"It's a big word," replied the other, "but you can tack it to my right here, and tell no lie. We can't dispute, so let's drop the matter. With that settled, I'm encouraged to pour out the story of why you see me here to-night, far from the madding crowd. Have you a stray tear? You'll need it. It's a sad touching story, concerned with haberdashery and a trusting heart, and a fair woman—fair, but, oh, how false!"

"Proceed," laughed Mr. Magee. "I'm an admirer of the vivid imagination. Don't curb yours, I beg of you."

"It's all straight," said the other in a hurt tone. "Every word true. My name is Joseph Bland. My profession, until love entered my life, was that of haberdasher and outfitter. In the city of Reuton, fifty miles from here, I taught the Beau Brummels of the thoroughfares what was doing in London in the necktie line. I sold them coats with padded shoulders, and collars high and awe inspiring. I was happy, twisting a piece of silk over my hand to show them how it would look on their heaving bosoms. And then—she came."

Mr. Bland puffed on his cigar.

"Yes," he said, "Arabella sparkled on the horizon of my life. When I have been here in the quiet for about two centuries, maybe I can do justice to her beauty. I won't attempt to describe her now. I loved her—madly. She said I made a hit with her. I spent on her the profits of my haberdashery. I whispered—marriage. She didn't scream. I had my wedding necktie picked out from the samples of a drummer from Troy." He paused and looked at Mr. Magee. "Have you ever stood, poised, on that brink?" he asked.

"Never," replied Magee. "But go on. Your story attracts me, strangely."

"From here on—the tear I spoke of, please. There flashed on the scene a man she had known and loved in Jersey City. I said flashed. He did—just that. A swell dresser—say, he had John Drew beat by two mauve neckties and a purple frock coat. I had a haberdashery back of me. No use. He out-dressed me. I saw that Arabella's love for me was waning. With his chamois-gloved hands that new guy fanned the ancient flame."

He paused. Emotion—or the smoke of the cigar—choked him.

"Let's make the short story shorter," he said. "She threw me down. In my haberdashery I thought it over. I was blue, bitter. I resolved on a dreadful step. In the night I wrote her a letter, and carried it down to the box and posted it. Life without Arabella, said the letter, was Shakespeare with Hamlet left out. It hinted at the river, carbolic acid, revolvers. Yes, I posted it. And then—"

"And then," urged Mr. Magee.

Mr. Bland felt tenderly of the horseshoe pin in his purple tie.

"This is just between us," he said. "At that point the trouble began. It came from my being naturally a very brave man. I could have died—easy. The brave thing was to live. To go on, day after day, devoid of Arabella— say, that took courage. I wanted to try it. I'm a courageous man, as I say."

"You seem so," Mr. Magee agreed.

"Lion-hearted," assented Mr. Bland. "I determined to show my nerve, and live. But there was my letter to Arabella. I feared she wouldn't appreciate my bravery—women are dull sometimes. It came to me maybe she would be hurt if I didn't keep my word, and die. So I had to—disappear. I had a friend mixed up in affairs at Baldpate. No, I can't give his name. I told him my story. He was impressed by my spirit, as you have been. He gave me a key he had—the key of the door opening from the east veranda into the dining-room. So I came up here. I came here to be alone, to forgive and forget, to be forgot. And maybe to plan a new haberdashery in distant parts."

"Was it your wedding necktie," asked Mr. Magee, "that you threw into the safe when you saw me coming?"

"No," replied Mr. Bland, sighing deeply. "A package of letters, written to me by Arabella at various times. I want to forget 'em. If I kept them on hand, I might look at them from time to time. My great courage might give way—you might find my body on the stairs. That's why I hid them."

Mr. Magee laughed, and stretched forth his hand.

"Believe me," he said, "your touching confidence in me will not be betrayed. I congratulate you on your narrative power. You want my story. Why am I here? I am not sure that it is worthy to follow yours. But it has its good points—as I have thought it out."

He went over to the table, and picked up a popular novel upon which his gaze had rested while the haberdasher spun his fabric of love and gloom. On the cover was a picture of a very dashing maiden.

"Do you see that girl?" he asked. "She is beautiful, is she not? Even Arabella, in her most splendid moments, could get a few points from her, I fancy. Perhaps you are not familiar with the important part such a picture plays in the success of a novel to-day. The truth is, however, that the noble art of fiction writing has come to lean more and more heavily on its illustrators. The mere words that go with the pictures grow less important every day. There are dozens of distinguished novelists in the country at this moment who might be haberdashers if it weren't for the long, lean, haughty ladies who are scattered tastefully through their works."

Mr. Bland stirred uneasily.

"I can see you are at a loss to know what my search for seclusion and privacy has to do with all this," continued Mr. Magee. "I am an artist. For years I have drawn these lovely ladies who make fiction salable to the masses. Many a novelist owes his motor-car and his country house to my brush. Two months ago, I determined to give up illustration forever, and devote my time to painting. I turned my back on the novelists. Can you imagine what happened?"

"My imagination's a little tired," apologized Mr. Bland.

"Never mind. I'll tell you. The leading authors whose work I had so long illustrated saw ruin staring them in the face. They came to me, on their knees, figuratively. They begged. They pleaded. They hid in the vestibule of my flat. I should say, my studio. They even came up in my dumb-waiter, having bribed the janitor. They wouldn't take no for an answer. In order to escape them and their really pitiful pleadings, I had to flee. I happened to have a friend involved in the management of Baldpate Inn. I am not at liberty to give his name. He gave me a key. So here I am. I rely on you to keep my secret. If you perceive a novelist in the distance, lose no time in warning me."

Mr. Magee paused, chuckling inwardly. He stood looking down at the lovelorn haberdasher. The latter got to his feet, and solemnly took Magee's hand.

"I—I—oh, well, you've got me beat a mile, old man," he said.

"You don't mean to say—" began the hurt Magee.

"Oh, that's all right," Mr. Bland assured him. "I believe every word of it. It's all as real as the haberdashery to me. I'll keep my eye peeled for novelists. What gets me is, when you boil our two fly-by-night stories down, I've come here to be alone. You want to be alone. We can't be alone here together. One of us must clear out."

"Nonsense," answered Billy Magee. "I'll be glad to have you here. Stay as long as you like."

The haberdasher looked Mr. Magee fully in the eye, and the latter was startled by the hostility he saw in the other's face.

"The point is," said Mr. Bland, "I don't want you here. Why? Maybe because you recall beautiful dames—on book covers—and in that way, Arabella. Maybe—but what's the use? I put it simply. I got to be alone— alone on Baldpate Mountain. I won't put you out to-night—"

"See here, my friend," cried Mr. Magee, "your grief has turned your head. You won't put me out to-night, or to-morrow. I'm here to stay. You're welcome to do the same, if you like. But you stay—with me. I know you are a man of courage—but it would take at least ten men of courage to put me out of Baldpate Inn."

They stood eying each other for a moment. Bland's thin lips twisted into a sneer. "We'll see," he said. "We'll settle all that in the morning." His tone took on a more friendly aspect "I'm going to pick out a downy couch in one of these rooms," he said, "and lay me down to sleep. Say, I could greet a blanket like a long-lost friend."

Mr. Magee proffered some of the covers that Quimby had given him, and accompanied Mr. Bland to suite ten, across the hall. He explained the matter of "stale air", and assisted in the opening of windows. The conversation was mostly facetious, and Mr. Bland's last remark concerned the fickleness of woman. With a brisk good night, Mr. Magee returned to number seven.

But he made no move toward the chilly brass bed in the inner room. Instead he sat a long time by the fire. He reflected on the events of his first few hours in that supposedly uninhabited solitude where he was to be alone with his thoughts. He pondered the way and manner of the flippant young man who posed as a lovelorn haberdasher, and under whose flippancy there was certainly an air of hostility. Who was Andy Rutter, down in Reuton? What did the young man mean when he asked if he should "close up shop"? Who was the "he" from whom came the orders? and most important of all, what was in the package now resting in the great safe?

Mr. Magee smiled. Was this the stuff of which solitude was made? He recalled the ludicrous literary tale he had invented to balance the moving fiction of Arabella, and his smile grew broader. His imagination, at least, was in a healthy state. He looked at his watch. A quarter of twelve. Probably they were having supper at the Plaza now, and Helen Faulkner was listening to the banalities of young Williams. He settled in his seat to think of Miss Faulkner. He thought of her for ten seconds; then stepped to the window.

The moon had risen, and the snowy roofs of Upper Asquewan Falls sparkled in the lime-light of the heavens. Under one of those roofs was the girl of the station—weeping no more, he hoped. Certainly she had eyes that held even the least susceptible—to which class Mr. Magee prided himself he belonged. He wished he might see her again; might talk to her without interruption from that impossible "mamma."

Mr. Magee turned back into the room. His fire was but red glowing ashes. He threw off his dressing-gown, and began to unlace his shoes.

"There *has* been too much crude melodrama in my novels," he reflected. "It's so easy to write. But I'm going to get away from all that up here. I'm going—"

Mr. Magee paused, with one shoe poised in his hand. For from below came the sharp crack of a pistol, followed by the crash of breaking glass.

CHAPTER III

BLONDES AND SUFFRAGETTES

r. Magee slipped into his dressing gown, seized a candle, and like the boy in the nursery rhyme with one shoe off and one shoe on, ran into the hall. All was silent and dark below. He descended to the landing, and stood there, holding the candle high above his head. It threw a dim light as far as the bottom of the stairs, but quickly lost the battle with the shadows that lay beyond.

"Hello," the voice of Bland, the haberdasher, came out of the blackness. "The Goddess of Liberty, as I live! What's your next imitation?"

"There seems to be something doing," said Mr. Magee.

Mr. Bland came into the light, partially disrobed, his revolver in his hand.

"Somebody trying to get in by the front door," he explained. "I shot at him to scare him away. Probably one of your novelists."

"Or Arabella," remarked Mr. Magee, coming down.

"No," answered Bland. "I distinctly saw a derby hat."

With Mr. Magee descended the yellow candlelight, and brushing aside the shadows of the hotel office, it revealed a mattress lying on the floor close to the clerk's desk, behind which stood the safe. On the mattress was the bedding Magee had presented to the haberdasher, hastily thrown back by the lovelorn one on rising.

"You prefer to sleep down here," Mr. Magee commented.

"Near the letters of Arabella—yes," replied Bland. His keen eyes met Magee's. There was a challenge in them.

Mr. Magee turned, and the yellow light of the candle flickered wanly over the great front door Even as he looked at it, the door was pushed open, and a queer figure of a man stood framed against a background of glittering snow. Mr. Bland's arm flew up.

"Don't shoot," cried Magee.

"No, please don't," urged the man in the doorway. A beard, a pair of round owlish spectacles, and two ridiculous ear-muffs, left only a suggestion of face here and there. He closed the door and stepped into the room. "I have every right here, I assure you, even though my arrival is somewhat unconventional. See—I have the key." He held up a large brass key that was the counterpart of the one Hal Bentley had bestowed upon Mr. Magee in that club on far-off Forty-fourth Street.

"Keys to burn," muttered Mr. Bland sourly.

"I bear no ill will with regard to the shooting," went on the newcomer. He took off his derby hat and ruefully regarded a hole through the crown. His bald head seemed singularly frank and naked above a face of so many disguises. "It is only natural that men alone on a mountain should defend themselves from invaders at two in the morning. My escape was narrow, but there is no ill will."

He blinked about him, his breath a white cloud in the cold room.

"Life, young gentlemen," he remarked, setting down his bag and leaning a green umbrella against it, "has its surprises even at sixty-two. Last night I was ensconced by my own library fire, preparing a paper on the Pagan Renaissance. To-night I am on Baldpate Mountain, with a perforation in my hat."

Mr. Bland shivered. "I'm going back to bed," he said in disgust.

"First," went on the gentleman with the perforated derby, "permit me to introduce myself. I am Professor Thaddeus Bolton, and I hold the Chair of Comparative Literature in a big eastern university."

Mr. Magee took the mittened hand of the professor.

"Glad to see you, I'm sure," he said. "My name is Magee. This is Mr. Bland—he is impetuous but estimable. I trust you will forgive his first salute. What's a bullet among gentlemen? It seems to me that as explanations may be lengthy and this room is very cold, we would do well to go up to my room, where there is a fire."

"Delighted," cried the old man. "A fire. I long to see one. Let us go to your room, by all means."

Mr. Bland sulkily stalked to his mattress and secured a gaily colored bed quilt, which he wound about his thin form.

"This is positively the last experience meeting I attend to-night," he growled.

They ascended to number seven. Mr. Magee piled fresh logs on the fire; Mr. Bland saw to it that the door was not tightly closed. The professor removed, along with other impedimenta, his ear tabs, which were connected by a rubber cord. He waved them like frisky detached ears before him.

"An old man's weakness," he remarked. "Foolish, they may seem to you. But I assure you I found them useful companions in climbing Baldpate Mountain at this hour."

He sat down in the largest chair suite seven owned, and from its depths smiled benignly at the two young men.

"But I am not here to apologize for my apparel, am I? Hardly. You are saying to yourselves 'Why is he here?' Yes, that is the question that disturbs you. What has brought this domesticated college professor scampering from the Pagan Renaissance to Baldpate Inn? For answer, I must ask you to go back with me a week's time, and gaze at a picture from the rather dreary academic kaleidoscope that is my life.

"I am seated back of a desk on a platform in a bare yellow room. In front of me, tier on tier, sit a hundred young men in various attitudes of inattention. I am trying to tell them something of the ideal poetry that marked the rebirth of the Saxon genius. They are bored. I—well, gentlemen, in confidence, even the mind of a college professor has been known to wander at times from the subject in hand. And then—I begin to read a poem—a poem descriptive of a woman dead six hundred years and more. Ah, gentlemen—"

He sat erect on the edge of his great chair. Back of the thick lenses of his spectacles he had eyes that still could flash.

"This is not an era of romance," he said. "Our people grub in the dirt for the dollar. Their visions perish. Their souls grow stale. Yet, now and then, at most inopportune times, comes the flash that reveals to us the glories that might be. A gentleman of my acquaintance caught a glimpse of perfect happiness while he was in the midst of an effort to corner the pickle market. Another evolved the scheme of a perfect ode to the essential purity of woman in—a Broadway restaurant. So, like lightning across the blackest sky, our poetic moments come."

Mr. Bland wrapped his gay quilt more securely about him. Mr. Magee smiled encouragement on the newest raconteur.

"I shall be brief," continued Professor Bolton. "Heaven knows that pedagogic room was no place for visions, nor were those athletic young men fit companions for a soul gone giddy. Yet—I lost my head. As I read on there returned to my heart a glow I had not known in forty years. The bard spoke of her hair:

"'Her yellow lockes, crisped like golden wyre, About her shoulders weren loosely shed'

and I saw, as in a dream—ahem, I can trust you, gentlemen—a girl I supposed I had forever forgot in the mold and dust of my later years. I will not go further into the matter. My wife's hair is black.

"And reading on, but losing the thread of the poet's eulogy in the golden fabric of my resurrected dream, it came to me to compare that maid I knew in the long ago with the women I know to-day. Ah, gentlemen! Lips, made but for smiling, fling weighty arguments on the unoffending atmosphere. Eyes, made to light with that light that never was by land or sea, blaze instead with what they call the injustice of woman's servitude. White hands, made to find their way to the hands of some young man in the moonlight, carry banners in the dusty streets. It seemed I saw the blue eyes of that girl of long ago turned, sad, rebuking, on her sisters of to-day. As I finished reading, my heart was awhirl. I said to the young men before me:

"'There *was* a woman, gentlemen—a woman worth a million suffragettes.'

"They applauded. The fire in me died down. Soon I was my old meek, academic self. The vision had left no trace. I dismissed my class and went home. I found that my wife—she of the black hair—had left my slippers by the library fire. I put them on, and plunged into a pamphlet lately published by a distinguished member of a German university faculty. I thought the incident closed forever."

He gazed sorrowfully at the two young men.

"But, gentlemen, I had not counted on that viper that we nourish in our bosom—the American newspaper. At present I will not take time to denounce the press. I am preparing an article on the subject for a respectable weekly of select circulation. Suffice it to record what happened. The next day an evening paper appeared with a huge picture of me on its front page, and the hideous statement that this was the Professor Bolton who had said that 'One Peroxide Blonde Is Worth a Million Suffragettes'.

"Yes, that was the dreadful version of my remark that was spread broadcast. Up to the time that story appeared, I had no idea as to what sort of creature the peroxide blonde might be. I protested, of course. I might as well have tried to dam a tidal wave with a table fork. The wrath of the world swept down upon me. I was deluged with telegrams, editorials, letters, denouncing me. Firm-faced females lay in wait for me and waved umbrellas in my eyes. Even my wife turned from me, saying that while she did not ask me to hold her views on the question of suffrage, she thought I might at least refrain from publicly commending a type of woman found chiefly in musical comedy choruses. I received a note from the president of the university, asking me to be more circumspect in my remarks. Me— Thadeus Bolton—the most conservative man on earth by instinct!

"And still the denunciations of me poured in; still women's clubs held meetings resolving against me; still a steady stream of reporters flowed through my life, urging me to state my views further, to name the ten greatest blondes in history, to—heaven knows what. Yesterday I resolved I Could stand it no longer. I determined to go away until the whole thing was forgotten. 'But', they said to me, 'there is no place, on land or sea, where the reporters will not find you'. I talked the matter over with my old friend, John Bentley, owner of Baldpate Inn, and he in his kindness gave me the key to this hostelry."

The old man paused and passed a silk handkerchief over his bald head.

"That, sirs," he said, "is my story. That is why you see me on Baldpate Mountain this chill December morning. That is why loneliness can have no terrors, exile no sorrows, for me. That is why I bravely faced your revolver-shots. Again let me repeat, I bear no malice on that score. You have ruined a new derby hat, and the honorarium of professor even at a leading university is not such as to permit of many purchases in that line. But I forgive you freely. Even at the cannon's mouth I would have fled from reputation, to paraphrase the poet."

Wisely Professor Bolton blinked about him. Mr. Bland was half asleep in his chair, but Mr. Magee was quick with sympathy.

"Professor," he said, "you are a much suffering man. I feel for you. Here, I am sure, you are safe from reporters, and the yellow journals will soon forget you in their discovery of the next distorted wonder. Briefly, Mr. Bland and myself will outline the tangle of events that brought us to the inn—"

"Briefly is right," broke in Bland. "And then it's me for that mountainous mattress of mine. I can rattle my story off in short order, and give you the fine points to-morrow. Up to a short time ago—"

But Billy Magee interrupted. An idea, magnificent delicious, mirthful, had come to him. Why not? He chuckled inwardly, but his face was most serious.

"I should like to tell my story first, if you please," he said.

The haberdasher grunted. The professor nodded. Mr. Magee looked Bland squarely in the eye, strangled the laugh inside him, and began:

"Up to a short time ago I was a haberdasher in the city of Reuton. My name, let me state, is Magee—William Magee. I fitted the gay shoulder-blades of Reuton with clothing from the back pages of the magazines, and as for neckties—"

Mr. Bland's sly eyes had opened wide. He rose to a majestic height— majestic considering the bed quilt.

"See here—" he began.

"Please don't interrupt," requested Mr. Magee sweetly. "I was, as I have said, a happy carefree haberdasher. And then—she entered my life. Arabella was her name. Ah, Professor, you lady of the yellow locks, crisped liken golden wire—even she must never in my presence be compared with Arabella. She—she had—a—face—Noah Webster couldn't have found words to describe it. And her heart was true to yours truly—at least I thought that it was."

Mr. Magee rattled on. The haberdasher, his calling and his tragedy snatched from him by the humorous Magee, retired with sullen face into his bed quilt. Carefully Mr. Magee led up to the coming of the man from Jersey City; in detail he laid bare the duel of haberdashery fought in the name of the fair Arabella. As he proceeded, his enthusiasm grew. He added fine bits that had escaped Mr. Bland. He painted with free hand the picture of tragedy's dark hour; the note hinting at suicide he gave in full. Then he told of how his courage grew again, of how he put the cowardice of death behind him, resolved to dare all—and live. He finished at last, his voice husky with emotion. Out of the corner of his eye he glanced triumphantly at Bland. That gentleman was gazing thoughtfully at the blazing logs.

"You did quite right," commented Professor Bolton, "in making up your mind to live. I congratulate you on your common sense. And perhaps, as the years go by, you will realize that had you married your Arabella, you would not have found life all honey and roses. She was fickle, unworthy of you. Soon you will forget. Youth—ah, youth throws off its sorrow like a cloak. A figure not original with me. And now—the gentleman in the— er—the bed quilt. Has he, too, a story?"

"Yes," laughed Mr. Magee, "let's hear now from the gentleman in the bed quilt. Has he, too, a story? And if so, what is it?"

He smiled delightedly into the eyes of Bland. What would the ex-haberdasher do, shorn of his fictional explanation? Would he rise in his wrath and denounce the man who had stolen his Arabella? Mr. Bland smiled back. He stood up. And a contingency that had not entered Mr. Magee's mind came to be.

Mr. Bland walked calmly to the table, and picked up a popular novel that lay thereon. On its cover was the picture of a very beautiful maiden.

"See that dame?" he inquired of the professor. "Sort of makes a man sit up and take notice, doesn't she? Even the frost-bitten haberdasher here has got to admit that in some ways she has this Arabella person looking like a faded chromo in your grandmother's parlor on a rainy afternoon. Ever get any notion, Professor, the way a picture like that boosts a novel in the busy marts of trade? No? Well—"

Mr. Bland continued. Mr. Magee leaned back, overjoyed, in his chair. Here was a man not to be annoyed by the mere filching of his story. Here was a man with a sense of humor—an opponent worthy his foe's best efforts. In his rôle of a haberdasher overcome with woe, Mr. Magee listened.

"I used to paint dames like that," Bland was saying to the dazed professor. He explained how his pictures had enabled many a novelist to "eat up the highway in a buzz-wagon." As he approached the time when the novelists besieged him, he gave full play to his imagination. One, he said, sought out his apartments in an aeroplane.

"Say, Professor," he finished, "we're in the same boat. Both hiding from writers. A fellow that's spent his life selling neckties—well, he can't exactly appreciate our situation. There's what you might call a bond between you and me. D'ye know, I felt drawn to you, just after I fired that first shot. That's why I didn't blaze away again. We're going to be great friends—I can read it in the stars."

He took the older man's hand feelingly, shook it, and walked away, casting a covert glance of triumph at Mr. Magee.

The face of the holder of the Crandall Chair of Comparative Literature was a study. He looked first at one young man, then at the other. Again he applied the handkerchief to his shining head.

"All this is very odd," he said thoughtfully. "A man of sixty-two— particularly one who has long lived in the uninspired circle surrounding a university—has not the quick wit of youth. I'm afraid I don't—but no matter. It's very odd, though."

He permitted Mr. Magee to escort him into the hall, and to direct his search for a bed that should serve him through the scant remainder of the night. Overcoats and rugs were pressed into service as cover. Mr. Bland blithely assisted.

"If I see any newspaper reporters," he assured the professor on parting, "I'll damage more than their derbies."

"Thank you," replied the old man heartily. "You are very kind. To-morrow we shall become better acquainted. Good night."

The two young men came out and stood in the hallway. Mr. Magee spoke in a low tone.

"Forgive me," he said, "for stealing your Arabella."

"Take her and welcome," said Bland. "She was beginning to bore me, anyhow. And I'm not in your class as an actor." He came close to Magee. In the dim light that streamed out from number seven the latter saw the look on his face, and knew that, underneath all, this was a very much worried young man.

"For God's sake," cried Bland, "tell me who you are and what you're doing here. In three words—tell me."

"If I did," Mr. Magee replied, "you wouldn't believe me. Let such minor matters as the truth wait over till to-morrow."

"Well, anyhow," Bland said, his foot on the top step, "we are sure of one thing—we don't trust each other. I've got one parting word for you. Don't try to come down-stairs to-night. I've got a gun, and I ain't afraid to shoot."

He paused. A look of fright passed over his face. For on the floor above they both heard soft footsteps—then a faint click, as though a door had been gently closed.

"This inn," whispered Bland, "has more keys than a literary club in a prohibition town. And every one's in use, I guess. Remember. Don't try to come down-stairs. I've warned you. Or Arabella's cast-off Romeo may be found with a bullet in him yet."

"I shan't forget, what you say," answered Mr. Magee. "Shall we look about up-stairs?"

Bland shook his head.

"No," he said. "Go in and go to bed. It's the down-stairs that—that concerns me. Good night."

He went swiftly down the steps, leaving Mr. Magee staring wonderingly after him. Like a wraith he merged with the shadows below. Magee turned slowly, and entered number seven. A fantastic film of frost was on the windows; the inner room was drear and chill. Partially undressing, he lay down on the brass bed and pulled the covers over him.

The events of the night danced in giddy array before him as he closed his eyes. With every groan Baldpate Inn uttered in the wind he started up, keen for a new adventure. At length his mind seemed to stand still, and there remained of all that amazing evening's pictures but one—that of a girl in a blue corduroy suit who wept—wept only that her smile might be the more dazzling when it flashed behind the tears. "With yellow locks, crisped like golden wire," murmured Mr. Magee. And so he fell asleep.

CHAPTER IV

A PROFESSIONAL HERMIT APPEARS

Every morning at eight, when slumber's chains had bound Mr. Magee in his New York apartments, he was awakened by a pompous valet named Geoffrey whom he shared with the other young men in the building. It was Geoffrey's custom to enter, raise the curtains, and speak of the weather in a voice vibrant with feeling, as of something he had prepared himself and was anxious to have Mr. Magee try. So, when a rattling noise came to his ear on his first morning at Baldpate Inn, Mr. Magee breathed sleepily from the covers: "Good morning, Geoffrey."

But no cheery voice replied in terms of sun, wind, or rain. Surprised, Mr. Magee sat up in bed. About him, the maple-wood furniture of suite seven stood shivering in the chill of a December morning. Through the door at his left he caught sight of a white tub into which, he recalled sadly, not even a Geoffrey could coax a glittering drop. Yes—he was at Baldpate Inn. He remembered—the climb with the dazed Quimby up the snowy road, the plaint of the lovelorn haberdasher, the vagaries of the professor with a penchant for blondes, the mysterious click of the door-latch on the floor above. And last of all—strange that it should have been last—a girl in blue corduroy somewhat darker than her eyes, who wept amid the station's gloom.

"I wonder," reflected Mr. Magee, staring at the very brassy bars at the foot of his bed, "what new variations on seclusion the day will bring forth?"

Again came the rattling noise that had awakened him. He looked toward the nearest window, and through an unfrosted corner of the pane he saw the eyes of the newest variation staring at him in wonder. They were dark eyes, and kindly; they spoke a desire to enter.

Rising from his warm retreat, Mr. Magee took his shivering way across the uncarpeted floor and unfastened the window's catch. From the blustering balcony a plump little man stepped inside. He had a market basket on his arm. His face was a stranger to razors; his hair to shears. He reminded Mr. Magee of the celebrated doctor who came every year to the small town of his boyhood, there to sell a wonderful healing herb to the crowds on the street corner.

Magee dived hastily back under the covers. "Well?" he questioned.

"So you're the fellow," remarked the little man in awe. He placed the basket on the floor; it appeared to be filled with bromidic groceries, such as the most subdued householder carries home.

"Which fellow?" asked Mr. Magee.

"The fellow Elijah Quimby told me about," explained he of the long brown locks. "The fellow that's come up to Baldpate Inn to be alone with his thoughts."

"You're one of the villagers, I take it," guessed Mr. Magee.

"You're dead wrong. I'm no villager. My instincts are all in the other direction—away from the crowd. I live up near the top of Baldpate, in a little shack I built myself. My name's Peters—Jake Peters—in the winter. But in the summer, when the inn's open, and the red and white awnings are out, and the band plays in the casino every night—then I'm the Hermit of Baldpate Mountain. I come down here and sell picture post-cards of myself to the ladies."

Mr. Magee appeared overcome with mirth.

"A professional hermit, by the gods!" he cried. "Say, I didn't know Baldpate Mountain was fitted up with all the modern improvements. This is great luck. I'm an amateur at the hermit business, you'll have to teach me the fine points. Sit down."

"Just between ourselves, I'm not a regular hermit," said the plump bewhiskered one, sitting gingerly on the edge of a frail chair. "Not one of these 'all for love of a woman' hermits you read about in books. Of course, I have to pretend I am, in summer, in order to sell the cards and do my whole duty by the inn management. A lot of the women ask me in soft tones about the great disappointment that drove me to old Baldpate, and I give 'em various answers, according to how I feel. Speaking to you as a friend, and considering the fact that it's the dead of winter, I may say there was little or no romance in my life. I married early, and stayed married a long time. I came up here for peace and quiet, and because I felt a man ought to read something besides time-tables and tradesmen's bills, and have something over his head besides a first and second mortgage."

"Back to nature, in other words," remarked Mr. Magee.

"Yes, sir—back with a rush. I was down to the village this morning for a few groceries, and I stopped off at Quimby's, as I often do. He told me about you. I help him a lot around the inn, and we arranged I was to stop in and start your fire, and do any other little errands you might want done. I thought we ought to get acquainted, you and me, being as we're both literary men, after a manner of speaking."

"No?" cried Mr. Magee.

"Yes," said the Hermit of Baldpate. "I dip into that work a little now and then. Some of my verses on the joys of solitude have appeared in print—on the post-cards I sell to the guests in the summer. But my life-work, as you might call it, is a book I've had under way for some time. It's called simply *Woman*. Just that one word—but, oh, the meaning in it! That book is going to prove that all the trouble in the world, from the beginning of time, was caused by females. Not just say so, mind you. Prove it!"

"A difficult task, I'm afraid," smiled Magee.

"Not difficult—long," corrected the hermit. "When I started out, four years ago, I thought it would just be a case of a chapter on Eve, and honorable mention for Cleopatra and Helen of Troy, and a few more like that, and the thing would be done. But as I got into the subject, I was fairly buried under new evidence. Then Mr. Carnegie came along and gave Upper Asquewan Falls a library. It's wonderful to think the great works that man will be responsible for. I've dedicated *Woman* to him. Since the new library, I've dug up information about a thousand disasters I never dreamed of before, and I contend that if you go back a ways in any one of 'em, you'll find the fluffy little lady that started the whole rumpus. So I hunt the woman. I reckon the French would call me the greatest *cherchez la femme* in history."

"A fascinating pursuit," laughed Mr. Magee. "I'm glad you've told me about it, and I shall watch the progress of the work with interest. Although I can't say that I entirely agree with you. Here and there is a woman who more than makes amends for whatever trouble her sisters have caused. One, for instance, with golden hair, and eyes that when they weep—"

"You're young," interrupted the little man, rising. "There ain't no use to debate it with you. I might as well try to argue with a storm at sea. Some men keep the illusion to the end of their days, and I hope you're one. I reckon I'll start your fire."

He went into the outer room, and Mr. Magee lay for a few moments listening to his preparations about the fireplace. This was comfort, he thought. And yet, something was wrong. Was it the growing feeling of emptiness inside? Undoubtedly. He sat up in bed and leaning over, gazed into the hermit's basket. The packages he saw there made his feeling of emptiness the more acute.

"I say, Mr. Peters," he cried, leaping from bed and running into the other room, where the hermit was persuading a faint blaze, "I've an idea. You can cook, can't you?"

"Cook?" repeated the hermit. "Well, yes, I've had to learn a few things about it, living far from the rathskellars the way I do."

"The very man," rejoiced Mr. Magee. "You must stay here and cook for me—for us."

"Us?" asked the hermit, staring.

"Yes. I forgot to tell you. After Mr. Quimby left me last night, two other amateur hermits hove in view. One is a haberdasher with a broken heart—"

"Woman," cried the triumphant Peters.

"Name, Arabella," laughed Magee. "The other's a college professor who made an indiscreet remark about blondes. You won't mind them, I'm sure, and they may be able to help you a lot with your great work."

"I don't know what Quimby will say," studied the hermit. "I reckon he'll run 'em out. He's against this thing—afraid of fire."

"Quimby will come later," Mr. Magee assured him, drawing on a dressing-gown. "Just now the idea is a little water in yonder tub, and a nice cheerful breakfast after. It's going to pay you a lot better than selling post-cards to romantic ladies, I promise you. I won't take you away from a work for which the world is panting without more than making it up to you financially. Where do you stand as a coffee maker?"

"Wait till you taste it," said Peters reassuringly. "I'll bring you up some water."

He started for the door, but Mr. Magee preceded him.

"The haberdasher," he explained, "sleeps below, and he's a nervous man. He might commit the awful error of shooting the only cook on Baldpate Mountain."

Mr. Magee went out into the hall and called from the depths the figure of Bland, fully attired in his flashy garments, and looking tawdry and tired in the morning light.

"I've been up hours," he remarked. "Heard somebody knocking round the kitchen, but I ain't seen any breakfast brought in on a silver tray. My inside feels like the Mammoth Cave."

Mr. Magee introduced the Hermit of Baldpate.

"Pleased to meet you," said Bland. "I guess it was you I heard in the kitchen. So you're going to cater to this select few, are you? Believe me, you can't get on the job any too soon to suit me."

Out of a near-by door stepped the black-garbed figure of Professor Thaddeus Bolton, and him Mr. Magee included in the presentation ceremonies. After the hermit had disappeared below, burdened with his market basket and the supplies Mr. Magee had brought the night before, the three amateurs at the hermit game gathered by the fire in number seven, and Mr. Bland spoke feelingly:

"I don't know where you plucked that cook, but believe me, you get a vote of thanks from yours truly. What is he—an advertisement for a hair restorer?"

"He's a hermit," explained Magee, "and lives in a shack near the mountain-top. Hermits and barbers aren't supposed to mix. He's also an author, and is writing a book in which he lays all the trouble of the ages at the feet of woman. Please treat him with the respect all these dignified activities demand."

"A writer, you say," commented Professor Bolton. "Let us hope it will not interfere with his cooking abilities. For even I, who am not much given to thought about material things, must admit the presence of a gnawing hunger within."

They talked little, being men unfed, while Jake Peters started proceedings in the kitchen, and tramped up-stairs with many pails of water. Mr. Magee requested warm water for shaving; whereupon he was regarded with mingled emotions by his companions.

"You ain't going to see any skirts up here," Mr. Bland promised him. And Mr. Peters, bringing the water from below, took occasion to point out that shaving was one of man's troubles directly attributable to woman's presence in the world.

At length the hermit summoned them to breakfast, and as they descended the broad stair the heavenly odor of coffee sent a glow to their hearts. Peters had built a rousing fire in the big fireplace opposite the clerk's desk in the office, and in front of this he had placed a table which held promise of a satisfactory breakfast. As the three sat down, Mr. Bland spoke:

"I don't know about you, gentlemen, but I could fall on Mr. Peters' neck and call him blessed."

The gentleman thus referred to served them genially. He brought to Mr. Magee, between whom and himself he recognized the tie of authorship, a copy of a New York paper that he claimed to get each morning from the station agent, and which helped him greatly, he said, in his eternal search for the woman. As the meal passed, Mr. Magee glanced it through. Twice he looked up from it to study keenly his queer companions at Baldpate Inn. Finally he handed it across the table to the haberdasher. The dull yellow sun of a winter morning drifted in from the white outdoors; the fire sputtered gaily in the grate. Also, Mr. Peters' failing for literature interfered in no way with his talents as cook. The three finished the repast in great good humor, and Mr. Magee handed round cigars.

"Gentlemen," he remarked, pushing back his chair, "we find ourselves in a peculiar position. Three lone men, knowing nothing of one another, we have sought the solitude of Baldpate Inn at almost the same moment. Why? Last night, before you came, Professor Bolton, Mr. Bland gave me as his reason for being here the story of Arabella, which I afterward appropriated as a joke and gave as my own reason. I related to Mr. Bland the fiction about the artist and the besieging novelists. We swapped stories when you came—it was our merry little method of doubting each other's word. Perhaps it was bad taste. At any rate, looking at it in the morning light, I am inclined to return Mr. Bland's Arabella, and no questions asked. He is again the lovelorn haberdasher. I am inclined to believe, implicitly, your story. That is my proposition. No doubts of one another. We are here for whatever reasons we say we are."

The professor nodded gravely.

"Last night," went on Mr. Magee, "there was some talk between Mr. Bland and myself about one of us leaving the inn. Mr. Bland demanded it. I trust he sees the matter differently this morning. I for one should be sorry to see him go."

"I've changed my mind," said Mr. Bland. The look on his thin face was not a pleasant one. "Very good," went on Mr. Magee. "I see no reason why we should not proceed on friendly terms. Mr. Peters has agreed to cook for us. He can no doubt be persuaded to attend to our other wants. For his services we shall pay him generously, in view of the circumstances. As for Quimby—I leave you to make your peace with him."

"I have a letter to Mr. Quimby from my old friend, John Bentley," said the professor, "which I am sure will win me the caretaker's warm regard."

Mr. Magee looked at Bland.

"I'll get Andy Rutter on the wire," said that gentleman. "Quimby will listen to him, I guess."

"Maybe," remarked Magee carelessly. "Who is Rutter?"

"He's manager of the inn when it's open," answered Bland. He looked suspiciously at Magee. "I only know him slightly," he added.

"Those matters you will arrange for yourselves," Mr. Magee went on. "I shall be very glad of your company if you can fix it to stay. Believe it or not—I forgot, we agreed to believe, didn't we?—I am here to do some writing. I'm going up to my room now to do a little work. All I ask of you gentlemen is that, as a favor to me, you refrain from shooting at each other while I am gone. You see, I am trying to keep crude melodrama out of my stuff."

"I am sure," remarked Professor Bolton, "that the use of firearms as a means of social diversion between Mr. Bland and myself is unthought of."

"I hope so," responded Magee. "There, then, the matter rests. We are here—that is all." He hesitated, as though in doubt. Then, with a decisive motion, he drew toward him the New York paper. With his eyes on the head-lines of the first page, he continued: "I shall demand no further explanations. And except for this once, I shall make no reference to this story in the newspaper, to the effect that early yesterday morning, in a laboratory at one of our leading universities, a young assistant instructor was found dead under peculiar circumstances." He glanced keenly at the bald-headed little man across from him. "Nor shall I make conversation of the fact," he added, "that the professor of chemistry at the university, a man past middle age, respected highly in the university circle, is missing."

An oppressive silence followed this remark. Mr. Bland's sly eyes sought quickly the professor's face. The older man sat staring at his plate; then he raised his head and the round spectacles were turned full on Magee.

"You are very kind," said Professor Bolton evenly.

"There is another story in this paper," went on Mr. Magee, glancing at the haberdasher, "that, it seems to me, I ought to taboo as table talk at Baldpate Inn. It relates that a few days ago the youthful cashier of a bank in a small Pennsylvania town disappeared with thirty thousand dollars of the bank's funds. No," he concluded, "we are simply here, gentlemen, and I am very glad to let it go at that."

Mr. Bland sneered knowingly.

"I should think you would be," he said. "If you'll turn that paper over you'll read on the back page that day before yesterday a lot of expensive paintings in a New York millionaire's house were cut from their frames, and that the young artist who was doing retouching in the house at the time has been just careless enough not to send his address to the police. It's a small matter, of course, and the professor and I will never mention it again."

Mr. Magee threw back his head and laughed heartily.

"We understand one another, it seems," he said. "I look forward to pleasant companionship where I had expected solitude. You will excuse me now—there is the work to which I referred. Ah, here's Peters," he added as the hermit entered through the dining-room door at the side of the stairs.

"All finished, gentlemen?" he asked, coming forward. "Now, this is solid comfort, ain't it? I reckon when you get a few days of this, you'll all become hermits, and build yourselves shacks on the mountain. Solid comfort. No woman to make you put on overshoes when you go out, or lecture you about the effects of alcohol on the stomach. Heaven, I call it."

"Peters," said Mr. Magee, "we have been wondering if you will stay on here and cook for us. We need you. How about it?"

"Well—I'll be glad to help you out," the hermit replied. "I guess I can manage to give satisfaction, seeing there ain't no women around. If there was, I wouldn't think of it. Yes, I'll stay and do what I can to boost the hermit life in your estimation. I—"

He stopped. His eyes were on the dining-room door, toward which Mr. Magee's back was turned. The jaw of Peters fell, and his mouth stood wide open. Behind the underbrush of beard a very surprised face was discernible.

Mr. Magee turned quickly. A few feet inside the door stood the girl of the station, weeping no more, but radiant with smiles. Back of her was the determined impossible companion of yesterday.

"Oh, mamma," laughed the girl, "we're too late for breakfast! Isn't it a shame?"

Mr. Bland's lean hands went quickly to adjust his purple tie. Professor Bolton looked every inch the owl as he blinked in dazed fashion at the blue corduroy vision. Gingerly Mr. Peters set down the plates he had taken from the table, still neglecting his open mouth.

Mr. Magee rose from the table, and went forward with outstretched hand.

CHAPTER V

THE MAYOR CASTS A SHADOW BEFORE

"From tears to smiles," said Mr. Magee, taking the girl's hand. "What worked the transformation? Not the Commercial House, I know, for I passed it last evening."

"No, hardly the Commercial House," laughed the girl. "Rather the sunshine of a winter morning, the brisk walk up the mountain, and the sight of the Hermit of Baldpate with eyes like saucers staring at a little girl who once bought his postal cards."

"Then you know Mr. Peters?" inquired Magee.

"Is that his name? You see, I never met him in private life—he was just the hermit when I knew him. I used to come to Baldpate in the summers, and send his cards back to the folks at home, and dream dreams of his love-story when from my window I saw the light of his shack at night. I'm so glad to meet Mr. Peters informally."

She held out her hand, but Peters, by long practise wary of women, had burdened himself with breakfast plates which prevented his clasping it. He muttered "How d'ye do?" and fled toward the door, narrowly averting what would have proved a serious collision with the large woman on the way.

"Mr. Peters meets so few of your sex in winter," Magee apologized, "you must pardon his clumsiness. This gentleman"—he indicated the professor, who arose—"is Thaddeus Bolton, a distinguished member of a certain university faculty, who has fled to Baldpate to escape the press of America. And this is Mr. Bland, who hides here from the world the scars of a broken heart. But let us not go into details."

The girl smiled brightly. "And you—" she asked.

"William Hallowell Magee," he returned, bowing low. "I have a neat little collection of stories accounting for my presence here, from which I shall allow you to choose later. Not to mention the real one, which is simple almost to a fault."

"I am so happy to meet you all," said the girl. "We shall no doubt become very good friends. For mamma and I have also come to Baldpate Inn—to stay."

Mr. Bland opened wide his usually narrow eyes, and ran his hand thoughtfully over his one day's beard. Professor Bolton blinked his astonishment. Mr. Magee smiled.

"I, for one, am delighted to hear it," he said.

"My name," went on the girl, "is Mary Norton. May I present my mother, Mrs. Norton?"

The older woman adopted what was obviously her society manner. Once again Mr. Magee felt a pang of regret that this should be the parent of a girl so charming.

"I certainly am pleased to meet you all," she said in her heavy voice. "Ain't it a lovely morning after the storm? The sun's almost blinding."

"Some explanation," put in Miss Norton quickly, "is due you if I am to thrust myself thus upon you. I am perfectly willing to tell why I am here— but the matter mustn't leak out. I can trust you, I'm sure."

Mr. Magee drew up chairs, and the two women were seated before the fire.

"The bandits of Baldpate," he remarked flippantly, glancing at the two men, "have their own code of honor, and the first rule is never to betray a pal."

"Splendid!" laughed the girl. "You said, I believe, that Professor Bolton was fleeing from the newspapers. I am fleeing for the newspapers—to attract their attention—to lure them into giving me that thing so necessary to a woman in my profession, publicity. You see, I am an actress. The name I gave you is not my stage name. That, perhaps, you would know. I employ a gentleman to keep me before the public as much as possible. It's horrid, I know, but it means bread and butter to me. That gentleman, my press-agent, evolved the present scheme—a mysterious disappearance."

She paused and looked at the others. Mr. Magee surveyed her narrowly. The youthful bloom of her cheek carried to him no story of grease paint; her unaffected manner was far from suggesting anything remotely connected with the stage. He wondered.

"I am to disappear completely for a time," she went on. "'As though the earth had swallowed me' will be the good old phrase of the reporters. I am to linger here at Baldpate Inn, a key to which my press-agent has secured for me. Meanwhile, the papers will speak tearfully of me in their head-lines—at least, I hope they will. Can't you just see them—those head-lines? 'Beautiful Actress Drops from Sight'." She stopped, blushing. "Every woman who gets into print, you know, is beautiful."

"But it'd be no lie in your case, dearie," put in Mrs. Norton, feeling carefully of her atrociously blond store hair.

"Your mother takes the words from my mouth," smiled Mr. Magee. "Guard as they will against it, the newspapers let the truth crop out occasionally. And this will be such an occasion."

"From what part of Ireland do you come?" laughed the girl. She seemed somewhat embarrassed by her mother's open admiration. "Well, setting all blarney aside, such will be the head-lines. And when the last clue is exhausted, and my press-agent is the same, I come back to appear in a new play, a well-known actress. Of such flippant things is a Broadway reputation built."

"We all wish you success, I'm sure." Mr. Magee searched his memory in vain for this "actress's" name and fame. Could it be possible, he wondered, at this late day, that any one would try for publicity by such an obvious worn-out road? Hardly. The answer was simple. Another fable was being spun from whole cloth beneath the roof of Baldpate Inn. "We have a New York paper here," he went on, "but as yet there seems to be no news of your sad disappearance."

"Wouldn't it be the limit if they didn't fall for it?" queried the older woman.

"Fall for it," repeated Professor Bolton, not questioningly, but with the air of a scientist about to add a new and rare specimen to his alcohol jar.

"She means, if they didn't accept my disappearance as legitimate news," explained the girl "That would be very disappointing. But surely there was no harm in making the experiment."

"They're a clever lot, those newspaper guys," sneered Mr. Bland, "in their own opinion. But when you come right down to it, every one of 'em has a nice little collection of gold bricks in his closet. I guess you've got them going. I hope so."

"Thank you," smiled the girl. "You are very kind. You are here, I understand, because of an unfortunate—er—affair of the heart?"

Mr. Bland smoothed back his black oily hair from his forehead, and smirked. "Oh, now—" he protested.

"Arabella," put in Mr. Magee, "was her name. The beauties of history and mythology hobbled into oblivion at sight of her."

"I'm quick to forget," insisted Mr. Bland.

"That does you no credit, I'm sure," replied the girl severely. "And now, mamma, I think we had better select our rooms—"

She paused. For Elijah Quimby had come in through the dining-room door, and stood gazing at the group before the fire, his face reflecting what Mr. Magee, the novelist, would not have hesitated a moment in terming "mingled emotions".

"Well," drawled Mr. Quimby. He strode into the room. "Mr. Magee," he said, "that letter from Mr. Bentley asked me to let you stay at Baldpate Inn. There wasn't anything in it about your bringing parties of friends along."

"These are not friends I've brought along," explained Magee. "They're simply some more amateur hermits who have strolled in from time to time. All have their individual latch-keys to the hermitage. And all, I believe, have credentials for you to examine."

Mr. Quimby stared in angry wonder.

"Is the world crazy?" he demanded. "Any one 'd think it was July, the way people act. The inn's closed, I tell you. It ain't running."

Professor Bolton rose from his chair.

"So you are Quimby," he said in a soothing tone. "I'm glad to meet you at last. My old friend John Bentley has spoken of you so often. I have a letter from him." He drew the caretaker to one side, and took an envelope from his pocket. The two conversed in low tones.

Quickly the girl in the corduroy suit leaned toward Mr. Magee. She whispered, and her tone was troubled:

"Stand by me. I'm afraid I'll need your help."

"What's the matter?" inquired Magee.

"I haven't much of any right here, I guess. But I had to come."

"But your key?"

"I fear my—my press-agent—stole it."

A scornful remark as to the antiquated methods of that mythical publicity promoter rose to Mr. Magee's lips, but before he spoke he looked into her eyes. And the remark was never made. For in their wonderful depths he saw worry and fear and unhappiness, as he had seen them there amid tears in the station.

"Never mind," he said very gently, "I'll see you through."

Quimby was standing over Mr. Bland. "How about you?" he asked.

"Call up Andy Rutter and ask about me," replied Bland, in the tone of one who prefers war to peace.

"I work for Mr. Bentley," said Quimby. "Rutter hasn't any authority here. He isn't to be manager next season, I understand. However the professor wants me to let you stay. He says he'll be responsible." Mr. Bland looked in open-mouthed astonishment at the unexpected sponsor he had found. "And you?" went on Quimby to the women.

"Why—" began Miss Norton.

"Absolutely all right," said Mr. Magee. "They come from Hal Bentley, like myself. He's put them in my care. I'll answer for them." He saw the girl's eyes; they spoke her thanks.

Mr. Quimby shook his head as one in a dream.

"All this is beyond me—way beyond," he ruminated. "Nothing like it ever happened before that I've heard of. I'm going to write all about it to Mr. Bentley, and I suppose I got to let you stay till I hear from him. I think he ought to come up here, if he can."

"The more the merrier," said Mr. Magee, reflecting cheerfully that the Bentleys were in Florida at last accounts.

"Come, mamma," said Miss Norton, rising, "let's go up and pick out a suite. There's one I used to have a few years ago—you can see the hermit's shack from the windows. By the way, Mr. Magee, will you send Mr. Peters up to us? He may be able to help us get settled."

"Ahem," muttered Mr. Magee, "I—I'll have a talk with Peters. To be quite frank, I anticipate trouble. You see, the Hermit of Baldpate doesn't approve of women—"

"Don't approve of women," cried Mrs. Norton, her green eyes flashing. "Why not, I'd like to know?"

"My dear madam," responded Mr. Magee, "only echo answers, and it but vacuously repeats, 'Why not?'. That, however, is the situation. Mr. Peters loathes the sex. I imagine that, until to-day, he was not particularly happy in the examples of it he encountered. Why, he has even gone so far as to undertake a book attributing all the trouble of the world to woman."

"The idiot!" cried Mrs. Norton.

"Delicious!" laughed the girl.

"I shall ask Peters to serve you," said Magee. "I shall appeal to his gallant side. But I must proceed gently. This is his first day as our cook, and you know how necessary a good first impression is with a new cook. I'll appeal to his better nature."

"Don't do it," cried the girl. "Don't emphasize us to him in any way, or he may exercise his right as cook and leave. Just ignore us. We'll play at being our own bell-boys."

"Ignore you," cried Mr. Magee. "What Herculean tasks you set. I'm not equal to that one." He picked up their traveling-bags and led the way up-stairs. "I'm something of a bell-boy myself, when roused," he said.

The girl selected suite seventeen, at the farther end of the corridor from Magee's apartments. "It's the very one I used to have, years and years ago—at least two or three years ago," she said. "Isn't it stupid? All the furniture in a heap."

"And cold," said Mrs. Norton. "My land, I wish I was back by my own fire."

"I'll make you regret your words, Mrs. Norton," cried Magee. He threw up the windows, pulled off his coat, and set to work on the furniture. The girl bustled about, lightening his work by her smile. Mrs. Norton managed to get consistently in the way. When he had the furniture distributed, he procured logs and tried his hand at a fire. Then he stood, his black hair disheveled, his hands soiled, but his heart very gay, before the girl of the station.

"I hope you don't expect a tip," she said, laughing.

"I do," he said, coming closer, and speaking in a voice that was not for the ear of the chaperon. "I want a tip on this—do you really act?"

She looked at him steadily.

"Once," she said, "when I was sixteen, I appeared in an amateur play at school. It was my first and last appearance on the stage."

"Thanks, lady," remarked Mr. Magee in imitation of the bell-boy he was supposed to be. He sought number seven. There he made himself again presentable, after which he descended to the office.

Mr. Bland sat reading the New York paper before the fire. From the little card-room and the parlor, the two rooms to the right and left of the hotel's front door, Quimby had brought forth extra chairs. He stood now by the large chair that held Professor Bolton, engaged in conversation with that gentleman.

"Yes," he was saying, "I lived three years in Reuton and five years in New York. It took me eight years—eight years to realize the truth."

"I heard about it from John Bentley," the professor said gently.

"He's been pretty kind to me, Mr. Bentley has," replied Quimby. "When the money was all gone, he offered me this job. Once the Quimbys owned most of the land around Baldpate Mountain. It all went in those eight years. To think that it took all those years for me to find it out."

"If I'm not impertinent, Quimby," put in Magee, "to find what out?"

"That what I wanted, the railroad men didn't want," replied Quimby bitterly, "and that was—the safety of the public. You see, I invented a new rail joint, one that was a great improvement on the old kind. I had sort of an idea, when I was doing it—an idea of service to the world—you know. God, what a joke! I sold all the Quimby lands, and went to Reuton, and then to New York, to place it. Not one of the railroad men but admitted that it was an improvement, and a big one—and not one but fought like mad to keep me from getting it down where the public would see it. They didn't want the expense of a change."

Mr. Quimby looked out at the sunlit stretch of snow.

"Eight years," he repeated, "I fought and pleaded. No, I begged—that was the word—I begged. You'd be surprised to know the names of some of the men who kept me waiting in their private offices, and sneered at me over their polished desks. They turned me down—every one. Some of them played me—as though I'd been a fish. They referred me to other ends of the same big game, laughing in their sleeves, I guess, at the knowledge of how hopeless it was. Oh, they made a fine fool of me."

"You might have put down some of your joints at your own expense," suggested the professor.

"Didn't I try?" cried Quimby. "Do you think they'd let me? No, the public might see them and demand them everywhere. Once, I thought I had convinced somebody. It was down in Reuton—the Suburban Railway." There was a rustle as Mr. Bland let his paper fall to the floor. "Old Henry Thornhill was president of the road—he is yet, I guess—but young Hayden and a fellow named David Kendrick were running it. Kendrick was on my side—he almost had Hayden. They were going to let me lay a stretch of track with my joints. Then—something happened. Maybe you remember. Kendrick disappeared in the night—he's never been seen since."

"I do remember," said the professor softly.

"Hayden turned me down," went on Quimby. "The money was all gone. So I came back to Upper Asquewan—caretaker of an inn that overlooks the property my father owned—the property I squandered for a chance to save human lives. It's all like a dream now—those eight years. And it nearly drives me mad, sometimes, to think that it took me eight years—eight years to find it out. I'll just straighten things around a bit."

He moved away, and the men sat in silence for a time. Then the professor spoke very gently:

"Poor devil—to have had his dream of service—and then grow old on Baldpate."

The two joined Mr. Bland by the fire. Mr. Magee had put from his mind all intention of work. The maze of events through which he wandered held him bewildered and enthralled. He looked at the haberdasher and the university scholar and asked himself if they were real, or if he was still asleep in a room on a side street in New York, waiting for the cheery coming of Geoffrey. He asked himself still more perplexedly if the creature that came toward him now through the dining-room door was real—the hairy Hermit of Baldpate, like a figure out of some old print, his market basket on his arm again, his coat buttoned to the chin.

"Well, everything's shipshape in the kitchen," announced the hermit cheerfully. "I couldn't go without seeing to that. I wish you the best of luck, gentlemen—and good-by."

"Good-by?" cried the professor.

"By the gods, he's leaving us," almost wept Mr. Bland.

"It can't be," said Mr. Magee.

"It has to be," said the Hermit of Baldpate, solemnly shaking his head. "I'd like to stay with you, and I would of, if they hadn't come. But here they are—and when women come in the door, I fly out of the window, as the saying is."

"But, Peters," pleaded Magee, "you're not going to leave us in the hole like this?"

"Sorry," replied Peters, "I can please men, but I can't please women. I tried to please one once—but let the dead past bury its dead. I live on Baldpate in a shack to escape the sex, and it wouldn't be consistent for me to stay here now. I got to go. I hate to, like a dog, but I got to."

"Peters," said Mr. Magee, "I'm surprised. After giving your word to stay! And who knows—you may be able to gather valuable data for your book. Stick around. These women won't bother you. I'll make them promise never to ask about the love-affair you didn't have—never even to come near you. And we'll pay you beyond the dreams of avarice of a Broadway chef. Won't we, gentlemen?"

The others nodded. Mr. Peters visibly weakened.

"Well—" he began. "I—" His eyes were on the stair. Mr. Magee also looked in that direction and saw the girl of the station smiling down. She no longer wore coat and hat, and the absence of the latter revealed a glory of golden hair that became instantly a rival to the sunshine in that drear bare room.

"No, Peters," she said, "you mustn't go. We couldn't permit it. Mamma and I will go."

She continued to smile at the obviously dazzled Peters. Suddenly he spoke in a determined tone:

"No—don't do that. I'll stay." Then he turned to Magee, and continued for that gentleman's ear alone: "Dog-gone it, we're all alike. We resolve and resolve, and then one of them looks at us, and it's all forgot. I had a friend who advertised for a wife, leastways, he was a friend until he advertised. He got ninety-two replies, seventy of 'em from married men advising against the step. 'I'm cured,' he says to me. 'Not for me.' Did he keep his word? No. A week after he married a widow just to see if what the seventy said was true. I'm mortal. I hang around the buzz-saw. If you give me a little money, I'll go down to the village and buy the provisions for lunch."

Gleefully Mr. Magee started the hermit on his way, and then went over to where the girl stood at the foot of the stairs.

"I promised him," he told her, "you'd ask no questions regarding his broken heart. It seems he hasn't any."

"That's horrid of him, isn't it?" she smiled. "Every good hermit is equipped with a broken heart. I certainly shan't bother him. I came down to get some water."

They went together to the kitchen, found a pail, and filled it with icy water from the pump at the rear of the inn. Inside once more, Mr. Magee remarked thoughtfully:

"Who would have guessed a week ago that to-day I would be climbing the broad staircase of a summer hotel carrying a pail of water for a lady fair?"

They paused on the landing.

"There are more things in heaven and earth, Horatio," smiled the girl, "than are dreamed of, even by novelists." Mr. Magee started. Had she recognized him as the Magee of light fiction? It seemed hardly likely; they read his books, but they rarely remembered his name. Her face went suddenly grave. She came closer. "I can't help wondering," she said, "which side you are on?"

"Which side of what?" asked Magee.

"Why, of this," she answered, waving her hand toward the office below.

"I don't understand," objected Mr. Magee.

"Let's not be silly," she replied. "You know what brought me here. I know what brought you. There are three sides, and only one is honest. I hope, so very much, that you are on that side."

"Upon my word—" began Magee.

"Will it interest you to know," she continued, "I saw the big mayor of Reuton in the village this morning? With him was his shadow, Lou Max. Let's see—you had the first key, Mr. Bland the second, the professor the third, and I had the fourth. The mayor has the fifth key, of course. He'll be here soon."

"The mayor," gasped Mr. Magee. "Really, I haven't the slightest idea what you mean. I'm here to work—"

"Very well," said the girl coldly, "if you wish it that way." They came to the door of seventeen, and she took the pail from Mr. Magee's hand. "Thanks."

"'Where are you going, my pretty maid?'" asked Magee, indicating the pail.

"'"I'll see you at luncheon, sir," she said,'" responded Miss Norton, and the door of seventeen slammed shut.

Mr. Magee returned to number seven, and thoughtfully stirred the fire. The tangle of events bade fair to swamp him.

"The mayor of Reuton," he mused, "has the fifth key. What in the name of common sense is going on? It's too much even for melodramatic me." He leaned back in his chair. "Anyhow, I like her eyes," he said. "And I shouldn't want to be quoted as disapproving of her hair, either. I'm on her side, whichever it may be."

CHAPTER VI

GHOSTS OF THE SUMMER CROWD

"I wonder," Miss Norton smiled up into Mr. Magee's face, "if you ever watched the people at a summer hotel get set on their mark for the sprint through the dining-room door?"

"No," answered Magee, "but I have visited the Zoo at meal-time. They tell me it is much the same."

"A brutal comparison," said the girl. "But just the same I'm sure that the head waiter who opens the door here at Baldpate must feel much the same at the moment as the keeper who proffers the raw meat on the end of the pitchfork. He faces such a wild determined mob. The front rank is made up of hard-faced women worn out by veranda gossip. Usually some stiff old dowager crosses the tape first. I was thinking that perhaps we resembled that crowd in the eyes of Mr. Peters now."

It was past one o'clock, and Mr. Magee with his four mysterious companions stood before the fire in the office, each with an eager eye out for the progress of the hermit, who was preparing the table beside them. Through the kindness of Quimby, the board was resplendent with snowy linen.

"We may seem over-eager," commented Professor Bolton. "I have no doubt we do. It is only natural. With nothing to look forward to but the next meal, the human animal attaches a preposterous importance to his feeding. We are in the same case as the summer guests—"

"Are we?" interrupted Mr. Magee. "Have we nothing but the next meal to look forward to? I think not. I haven't. I've come to value too highly the capacity for excitement of Baldpate Inn in December. I look forward to startling things. I expect, before the day is out, at least two gold-laced kings, an exiled poet, and a lord mayor, all armed with keys to Baldpate Inn and stories strange and unconvincing."

"Your adventures of the last twenty-four hours," remarked the professor, smiling wanly, "have led you to expect too much. I have made inquiries of Quimby. There are, aside from his own, but seven keys in all to the various doors of Baldpate Inn. Four are here represented. It is hardly likely that the other three will send delegates, and if they should, you have but a slim chance for kings and poets. Even Baldpate's capacity for excitement, you see, is limited by the number of little steel keys which open its portals to exiles from the outside world. I am reminded of the words of the philosopher—"

"Well, Peters, old top," broke in Mr. Bland in robust tones, "isn't she nearly off the fire?"

"Now see here," said the hermit, setting down the armful of dishes with which he had entered the office, "I can't be hurried. I'm all upset, as it is. I can't cook to please women—I don't pretend to. I have to take all sorts of precautions with this lunch. Without meaning to be impolite, but just because of a passion for cold facts, I may say that women are faultfinding."

"I'm sure," said Miss Norton sweetly, "that I shall consider your luncheon perfect."

"They get more faultfinding as they get older," replied Mr. Peters ungallantly, glancing at the other woman.

Mrs. Norton glared.

"Meaning me, I suppose," she rasped. "Well, don't worry. I ain't going to find anything wrong."

"I ain't asking the impossible," responded Mr. Peters. "I ain't asking you not to find anything wrong. I'm just asking you not to mention it when you do." He retired to the kitchen.

Mrs. Norton caressed her puffs lovingly.

"What that man needs," she said, "is a woman's guiding hand. He's lived alone too long. I'd like to have charge of him for a while. Not that I wouldn't be kind—but I'd be firm. If poor Norton was alive to-day he'd testify that I was always kindness itself. But I insisted on his living up to his promises. When I was a girl I was mighty popular. I had a lot of admirers."

"No one could possibly doubt that," Mr. Magee assured her.

"Then Norton came along," she went on, rewarding Magee with a smile, "and said he wanted to make me happy. So I thought I'd let him try. He was a splendid man, but there's no denying that in the years we were married he sometimes forgot what he started out to do. I always brought him up sharp. 'Your great desire,' I told him, 'is to make me happy. I'd keep on the job if I was you!' And he did, to the day of his death. A perfectly lovely man, though careless in money matters. If he hadn't had that failing I wouldn't be—"

Miss Norton, her cheeks flushed, broke in hurriedly.

"Mamma, these gentlemen can't be at all interested." Deftly she turned the conversation to generalities.

Mr. Peters at last seated the winter guests of Baldpate Inn, and opened his luncheon with a soup which he claimed to have wrested from a can. This news drew from Professor Bolton a learned discourse on the tinned aids to the hermit of to-day. He pictured the seeker for solitude setting out for a desert isle, with canned foods for his body and canned music for his soul. "Robinson Crusoe," he said, "should be rewritten with a can-opener in the leading rôle." Mrs. Norton gave the talk a more practical turn by bringing up the topic of ptomaine poisoning.

While the conversation drifted on, Mr. Magee pondered in silence the weird mesh in which he had become involved. What did it all mean? What brought these people to Baldpate Christmas week? His eyes sought the great safe back of the desk, and stayed there a long time. In that safe, he was sure, lay the answer to this preposterous riddle. When his thoughts came back to the table he found Mr. Bland eying him narrowly. There was a troubled look on the haberdasher's lean face that could never be ascribed to the cruelty of Arabella.

The luncheon over, Miss Norton and her mother prepared to ascend to their rooms. Mr. Magee maneuvered so as to meet the girl at the foot of the stairs.

"Won't you come back," he whispered softly, "and explain things to a poor hermit who is completely at sea?"

"What things?" she asked.

"What it all means," he whispered. "Why you wept in the station, why you invented the story of the actress, why you came here to brighten my drab exile—what this whole comedy of Baldpate Inn amounts to, anyhow? I assure you I am as innocent of understanding it as is the czar of Russia on his golden throne."

She only looked at him with unbelieving eyes.

"You can hardly expect me to credit that," she said. "I must go up now and read mamma into the pleasant land of thin girlish figures that is her afternoon siesta. I may come back and talk to you after a while, but I don't promise to explain."

"Come back," pleaded Mr. Magee. "That is all I ask."

"A tiny boon," she smiled. "I grant it."

She followed the generous figure of the other woman up the stair and, casting back a dazzling smile from the landing, disappeared. Mr. Magee turned to find Professor Bolton discoursing to Mr. Bland on some aspects of the Pagan Renaissance. Mr. Bland's face was pained.

"That's great stuff, Professor," he said, "and usually I'd like it. But just now—I don't seem in the mood, somehow. Would you mind saving it for me till later?"

"Certainly," sighed the professor. Mr. Bland slouched into the depths of his chair. Professor Bolton turned his disappointed face ceilingward. Laughing, Mr. Magee sought the solitude of number seven.

"After all, I'm here to work," he told himself. "Alarms and excursions and blue eyes must not turn me from my task. Let's see—what was my task? A deep heart-searching novel, a novel devoid of rabid melodrama. It becomes more difficult every minute here at Baldpate Inn. But that should only add more zest to the struggle. I devote the next two hours to thought."

He pulled his chair up before the blazing hearth, and gazed into the red depths. But his thoughts refused to turn to the masterpiece that was to be born on Baldpate. They roamed to far-off Broadway; they strolled with Helen Faulkner—the girl he meant to marry if he ever got round to it—along dignified Fifth Avenue. Then joyously they trooped to a far more alluring, more human girl, who pressed a bit of cambric to her face in a railway station, while a ginger-haired agent peeped through the bars. How ridiculously small that bit of cambric had been to hide so much beauty. Soon Mr. Magee's thoughts were climbing Baldpate Mountain, there to wander in a mystic maze of ghostly figures which appeared from the shadows, holding aloft in triumph gigantic keys. Mr. Magee had slept but little the night before. The quick December dusk filled number seven when he awoke with a start.

He remembered that he had asked the girl to come back to the office, and berated himself to think that probably she had done so only to find that he was not there. Hastily straightening his tie, and dashing the traces of sleep from his eyes with the aid of cold water, he ran down-stairs.

The great bare room was in darkness save for the faint red of the fire. Before the fireplace sat the girl of the station, her hair gleaming with a new splendor in that light. She looked in mock reproval at Mr. Magee.

"For shame," she said, "to be late at the trysting-place."

"A thousand pardons," Mr. Magee replied. "I fell asleep and dreamed of a girl who wept in a railway station—and she was so altogether charming I could not tear myself away."

"I fear," she laughed, "you are old in the ways of the world. A passion for sleep seems to have seized the hermits. The professor has gone to his room for that purpose. And Mr. Bland, his broken heart forgot, slumbers over there." She pointed to the haberdasher inert in a big chair drawn up near the clerk's desk. "Only you and I in all the world awake."

"Pretty lonesome, isn't it?" Mr. Magee glanced over his shoulder at the shadows that crept in on them.

"I was finding it very busy when you came," she answered. "You see, I have known the inn when it was gay with summer people, and as I sat here by the fire I pretended I saw the ghosts of a lot of the people I knew flitting about in the dusk. The rocking-chair fleet sailed by—"

"The what?"

"Black flag flying, decks cleared for action—I saw the rocking-chair fleet go by." She smiled faintly. "We always called them that. Bitter, unkind old women who sat hour after hour on the veranda, and rocked and gossiped, and gossiped and rocked. All the old women in the world seem to gather at summer hotels. And, oh, the cruel mouths the fleet had—just thin lines of mouths—I used to look at them and wonder if any one had ever kissed them."

The girl's eyes were very large and tender in the firelight.

"And I saw some poor little ghosts weeping in a corner," she went on; "a few that the fleet had run down and sunk in the sea of gossip. A little ghost whose mother had not been all she should have been, and the fleet found it out, and rocked, and whispered, and she went away. And a few who were poor—the most terrible of sins—to them the fleet showed no mercy. And a fine proud girl, Myra Thornhill, who was engaged to a man named Kendrick, and who never dared come here again after Kendrick suddenly disappeared, because of the whispered dishonors the fleet heaped upon his head."

"What wicked women!" said Magee.

"The wickedest women in the world," answered the girl. "But every summer resort must have its fleet. I doubt if any other ever had its admiral, though—and that makes Baldpate supreme."

"Its admiral?"

"Yes. He isn't really that, I imagine—sort of a vice, or an assistant, or whatever it is, long ago retired from the navy. Every summer he comes here, and the place revolves about him. It's all so funny. I wonder if any other crowd attains such heights of snobbishness as that at a summer resort? It's the admiral this, and the admiral that, from the moment he enters the door. Nearly every day the manager of Baldpate has a new picture of the admiral taken, and hangs it here in the hotel. I'll show them to you when it's light. There's one over there by the desk, of the admiral and the manager together, and the manager has thrown his arm carelessly over the admiral's shoulder with 'See how well I know him' written all over his stupid face. Oh, what snobs they are!"

"And the fleet?" asked Mr. Magee.

"Worships him. They fish all day for a smile from him. They keep track of his goings and comings, and when he is in the card-room playing his silly old game of solitaire, they run down their victims in subdued tones so as not to disturb him."

"What an interesting place," said Mr. Magee. "I must visit Baldpate next summer. Shall—shall you be here?"

"It's so amusing," she smiled, ignoring the question. "You'll enjoy it. And it isn't all fleet and admiral. There's happiness, and romance, and whispering on the stairs. At night, when the lights are all blazing, and the band is playing waltzes in the casino, and somebody is giving a dinner in the grill-room, and the girls flit about in the shadows looking too sweet for words—well, Baldpate Inn is a rather entrancing spot. I remember those nights very often now."

Mr. Magee leaned closer. The flicker of the firelight on her delicate face, he decided, was an excellent effect.

"I can well believe you do remember them," he said. "And it's no effort at all to me to picture you as one of those who flitted through the shadows—too sweet for words. I can see you the heroine of whispering scenes on the stair. I can see you walking with a dazzled happy man on the mountain in the moonlight. Many men have loved you."

"Are you reading my palm?" she asked, laughing.

"No—your face," answered Mr. Magee. "Many men have loved you, for very few men are blind. I am sorry I was not the man on the stair, or on the mountain in the moonlight. Who knows—I might have been the favored one for my single summer of joy."

"The autumn always came," smiled the girl.

"It would never have come for me," he answered. "Won't you believe me when I say that I have no part in this strange drama that is going on at Baldpate? Won't you credit it when I say that I have no idea why you and the professor and Mr. Bland are here—nor why the Mayor of Reuton has the fifth key? Won't you tell me what it all means?"

"I mustn't," she replied, shaking her head. "I can trust no one—not even you. I mustn't believe that you don't know—it's preposterous. I must say over and over—even he is simply—will you pardon me—flirting, trying to learn what he can learn. I must."

"You can't even tell me why you wept in the station?"

"For a simple silly reason. I was afraid. I had taken up a task too big for me by far—taken it up bravely when I was out in the sunlight of Reuton. But when I saw Upper Asquewan Falls, and the dark came, and that dingy station swallowed me up, something gave way inside me and I felt I was going to fail. So—I cried. A woman's way."

"If I were only permitted to help—" Mr. Magee pleaded.

"No—I must go forward alone. I can trust no one, now. Perhaps things will change. I hope they will."

"Listen," said Mr. Magee. "I am telling you the truth. Perhaps you read a novel called *The Lost Limousine*." He was resolved to claim its authorship, tell her of his real purpose in coming to Baldpate, and urge her to confide in him regarding the odd happenings at the inn.

"Yes," said the girl before he could continue. "I did read it. And it hurt me. It was so terribly insincere. The man had talent who wrote it, but he seemed to say: 'It's all a great big joke. I don't believe in these people myself. I've just created them to make them dance for you. Don't be fooled—it's only a novel.' I don't like that sort of thing. I want a writer really to mean all he says from the bottom of his heart."

Mr. Magee bit his lip. His determination to claim the authorship of *The Lost Limousine* was quite gone.

"I want him to make me feel with his people," the girl went on seriously. "Perhaps I can explain by telling you of something that happened to me once. It was while I was at college. There was a blind girl in my class and one night I went to call on her. I met her in the corridor of her dormitory. Somebody had just brought her back from an evening lecture, and left her there. She unlocked her door, and we went in. It was pitch dark in the room—the first thing I thought of was a light. But she—she just sat down and began to talk. She had forgot to light the gas."

The girl paused, her eyes very wide, and it seemed to Mr. Magee that she shivered slightly.

"Can you imagine it?" she asked. "She chatted on—quite cheerfully as I remember it. And I—I stumbled round and fell into a chair, cold and trembly and sick with the awful horror of blindness, for the first time in my life. I thought I had imagined before what it was to be blind—just by shutting my eyes for a second. But as I sat there in the blackness, and listened to that girl chatter, and realized that it had never occurred to her to light a lamp—then for the first time—I knew—I knew."

Again she stopped, and Mr. Magee, looking at her, felt what he had never experienced before—a thrill at a woman's near presence.

"That's what I ask of a writer," she said, "that he make me feel for his people as I felt for that girl that night. Am I asking too much? It need not be for one who is enmeshed in tragedy—it may be for one whose heart is as glad as a May morning. But he must make me feel. And he can't do that if he doesn't feel himself, can he?"

William Hallowell Magee actually hung his head.

"He can't," he confessed softly. "You're quite right. I like you immensely—more than I can say. And even if you feel you can't trust me, I want you to know that I'm on your side in whatever happens at Baldpate Inn. You have only to ask, and I am your ally."

"Thank you," she answered. "I may be very glad to ask. I shall remember." She rose and moved toward the stairs. "We had better disperse now. The rocking-chair fleet will get us if we don't watch out." Her small slipper was on the first step of the stair, when they heard a door slammed shut, and the sound of steps on the bare floor of the dining-room. Then a husky voice called "Bland".

Mr. Magee felt his hand grasped by a much smaller one, and before he knew it he had been hurried to the shadows of the landing. "The fifth key," whispered a scared little voice in his ear. And then he felt the faint brushing of finger-tips across his lips. A mad desire seized him to grasp those fingers and hold them on the lips they had scarcely touched. But the impulse was lost in the thrill of seeing the dining-room door thrown open and a great bulk of a man cross the floor of the office and stand beside Bland's chair. At his side was a thin waif who had not unjustly been termed the mayor of Reuton's shadow.

"Asleep," bellowed the big man. "How's this for a watch-dog, Lou?"

"Right on the job, ain't he?" sneered the thin one.

Mr. Bland started suddenly from slumber, and looked up into the eyes of the newcomers.

"Hello, Cargan," he said. "Hello, Lou. For the love of heaven, don't shout so. The place is full of them."

"Full of what?" asked the mayor.

"Of spotters, maybe—I don't know what they are. There's an old high-brow and a fresh young guy, and two women."

"People," gasped the mayor. "People—here?"

"Sure."

"You're asleep, Bland."

"No I'm not, Cargan," cried the haberdasher. "Look around for yourself. The inn's overrun with them."

Cargan leaned weakly against a chair.

"Well, what do you know about that," he said. "And they kept telling me Baldpate Inn was the best place—say, this is one on Andy Rutter. Why didn't you get it out and beat it?"

"How could I?" Mr. Bland asked. "I haven't got the combination. The safe was left open for me. That was the agreement with Rutter."

"You might have phoned us not to come," remarked Lou, with an uneasy glance around.

Mr. Cargan hit the mantelpiece with his huge fist.

"By heaven, no," he cried. "I'll lift it from under their very noses. I've done it before—I can do it now. I don't care who they are. They can't touch me. They can't touch Jim Cargan. I ain't afraid."

Mr. Magee, on the landing, whispered into his companion's ear. "I think I'll go down and greet our guests." He felt her grasp his arm suddenly, as though in fear, but he shook off her hand and debonairly descended to the group below.

"Good evening, gentlemen," he said suavely. "Welcome to Baldpate! Please don't attempt to explain—we're fed up on explanations now. You have the fifth key, of course. Welcome to our small but growing circle."

The big man advanced threateningly. Mr. Magee saw that his face was very red, his neck very thick, but his mouth a cute little cupid's bow that might well have adorned a dainty baby in the park.

"Who are you?" bellowed the mayor of Reuton in a tone meant to be cowering.

"I forget," replied Mr. Magee easily. "Bland, who am I to-day? The cast-off lover of Arabella, the fleeing artist, or the thief of portraits from a New York millionaire's home? Really, it doesn't matter. We shift our stories from time to time. As the first of the Baldpate hermits, however, it is my duty to welcome you, which I hereby do."

The mayor pointed dramatically to the stair.

"I give you fifteen minutes," he roared, "to pack up and get out. I don't want you here. Understand?"

To Cargan's side came the slinking figure of Lou Max. His face was the withered yellow of an old lemon; his garb suggested shop-windows on dirty side streets; unpleasant eyes shifted behind a pair of gold-rimmed glasses. His attitude was that of the dog who crouches by its master.

"Clear out," he snarled.

"By no means," replied Magee, looking the mayor squarely in the eye. "I was here first. I'm here to stay. Put me out, will you? Well, perhaps, after a fight. But I'd be back in an hour, and with me whatever police Upper Asquewan Falls owns to."

He saw that the opposing force wavered at this.

"I want no trouble, gentlemen," he went on. "Believe me, I shall be happy to have your company to dinner. Your command that I withdraw is ill-timed, not to say ill-natured and impolite. Let us all forget it."

The mayor of Reuton turned away, and his dog slid into the shadows.

"Have I your promise to stay to dinner?" went on Magee. No answer came from the trio in the dusk. "Silence gives consent," he added gaily. "You must excuse me while I dress. Bland, will you inform Mr. Peters that we are to have company to dinner? Handle him gently. Emphasize the fact that our guests are men."

He ran up the stairs. At the top of the second flight he met the girl, and her eyes, he thought, shone in the dark.

"Oh, I'm so glad," she whispered.

"Glad of what?" asked Magee.

"That you are not on their side," she answered.

Mr. Magee paused at the door of number seven.

"I should say not," he remarked. "Whatever it's all about, I should say not. Put on your prettiest gown, my lady. I've invited the mayor to dinner."

CHAPTER VII

THE MAYOR BEGINS A VIGIL

One summer evening, in dim dead days gone by, an inexperienced head waiter at Baldpate Inn had attempted to seat Mrs. J. Sanderson Clark, of Pittsburgh, at the same table with the unassuming Smiths, of Tiffin, Ohio. The remarks of Mrs. Clark, who was at the time busily engaged in trying to found a first family, lingered long in the memory of those who heard them. So long, in fact, that Miss Norton, standing with Mr. Magee in the hotel office awaiting the signal from Peters that dinner was ready, could repeat them almost verbatim. Mr. Magee cast a humorous look about.

"Lucky the manners and customs of the summer folks aren't carried over into the winter," he said. "Imagine a Mrs. Clark asked to sit at table with the mayor of Reuton and his picturesque but somewhat soiled friend, Mr. Max. I hope the dinner is a huge success."

The girl laughed.

"The natural nervousness of a host," she remarked. "Don't worry. The hermit and his tins won't fail you."

"It's not the culinary end that worries me," smiled Magee. "It's the repartee and wit. I want the mayor to feel at home. Do you know any good stories ascribed to Congressman Jones, of the Asquewan district?"

Together they strolled to a window. The snow had begun to fall again, and the lights of the little hamlet below showed but dimly through the white blur.

"I want you to know," said the girl, "that I trust you now. And when the time comes, as it will soon—to-night—I am going to ask you to help me. I may ask a rather big thing, and ask you to do it blindly, just trusting in me, as I refused to trust in you." She stopped and looked very seriously into Mr. Magee's face.

"I'm mighty glad," he answered in a low tone. "From the moment I saw you weeping in the station I've wanted to be of help to you. The station agent advised me not to interfere. He said to become involved with a weeping woman meant trouble. The fool. As though any trouble—"

"He was right," put in the girl, "it probably will mean trouble."

"As though any storm," finished Mr. Magee "would not be worth the rainbow of your smile at the end."

"A very fancy figure," laughed she. "But storms aren't nice."

"There are a few of us," replied Magee, "who can be merry through the worst of them because of the rainbow to come."

For answer, she flattened her finely-modeled nose into shapelessness against the cold pane. Back of them in the candle-lighted room, the motley crew of Baldpate's winter guests stood about in various attitudes of waiting. In front of the fire the holder of the Chair of Comparative Literature quoted poetry to Mrs. Norton, and probably it never occurred to the old man that the woman to whom he talked was that nightmare of his life—a peroxide blonde. Ten feet away in the flickering half-light, the immense bulk of the mayor of Reuton reposed on the arm of a leather couch, and before him stood his lithe unpleasant companion, Lou Max, side by side with Mr. Bland, whose talk of haberdashery was forever stilled. The candles sputtered, the storm angrily rattled the windows; Mr. Peters flitted like a hairy wraith about the table. So the strange game that was being played at Baldpate Inn followed the example of good digestion and waited on appetite.

What Mr. Magee flippantly termed his dinner party was seated at last, and there began a meal destined to linger long in the memories of those who partook if it. Puzzled beyond words, the host took stock of his guests. Opposite him, at the foot of the table, he could see the lined tired face of Mrs. Norton, dazed, uncomprehending, a little frightened. At his right the great red acreage of Cargan's face held defiance and some amusement; beside it sneered the cruel face of Max; beyond that Mr. Bland's countenance told a story of worry and impotent anger. And on Mr. Magee's left sat the professor, bearded, spectacled, calm, seemingly undisturbed by this queer flurry of events, beside the fair girl of the station who trusted Magee at last. In the first few moments of silence Mr. Magee compared her delicate features with the coarse knowing face of the woman at the table's foot, and inwardly answered "No."

Without the genial complement of talk the dinner began. Mr. Peters appeared with another variety of his canned soup, whereupon the silence was broken by the gastronomic endeavors of Mr. Max and the mayor. Mr. Magee was reflecting that conversation must be encouraged, when Cargan suddenly spoke.

"I hope I ain't putting you folks out none," he remarked with obvious sarcasm. "It ain't my habit to drop in unexpected like this. But business—"

"We're delighted, I'm sure," said Mr. Magee politely.

"I suppose you want to know why I'm here," the mayor went on. "Well—" he hesitated—"it's like this—"

"Dear Mr. Cargan," Magee broke in, "spare us, I pray. And spare yourself. We have had explanations until we are weary. We have decided to drop them altogether, and just to take it for granted that, in the words of the song, we're here because we're here."

"All right," replied Cargan, evidently relieved. "That suits me. I'm tired explaining, anyhow. There's a bunch of reformers rose up lately in Reuton—maybe you've heard about 'em. A lovely bunch. A white necktie and a half-portion of brains apiece. They say they're going to do for me at the next election."

Mr. Max laughed harshly from the vicinity of his soup.

"They wrote the first joke book, them people," he said.

"Well," went on Cargan, "there ain't nobody so insignificant and piffling that people won't listen to 'em when they attack a man in public life. So I've had to reply to this comic opera bunch, and as I say, I'm about wore out explaining. I've had to explain that I never stole the town I used to live in in Indiana, and that I didn't stick up my father with a knife. It gets monotonous. So I'm much obliged to you for passing the explanations up. We won't bother you long, me and Lou. I got a little business here, and then we'll mosey along. We'll clear out about nine o'clock."

"No," protested Magee. "So soon? We must make it pleasant for you while you stay. I always hate hosts who talk about their servants—I have a friend who bores me to death because he has a Jap butler he believes was at Mukden. But I think I am justified in calling your attention to ours—Mr. Peters, the Hermit of Baldpate Mountain. Cooking is merely his avocation. He is writing a book."

"That guy," remarked Cargan, incredulous.

"What do you know about that?" asked Mr. Bland. "It certainly will get a lot of hot advertising if it ever appears. It's meant to prove that all the trouble in the world has been caused by woman."

The mayor considered.

"He's off—he's nutty, that fellow," he announced. "It ain't women that cause all of the trouble."

"Thank you, Mr. Cargan," said Miss Norton, smiling.

"Anybody'd know it to look at you, miss," replied the mayor in his most gallant manner. Then he added hastily: "And you, ma'am," with a nod in the other woman's direction.

"I don't know as I got the evidence in my face," responded Mrs. Norton easily, "but women don't make no trouble, I know that. I think the man's crazy, myself, and I'd tell him so if he wasn't the cook." She paused, for Peters had entered the room. There was silence while he changed the courses. "It's getting so now you can't say the things to a cook you can to a king," she finished, after the hermit had retired.

"Ahem—Mr. Cargan," put in Professor Bolton, "you give it as your opinion that woman is no trouble-maker, and I must admit that I agree with your premise in general, although occasionally she may cause a—a slight annoyance. Undeniably, there is a lot of trouble in the world. To whose efforts do you ascribe it?"

The mayor ran his thick fingers through his hair.

"I got you," he said, "and I got your answer, too. Who makes the trouble? Who's made it from the beginning of time? The reformers, Doc. Yes, sir. Who was the first reformer? The snake in the garden of Eden. This hermit guy probably has that affair laid down at woman's door. Not much. Everything was running all right around the garden, and then the snake came along. It's a twenty to one shot he'd just finished a series of articles on 'The Shame of Eden' for a magazine. 'What d'ye mean?' he says to the woman, 'by letting well enough alone? Things are all wrong here. The present administration is running everything into the ground. I can tell you a few things that will open your eyes. What's that? What you don't know won't hurt you? The old cry', he says, 'the old cry against which progressives got to fight,' he says. 'Wake up. You need a change here. Try this nice red apple, and you'll see things the way I do.' And the woman fell for it. You know what happened."

"An original point of view," said the dazed professor.

"Yes, Doc," went on Mr. Cargan, evidently on a favorite topic, "it's the reformers that have caused all the trouble, from that snake down. Things are running smooth, folks all prosperous and satisfied—then they come along in their gum shoes and white neckties. And they knock away at the existing order until the public begins to believe 'em and gives 'em a chance to run things. What's the result? The world's in a worse tangle than ever before."

"You feel deeply on the subject, Mr. Cargan," remarked Magee.

"I ought to," the mayor replied. "I ain't no writer, but if I was, I'd turn out a book that would drive this whiskered hermit's argument to the wall. Woman—bah! The only way women make trouble is by falling for the reform gag."

Mr. Peters here interrupted with the dessert, and through that course Mr. Cargan elaborated on his theory. He pointed out how, in many states, reform had interrupted the smooth flow of life, set everything awhirl, and cruelly sent "the boys" who had always been faithful out into the cold world seeking the stranger, work. While he talked, the eyes of Lou Max looked out at him from behind the incongruous gold-rimmed glasses, with the devotion of the dog to its master clearly written in them. Mr. Magee had read many articles about this picturesque Cargan who had fought his way with his fists to the position of practical dictator in the city of Reuton. The story was seldom told without a mention of his man Max—Lou Max who kept the south end of Reuton in line for the mayor, and in that low neighborhood of dives and squalor made Cargan's a name to conjure with. Watching him now, Mr. Magee marveled at this cheap creature's evident capacity for loyalty.

"It was the reformers got Napoleon," the mayor finished. "Yes, they sent Napoleon to an island at the end. And him without an equal since the world began."

"Is your—begging your pardon—is your history just straight?" demurred Professor Bolton timidly.

"Is it?" frowned Cargan. "You can bet it is. I know Napoleon from the cradle to the grave. I ain't an educated man, Doc—I can hire all the educated men I want for eighteen dollars a week—but I'm up on Bonaparte."

"It seems to me," Miss Norton put in, "I have heard—did I read it in a paper?—that a picture of Napoleon hangs above your desk. They say that you see in your own career, a similarity to his. May I ask—is it true?"

"No, miss," replied Cargan. "That's a joking story some newspaper guy wrote up. It ain't got no more truth in it than most newspaper yarn. No, I ain't no Napoleon. There's lots of differences between us—one in particular." He raised his voice, and glared at the company around the table. "One in particular. The reformers got Napoleon at the end."

"But the end is not yet," suggested Mr. Magee, smiling.

Mr. Cargan gave him a sudden and interested look.

"I ain't worrying," he replied. "And don't you, young fellow."

Mr. Magee responded that he was not one to indulge in needless worry, and a silence fell upon the group. Peters entered with coffee, and was engaged in pouring it when Mr. Bland started up wildly from the table with an expression of alarm on his face.

"What's that?" he cried.

The others looked at him in wonder.

"I heard steps up-stairs," he declared.

"Nonsense," said Mr. Cargan, "you're dreaming. This peace and quiet has got to you, Bland."

Without replying, Mr. Bland rose and ran up the stair. In his absence the Hermit of Baldpate spoke into Magee's ear.

"I ain't one to complain," he said; "livin' alone as much as I do I've sort of got out of the habit, having nobody to complain to. But if folks keep coming and coming to this hotel, I've got to resign as cook. Seems as though every few minutes there's a new face at the table, and it's a vital matter to me."

"Cheer up, Peters," whispered Mr. Magee. "There are only two more keys to the inn. There will be a limit to our guests."

"What I'm getting at is," replied Mr. Peters, "there's a limit to my endurance."

Mr. Bland came down-stairs. His face was very pale as he took his seat, but in reply to Cargan's question he remarked that he must have been mistaken.

"It was the wind, I guess," he said.

The mayor made facetious comment on Mr. Bland's "skittishness", and Mr. Max also indulged in a gibe or two. These the haberdasher met with a wan smile. So the dinner came to an end, and the guests of Baldpate sat about while Mr. Peters removed all traces of it from the table. Mr. Magee sought to talk to Miss Norton, but found her nervous and distrait.

"Has Mr. Bland frightened you?" he asked.

She shook her head. "I have other things to think of," she replied.

Mr. Peters shortly bade the company good-by for the night, with the warmly expressed hope in Mr. Magee's ear that there would be no further additions to the circle in the near future. When he had started off through the snow for his shack, Mr. Cargan took out his watch.

"You've been pretty kind to us poor wanderers already," he said. "I got one more favor to ask. I come up here to see Mr. Bland. We got some business to transact, and we'd consider it a great kindness if you was to leave us alone here in the office."

Mr. Magee hesitated. He saw the girl nod her head slightly, and move toward the stairs.

"Certainly, if you wish," he said. "I hope you won't go without saying good-by, Mr. Cargan."

"That all depends," replied the mayor. "I've enjoyed knowing you, one and all. Good night."

The women, the professor and Mr. Magee moved up the broad stairway. On the landing Mr. Magee heard the voice of Mrs. Norton, somewhere in the darkness ahead.

"I'm worried, dearie—real worried."

"Hush," came the girl's voice. "Mr. Magee-we'll meet again—soon."

Mr. Magee seized the professor's arm, and together they stood in the shadows.

"I don't like the looks of things," came Bland's hoarse complaint from below. "What time is it?"

"Seven-thirty." Cargan answered. "A good half-hour yet."

"There was somebody on the second floor when I went up," Bland continued. "I saw him run into one of the rooms and lock the door."

"I've got charge now," the mayor reassured him, "don't you worry."

"There's something doing." This seemed to be Max's voice.

"There sure is," laughed Cargan. "But what do I care? I own young Drayton. I put him where he is. I ain't afraid. Let them gumshoe round as much as they want to. They can't touch me."

"Maybe not," said Bland. "But Baldpate Inn ain't the grand idea it looked at first, is it?"

"It's a hell of an idea," answered Cargan. "There wasn't any need of all this folderol. I told Hayden so. Does that phone ring?"

"No—it'll just flash a light, when they want us," Bland told him.

Mr. Magee and Professor Bolton continued softly up the stairs, and in answer to the former's invitation, the old man entered number seven and took a chair by the fire.

"It is an amazing tangle," he remarked, "in which we are involved. I have no idea what your place is in the scheme of things up here. But I assume you grasp what is going on, if I do not. I am not so keen of wit as I once was."

"If you think," answered Mr. Magee, proffering a cigar, "that I am in on this little game of 'Who's Who', then you are vastly mistaken. As a matter of fact, I am as much in the dark as you are."

The professor smiled.

"Indeed," he said in a tone that showed his unbelief. "Indeed."

He was deep in a discussion of the meters of the poet Chaucer when there came a knock at the door, and Mr. Lou Max's unpleasant head was thrust inside.

"I been assigned," he said, "to sit up here in the hall and keep an eye out for the ghost Bland heard tramping about. And being of a sociable nature, I'd like to sit in your doorway, if you don't mind."

"By all means," replied Magee. "Here's a chair. Do you smoke?"

"Thanks." Mr. Max placed the chair sidewise in the doorway of number seven, and sat down. From his place he commanded a view of

Mr. Magee's apartments and of the head of the stairs. With his yellow teeth he viciously bit the end from the cigar. "Don't let me interrupt the conversation, gentlemen," he pleaded.

"We were speaking," said the professor calmly, "of the versification of Chaucer. Mr. Magee—"

He continued his discussion in an even voice, Mr. Magee leaned back in his chair and smiled in a pleased way at the settings of the stage: Mr. Max in a cloud of smoke on guard at his door; the mayor and Mr. Bland keeping vigil by a telephone switchboard in the office below, watching for the flash of light that should tell them some one in the outside world wanted to speak to Baldpate Inn; a mysterious figure who flitted about in the dark; a beautiful girl who was going to ask Mr. Magee to do her a service, blindly trusting her.

The professor droned on monotonously. Once Mr. Magee interrupted to engage Lou Max in spirited conversation. For, through the squares of light outside the windows, he had seen the girl of the station pass hurriedly down the balcony, the snowflakes falling white on her yellow hair.

CHAPTER VIII

MR. MAX TELLS A TALE OF SUSPICION

An hour passed. Mr. Max admitted when pressed that a good cigar soothed the soul, and accepted another from Magee's stock. The professor continued to talk. Obviously it was his favorite diversion. He seemed to be quoting from addresses; Mr. Magee pictured him on a Chautauqua platform, the white water pitcher by his side.

As he talked, Mr. Magee studied that portion of his delicate scholarly face that the beard left exposed to the world. What part had Thaddeus Bolton, holder of the Crandall Chair of Comparative Literature, in this network of odd alarms? Why was he at Baldpate? And why was he so little moved by the rapid changes in the make-up of the inn colony—changes that left Mr. Magee gasping? He took them as calmly as he would take his grapefruit at the breakfast-table. Only that morning Mr. Magee, by way of experiment, had fastened upon him the suspicion of murder, and the old man had not flickered an eyelash. Not the least strange of all the strange figures that floated about Baldpate, Mr. Magee reflected, was this man who fiddled now with Chaucer while, metaphorically, Rome burned. He could not make it out.

Mr. Max inserted a loud yawn into the professor's discourse.

"Once I played chess with a German," he said, "and another time I went to a lecture on purifying politics, but I never struck anything so monotonous as this job I got now."

"So sorry," replied Magee, "that our company bores you."

"No offense," remarked the yellow-faced one. "I was just thinking as I set here how it all comes of people being suspicious of one another. Now I've always held that the world would be a better place if there wasn't no suspicion in it. Nine times out of ten the suspicion ain't got a leg to stand on—if suspicion can be said to have a leg."

Evidently Mr. Max desired the floor; graciously Professor Bolton conceded it to him.

"Speaking of suspicion," continued the drab little man on the threshold, turning his cigar thoughtfully between his thin lips, "reminds me of a case told me by Pueblo Sam, a few years ago. In some ways it's real funny, and in others it's sad as hell. Pueblo Sam was called in them terms because he'd never been west of Sixth Avenue. He was a swell refined gentleman who lived by his wits, and he had considerable."

"A confidence man," suggested Magee.

"Something along that order," admitted Mr. Max, "but a good sport among his friends, you understand. Well, this case of suspicion Sam tells me about happened something like this. One scorching hot day in summer Sam gets aboard the Coney boat, his idea being to put all business cares away for an hour or two, and just float calm and peaceful down the bay, and cool off. So he grabs out a camp chair and hustles through the crowd up to the top deck, beside the pilot's hangout, and sits down to get acquainted with the breeze, if such there was.

"Well, he'd been sitting there about ten minutes, Sam tells me, when along came about the easiest picking that ever got loose from the old homestead—"

"I beg your pardon," protested Professor Bolton.

"The ready money, the loosened kale, the posies in the garden waiting to be plucked," elucidated Mr. Max. "This guy, Sam says, was such a perfect rube he just naturally looked past him to see if there was a trail of wisps of hay on the floor. For a while Sam sits there with a grouch as he thought how hard it was to put business aside and get a little rest now and then, and debating whether, being on a vacation, as it was, he'd exert himself enough to stretch forth his hand and take whatever money the guy had. While he was arguing the matter with himself, the jay settled the question by coming over and sitting down near him.

"He's in the city, he tells Sam, to enjoy the moving pictures of the streets, and otherwise forget the trees back home that grow the cherries in the bottom of the cocktail glasses. 'And believe me,' he says to Sam, 'there ain't none of those confidence men going to get me. I'm too wise,' he says.

"'I'll bet money you are,' Sam tells him laughing all over at the fish that was fighting to get into the net.

"'Yes, siree,' says the last of the Mohicans, 'they can't fool me. I can tell them as fur away as I can see 'em, and my eyesight's perfect. One of 'em comes up to me in City Hall park and tries to sell me some mining stock. I guess he ain't recovered yet from what I said to him. I tell you, they can't fool Mark Dennen,' says the guy.

"Sam told me that at them words he just leaned back in his seat and stared at the jay and whistled under his breath. Years ago, it seemed, Sam had lived in the town of Readsboro, Vermont, and run up and down the streets with one suspender and a stone bruise, and the kid that had run with him was Mark Dennen. And Sam says he looked at this guy from the woods that was running round crying to high heaven he needed a guardian, and he sees that sure enough it was the tow-head Mark Dennen and—Sam told me—something seemed to bust inside him, and he wanted to stretch out his arms and hug this guy.

"'Mark Dennen,' shouts Sam, 'as I live. Of Readsboro, Vermont. The kid I used to play with under the arc lights—don't you remember me?'

"But Sam says the guy just looked him straight in the eye and shut his jaw, and says: 'I suppose you'll be asking after my brother George next?'

"'You ain't got any brother George, you idiot,' laughs Sam. He told me he was thinking how he'd treat his old friend Mark to a dinner that would go down in history in Readsboro. 'Mark, you old rascal,' he says, 'don't you remember me—don't you remember little Sam Burns that used to play andy-over with you, and that stole your girl in 1892? Don't you remember the old days in Readsboro?' He was all het up by this time, Sam tells me, and all the old memories came creeping back, and he kept thinking he never was so glad to run across anybody in his life. 'You remember little Sam Burns, don't you?' he asks once more.

"But this guy just looks back into Sam's eye with his own cold as steel, and he says, says he: 'You're pretty clever, mister, but you don't fool me. No, you don't come any games on Mark Dennen.'

"'But, Mark,' says Sam, 'I swear to you by all that's holy that I'm that kid—I'm Sam Burns. What proof do you want? Do you remember old Ed Haywood that used to keep the drug store right across from the post-office? The guy that never washed his windows? I do. And Miss Hunter that taught the sixth grade school when we went there—a little woman with washed-out gray eyes and a broken front tooth? And that pretty little girl, Sarah somebody—wait a minute, I'll get it or bust—Sarah—Sarah—Sarah Scott, you used to be so sweet on? Did you marry her, Mark? And old Lafe Perkins, who used to be on hand whenever there was any repairs being made anywhere—rheumatism and a cane and a high squeaky voice that he used to exercise giving orders about things that wasn't any of his business. Why, Mark, I remember 'em all. Good lord, man,' says Sam, 'do you want any more proof?'

"But this country blockhead just looked Sam up and down, and remarks judicious: 'It's certainly wonderful how you know all these things. Wonderful. But you can't fool me,' he says, 'you can't fool Mark Dennen.'"

Mr. Max paused in his narrative for a moment. The sound of voices came up from the office of Baldpate Inn. One, that of the mayor, boomed loudly and angrily. In an evident desire to drown it, Mr. Max went on with spirit:

"Well, gentlemen, it got to be a point of honor, as you might say, for Sam to convince that guy. He told me he never wanted anything so much in his life as for Mark Dennen to give in. It was a hot afternoon, and he'd come aboard that boat for a rest, but he peeled off his collar and started in. He gave Mark Dennen the number of bricks in the Methodist Church, as reported in the Readsboro *Citizen* at the time it was built. He told him the name of the piece Mark's sister recited at the school entertainment in the spring of 1890. He bounded on all four sides the lot where the circuses played when they came to Readsboro. He named every citizen of the town, living or dead, that ever got to be known outside his own family, and he brought children into the world and married them and read the funeral service over them, and still that bonehead from the woods sat there, his mouth open, and says: 'It's beyond me how you know all that. You New

Yorkers are slicker then I give ye credit for. But you can't fool me. You ain't Sam Burns. Why, I went to school with him.'

"They was drawing near Coney now," went on Mr. Max, "and Sam's face was purple and he was dripping with perspiration, and rattling off Readsboro happenings at the rate of ten a second, but that Mark Dennen he sat there and wouldn't budge from his high horse. So they came up to the pier, Sam almost weeping real tears and pleading like his heart would break: 'Mark, don't you remember that time we threw little Bill Barnaby into the swimming hole, and he couldn't swim a stroke and nearly drowned on us?' and still getting the stony face from his old pal.

"And on the pier this Dennen held out his hand to Sam, who was a physical wreck and a broken man by this time, and says: 'You sure are cute, mister. I'll have great times telling this in Readsboro. Once you met one too smart for ye, eh? Much obliged for your company, anyhow!' And he went away and left Sam leaning against the railing, with no faith in human nature no more. 'I hope somebody got to him,' says Sam to me, 'and got to him good. He's the kind that if you work right you can sell stock in a company for starting roof gardens on the tops of the pyramids in Egypt. I'd trimmed him myself,' says Sam to me, 'but I hadn't the heart.'"

Mr. Max finished, and again from below came the sound of voices raised in anger.

"An interesting story, Mr. Max," commented Professor Bolton. "I shall treasure it."

"Told with a remarkable feeling for detail," added Mr. Magee. "In fact, it seems to me that only one of the two participants in it could remember all the fine points so well. Mr. Max, you don't exactly look like Mark Dennen to me, therefore—if you will pardon the liberty—"

"I get you," replied Max sadly. "The same old story. Suspicion— suspicion everywhere. It does a lot of harm, believe me. I wouldn't—"

He jumped from his chair and disappeared, for the voice of Cargan had hailed him from below. Mr. Magee and the professor with one accord followed. Hiding in the friendly shadows of the landing once again, they heard the loud tones of the mayor's booming voice, and the softer tones of Bland's.

"How about this?" bellowed the mayor. "Hayden's squealed. Phones to Bland—not to me. Whines about the courts—I don't know what rot. He's squealed. He didn't phone the combination."

"The rat!" screamed Mr. Max.

"By the Lord Harry," said the mayor, "I'll have it open, anyhow. I've earned what's in there, fair and—I've earned it. I'm going to have it, Max."

"See here, Cargan—" put in Mr. Bland.

"Keep out of the way, you," cried Cargan. "And put away that pop-gun before you get hurt. I'm going to have what's mine by justice. That safe comes open to-night. Max, get your satchel."

Mr. Magee and the professor turned and ascended to the second floor. In front of number seven they paused and looked into each other's eyes. Professor Bolton shrugged his shoulders.

"I'm going to bed," he said, "and I advise you to do the same."

"Yes," replied Mr. Magee, but had no idea what he had said. As for the old man's advice, he had no intention of taking it. Melodrama—the thing he had come to Baldpate Inn to forget forever—raged through that home of solitude. Men spoke of guns, and swore, and threatened. What was it all about? And what part could he play in it all?

He entered number seven, and paused in amazement. Outside one of his windows Miss Norton stood, rapping on the glass for him to open. When he stood facing her at last, the window no longer between, he saw that her face was very pale and that her chin trembled as it had in the station.

"What is it?" cried Magee.

"I mustn't come in," she answered. "Listen. You said you wanted to help me. You can do so now. I'll explain everything later—this is all I need tell you just at present. Down-stairs in the safe there's a package containing two hundred thousand dollars. Do you hear—two hundred thousand. I must have that package. Don't ask me why. I came here to get it—I must have it. The combination was to have been phoned to Cargan at eight o'clock. I was hiding outside the window. Something went wrong—they didn't phone it. He's going to open the safe by force. I heard him say so. I couldn't wait to hear more—I saw him."

"Who?" asked Mr. Magee.

"I don't know—a tall black figure—hiding outside a window like myself. The man with one of the other keys, I suppose. The man Mr. Bland heard walking about to-night. I saw him and I was terribly frightened. It's all right when you know who the other fellow is, but when—it's all so creepy—I was afraid. So I ran—here."

"The thing to do," approved Mr. Magee. "Don't worry. I'll get the money for you. I'll get it if I have to slay the city administration of Reuton in its tracks."

"You trust me?" asked the girl, with a little catch in her voice. The snow lay white on her hair; even in the shadows her eyes suggested June skies. "Without knowing who I am, or why I must have this money—you'll get it for me?"

"Some people," said Mr. Magee, "meet all their lives long at pink little teas, and never know one another, while others just smile at each other across a station waiting-room—that's enough."

"I'm so glad," whispered the girl. "I never dreamed I'd meet any one like you—up here. Please, oh, please, be very careful. Neither Cargan nor Max is armed. Bland is. I should never forgive myself if you were hurt. But you won't be—will you?"

"I may catch cold," laughed Mr. Magee; "otherwise I'll be perfectly safe." He went into the room and put on a gay plaid cap. "Makes me look like Sherlock Holmes," he smiled at the girl framed in the window. When he turned to his door to lock it, he discovered that the key was gone and that it had been locked on the outside. "Oh, very well," he said flippantly. He buttoned his coat to the chin, blew out the candles in number seven, and joined the girl on the balcony.

"Go to your room," he said gently. "Your worries are over. I'll bring you the golden fleece inside an hour."

"Be careful," she whispered, "Be very careful, Mr.—Billy."

"Just for that," cried Magee gaily, "I'll get you *four* hundred thousand dollars."

He ran to the end of the balcony, and dropping softly to the ground, was ready for his first experiment in the gentle art of highway robbery.

CHAPTER IX

MELODRAMA IN THE SNOW

The justly celebrated moon that in summer months shed so much glamour on the romances of Baldpate Inn was no where in evidence as Mr. Magee crept along the ground close to the veranda. The snow sifted down upon him out of the blackness above; three feet ahead the world seemed to end.

"A corking night," he muttered humorously, "for my debut in the hold-up business."

He swung up over the rail on to the veranda, and walked softly along it until he came to a window opening into the office. Cautiously he peered in. The vast lonely room was lighted by a single candle. At the foot of the broad stair he could discern a great bulk, seated on the lowest step, which he correctly took to be the mayor of Reuton. Back of the desk, on which stood the candle, Mr. Max's head and shoulders were visible. He was working industriously in the immediate vicinity of the safe door. Occasionally he consulted the small traveling-bag that stood on the desk. Many other professions had claimed Mr. Max before his advent into Reuton politics; evidently he was putting into operation the training acquired in one of them. Mr. Bland was nowhere in sight.

Shivering with cold and excitement, Mr. Magee leaned against the side of Baldpate Inn and waited. Mr. Max worked eagerly, turning frequently to his bag as a physician might turn to his medicine-case. No word was spoken in the office. Minutes passed. The bulk at the foot of the stairs surged restlessly. Mr. Max's operations were mostly hidden by the desk at which, in summer, timid old ladies inquired for their mail. Having time to think, Mr. Magee pictured the horror of those ladies could they come up to the desk at Baldpate now.

Suddenly Mr. Max ran out into the center of the office. Almost on the instant there was a white puff of smoke and a roar. The inn seemed about to roll down the mountain after all those years of sticking tight. The mayor looked apprehensively up the stair behind him; Mr. Max ran to the open safe door and came back before the desk with a package in his hand. After examining it hastily, Mr. Cargan placed the loot in his pocket. The greedy eyes of Max followed it for a second; then he ran over and gathered up his tools. Now they were ready to depart. The mayor lifted the candle from the desk. Its light fell on a big chair by the fire, and Mr. Magee saw in that chair the figure of Mr. Bland, bound and gagged.

Mr. Cargan and his companion paused, and appeared to address triumphant and jesting comment in Mr. Bland's direction. Then they buttoned their coats and, holding aloft the candle, disappeared through the dining-room door.

"I must have that package." Standing on the balcony of Baldpate Inn, her yellow hair white with snow, her eyes shining even in shadow, thus had the lady of this weird drama spoken to Mr. Magee. And gladly he had undertaken the quest. Now, he knew, the moment had come to act. Max he could quickly dispose of, he felt; Cargan would require time and attention.

He hurried round to the front door of the inn, and taking the big key from his pocket, unlocked it as a means of retreat where the men he was about to attack could not follow. Already he heard their muffled steps in the distance. Crossing the veranda, he dropped down into the snow by the side of the great stone steps that led to Baldpate Inn's chief entrance.

He heard Cargan and Max on the veranda just above his head. They were speaking of trains to Reuton. In great good humor, evidently, they started down the steps. Mr. Magee crouched, resolved that he would spring the moment they reached the ground. They were on the last step—now!

Suddenly from the other side of the steps a black figure rose, a fist shot out, and Mr. Max went spinning like a whirling dervish down the snowy path, to land in a heap five feet away. The next instant the mayor of Reuton and the black figure were locked in terrific conflict. Mr. Magee, astounded by this turn of affairs, could only stand and stare through the dark.

For fifteen seconds, muttering, slipping, grappling, the two figures waltzed grotesquely about in the falling snow. Then the mayor's feet slid from under him on the treacherous white carpet, and the two went down together. As Mr. Magee swooped down upon them he saw the hand of the stranger find the mayor's pocket, and draw from it the package that had been placed there in the office a few moments before.

Unfortunately for the demands of the drama in which he had become involved, Mr. Magee had never been an athlete at the university. But he was a young man of average strength and agility, and he had the advantage of landing most unexpectedly on his antagonist. Before that gentleman realized what had happened, Magee had wrenched the package from his hand, thrown him back on the prostrate form of the highest official of Reuton, and fled up the steps. Quickly the stranger regained his feet and started in pursuit, but he arrived at the great front door of Baldpate Inn just in time to hear the lock click inside.

Safe for the moment behind a locked door, Mr. Magee paused to get his breath. The glory of battle filled his soul. It was not until long afterward that he realized the battle had been a mere scuffle in the dark. He felt his cheeks burn with excitement like a sweet girl graduate's—the cheeks of a man who had always prided himself he was the unmoved cynic in any situation.

With no thought for Mr. Bland, bound in his uneasy chair, Mr. Magee hurried up the broad staircase of Baldpate. Now came the most gorgeous scene of all. A fair-haired lady; a knight she had sent forth to battle; the knight returned. "You asked me to bring you this, my lady." Business of surprise and joy on the lady's part—business also, perhaps, of adoration for the knight.

At the right of the stairs lay seventeen and the lady, at the left a supposedly uninhabited land. As Mr. Magee reached the second floor, blithely picturing the scene in which he was to play so satisfactory a part— he paused. For half-way down the corridor to the left an open door threw a faint light into the hall, and in that light stood a woman he had never seen before. In this order came Mr. Magee's impressions of her, fur-coated, tall, dark, handsome, with the haughty manner of one engaging a chauffeur.

"I beg your pardon," she said, "but are you by any chance Mr. Magee?"

The knight leaned weakly against the wall and tried to think.

"I—I am," he managed to say.

"I'm so glad I've found you," replied the girl. It seemed to the dazed Magee that her dark eyes were not overly happy. "I can not ask you in, I'm afraid. I do not know the custom on such an occasion—does anybody? I am alone with my maid. Hal Bentley, when I wrote to him for a key to this place, told me of your being here, and said that I was to put myself under your protection."

Mr. Magee arranged a bow, most of which was lost in the dark.

"Delighted, I'm sure," he murmured.

"I shall try not to impose on you," she went on. "The whole affair is so unusual as to be almost absurd. But Mr. Bentley said that you were—very kind. He said I might trust you. I am in great trouble. I have come here to get something—and I haven't the least idea how to proceed. I came because I must have it—so much depends on it."

Prophetically Mr. Magee clutched in his pocket the package for which he had done battle.

"I may be too late." The girl's eyes grew wide. "That would be terribly unfortunate. I do not wish you to be injured serving me—" She lowered her voice. "But if there is any way in which you can help me in—in this difficulty—I can never be grateful enough. Down-stairs in the safe there is, I believe, a package containing a large sum of money."

Mr. Magee's hand closed convulsively in his pocket.

"If there is any way possible," said the girl, "I must obtain that package. I give you my word I have as much right to it as any one who will appear at the inn. The honor and happiness of one who is very dear to me is involved. I ask you—made bold as I am by my desperation and Hal Bentley's assurances—to aid me if you find you can."

With the eyes of a man in a dream Mr. Magee looked into the face of the latest comer to Baldpate.

"Hal Bentley is an old friend and a bully chap," he said. "It will be a great pleasure to serve a friend of his." He paused, congratulating himself that these were words, idle words. "When did you arrive, may I ask?"

"I believe you were having dinner when I came," she answered. "Mr. Bentley gave me a key to the kitchen door, and we found a back stairway. There seemed to be a company below—I wanted to see only you."

"I repeat," said Mr. Magee, "I shall be happy to help you, if I can." His word to another lady, he reflected, was binding. "I suggest that there is no harm in waiting until morning."

"But—I am afraid it was to-night—" she began.

"I understand," Magee replied. "The plans went wrong. You may safely let your worries rest until to-morrow." He was on the point of adding something about relying on him, but remembered in time which girl he was addressing. "Is there anything I can do to make you more comfortable?"

The girl drew the fur coat closer about her shoulders. She suggested to Magee a sheltered luxurious life—he could see her regaling young men with tea before a fireplace in a beautiful room—insipid tea in thimble-like cups.

"You are very kind," she said. "I hardly expected to be here the night through. It is rather cold, but I am sure we have rugs and coats enough."

Mr. Magee's duty was clear.

"I'll build you a fire," he announced. The girl seemed distressed at the thought.

"No, I couldn't let you," she said. "I am sure it isn't necessary. I will say good night now."

"Good night. If there is anything I can do—"

"I shall tell you," she finished, smiling. "I believe I forgot to give you my name. I am Myra Thornhill, of Reuton. Until to-morrow." She went in and closed the door.

Mr. Magee sat limply down on the cold stair. All the glory was gone from the scene he had pictured a moment ago. He had the money, yes, the money procured in valiant battle, but at the moment he bore the prize to his lady, another appeared from the dark to claim it. What should he do?

He got up and started for number seventeen. The girl who waited there was very charming and attractive—but what did he know about her? What did she want with this money? He paused This other girl came from

Hal Bentley, a friend of friends. And she claimed to have every right to this precious package. What were her exact words?

Why not wait until morning? Perhaps, in the cold gray dawn, he would see more clearly his way through this preposterous tangle. Anyhow, it would be dangerous to give into any woman's keeping just then a package so earnestly sought by desperate men. Yes, he would wait until morning. That was the only reasonable course.

Reasonable? That was the word he used. A knight prating of the reasonable!

Mr. Magee unlocked the door of number seven and entered. Lighting his candles and prodding the fire, he composed a note to the waiting girl in seventeen:

"Everything all right. Sleep peacefully. I am on the job. Will see you to-morrow. Mr.—Billy."

Slipping this message under her door, the ex-knight hurried away to avoid an interview, and sat down in his chair before the fire.

"I must think," he muttered. "I must get this thing straight."

For an hour he pondered, threshing out as best he could this mysterious game in which he played a leading part unequipped with a book of rules. He went back to the very beginning—even to the station at Upper Asquewan Falls where the undeniable charm of the first of these girls had won him completely. He reviewed the arrival of Bland and his babble of haberdashery, of Professor Bolton and his weird tale of peroxide blondes and suffragettes, of Miss Norton and her impossible mother, of Cargan, hater of reformers, and Lou Max, foe of suspicion. He thought of the figure in the dark at the foot of the steps that had fought so savagely for the package now in his own pocket—of the girl who had pleaded so convincingly on the balcony for his help—of the colder, more sophisticated woman who came with Hal Bentley's authority to ask of him the same favor. Myra Thornhill? He had heard the name, surely. But where?

Mr. Magee's thoughts went back to New York. He wondered what they would say if they could see him now, whirling about in a queer romance not of his own writing—he who had come to Baldpate Inn to get away from mere romancing and look into men's hearts, a philosopher. He laughed out loud.

"To-morrow is another day," he reflected. "I'll solve this whole thing then. They can't go on playing without me—I've got the ball."

He took the package from his pocket. Its seals had already been broken. Untying the strings, he began carefully to unwrap the paper—the thick yellow banking manila, and then the oiled inner wrapping. So finally he opened up the solid mass of—what? He looked closer. Crisp, beautiful, one thousand dollar bills. Whew! He had never seen a bill of this size before. And here were two hundred of them.

He wrapped the package up once more, and prepared for bed. Just as he was about to retire, he remembered Mr. Bland, bound and gagged below. He went into the hall with the idea of releasing the unlucky haberdasher, but from the office rose the voices of the mayor, Max, and Bland himself. Peace, evidently, had been declared between them. Mr. Magee returned to number seven, locked all the windows, placed the much-sought package beneath his pillow, and after a half-hour of puzzling and tossing, fell asleep.

It was still quite dark when he awoke with a start. In the blackness he could make out a figure standing by the side of his bed. He put his hand quickly beneath his pillow; the package was still there.

"What do you want?" he asked, sitting up in bed.

For answer, the intruder sprang through the door and disappeared in the darkness of the outer room. Mr. Magee followed. One of his windows slammed back and forth in the wind. Slipping on a dressing-gown and lighting a candle, he made an investigation. The glass above the lock had been broken. Outside, in the snow on the balcony, were recent footprints.

Sleepily Mr. Magee procured the precious package and put it in the pocket of his gown. Then drawing on his shoes, he added a greatcoat to his equipment, took a candle, and went out on to the balcony.

The storm had increased; the snow flurried and blustered; the windows of Baldpate Inn rattled wildly all about. It was difficult to keep the candle burning in that wind. Mr. Magee followed the footprints along the east side of the inn to the corner, then along the more sheltered rear, and finally to the west side. On the west was a rather unlovely annex to the main building, which increasing patronage had made necessary. It was connected with the inn by a covered passageway from the second floor balcony. At the entrance to this passageway the footprints stopped.

Entering the dark passageway, Mr. Magee made his way to the door of the annex. He tried it. It was locked. But as he turned away, he heard voices on the other side.

Mr. Magee had barely enough time to extinguish his candle and slip into the shadows of the corner. The door of the annex opened. A man stepped out into the passageway. He stood there The light from a candle held by some one in the doorway whom Mr. Magee could not see fell full upon his face—the bespectacled wise face of Professor Thaddeus Bolton.

"Better luck next time," said the professor.

"Keep an eye an him," said the voice from inside. "If he tries to leave the inn there'll be a big row. We must be in on it—and win."

"I imagine," said Professor Bolton, smiling his academic smile, "that the inmates of Baldpate will make to-morrow a rather interesting day for him."

"It will be an interesting day for every one," answered the voice.

"If I should manage to secure the package, by any chance," the professor went on, "I shall undoubtedly need your help in getting away with it. Let us arrange a signal. Should a window of my room be open at any time to-morrow, you will know the money is in my hands."

"Very good," replied the other. "Good night—and good luck."

"The same to you," answered Professor Bolton. The door was closed, and the old man moved off down the passageway.

After him crept Mr. Magee. He followed the professor to the east balcony, and saw him pause at the open window of number seven. There the old man looked slyly about, as though in doubt. He peered into the room, and one foot was across the sill when Mr. Magee came up and touched him on the arm.

Professor Bolton leaped in evident fright out upon the balcony.

"It's—it's a wonderful night," he said. "I was out for a little walk on the balcony, enjoying it. Seeing your open window, I was afraid—"

"The night you speak so highly of," replied Mr. Magee, "is at your left. You have lost your way. Good night, Professor."

He stepped inside and closed the window. Then he pulled down the curtains in both rooms of his suite, and spent some time exploring. Finally he paused before the fireplace, and with the aid of a knife unloosed a brick.

Under this he placed the package of money, removing the traces of his act as best he could.

"Now," he said, standing up, "I'm a regular hermit with a buried treasure, as per all hermit specifications. To-morrow I'm going to hand my treasure to somebody—it's too much for a man who came up here to escape the excitement and melodrama of the world."

He looked at his watch. It was past three o'clock. Entering the inner room, for the second time that night he sought to sleep. "They can't play without me—I've got the ball," he repeated with a smile. And, safe in this thought, he closed his eyes, and slumbered.

CHAPTER X

THE COLD GRAY DAWN

The gayest knight must have a morning after. Mr. Magee awakened to his to find suite seven wrapped again in its favorite polar atmosphere. Filling the door leading to the outer room, he beheld the cause of his awakening—the mayor of Reuton. Mr. Cargan regarded him with the cold steely eye of a Disraeli in action, but when he spoke he opened the jaws of a cocktail mixer.

"Well, young fellow," he remarked, "it seems to me it was time you got up and faced the responsibilities of the day. First of which, I may mention, is a little talk with me."

He stepped into the room, and through the doorway he vacated Mr. Max came slinking. The unlovely face of the foe of suspicion was badly bruised, and he looked upon the world with no cheerful eye. Pushing aside one of the frail bedroom chairs as untrustworthy, the mayor sat down on the edge of Mr. Magee's bed. It creaked in protest.

"You used us pretty rough last night in the snow," Cargan went on. "That's why I ain't disposed to go in for kid gloves and diplomacy this morning. It's my experience that when you're dealing with a man who's got the good old Irish name of Magee, it's best to hit first and debate afterward."

"I—I used you roughly, Mr. Cargan?" said Magee.

"No debate, mind you," protested the mayor. "Lou and me are making this morning call to inquire after a little package that went astray somewhere last night. There's two courses open to you—hand over the package or let us take it. I'll give you a tip—the first is the best. If we have to take it, we might get real rough in our actions."

Mr. Max slipped closer to the bed, an ugly look on his face. The mayor glared fixedly into Magee's eyes. The knight who fought for fair ladies in the snow lay on his pillow and considered briefly.

"I get what I go after," remarked Cargan emphatically.

"Yes," sparred Magee, "but the real point is keeping what you get after you've gone after it. You didn't make much of an impression on me last night in that line, Mr. Cargan."

"I never cared much for humor," replied the mayor, "especially at this early hour of the morning."

"And I hate a fresh guy," put in Max, "like poison."

"I'm not fresh," Mr. Magee smiled, "I'm stating facts. You say you've come for that package. All right—but you've come to the wrong room. I haven't got it."

"The hell you haven't," roared the mayor. "Lou, look about a bit."

"Look about all you like," agreed Magee. "You won't find it. Mr. Cargan, I admit that I laid for you last night. I saw you open the safe according to the latest approved methods, and I saw you come forth with a package of money. But I wasn't rough with you. I might have been, to be frank, but somebody beat me to it."

"Who?"

"The man with the seventh key, I suppose. The man Bland heard walking about last night when we were at dinner. Don't tell me you didn't see him in that mix-up at the foot of the steps?"

"Well—I did think there was another guy," the mayor answered, "but Lou said I was crazy."

"Lou does you an injustice. There was another guy, and if you are anxious to recover your precious package, I advise you to wake him up to the responsibilities of the day, not me."

The mayor considered. Mr. Max, who had hastily made the rounds of the three rooms, came back with empty hands.

"Well," said the mayor, "I might as well admit it. I'm up in the air. I don't know just at this minute where to get off. But that state of affairs don't last long with me, young fellow. I'll go to the bottom of this before the day is out, believe me. And if I can't do anything else, I'll take you back to Reuton myself and throw you in jail for robbery."

"I wouldn't do that," smiled Magee. "Think of the awful job of explaining to the white necktie crowd how you happened to be dynamiting a safe on Baldpate Mountain at midnight."

"Oh, I guess I can get around that," said the mayor. "That money belongs to a friend of mine—Andy Rutter. I happen to go to the inn for a little rest, and I grab you dynamiting the safe. I'll keep an eye on you to-day, Mr. Magee. And let me tell you now that if I catch you or any of the bunch that's with you trying to make a getaway from Baldpate, there's going to be a war break out."

"I don't know about the other hermits," laughed Magee, "but personally, I expect to be here for several weeks to come. Whew! It's cold in here. Where's the hermit? Why hasn't he been up to fix my fire?"

"Yes, where is he?" repeated Mr. Cargan. "That's what everybody'd like to know. He hasn't showed up. Not a sign of breakfast, and me as hollow as a reformer's victory."

"He's backslid," cried Magee.

"The quitter," sneered Max. "It's only a quitter would live on the mountain in a shack, anyhow."

"You're rather hard on poor old Peters," remarked Magee, "but when I think that I have to get up and dress in a refrigerating plant—I can't say I blame you. If only the fire were lighted—"

He smiled his most ingratiating smile on his companion.

"By the way, Mr. Cargan, you're up and dressed. I've read a lot of magazine articles about you, and they one and all agree that you're a good fellow. You'll find kindling and paper beside the hearth."

"What!" The mayor's roar seemed to shake the windows. "Young man, with a nerve like yours, you could wheedle the price of a battleship from Carnegie. I—I—" He stood for a moment gazing almost in awe at Magee. Then he burst forth into a whole-souled laugh. "I am a good fellow," he said. "I'll show you."

He went into the other room, and despite the horrified protests of Lou Max, busied himself amid the ashes of the fireplace. When he had a blaze under way, Mr. Magee came shivering from the other room and held out his hand.

"Mr. Cargan," he laughed, "you're a prince." He noted with interest that the mayor's broad shoes were mighty near two hundred thousand, dollars.

While Mr. Magee drew on his clothes, the mayor and Max sat thoughtfully before the fire, the former with his pudgy hands folded over the vast expanse where no breakfast reposed. Mr. Magee explained to them that the holder of the sixth key had arrived.

"A handsome young lady," he remarked; "her name is Myra Thornhill."

"Old Henry Thornhill's daughter," reflected the mayor. "Well, seems I've sort of lost the habit of being surprised now. I tell you, Lou, we're breaking into the orchid division up here."

While Mr. Magee shaved—in ice-cold water, another black mark against the Hermit of Baldpate—he turned over in his mind the events of the night before. The vigil in the office, the pleading of the fair girl on the balcony, the battle by the steps, the sudden appearance of Miss Thornhill, the figure in his room, the conversation by the annex door—like a moving picture film the story of that weird night unrolled itself. The film was not yet at an end. He had given himself the night to think. Soon he would stand before the girl of the station; soon he must answer her questions. What was he to do with the fortune that lay beneath the feet of the mayor of Reuton at this minute? He hardly knew.

He was ready to descend at last, and came into the parlor of his suite with greatcoat and hat. In reply to Mr. Cargan's unasked question, he said:

"I'm going up the mountain presently to reason with our striking cook."

"You ain't going to leave this inn, Magee," said the mayor.

"Not even to bring back a cook. Come, Mr. Cargan, be reasonable. You may go with me, if you suspect my motives."

They went out into the hall, and Mr. Magee passed down the corridor to the farther end, where he rapped on the door of Miss Thornhill's room. She appeared almost immediately, buried beneath furs and wraps.

"You must be nearly frozen," remarked Mr. Magee pityingly. "You and your maid come down to the office. I want you to meet the other guests."

"I'll come," she replied. "Mr. Magee, I've a confession to make. I invented the maid. It seemed so horribly unconventional and shocking—I couldn't admit that I was alone. That was why I wouldn't let you build a fire for me."

"Don't worry," smiled Magee. "You'll find we have all the conveniences up here. I'll present you to a chaperon shortly—a Mrs. Norton, who is here with her daughter. Allow me to introduce Mr. Cargan and Mr. Max."

The girl bowed with a rather startled air, and Mr. Cargan mumbled something that had "pleasure" in it. In the office they found Professor Bolton and Mr. Bland sitting gloomily before the fireplace.

"Got the news, Magee?" asked the haberdasher. "Peters has done a disappearing act."

It was evident to Magee that everybody looked upon Peters as his creature, and laid the hermit's sins at his door. He laughed.

"I'm going to head a search party shortly," he said. "Don't I detect the odor of coffee in the distance?"

"Mrs. Norton," remarked Professor Bolton dolefully, "has kindly consented to do what she can."

The girl of the station came through the dining-room door. It was evident she had no share in the general gloom that the hermit's absence cast over Baldpate. Her eyes were bright with the glories of morning on a mountain; in their depths there was no room for petty annoyances.

"Good morning," she said to Mr. Magee. "Isn't it bracing? Have you been outside? Oh, I—"

"Miss Norton—Miss Thornhill," explained Magee. "Miss Thornhill has the sixth key, you know. She came last night without any of us knowing."

With lukewarm smiles the two girls shook hands. Outwardly the glances they exchanged were nonchalant and casual, but somehow Mr. Magee felt that among the matters they established were social position, wit, cunning, guile, and taste in dress.

"May I help with the coffee?" asked Miss Thornhill.

"Only to drink it," replied the girl of the station. "It's all made now, you see."

As if in proof of this, Mrs. Norton appeared in the dining-room door with a tray, and simultaneously opened an endless monologue:

"I don't know what you men will say to this, I'm sure—nothing in the house but some coffee and a few crackers—not even any canned soup, and I thought from the way things went yesterday he had ten thousand cans of it at the very least—but men are all alike—what name did you say?—oh yes, Miss Thornhill, pleased to meet you, I'm sure—excuse my not shaking hands—as I was saying, men are all alike—Norton thought if he brought home a roast on Saturday night it ought to last the week out—"

She rattled on. Unheeding her flow of talk, the hermits of Baldpate Inn swallowed the coffee she offered. When the rather unsatisfactory substitute for breakfast was consumed, Mr. Magee rose briskly.

"Now," he said, "I'm going to run up to the hermit's shack and reason with him as best I can. I shall paint in touching colors our sad plight. If the man has an atom of decency—"

"A walk on the mountain in the morning," said Miss Thornhill quickly. "Splendid. I—"

"Wonderful," put in Miss Norton. "I, for one, can't resist. Even though I haven't been invited, I'm going along." She smiled sweetly. She had beaten the other girl by the breadth of a hair, and she knew it. New glories shone in her eyes.

"Good for you!" said Magee. The evil hour of explanations was at hand, surely. "Run up and get your things."

While Miss Norton was gone, Mr. Cargan and Lou Max engaged in earnest converse near a window. After which Mr. Max pulled on his overcoat.

"I ain't been invited either," he said, "but I reckon I'll go along. I always wanted to see what a hermit lived like when he's really buckled down to the hermit business. And then a walk in the morning has always been my first rule for health. You don't mind, do you?"

"Who am I," asked Magee, "that I should stand between you and health? Come along, by all means."

With the blue corduroy suit again complete, and the saucy hat perched on her blond head, Miss Norton ran down the stairs and received the news that Mr. Max also was enthralled by the possibilities of a walk up Baldpate. The three went out through the front door, and found under the snow a hint of the path that led to the shack of the post-card merchant.

"Will you go ahead?" asked Magee of Max.

"Sorry," grinned Max, "but I guess I'll bring up the rear."

"Suspicion," said Mr. Magee, shaking his head, "has caused a lot of trouble in the world. Remember the cruelty practised on Pueblo Sam."

"I do," replied Mr. Max, "and it nearly breaks my heart. But there's a little matter I forgot to mention last night. Suspicion is all right in its place."

"Where's that?" asked Mr. Magee.

Mr. Max tapped his narrow chest. "Here," he said. So the three began the climb, Mr. Magee and the girl ahead, Mr. Max leering at their heels.

The snow still fell, and the picture of the world was painted in grays and whites. At some points along the way to the hermit's abode it had drifted deep; at others the foot-path was swept almost bare by the wind. For a time Mr. Max kept so close that the conversation of the two in the lead was necessarily of the commonplaces of the wind and sky and mountain.

Covertly Mr. Magee glanced at the girl striding along by his side. The red flamed in her cheeks; her long lashes were flecked with the white of the snow; her face was such a one as middle-aged men dream of while their fat wives read the evening paper's beauty hints at their side. Far beyond the ordinary woman was she desirable and pleasing. Mr. Magee told himself he had been a fool. For he who had fought so valiantly for her heart's desire at the foot of the steps had faltered when the time came to hand her the prize. Why? What place had caution in the wild scheme of the night before? None, surely. And yet he, dolt, idiot, coward, had in the moment of triumph turned cautious. Full confession, he decided, was the only way out.

Mr. Max was panting along quite ten feet behind. Over her shoulder the girl noted this; she turned her questioning eyes on Magee; he felt that his moment had come.

"I don't know how to begin," muttered the novelist whose puppets' speeches had always been so apt. "Last night you sent me on a sort of— quest for the golden fleece. I didn't know who had been fleeced, or what the idea was. But I fared forth, as they say. I got it for you—"

The eyes of the girl glowed happily. She was beaming.

"I'm so glad," she said. "But why—why didn't you give it to me last night? It would have meant so much if you had."

"That," replied Mr. Magee, "is what I'm coming to—very reluctantly. Did you note any spirit of caution in the fellow who set forth on your quest, and dropped over the balcony rail? You did not. I waited on the porch and saw Max tap the safe. I saw him and Cargan come out. I waited for them. Just as I was about to jump on them, somebody—the man with the seventh key, I guess—did it for me. There was a scuffle. I joined it. I emerged with the package everybody seems so interested in."

"Yes," said the girl breathlessly. "And then—"

"I started to bring it to you," went on Magee, glancing over his shoulder at Max. "I was all aglow with romance, and battle, and all that sort of thing. I pictured the thrill of handing you the thing you had asked. I ran up-stairs. At the head of the stairs—I saw her."

The light died in her eyes. Reproach entered there.

"Yes," continued Magee, "your knight errant lost his nerve. He ceased to run on schedule. She, too, asked me for that package of money."

"And you gave it to her," said the girl scornfully.

"Oh, no," answered Magee quickly. "Not so bad as that. I simply sat down on the steps and thought. I got cautious. I decided to wait until to-day. I—I did wait."

He paused. The girl strode on, looking straight ahead. Mr. Magee thought of adding that he had felt it might be dangerous to place a package so voraciously desired in her frail hands. He decided he'd better not, on second thought.

"I know," he said, "what you think. I'm a fine specimen of a man to send on a hunt like that. A weak-kneed mollycoddle who passes into a state of coma at the crucial moment. But—I'm going to give you that package yet."

The girl turned her head. Mr. Magee saw that her eyes were misty with tears.

"You're playing with me," she said brokenly. "I might have known. And I trusted you. You're in the game with the others—and I thought you weren't. I staked my whole chance of success on you—now you're making sport of me. You never intended to give me that money—you don't intend to now."

"On my word," cried Magee, "I do intend to give it to you. The minute we get back to the inn. I have it safe in my room."

"Give it to her," said the girl bitterly. "Why don't you give it to her?"

Oh, the perversity of women!

"It's you I want to give it to," replied Magee warmly. "I don't know what was the matter with me last night. I was a fool. You don't believe in me, I know—" Her face was cold and expressionless.

"And I wanted to believe in you—so much," she said.

"Why did you want to?" cried Magee. "Why?"

She plodded on through the snow.

"You must believe," he pleaded. "I don't know what all this is about—on my word of honor. But I want to give you that money, and I will—the minute we get back to the inn. Will you believe then? Will you?"

"I hate you," said the girl simply.

She should not have said that. As far back as he could remember, such opposition had stirred Mr. Magee to wild deeds. He opened his mouth and words flowed forth. What were the words?

"I love you! I love you! Ever since that moment in the station I have loved you! I love you!"

Faintly he heard himself saying it over and over. By the gods, he was proposing! Inanely, in words of one syllable, as the butcher's boy might have told his love to the second kitchen maid.

"I love you," he continued. Idiot!

Often Mr. Magee had thought of the moment when he would tell his love to a woman. It was a moment of dim lights, music perhaps in the distance, two souls caught up in the magic of the moonlit night—a pretty graceful speech from him, a sweet gracious surrender from the girl. And this—instead.

"I love you." In heaven's name, was he never going to stop saying it? "I want you to believe."

Bright morning on the mountain, a girl in an angry mood at his side, a seedy chaperon on his trail, an erring cook ahead. Good lord! He recalled that a fellow novelist, whose love scenes were regarded as models by young people suffering the tender passion, had once confessed that he proposed to his wife on a street-car, and was accepted just as the conductor handed him his transfers. Mr. Magee had been scornful. He could never be scornful again. By a tremendous effort he avoided repeating his childish refrain.

The girl deliberately stopped. There was never less of sweet gracious surrender in a suffragette hurling a stone through a shop-keeper's window.

She eyed Mr. Magee pityingly, and they stood until Mr. Max caught up with them.

"So that's the hermit's shack," said Max, indicating the little wooden hut at which they had arrived. "A funny place for a guy to bury himself. I should think he'd get to longing for the white lights and the table d'hôtes with red wine."

"A very unromantic speech," reproved the girl. "You should be deeply thrilled at the thought of penetrating the secrets of the hermitage. I am. Are you, Mr. Magee?"

She smiled up at Magee, and he was in that state where he thought that in the blue depths of her eyes he saw the sunny slopes of the islands of the blest.

"I—" he caught himself in time. He would not be idiot enough to babble it again. He pulled himself together. "I'm going to make you believe in me," he said, with a touch of his old jauntiness.

Mr. Max was knocking with characteristic loudness at the hermit's door.

CHAPTER XI

A FALSEHOOD UNDER THE PALMS

"Make me a willow cabin at your gate," quoted Mr. Magee, looking at the hermit's shack with interest.

"U-m-m," replied Miss Norton. Thus beautiful sentiments frequently fare, even at the hands of the most beautiful. Mr. Magee abandoned his project of completing the speech.

The door of the hermit's abode opened before Mr. Max's masterful knock, and the bearded little man appeared on the threshold. He was clad in a purple dressing-gown that suggested some woman had picked it. Surely no man could have fallen victim to that riot of color.

"Come in," said the hermit, in a tone so colorless it called added attention to the gown. "Miss, you have the chair. You'll have to be contented with that soap-box davenport, gentlemen. Well?"

He stood facing them in the middle of his hermitage. With curious eyes they examined its architecture. Exiled hands had built it of poles and clay and a reliable brand of roofing. In the largest room, where they sat, were chairs, a table, and a book-shelf hammered together from stray boards— furniture midway between that in a hut on a desert isle and that of a home made happy from the back pages of a woman's magazine. On the wall were various posters that defined the hermit's taste in art as inflammatory, bold, arresting. Through one door at the rear they caught a glimpse of a tiny kitchen; through another the white covering of a hall-room cot could be seen.

"Well?" repeated Mr. Peters. "I suppose you're a delegation, so to speak?"

"A cold unfeeling word," objected Mr. Magee.

"We have come to plead"—began Miss Norton, turning her eyes at their full candle-power on the hermit's bearded face.

"I beg pardon, miss," interrupted Mr. Peters, "but it ain't any use. I've thought it all out—in the night watches, as the poet says. I came up here to be alone. I can't be a hermit and a cook, too. I can't and be true to myself. No, you'll have to accept my resignation, to take effect at once."

He sat down on an uncertain chair and regarded them sorrowfully. His long well-shaped fingers clutched the cord of the purple gown.

"It isn't as though we were asking you to give up the hermit business for good," argued Magee. "It's just for a short time—maybe only for a few days. I should think you would welcome the diversion."

Mr. Peters shook his head vigorously. The brown curls waved flippantly about his shoulders.

"My instincts," he replied, "are away from the crowd. I explained that to you when we first met, Mr. Magee."

"Any man," commented Mr. Max, "ought to be able to strangle his instincts for a good salary, payable in advance."

"You come here," said the hermit with annoyance, "and you bring with you the sentiments of the outside world—the world I have foresworn. Don't do it. I ask you."

"I don't get you," reflected Mr. Max. "No, pal, I don't quite grab this hermit game. It ain't human nature, I say. Way up here miles from the little brass rail and the sporting extra, and other things that make life worth living. It's beyond me."

"I'm not asking your approval," replied the hermit. "All I ask is to be let alone."

"Let me speak," said Miss Norton. "Mr. Peters and I have been friends, you might say, for three years. It was three years ago my awed eyes first fell upon him, selling his post-cards at the inn. He was to me then—the true romance—the man to whom the world means nothing without a certain woman at his side. That is what he has meant to all the girls who came to Baldpate. He isn't going to shatter my ideal of him—he isn't going to refuse a lady in distress. You will come for just a little while, won't you, Mr. Peters?"

But Peters shook his head again.

"I dislike women as a sex," he said, "but I've always been gentle and easy with isolated examples of 'em. It ain't my style to turn 'em down. But this is asking too much. I'm sorry. But I got to be true to my oath—I got to be a hermit."

"Maybe," sneered Mr. Max, "he's got good reason for being a hermit. Maybe there's brass buttons and blue uniforms mixed up in it."

"You come from the great world of suspicion," answered the hermit, turning reproving eyes upon him. "Your talk is natural—it goes with the life you lead. But it isn't true."

"And Mr. Max is the last who should insinuate," rebuked Mr. Magee. "Why, only last night he denounced suspicion, and bemoaned the fact that there is so much of it in the world."

"Well he might," replied the hermit. "Suspicion is the key-note of modern life—especially in New York." He drew the purple dressing-gown closer about his plump form. "I remember the last time I was in the big town, seeing a crowd of men in the grill-room of the Hoffman House. One of them—long, lean, like an eel—stooped down and whispered in the ear of a little fellow with a diamond horseshoe desecrating his haberdashery, and pointing to another man near by. 'No, I won't,' says the man with the diamonds, 'I don't introduce nobody to nobody. Let every man play his own game, I say.' That's New York. That's the essence of the town. 'I introduce nobody to nobody.'"

"It seems odd," remarked Mr. Magee, "to hear you speak of the time you walked on pavements."

"I haven't always been on Baldpate Mountain," replied the hermit. "Once I, too, paid taxes and wore a derby hat and sat in barbers' chairs. Yes, I sat in 'em in many towns, in many corners of this little round globe. But that's all over now."

The three visitors gazed at Mr. Peters with a new interest.

"New York," said Mr. Max softly, as a better man might have spoken the name of the girl he loved. "Its a great little Christmas tree. The candles are always burning and the tinsel presents always look good to me."

The hermit's eyes strayed far away—down the mountain—and beyond.

"New York," said he, and his tone was that in which Max had said the words. "A great little Christmas tree it is, with fine presents for the reaching. Sometimes, at night here, I see it as it was four years ago—I see the candles lit on the Great White Way—I hear the elevated roar, and the newsboys shout, and Diamond Jim Brady applauding at a musical comedy's first night. New York!"

Mr. Max rose pompously and pointed a yellow finger at the Hermit of Baldpate Mountain.

"I got you!" he cried in triumph. "I'm wise! You want to go back."

A half-hearted smile crossed the visible portion of the hermit's face.

"I guess I'm about the poorest liar in the world," he said. "I never got away with but one lie in my life, and that was only for a little while. It was a masterpiece while it lasted, too. But it was my only hit as a liar. Usually I fail, as I have failed now. I lied when I said I couldn't cook for you because I had to be true to my hermit's oath. That isn't the reason. I'm afraid."

"Afraid?" echoed Mr. Magee.

"Scared," said Mr. Peters, "of temptation. Your seventh son of a seventh son friend here has read my palm O. K. I want to go back. Not in the summer, when the inn blazes like Broadway every evening, and I can sit here and listen to the latest comic opera tunes come drifting up from the casino, and go down and mingle with the muslin brigade any time I want, and see the sympathetic look in their eyes as they buy my postals. It ain't then I want to go back. It's when fall comes, and the trees on the mountain are bare, and Quimby locks up the inn, and there's only the wind and me on the mountain—then I get the fever. I haven't the post-card trade to think of—so I think of Ellen, and New York. She's—my wife. New York—it's my town.

"That's why I can't come among you to cook. It'd be leading me into temptation greater than I could stand. I'd hear your talk, and like as not when you went away I'd shave off this beard, and burn the manuscript of *Woman*, and go down into the marts of trade. Last night I walked the floor till two. I can't stand such temptation."

Mr. Peters' auditors regarded him in silence. He rose and moved toward the kitchen door.

"Now you understand how it is," he said. "Perhaps you will go and leave me to my baking."

"One minute," objected Mr. Magee. "You spoke of one lie—your masterpiece. We must hear about that."

"Yes—spin the yarn, pal," requested Mr. Max.

"Well," said the hermit reluctantly, "if you're quite comfortable—it ain't very short."

"Please," beamed Miss Norton.

With a sigh the Hermit of Baldpate Mountain sank upon a most unsocial seat and drew his purple splendor close.

"It was like this," he began. "Five years ago I worked for a fruit company, and business sent me sliding along the edges of strange seas and picture-book lands. I met little brown men, and listened to the soft swish of the banana growing, and had an orchestra seat at a revolution or two. Don't look for a magazine story about overthrown tyrants, or anything like that. It's just a quiet little lie I'm speaking of, told on a quiet little afternoon, by the sands of a sea as blue as Baldpate Inn must have been this morning when I didn't show up with breakfast.

"Sitting on those yellow sands the afternoon I speak of, wearing carpet slippers made for me by loving, so to speak, hands, I saw Alexander McMann come along. He was tall and straight and young and free, and I envied him, for even in those days my figure would never have done in a clothing advertisement, owing to the heritage of too many table d'hôtes about the middle. Well, McMann sat at my side, and little by little, with the sea washing sad-like near by, I got from him the story of his exile, and why.

"I don't need to tell you it was woman had sent him off for the equator. This one's name was Marie, I think, and she worked at a lunch-counter in Kansas City. From the young man's bill-of-fare description of her, I gathered that she had cheeks like peaches and cream, but a heart like a lunch-counter doughnut, which is hard.

"'She cast you off?' I asked.

"'She threw me down,' said he.

"Well, it seems he'd bought a ticket for that loud-colored country where I met him, and come down there to forget. 'I could buy the ticket,' he said, 'as soon as I learned how to pronounce the name of this town. But I can't forget. I've tried. It's hopeless.' And he sat there looking like a man whose best friend has died, owing him money. I won't go into his emotions. Mr. Bland, up at the inn, is suffering them at the present moment, I'm told. They're unimportant; I'll hurry on to the lie. I simply say he was sorrowful, and it seemed to me a crime, what with the sun so bright, and the sea so blue, and the world so full of a number of things. Yes, it certainly was a crime, and I decided he had to be cheered up at any cost. How? I thought a while, gazing up at the sky, and then it came to me—the lie—the great glorious lie—and I told it."

The hermit looked in defiance round the listening circle.

"'You're chuck full of sorrow now,' I said to McMann, 'but it won't last long.' He shook his head. 'Nonsense,' I told him. 'Look at me. Do you see me doing a heart-bowed-down act under the palms? Do you find anything but joy in my face?' And he couldn't, the lie unfolding itself in such splendor to me. 'You?' he asked. 'Me,' I said. 'Ten years ago I was where you are to-day. A woman had spoken to me as Mabel—or Marie— or what was it?—spoke to you.'

"I could see I had the boy interested. I unfolded my story, as it occurred to me at the moment. 'Yes,' said I, 'ten years ago I saw her first. Dancing as a butterfly dances from flower to flower. Dancing on the stage—a fairy sprite. I loved her—worshiped her. It could never be. There in the dark of the wings, she told me so. And she shed a tear—a sweet tear of sorrow at parting.

"'I went to my room,' I told McMann, 'with a lot of time-tables and steamship books. Bright red books—the color came off on my eager hands. I picked out a country, and sailed away. Like you, I thought I could never be happy, never even smile, again. Look at me.'

"He looked. I guess my face radiated bliss. The idea was so lovely. He was impressed—I could see it. 'I'm supremely happy,' I told him. 'I am my own master. I wander where I will. No woman tells me my hour for going out, or my hour for coming in. I wander. For company I have her picture—as I saw her last—with twinkling feet that never touched earth. As the spirit moves, I go. You can move the memory of a woman in a flash, my boy, but it takes two months to get the real article started, and then like as not she's forgot everything of importance. Ever thought of that? You should. You're going to be as happy as I am. Study me. Reflect.' I waved my carpet-slippered feet toward the palms. I had certainly made an impression on Alexander McMann.

"As we walked back over the sands and grass-grown streets to the hotel, his heart got away from that cupid's lunch-counter, and he was almost cheerful. I was gay to the last, but as I parted from him my own heart sank. I knew I had to go back to her, and that she would probably give me a scolding about the carpet slippers. I parted from McMann with a last word of cheer. Then I went to the ship—to her. My wife. That was the lie, you understand. She traveled everywhere with me. She never trusted me.

"We were due to sail that night, and I was glad. For I worried some over what I had done. Suppose my wife and Alexander McMann should meet. An estimable woman, but large, determined, little suggesting the butterfly of the footlights I married, long before. We had a bad session over the carpet slippers. The boat was ready to sail, when McMann came aboard. He carried a bag, and his face shone.

"'She's sent for me,' he said. 'Marie wants me. I got a letter from my brother. I'll blow into Kansas like a cyclone, and claim her.'

"I was paralyzed. At that minute a large black figure appeared on deck. It headed for me. 'Jake,' it says, 'you've sat up long enough. Go below now.'

"McMann's face was terrible. I saw it was all up. 'I lied, McMann,' I explained. 'The idea just came to me, it fascinated me, and I lied. She did turn me down—there in the wings. And she shed that tear I spoke of, too. But, when I was looking over the railroad folders, she sent for me. I went— on the wings of love. It was two blocks—but I went on the wings of love. We've been married twenty years. Forgive me, McMann!'

"McMann turned around. He picked up the bag. I asked where he was going. 'Ashore,' he said, 'to think. I may go back to Kansas City—I may. But I'll just think a bit first.' And he climbed into the ship's boat. I never saw him again."

The hermit paused, and gazed dreamily into space.

"That," he said, "was my one great lie, my masterpiece. A year afterward I came up here on the mountain to be a hermit."

"As a result of it?" asked Miss Norton.

"Yes," answered Mr. Peters, "I told the story to a friend. I thought he was a friend—so he was, but married. My wife got to hear of it. 'So you denied my existence,' she said. 'As a joke,' I told her. 'The joke's on you,' she says. That was the end. She went her way, and I went mine. I'd just unanimously gone her way so long, I was a little dazed at first with my freedom. After fighting for a living alone for a time, I came up here. It's cheap. I get the solitude I need for my book. Not long ago I heard I could go back to her if I apologized."

"Stick to your guns," advised Mr. Max.

"I'm trying to," Mr. Peters replied. "But it's lonesome here—in winter. And at Christmas in particular. This dressing-gown was a Christmas present from Ellen. She picked it. Pretty, ain't it? You see why I can't come down and cook for you. I might get the fever for society, and shave, and go to Brooklyn, where she's living with her sister."

"But," said Mr. Magee, "we're in an awful fix. You've put us there. Mr. Peters, as a man of honor, I appeal to you. Your sense of fairness must tell you my appeal is just. Risk it one more day, and I'll have a cook sent up from the village. Just one day. There's no danger in that. Surely you can resist temptation one little day. A man of your character."

Miss Norton rose and stood before Mr. Peters. She fixed him with her eyes—eyes into which no man could gaze and go his way unmoved.

"Just one tiny day," she pleaded.

Mr. Peters sighed. He rose.

"I'm a fool," he said. "I can't help it. I'll take chances on another day. Though nobody knows where it'll lead."

"Brooklyn, maybe," whispered Lou Max to Magee in mock horror.

The hermit donned his coat, attended to a few household duties, and led the delegation outside. Dolefully he locked the door of his shack. The four started down the mountain.

"Back to Baldpate with our cook," said Mr. Magee into the girl's ear. "I know now how Cæsar felt when he rode through Rome with his ex-foes festooned about his chariot wheels."

Mr. Max again chose the rear, triumphantly escorting Mr. Peters. As Mr. Magee and the girl swung into the lead, the former was moved to recur to the topic he had handled so amateurishly a short time before.

"I'll make you believe in me yet," he said.

She did not turn her head.

"The moment we reach the inn," he went on "I shall come to you, with the package of money in my hand. Then you'll believe I want to help you—tell me you'll believe then."

"Very likely I shall," answered the girl without interest. "If you really do intend to give me that money—no one must know about it."

"No one shall know," he answered, "but you and me."

They walked on in silence. Then shyly the girl turned her head. Oh, most assuredly, she was desirable. Clumsy as had been his declaration, Mr. Magee resolved to stick to it through eternity.

"I'm sorry I spoke as I did," she said. "Will you forgive me?"

"Forgive you?" he cried. "Why, I—"

"And now," she interrupted, "let us talk of other things. Of ships, and shoes, and sealing-wax—"

"All the topics in the world," he replied, "can lead to but one with me—"

"Ships?" asked the girl.

"For honeymoons," he suggested.

"Shoes?"

"In some circles of society, I believe they are flung at bridal parties."

"And sealing-wax?"

"On the license, isn't it?" he queried.

"I'll not try you on cabbage and kings," laughed the girl. "Please, oh, please, don't fail me. You won't, will you?" Her face was serious. "You see, it means so very much to me."

"Fail you?" cried Magee. "I'd hardly do that now. In ten minutes that package will be in your hands—along with my fate, my lady."

"I shall be so relieved." She turned her face away, there was a faint flush in the cheek toward Mr. Magee. "And—happy," she whispered under her breath.

They were then at the great front door of Baldpate Inn.

CHAPTER XII

WOE IN NUMBER SEVEN

Inside, before the office fire, Miss Thornhill read a magazine in the indolent fashion so much affected at Baldpate Inn during the heated term; while the mayor of Reuton chatted amiably with the ponderously coy Mrs. Norton. Into this circle burst the envoys to the hermitage, flushed, energetic, snowflaked.

"Hail to the chef who in triumph advances!" cried Mr. Magee.

He pointed to the door, through which Mr. Max was leading the captured Mr. Peters.

"You got him, didyu?" rasped Mrs. Norton.

"Without the use of anesthetics," answered Magee. "Everybody ready for one of Mr. Peters' inimitable lunches?"

"Put me down at the head of the list," contributed the mayor.

Myra Thornhill laid down her magazine, and fixed her great black eyes upon the radiant girl in corduroy.

"And was the walk in the morning air," she asked, "all you expected?"

"All, and much more," laughed Miss Norton, mischievously regarding the man who had babbled to her of love on the mountain. "By the way, enjoy Mr. Peters while you can. He's back for just one day."

"Eat, drink, and be merry, for to-morrow the cook leaves, as the fellow says," supplemented Mr. Max, removing his overcoat.

"How about a quick lunch, Peters?" inquired Magee.

"Out of what, I'd like to know," put in Mrs. Norton. "Not a thing in the house to eat. Just like a man."

"You didn't look in the right place, ma'am," replied Mr. Peters with relish. "I got supplies for a couple of days in the kitchen."

"Well, what's the sense in hiding 'em?" the large lady inquired.

"It ain't hiding—it's system," explained Mr. Peters. "Something women don't understand." He came close to Mr. Magee, and whispered low: "You didn't warn me there was another of 'em."

"The last, on my word of honor," Magee told him.

"The last," sneered Mr. Peters. "There isn't any last up here." And with a sidelong glance at the new Eve in his mountain Eden, he turned away to the kitchen.

"Now," whispered Magee to Miss Norton, "I'll get you that package. I'll prove that it was for you I fought and bled the mayor of Reuton. Watch for our chance—when I see you again I'll have it in my pocket."

"You mustn't fail me," she replied. "It means so much."

Mr. Magee started for the stairs. Between him and them loomed suddenly the great bulk of Mr. Cargan. His hard menacing eyes looked full into Magee's.

"I want to speak to you, young fellow," he remarked.

"I'm flattered," said Magee, "that you find my company so enchanting. In ten minutes I'll be ready for another interview."

"You're ready now," answered the mayor, "even if you don't know it." His tone was that of one correcting a child. He took Mr. Magee's arm in a grip which recalled to that gentleman a fact the muckraking stories always dwelt on—how this Cargan had, in the old days, "put away his man" in many shady corners of a great city.

"Come over here," said Cargan. He led the way to a window. Over his shoulder Magee noted the troubled eyes of Miss Norton following. "Sit down. I've been trying to dope you out, and I think I've got you. I've seen your kind before. Every few months one of 'em breezes into Reuton, spends a whole day talking to a few rats I've had to exterminate from politics, and then flies back to New York with a ten-page story of my vicious career all ready for the linotypers. Yes, sir—I got you. You write sweet things for the magazines."

"Think so?" inquired Magee.

"Know it," returned the mayor heartily. "So you're out after old Jim Cargan's scalp again, are you? I thought that now, seeing stories on the corruption of the courts is so plentiful, you'd let the shame of the city halls alone for a while. But—well, I guess I'm what you guys call good copy. Big, brutal, uneducated, picturesque—you see I read them stories myself. How long will the American public stand being ruled by a man like this, when it might be authorizing pretty boys with kid gloves to get next to the good things? That's the dope, ain't it—the old dope of the reform gang—the ballyhoo of the bunch that can't let the existing order stand? Don't worry, I ain't going to get started on that again. But I want to talk to you serious— like a father. There was a young fellow like you once—"

"Like me?"

"Exactly. He was out working on long hours and short pay for the reform gang, and he happened to get hold of something that a man I knew—a man high up in public office—wanted, and wanted bad. The young fellow was going to get two hundred dollars for the article he was writing. My friend offered him twenty thousand to call it off. What'd the young fellow do?"

"Wrote the article, of course," said Magee.

"Now—now," reproved Cargan. "That remark don't fit in with the estimate I've made of you. I think you're a smart boy. Don't disappoint me. This young fellow I speak of—he was smart, all right. He thought the matter over. He knew the reform bunch, through and through. All glory and no pay, serving them. He knew how they chased bubbles, and made a lot of noise, and never got anywhere in the end. He thought it over, Magee, the same as you're going to do. 'You're on,' says this lad, and added five figures to his roll as easy as we'd add a nickel. He had brains, that guy."

"And no conscience," commented Magee.

"Conscience," said Mr. Cargan, "ain't worth much except as an excuse for a man that hasn't made good to give his wife. How much did you say you was going to get for this article?"

Mr. Magee looked him coolly in the eye.

"If it's ever written," he said, "it will be a two-hundred-thousand-dollar story."

"There ain't anything like that in it for you," replied the mayor. "Think over what I've told you."

"I'm afraid," smiled Magee, "I'm too busy to think."

He again crossed the office floor to the stairway. Before the fire sat the girl of the station, her big eyes upon him, pleadingly. With a reassuring smile in her direction, he darted up the stairs.

"And now," he thought, as he closed and locked the door of number seven behind him, "for the swag. So Cargan would give twenty thousand for that little package. I don't blame him."

He opened a window and glanced out along the balcony. It was deserted in either direction; its snowy floor was innocent of footprints. Re-entering number seven, he knelt by the fireplace and dug up the brick under which lay the package so dear to many hearts on Baldpate Mountain.

"I might have known," he muttered.

For the money was gone. He dug up several of the bricks, and rummaged about beneath them. No use. The fat little bundle of bills had flown. Only an ugly hole gaped up at him.

He sat down. Of course! What a fool he had been to suppose that such treasure as this would stay long in a hiding-place so obvious. He who had made a luxurious living writing tales of the chase of gems and plate and gold had bungled the thing from the first. He could hammer out on a typewriter wild plots and counter-plots—with a boarding-school girl's cupid busy all over the place. But he could not live them.

A boarding-school cupid! Good lord! He remembered the eyes of the girl in blue corduroy as they had met his when he turned to the stairs. What would she say now? On this he had gaily staked her faith in him. This was to be the test of his sincerity, the proof of his devotion. And now he must go to her, looking like a fool once more—go to her and confess that again he had failed her.

His rage blazed forth. So they had "got to him", after all. Who? He thought of the smooth crafty mountain of a man who had detained him a moment ago. Who but Cargan and Max, of course? They had found his childish hiding-place, and the money had come home to their eager hands. No doubt they were laughing slyly at him now.

Well, he would show them yet. He got up and walked the floor. Once he had held them up in the snow and spoiled their little game—he would do it again. How? When? He did not know. His soul cried for action of some sort, but he was up against a blind alley, and he knew it.

He unlocked the door of number seven. To go down-stairs, to meet the sweet eagerness of the girl who depended on him, to confess himself tricked—it took all the courage he had. Why had it all happened, anyhow? Confound it, hadn't he come up here to be alone with his thoughts? But, brighter side, it had given him her—or it would give him her before the last card was played. He shut his teeth tightly, and went down the stairs.

Mr. Bland had added himself to the group about the fire. Quickly the eyes of Miss Norton met Magee's. She was trembling with excitement. Cargan, huge, red, cheery, got in Magee's path once more.

"I'll annihilate this man," thought Magee.

"I've been figuring," said the mayor, "that was one thing he didn't have to contend with. No, sir, there wasn't any bright young men hunting up old Napoleon and knocking him in the monthly magazines. They didn't go down to Sardinia and pump it out of the neighbors that he started business on borrowed money, and that his father drank more than was good for him. They didn't run illustrated articles about the diamonds he wore, and moving pictures of him eating soup."

"No, I guess not," replied Magee abstractedly.

"I reckon there was a lot in *his* record wasn't meant for the newspapers," continued Cargan reflectively. "And it didn't get there. Nap was lucky. He had it on the reformers there. They couldn't squash him with the power of the press."

Mr. Magee broke away from the mayor's rehashed history, and hurried to Miss Norton.

"You promised yesterday," he reminded her, "to show me the pictures of the admiral."

"So I did," she replied, rising quickly. "To think you have spent all this time in Baldpate Inn and not paid homage to its own particular cock of the walk."

She led him to a portrait hanging beside the desk.

"Behold," she said, "the admiral on a sunny day in July. Note the starchy grandeur of him, even with the thermometer up in the clouds.

That's one of the things the rocking-chair fleet adores in him. Can you imagine the flurry at the approach of all that superiority? Theodore Roosevelt, William Faversham, and Richard Harding Davis all arriving together couldn't overshadow the admiral for a minute."

Mr. Magee gazed at the picture of a pompous little man, whose fierce mustache seemed anxious to make up for the lack of hair on his head.

"A bald hero at a summer resort," he commented, "it seems incredible."

"Oh, they think he lost his hair fighting for the flag," she laughed. "It's winter, and snowing, or I shouldn't dare *lèse-majesté*. And—over here—is the admiral on the veranda, playing it's a quarter deck. And here the great portrait—Andrew Rutter with a profaning arm over the admiral's shoulder. The old ladies make their complaints to Mr. Rutter in softer tones after seeing that picture."

"And this?" asked Magee, moving farther from the group by the fire.

"A precious one—I wonder they leave it here in winter. This is the admiral as a young man—clipped from a magazine article. Even without the mustache, you see, he had a certain martial bearing."

"And now he's the ruler of the queen's navee," smiled Magee. He looked about. "Is it possible to see the room where the admiral plays his famous game?"

"Step softly," she answered. "In here. There stands the very table."

They went into the small card-room at the right of the entrance to the office, and Mr. Magee quietly closed the door behind them. The time had come. He felt his heart sink.

"Well?" said the girl, with an eagerness she could not conceal.

Mr. Magee groped for words. And found—his old friends of the mountain.

"I love you," he cried desperately. "You must believe I want to help you. It looks rather the other way now, I'll admit. I want you to have that money. I don't know who you are, nor what this all means, but I want you to have it. I went up-stairs determined to give it to you—"

"Really." The word was at least fifty degrees below the temperature of the card-room.

"Yes, really. I won't ask you to believe—but I'm telling the truth. I went to the place where I had fatuously hid the money—under a brick of my fireplace. It was gone."

"How terribly unfortunate."

"Yes, isn't it?" Mr. Magee rejoiced that she took so calm a view of it. "They searched the room, of course. And they found the money. They're on top now. But I'm going—"

He stopped. For he had seen her face. She—taking a calm view of it? No, indeed. Billy Magee saw that she was furiously, wildly angry. He remembered always having written it down that beautiful women were even more beautiful in anger. How, he wondered, had he fallen into that error?

"Please do not bore me," she said through her teeth, "with any further recital of what you 'are going' to do. You seem to have a fatal facility in that line. Your record of accomplishment is pathetically weak. And—oh, what a fool I've been! I believed. Even after last night, I believed."

No, she was not going to cry. Hers was no mood for tears. What said the librettist? "There is beauty in the roaring of the gale, and the tiger when a-lashing of his tail." Such was the beauty of a woman in anger. And nothing to get enthusiastic about, thought Mr. Magee.

"I know," he said helplessly, "you're terribly disappointed. And I don't blame you. But you will find out that you've done me an injustice. I'm going—"

"One thing," said she, smiling a smile that could have cut glass, "you are going to do. I know that you won't fail this time, because I shall personally see you through with it. You're going to stop making a fool of me."

"Tell me," pleaded Billy Magee. "Tell me who you are—what this is all about. Can't you see I'm working in the dark? You must—"

She threw open the card-room door.

"An English officer," she remarked loudly, stepping out into the other room, "taught the admiral the game. At least, so he said. It added so much romance to it in the eyes of the rocking-chair fleet. Can't you see—India— the hot sun—the Kipling local color—a silent, tanned, handsome man eternally playing solitaire on the porch of the barracks? Has the barracks a porch?"

Roused, humiliated, baffled, Mr. Magee felt his cheeks burn.

"We shall see what we shall see," he muttered.

"Why coin the inevitable into a bromide," she asked.

Mr. Magee joined the group by the fire. Never before in his life had he been so determined on anything as he was now that the package of money should return to his keeping. But how? How trace through this maze of humans the present holder of that precious bundle of collateral? He looked at Mr. Max, sneering his lemon-colored sneer at the mayor's side; at the mayor himself, nonchalant as the admiral being photographed; at Bland, author of the Arabella fiction, sprawling at ease before the fire; at the tawdry Mrs. Norton, and at Myra Thornhill, who had by her pleading the night before made him ridiculous. Who of these had the money now? Who but Cargan and Max, their faces serene, their eyes eagerly on the preparations for lunch, their plans for leaving Baldpate Inn no doubt already made?

And then Mr. Magee saw coming down the stairs another figure—one he had forgot—Professor Thaddeus Bolton, he of the mysterious dialogue by the annex door. On the professor's forehead was a surprising red scratch, and his eyes, no longer hidden by the double convex lenses, stood revealed a washed-out gray in the light of noon.

"A most unfortunate accident," explained the old man. "Most distressing. I have broken my glasses. I am almost blind without them."

"How'd it happen, Doc?" asked Mr. Cargan easily.

"I came into unexpected juxtaposition with an open door," returned Professor Bolton. "Stupid of me, but I'm always doing it. Really, the agility displayed by doors in getting in my path is surprising."

"You and Mr. Max can sympathize with each other," said Magee, "I thought for a moment your injuries might have been received in the same cause."

"Don't worry, Doc," Mr. Bland soothed him, "we'll all keep a weather eye out for reporters that want to connect you up with the peroxide blondes."

The professor turned his ineffectual gaze on the haberdasher, and there was a startlingly ironic smile on his face.

"I know, Mr. Bland," he said, "that my safety is your dearest wish."

The Hermit of Baldpate announced that lunch was ready, and with the others Mr. Magee took his place at the table. Food for thought was also his. The spectacles of Professor Thaddeus Bolton were broken. Somewhere in the scheme of things those smashed lenses must fit. But where?

CHAPTER XIII

THE EXQUISITE MR. HAYDEN

I t was past three o'clock. The early twilight crept up the mountain, and the shadows began to lengthen in the great bare office of Baldpate Inn. In the red flicker of firelight Mr. Magee sat and pondered; the interval since luncheon had passed lazily; he was no nearer to guessing which of Baldpate Inn's winter guests hugged close the precious package. Exasperated, angry, he waited for he knew not what, restless all the while to act, but having not the glimmer of an inspiration as to what his course ought to be.

He heard the rustle of skirts on the stair landing, and looked up. Down the broad stairway, so well designed to serve as a show-window for the sartorial triumphs of Baldpate's gay summer people, came the tall handsome girl who had the night before set all his plans awry. In the swift-moving atmosphere of the inn she had hitherto been to Mr. Magee but a puppet of the shadows, a figure more fictitious than real. Now for the first time he looked upon her as a flesh-and-blood girl, noted the red in her olive cheeks, the fire in her dark eyes, and realized that her interest in that package of money might be something more than another queer quirk in the tangle of events.

She smiled a friendly smile at Magee, and took the chair he offered. One small slipper beat a discreet tattoo on the polished floor of Baldpate's office. Again she suggested to Billy Magee a house of wealth and warmth and luxury, a house where Arnold Bennett and the post-impressionists are often discussed, a house the head of which becomes purple and apoplectic at the mention of Colonel Roosevelt's name.

"Last night, Mr. Magee," she said, "I told you frankly why I had come to Baldpate Inn. You were good enough to say that you would help me if you could. The time has come when you can, I think."

"Yes?" answered Magee. His heart sank. What now?

"I must confess that I spied this morning," she went on. "It was rude of me, perhaps. But I think almost anything is excusable under the circumstances, don't you? I witnessed a scene in the hall above—Mr. Magee, I know who has the two hundred thousand dollars!"

"You know?" cried Magee. His heart gave a great bound. At last! And then—he stopped. "I'm afraid I must ask you not to tell me," he added sadly.

The girl looked at him in wonder. She was of a type common in Magee's world—delicate, finely-reared, sensitive. True, in her pride and haughtiness she suggested the snow-capped heights of the eternal hills. But at sight of those feminine heights Billy Magee had always been one to seize his alpenstock in a more determined grip, and climb. Witness his attentions to the supurb Helen Faulkner. He had a moment of faltering. Here was a girl who at least did not doubt him, who ascribed to him the virtues of a gentleman, who was glad to trust in him. Should he transfer his allegiance? No, he could hardly do that now.

"You ask me not to tell you," repeated the girl slowly.

"That demands an explanation," replied Billy Magee. "I want you to understand—to be certain that I would delight to help you if I could. But the fact is that before you came I gave my word to secure the package you speak of for—another woman. I can not break my promise to her."

"I see," she answered. Her tone was cool.

"I'm very sorry," Magee went on. "But as a matter of fact, I seem to be of very little service to any one. Just now I would give a great deal to have the information you were about to give me. But since I could not use it helping you, you will readily see that I must not listen. I'm sorry."

"I'm sorry, too," replied the girl. "Thank you very much—for telling me. Now I must—go forward—alone." She smiled unhappily.

"I'm afraid you must," answered Billy Magee.

On the stairs appeared the slim figure of the other girl. Her great eyes were wistful, her face was pale. She came toward them through the red firelight. Mr. Magee saw what a fool he had been to waver in his allegiance even for a moment. For he loved her, wanted her, surely. The snow-capped heights are inspiring, but far more companionable is the brook that sparkles in the valley.

"It's rather dull, isn't it?" asked Miss Norton of the Thornhill girl. By the side of the taller woman she seemed slight, almost childish. "Have you seen the pictures of the admiral, Miss Thornhill? Looking at them is our one diversion."

"I do not care to see them, thank you," Myra Thornhill replied, moving toward the stairs. "He is a very dear friend of my father." She passed up and out of sight.

Miss Norton turned away from the fire, and Mr. Magee rose hastily to follow. He stood close behind her, gazing down at her golden hair shimmering in the dark.

"I've just been thinking," he said lightly, "what an absolutely ridiculous figure I must be in your eyes, buzzing round and round like a bee in a bottle, and getting nowhere at all. Listen—no one has left the inn. While they stay, there's hope. Am I not to have one more chance—a chance to prove to you how much I care?"

She turned, and even in the dusk he saw that her eyes were wet.

"Oh, I don't know, I don't know," she whispered. "I'm not angry any more. I'm just—at sea. I don't know what to think—what to do. Why try any longer? I think I'll go away—and give up."

"You mustn't do that," urged Magee. They came back into the firelight. "Miss Thornhill has just informed me that she knows who has the package!"

"Indeed," said the girl calmly, but her face had flushed.

"I didn't let her tell me, of course."

"Why not?" Oh, how maddening women could be!

"Why not?" Magee's tone was hurt. "Because I couldn't use her information in getting the money for you."

"You are still 'going to' get the money for me?"

Maddening certainly, as a rough-edged collar.

"Of—" Magee began, but caught himself. No, he would prate no more of 'going to'. "I'll not ask you to believe it," he said, "until I bring it to you and place it in your hand."

She turned her face slowly to his and lifted her blue eyes.

"I wonder," she said. "I wonder."

The firelight fell on her lips, her hair, her eyes, and Mr. Magee knew that his selfish bachelorhood was at an end. Hitherto, marriage had been to him the picture drawn by the pathetic exiled master. "There are no more pleasant by-paths down which you may wander, but the road lies long and straight and dusty to the grave." What if it were so? With the hand of a girl like this in his, what if the pleasant by-paths of his solitude did bear hereafter the "No Thoroughfare" sign? Long the road might be, and he would rejoice in its length; dusty perhaps, but her smile through the dust would make it all worth while. He stooped to her.

"Give me, please," he said, "the benefit of the doubt." It was a poor speech compared to what was in his heart, but Billy Magee was rapidly learning that most of the pretty speeches went with puppets who could not feel.

Bland and Max came in from a brisk walk on the veranda. The mayor of Reuton, who had been dozing near the desk, stirred.

"Great air up here," remarked Mr. Max, rubbing his hands before the fire. "Ought to be pumped down into the region of the white lights. It sure would stir things up."

"It would put out the lights at ten p.m.," answered Mr. Magee, "and inculcate other wholesome habits of living disastrous to the restaurant impresarios."

Miss Norton rose and ascended the stairs. Still the protesting Magee was at her heels. At the head of the stair she turned.

"You shall have your final chance," she said. "The mayor, Max and Bland are alone in the office. I don't approve of eavesdropping at Baldpate in the summer—it has spoiled a lot of perfectly adorable engagements. But in winter it's different. Whether you really want to help me or not I'm sure I don't know, but if you do, the conversation below now might prove of interest."

"I'm sure it would," Magee replied.

"Well, I have a scheme. Listen. Baldpate Inn is located in a temperance county. That doesn't mean that people don't drink here—it simply means that there's a lot of mystery and romance connected with the drinking. Sometimes those who follow the god of chance in the card-room late at night grow thirsty. Now it happens that there is a trap-door in the floor of the card-room, up which drinks are frequently passed from the cellar. Isn't that exciting? A hotel clerk who became human once in my presence told me all about it. If you went into the cellar and hunted about, you might find that door and climb up into the card-room."

"A bully idea," agreed Mr. Magee. "I'll hurry down there this minute. I'm more grateful than you can guess for this chance. And this time—but you'll see."

He found the back stairs, and descended. In the kitchen the hermit got in his path.

"Mr. Magee," he pleaded, "I consider that, in a way, I work for you here. I've got something important to tell you. Just a minute—"

"Sorry," answered Magee, "but I can't possibly stop now. In an hour I'll talk to you. Show me the cellar door, and don't mention where I've gone, there's a good fellow."

Mr. Peters protested that his need of talk was urgent, but to no avail. Magee hurried to the cellar, and with the aid of a box of matches found a ladder leading to a door cut in the floor above. He climbed through dust and cobwebs, unfastened the catch, and pushed cautiously upward. In another minute he was standing in the chill little card-room. Softly he opened the card-room door about half an inch, and put his ear to it.

The three men were grouped very close at hand, and he heard Mr. Bland speaking in low tones:

"I'm talking to you boys as a friend. The show is over. There ain't no use hanging round for the concert—there won't be none. Go home and get some clean collars and a square meal."

"If you think I'm going to be shook off by any fairy story like that," said the mayor of Reuton "you're a child with all a child's touching faith."

"All right," replied Mr. Bland, "I thought I'd pass you the tip, that's all. It ain't nothing to me what you do. But it's all over, and you've lost out. I'm sorry you have—but I take Hayden's orders."

"Damn Hayden!" snarled the mayor. "It was his idea to make a three-act play out of this thing. He's responsible for this silly trip to Baldpate. This audience we've been acting for—he let us in for them."

"I know," said Bland. "But you can't deny that Baldpate Inn looked like the ideal spot at first. Secluded, off the beaten path, you know, and all that."

"Yes," sneered the mayor, "as secluded as a Sunday-school the Sunday before Christmas."

"Well, who could have guessed it?" went on Mr. Bland. "As I say, I don't care what you do. I just passed you the tip. I've got that nice little package of the long green—I've got it where you'll never find it. Yes, sir, it's returned to the loving hands of little Joe Bland, that brought it here first. It ain't going to roam no more. So what's the use of your sticking around?"

"How did you get hold of it?" inquired Mr. Lou Max.

"I had my eye on this little professor person," explained Mr. Bland. "This morning when Magee went up the mountain I trailed the high-brow to Magee's room. When I busted in, unannounced by the butler, he was making his getaway. I don't like to talk about what followed. He's an old man, and I sure didn't mean to break his glasses, nor scratch his dome of thought. There's ideas in that dome go back to the time of Anthony J. Chaucer. But—he's always talking about that literature chair of his—why couldn't he stay at home and sit in it? Anyhow, I got the bundle all right, all right. I wonder what the little fossil wants with it."

"The Doc's glasses *was* broke," said Max, evidently to the mayor of Reuton.

"Um-m," came Cargan's voice. "Bland, how much do you make working for this nice kind gentleman, Mr. Hayden?"

"Oh, about two thousand a year, with pickings," replied Bland.

"Yes?" went on Mr. Cargan. "I ain't no Charles Dana Gibson with words. My talk's a little rough and sketchy, I guess. But here's the outline, plain as I can make it. Two thousand a year from Hayden. Twenty thousand in two seconds if you hand that package to me."

"No," objected Bland. "I've been honest—after a fashion. I can't quite stand for that. I'm working for Hayden."

"Don't be a fool," sneered Max.

"Of course," said the mayor, "I appreciate your scruples, having had a few in my day myself, though you'd never think so to read the *Star*. But look at it sensible. The money belongs to me. If you was to hand it over you'd be just doing plain justice. What right has Hayden on his side? I did what was agreed—do I get my pay? No. Who are you to defeat the ends of justice this way? That's how you ought to look at it. You give me what's my due—and you put twenty thousand in your pocket by an honest act. Hayden comes. He asks for the bundle. You point to the dynamited safe. You did your best."

"No," said Bland, but his tone was less firm. "I can't go back on Hayden. No—it wouldn't—"

"Twenty thousand," repeated Cargan. "Ten years' salary the way you're going ahead at present. A lot of money for a young man. If I was you I wouldn't hesitate a minute. Think. What's Hayden ever done for you? He'll throw you down some day, the way he's thrown me."

"I—I—don't know—" wavered Bland. Mr. Magee, in the card-room, knew that Hayden's emissary was tottering on the brink.

"You could set up in business," whined Mr. Max. "Why, if I'd had that much money at your age, I'd be a millionaire to-day."

"You get the package," suggested the mayor, "take twenty thousand out, and slip the rest to me. No questions asked. I guess there ain't nobody mixed up in this affair will go up on the housetops and shout about it when we get back to Reuton."

"Well,—" began Bland. He was lost. Suddenly the quiet of Baldpate Mountain was assailed by a loud pounding at the inn door, and a voice crying, "Bland. Let me in."

"There's Hayden now," cried Mr. Bland.

"It ain't too late," came the mayor's voice, "You can do it yet. It ain't too late."

"Do what?" cried Bland in a firm tone. "You can't bribe me, Cargan." He raised his voice. "Go round to the east door, Mr. Hayden." Then he added, to Cargan: "That's my answer. I'm going to let him in."

"Let him in," bellowed the mayor. "Let the hound in. I guess I've got something to say to Mr. Hayden."

There came to Magee's ears the sound of opening doors, and of returning footsteps.

"How do you do, Cargan," said a voice new to Baldpate.

"Cut the society howdydoes," replied the mayor hotly. "There's a little score to be settled between me and you, Hayden. I ain't quite wise to your orchid-in-the-buttonhole ways. I don't quite follow them. I ain't been bred in the club you hang around—they blackballed me when I tried to get in. You know that. I'm a rough rude man. I don't understand your system. When I give my word, I keep it. Has that gone out of style up on the avenue, where you live?"

"There are conditions—" began Hayden.

"The hell there are!" roared Cargan. "A man's word's his word, and he keeps it to me, or I know the reason why. You can't come down to the City Hall with any new deal like this. I was to have two hundred thousand. Why didn't I get it?"

"Because," replied Hayden smoothly, "the—er—little favor you were to grant me in return is to be made useless by the courts."

"Can I help that?" the mayor demanded. "Was there anything about that in the agreement? I did my work. I want my pay. I'll have it, *Mister* Hayden."

Hayden's voice was cool and even as he spoke to Bland.

"Got the money, Joe?"

"Yes," Bland answered.

"Where?"

"Well—we'd better wait, hadn't we?" Bland's, voice was shaky.

"No. We'll take it and get out," answered Hayden.

"I want to see you do it," cried Cargan. "If you think I've come up here on a pleasure trip, I got a chart and a pointer all ready for your next lesson. And let me put you wise—this nobby little idea of yours about Baldpate Inn is the worst ever. The place is as full of people as if the regular summer rates was being charged."

"The devil it is!" cried Hayden. His voice betrayed a startled annoyance.

"It hasn't worried me none," went on the mayor. "They can't touch me. I own the prosecutor, and you know it. But it ain't going to do you any good on the avenue if you're seen here with me. Is it, Mr. Hayden?"

"The more reason," replied Hayden, "for getting the money and leaving at once. I'm not afraid of you, Cargan. I'm armed."

"I ain't," sneered the mayor. "But no exquisite from your set with his little air-gun ever scared me. You try to get away from here with that bundle and you'll find yourself all tangled up in the worst scrap that ever happened."

"Where's the money, Joe?" asked Hayden.

"You won't wait—" Bland begged.

"Wait to get my own money—I guess not. Show me where it is."

"Remember," put in Cargan, "that money's mine. And don't have any pipe dreams about the law—the law ain't called into things of this sort as a rule. I guess you'd be the last to call it. You'll never get away from here with my money."

Mr. Magee opened the card-room door farther, and saw the figure of the stranger Hayden confronting the mayor. Mr. Cargan's title of exquisite best described him. The newcomer was tall, fair, fastidious in dress and manner. A revolver gleamed in his hand.

"Joe," he said firmly, "take me to that money at once."

"It's out here," replied Bland. He and Hayden disappeared through the dining-room door into the darkness. Cargan and Max followed close behind.

Hot with excitement, Mr. Magee slipped from his place of concealment. A battle fit for the gods was in the air. He must be in the midst of it—perhaps again in a three-cornered fight it would be the third party that would emerge victorious.

In the darkness of the dining-room he bumped into a limp clinging figure. It proved to be the Hermit of Baldpate Mountain.

"I got to talk to you, Mr. Magee," he whispered in a frightened tremolo. "I got to have a word with you this minute."

"Not now," cried Magee, pushing him aside. "Later."

The hermit wildly seized his arm.

"No, now," he said. "There's strange goings-on, here, Mr. Magee. I got something to tell you—about a package of money I found in the kitchen."

Mr. Magee stood very still. Beside him in the darkness he heard the hermit's excited breathing.

CHAPTER XIV

THE SIGN OF THE OPEN WINDOW

Undecided, Mr. Magee looked toward the kitchen door, from behind which came the sound of men's voices. Then he smiled, turned and led Mr. Peters back into the office. The Hermit of Baldpate fairly trembled with news.

"Since I broke in on you yesterday morning," he said in a low tone as he took a seat on the edge of a chair, "one thing has followed another so fast that I'm a little dazed. I can't just get the full meaning of it all."

"You have nothing on me there, Peters," Magee answered. "I can't either."

"Well," went on the hermit, "as I say, through all this downpour of people, including women, I've hung on to one idea. I'm working for you. You give me my wages. You're the boss. That's why I feel I ought to give what information I got to you."

"Yes, yes," Mr. Magee agreed impatiently. "Go ahead."

"Where you find women," Peters continued, "there you find things beyond understanding. History—"

"Get to the point."

"Well—yes. This afternoon I was looking round through the kitchen, sort of reconnoitering, you might say, and finding out what I have to work with, for just between us, when some of this bunch goes I'll easily be persuaded to come back and cook for you. I was hunting round in the big refrigerator with a candle, thinking maybe some little token of food had been left over from last summer's rush—something in a can that time can not wither nor custom stale, as the poet says—and away up on the top shelf, in the darkest corner, I found a little package."

"Quick, Peters," cried Magee, "where is that package now?"

"I'm coming to that," went on the hermit, not to be hurried. "What struck me first about the thing was it didn't have any dust on it. 'Aha,' I says, or words to that effect. I opened it. What do you think was in it?"

"I don't have to think—I know," said Magee. "Money. In the name of heaven, Peters, tell me where you've got the thing."

"Just a minute, Mr. Magee. Let me tell it my way. You're right. There was money in that package. Lots of it. Enough to found a university, or buy a woman's gowns for a year. I was examining it careful-like when a shadow came in the doorway. I looked up—"

"Who?" asked Magee breathlessly.

"That little blinky-eyed Professor Bolton was standing there, most owlish and interested. He came into the refrigerator. 'That package you have in your hand, Peters,' he says, 'belongs to me. I put it in cold storage so it would keep. I'll take it now.' Well, Mr. Magee, I'm a peaceful man. I could have battered that professor into a learned sort of jelly if I'd wanted to. But I'm a great admirer of Mr. Carnegie, on account of the library, and I go in for peace. I knew it wasn't exactly the thing, but—"

"You gave him the package?"

"That's hardly the way I would put it, Mr. Magee. I made no outcry or resistance when he took it. 'I'm just a cook,' I says, 'in this house. I ain't the trusted old family retainer that retains its fortunes like a safety deposit vault.' So I let go the bundle. It was weak of me, I know, but I sort of got the habit of giving up money, being married so many years."

"Peters," said Mr. Magee, "I'm sorry your grip was so insecure, but I'm mighty glad you came to me with this matter."

"He told me I wasn't to mention it to anybody," replied the hermit, "but as I say, I sort of look on it that we were here first, and if our guests get to chasing untold wealth up and down the place, we ought to let each other in on it."

"Correct," answered Magee. "You are a valuable man, Peters. I want you to know that I appreciate the way you have acted in this affair." Four shadowy figures tramped in through the dining-room door. "I should say," he continued, "that the menu you propose for dinner will prove most gratifying."

"What—oh—yes, sir," said Peters. "Is that all?"

"Quite," smiled Magee. "Unless—just a minute, this may concern you—on my word, there's another new face at Baldpate."

He stood up, and in the light of the fire met Hayden. Now he saw that the face of the latest comer was scheming and weak, and that under a small blond mustache a very cruel mouth sought to hide. The stranger gazed at Magee with an annoyance plainly marked.

"A friend of mine—Mr.—er—Downs, Mr. Magee," muttered Bland.

"Oh, come now," smiled Magee. "Let's tell our real names. I heard you greeting your friend a minute ago. How are you, Mr. Hayden?"

He held out his hand. Hayden looked him angrily in the eyes.

"Who the devil are you?" he asked.

"Do you mean," said Magee, "that you didn't catch the name. It's Magee—William Hallowell Magee. I hold a record hereabouts, Mr. Hayden. I spent nearly an hour at Baldpate Inn—alone. You see, I was the first of our amiable little party to arrive. Let me make you welcome. Are you staying to dinner? You must."

"I'm not," growled Hayden.

"Don't believe him, Mr. Magee," sneered the mayor, "he doesn't always say what he means. He's going to stay, all right."

"Yes, you'd better, Mr. Hayden," advised Bland.

"Huh—delighted, I'm sure," snapped Hayden. He strolled over to the wall, and in the light of the fire examined a picture nonchalantly.

"The pride of our inn," Mr. Magee, following, explained pleasantly, "the admiral. It is within these very walls in summer that he plays his famous game of solitaire."

Hayden wheeled quickly, and looked Magee in the eyes. A flush crossed his face, leaving it paler than before. He turned away without speaking.

"Peters," said Magee, "you heard what Mr. Hayden said. An extra plate at dinner, please. I must leave you for a moment, gentlemen." He saw that their eyes followed him eagerly—full of suspicion, menacing. "We shall all meet again, very shortly."

Hayden slipped quickly between Magee and the stairs. The latter faced him smilingly, reflecting as he did so that he could love this man but little.

"Who are you?" said Hayden again. "What is your business here?"

Magee laughed outright, and turned to the other men.

"How unfortunate," he said, "this gentleman does not know the manners and customs of Baldpate in winter. Those are questions, Mr. Hayden, that we are never impolite enough to ask of one another up here." He moved on toward the stairs, and reluctantly Hayden got out of his path. "I am very happy," he added, "that you are to be with us at dinner. It will not take you long to accustom yourself to our ways, I'm sure."

He ran up the stairs and passed through number seven out upon the balcony. Trudging through the snow, he soon sighted the room of Professor Bolton. And as he did so, a little shiver that was not due to atmospheric conditions ran down his spine. For one of the professor's windows stood wide open, bidding a welcome to the mountain storm. Peters had spoken the truth. Once more that tight little, right little package was within Mr. Magee's ken.

He stepped through the open window, and closed it after him. By the table sat Professor Bolton, wrapped in coats and blankets, reading by the light of a solitary candle. The book was held almost touching his nose—a reminder of the spectacles that were gone. As Magee entered the old man looked up, and a very obvious expression of fright crossed his face.

"Good evening, Professor," said Magee easily. "Don't you find it rather cool with the window open?"

"Mr. Magee," replied the much wrapped gentleman, "I am that rather disturbing progressive—a fresh air devotee. I feel that God's good air was meant to be breathed, not barricaded from our bodies."

"Perhaps," suggested Magee, "I should have left the window open?"

The old man regarded him narrowly.

"I have no wish to be inhospitable," he replied. "But—if you please—"

"Certainly," answered Magee. He threw open the window. The professor held up his book.

"I was passing the time before dinner with my pleasant old companion, Montaigne. Mr. Magee, have you ever read his essay on liars?"

"Never," said Magee. "But I do not blame you for brushing up on it at the present time, Professor. I have come to apologize. Yesterday morning I referred in a rather unpleasant way to a murder in the chemical laboratory at one of our universities. I said that the professor of chemistry was missing. This morning's paper, which I secured from Mr. Peters, informs me that he has been apprehended."

"You need not have troubled to tell me," said the old man. He smiled his bleak smile.

"I did you an injustice," went on Magee.

"Let us say no more of it," pleaded Professor Bolton.

Mr. Magee walked about the room. Warily the professor turned so that the other was at no instant at his back. He looked so helpless, so little, so ineffectual, that Mr. Magee abandoned his first plan of leaping upon him there in the silence. By more subtle means than this must his purpose be attained.

"I suppose," he said, "your love of fresh air accounts for the strolls on the balcony at all hours of the night?"

The old man merely blinked at him.

"I mustn't stop," Magee continued. "I just wanted to make my apology, that's all. It was unjust of me. Murder—that is hardly in your line. By the way, were you by any chance in my room this morning, Professor Bolton?"

Silence.

"Pardon me," remarked the professor at last, "if I do not answer. In this very essay on—on liars, Montaigne has expressed it so well. 'And how much is a false speech less sociable than silence.' I am a sociable man."

"Of course," smiled Magee. He stood looking down at the frail old scholar before him, and considered. Of what avail a scuffle there in that chill room? The package was no doubt safely hidden in a corner he could not quickly find. No he must wait, and watch.

"Good-by, until dinner," he said, "and may you find much in your wise companion's book to justify your conduct."

He went out through the open window, and in another moment stood just outside Miss Norton's room. She put a startled head out at his knock.

"Oh, it's you," she said. "I can't invite you in. You might learn terrible secrets of the dressing-table—mamma is bedecking herself for dinner. Has anything happened?"

"Throw something over your head, Juliet," smiled Magee, "the balcony is waiting for you."

She was at his side in a moment, and they walked briskly along the shadowy white floor.

"I know who has the money," said Magee softly. "Simply through a turn of luck, I know. I realize that my protestations of what I am going to do have bored you. But it looks very much to me as if that package would be in your hands very soon."

She did not reply.

"And when I have got it, and have given it to you—if I do," he continued, "what then?"

"Then," she answered, "I must go away—very quickly. And no one must know, or they will try to stop me."

"And after that?"

"The deluge," she laughed without mirth.

Up above them the great trees of Baldpate Mountain waved their black arms constantly as though sparring with the storm. At the foot of the buried roadway they could see the lamps of Upper Asquewan Falls; under those lamps prosaic citizens were hurrying home with the supper groceries through the night. And not one of those citizens was within miles of guessing that up on the balcony of Baldpate Inn a young man had seized a young woman's hand, and was saying wildly: "Beautiful girl—I love you."

Yet that was exactly what Billy Magee was doing. The girl had turned her face away.

"You've known me just two days," she said.

"If I can care this much in two days," he said, "think—but that's old, isn't it? Sometime soon I'm going to say to you: 'Whose girl are you?' and you're going to look up at me with a little heaven for two in your eyes and say: 'I'm Billy Magee's girl.' So before we go any further I must confess everything—I must tell you who this Billy Magee is—this man you're going to admit you belong to, my dear."

"You read the future glibly," she replied. "Are your prophecies true, I wonder?"

"Absolutely. Some time ago—on my soul, it was only yesterday—I asked if you had read a certain novel called *The Lost Limousine*, and you said you had, and that—it wasn't sincere. Well, I wrote it—"

"Oh!" cried the girl.

"Yes," said Magee, "and I've done others like it. Oh, yes, my muse has been a *nouveau riche* lady in a Worth gown, my ambition a big red motor-car. I've been a 'scramble a cent, mister' troubadour beckoning from the book-stalls. It was good fun writing those things, and it brought me more money than was good for me. I'm not ashamed of them; they were all right as a beginning in the game. But the other day—I thought an advertisement did the trick—I turned tired of that sort, and I decided to try the other kind—the real kind. I thought it was an advertisement that did it—but I see now it was because you were just a few days away."

"Don't tell me," whispered the girl, "that you came up here to—to—"

"Yes," smiled Magee, "I came up here to forget forever the world's giddy melodrama, the wild chase for money through deserted rooms, shots in the night, cupid in the middle distance. I came here to do—literature—if it's in me to do it."

The girl leaned limply against the side of Baldpate Inn.

"Oh, the irony of it!" she cried.

"I know," he said, "it's ridiculous. I think all this is meant just for—temptation. I shall be firm. I'll remember your parable of the blind girl—and the lamp that was not lighted. I'll do the real stuff. So that when you say—as you certainly must some day—'I'm Billy Magee's girl' you can say it proudly."

"I'm sure," she said softly, "that if I ever do say it—oh, no, I didn't say I would"—for he had seized her hands quickly—"if I ever do say it—it will certainly be proudly. But now—you don't even know my name—my right one. You don't know what I do, nor where I come from, nor what I want with this disgusting bundle of money. I sort of feel, you know—that this is in the air at Baldpate, even in the winter time. No sooner have the men come than they begin to talk of—love—to whatever girls they find here—on this very balcony—down there under the trees. And the girls listen, for—it's in the air, that's all. Then autumn comes, and everybody laughs, and forgets. May not our autumn come—when I go away?"

"Never," cried Magee. "This is no summer hotel affair to me. It's a real in winter and summer love, my dear—in spring and fall—and when you go away, I'm going too, about ten feet behind."

"Yes," she laughed, "they talk that way at Baldpate—the last weeks of summer. It's part of the game." They had come to the side of the hotel on which was the annex, and the girl stopped and pointed. "Look!" she whispered breathlessly.

In a window of the annex had appeared for a moment a flickering yellow light. But only for a moment.

"I know," said Mr. Magee. "There's somebody in there. But that isn't important in comparison. This is no summer affair, dear. Look to the thermometer for proof. I love you. And when you go away, I shall follow."

"And the book—"

"I have found better inspiration than Baldpate Inn."

They walked along for a time in silence.

"You forget," said the girl, "you only know who has the money."

"I will get it," he answered confidently. "Something tells me I will. Until I do, I am content to say no more."

"Good-by," said the girl. She stood in the window of her room, while a harsh voice called "That you, dearie?" from inside. "And I may add," she smiled, "that in my profession—a following is considered quite—desirable."

She disappeared, and Mr. Magee, after a few minutes in his room, descended again to the office. In the center of the room, Elijah Quimby and Hayden stood face to face.

"What is it, Quimby?" asked Magee.

"I just ran up to see how things were going," Quimby replied, "and I find him here."

"Our latest guest," smiled Magee.

"I was just reminding Mr. Hayden," Quimby said, his teeth set, an angry light in his eyes, "that the last time we met he ordered me from his office. I told you, Mr. Magee, that the Suburban Railway once promised to make use of my invention. Then Mr. Kendrick went away—and this man took charge. When I came around to the offices again—he laughed at me. When I came the second time, he called me a loafer and ordered me out."

He paused, and faced Hayden again.

"I've grown bitter, here on the mountain," he said, "as I've thought over what you and men like you said to me—as I've thought of what might have been—and what was—yes, I've grown pretty bitter. Time after time I've gone over in my mind that scene in your office. As I've sat here thinking you've come to mean to me all the crowd that made a fool of me. You've come to mean to me all the crowd that said 'The public be damned' in my ear. I haven't ever forgot—how you ordered me out of your office."

"Well?" asked Hayden.

"And now," Quimby went on, "I find you trespassing in a hotel left in my care—the tables are turned. I ought to show you the door. I ought to put you out."

"Try it," sneered Hayden.

"No," answered Quimby, "I ain't going to do it. Maybe it's because I've grown timid, brooding over my failure. And maybe it's because I know who's got the seventh key."

Hayden made no reply. No one stirred for a minute, and then Quimby moved away, and went out through the dining-room door.

CHAPTER XV

TABLE TALK

The seventh key! Mr. Magee thrilled at the mention of it. So Elijah Quimby knew the identity and the mission of the man who hid in the annex. Did any one else? Magee looked at the broad acreage of the mayor's face, at the ancient lemon of Max's, at Bland's, frightened and thoughtful, at Hayden's, concerned but smiling. Did any one else know? Ah, yes, of course. Down the stairs the professor of Comparative Literature felt his way to food.

"Is dinner ready?" he asked, peering about.

The candles flickered weakly as they fought the stronger shadows; winter roared at the windows; somewhere above a door crashed shut. Close to its final scene drew the drama at Baldpate Inn. Mr. Magee knew it, he could not have told why. The others seemed to know it, too. In silence they waited while the hermit scurried along his dim way preparing the meal. In silence they sat while Miss Norton and her mother descended. Once there was a little flurry of interest when Miss Thornhill and Hayden met at the foot of the stairs.

"Myra!" Hayden cried. "In heaven's name—what does this mean?"

"Unfortunately," said the girl, "I know—all it means."

And Hayden fell back into the shadows.

Finally the attitude of the hermit suggested that the dinner was ready.

"I guess you might as well sit down," he remarked. "It's all fixed, what there is to fix. This place don't need a cook, it needs a commissary department."

"Peters," reproved Magee. "That's hardly courteous to our guests."

"Living alone on the mountain," replied the hermit from the dining-room door, "you get to have such a high regard for the truth you can't put courtesy first. You want to, but you haven't the heart."

The winter guests took their places at the table, and the second December dinner at Baldpate Inn got under way. But not so genially as on the previous night did it progress. On the faces of those about him Mr. Magee noted worry and suspicion; now and again menacing cold eyes were turned upon him; evidently first in the thoughts of those at table was a little package rich in treasure; and evidently first in the thoughts of most of them, as the probable holder of that package, was Mr. Magee himself. Several times he looked up to find Max's cat-like eyes upon him, sinister and cruel behind the incongruous gold-rimmed glasses; several times he saw Hayden's eyes, hostile and angry, seek his face. They were desperate; they would stop at nothing; Mr. Magee felt that as the drama drew to its close they saw him and him alone between them and their golden desires.

"Before I came up here to be a hermit," remarked Cargan contemporaneously with the removal of the soup, "which I may say in passing I ain't been able to be with any success owing to the popularity of the sport on Baldpate Mountain, there was never any candles on the table where I et. No, sir. I left them to the people up on the avenue—to Mr. Hayden and his kind that like to work in dim surroundings—I was always strong for a bright light on my food. What I'm afraid of is that I'll get the habit up here, and will be wanting Charlie to set out a silver candelabrum with my lager. Candles'd be quite an innovation at Charlie's, wouldn't they, Lou?"

"Too swell for Charlie's," commented Mr. Max. "Except after closing hours. I've seen 'em in use there then, but the idea wasn't glory and decoration."

"I hope you don't dislike the candles, Mr. Cargan," remarked Miss Norton. "They add such a lot to the romance of the affair, don't you think? I'm terribly thrilled by all this. The rattling of the windows, and the flickering light—two lines of a poem keep running through my head:

"'My lord he followed after one who whispered in his ear—The weeping of the candles and the wind is all I hear.'

I don't know who the lord was, nor what he followed—perhaps the seventh key. But the weeping candles and the wind seem so romantic—and so like Baldpate Inn to-night."

"If I had a daughter your age," commented Cargan, not unkindly, "she'd be at home reading Laura Jean Libbey by the fire, and not chasing after romance on a mountain."

"That would be best for her, I'm sure," replied the girl sweetly. "For then she wouldn't be likely to find out things about her father that would prove disquieting."

"Dearie!" cried Mrs. Norton. No one else spoke, but all looked at the mayor. He was busily engaged with his food. Smiling his amusement, Mr. Magee sought to direct the conversation into less personal channels.

"We hear so much about romance, especially since its widely advertised death," he said. "And to every man I ever met, it meant something different. Mr. Cargan, speaking as a broad-minded man of the world—what does romance mean to you?"

The mayor ran his fingers through his graying hair, and considered seriously.

"Romance," he reflected. "Well, I ain't much on the talk out of books. But here's what I see when you say that word to me. It's the night before election, and I'm standing in the front window of the little room on Main Street where the boys can always find me. Down the street I hear the snarl and rumble of bands, and pretty soon I see the yellow flicker of torches, like the flicker of that candle, and the bobbing of banners. And then— the boys march by. All the boys! Pat Doherty, and Bob Larsen, and Matt Sanders—all the boys! And when they get to my window they wave their hats and cheer. Just a fat old man in that window, but they'll go to the pavement with any guy that knocks him. They're loyal. They're for me. And so they march by—cheering and singing—all the boys—just for me to see and hear. Well—that—that's romance to me."

"Power," translated Mr. Magee.

"Yes, sir," cried the mayor. "I know I've got them. All the reformers in the world can't spoil my thrill then. They're mine. I guess old Napoleon knew that thrill. I guess he was the greatest romancer the world ever knew. When he marched over the mountains with his starving bunch—and looked back and saw them in rags and suffering—for him—well I reckon old Nap was as close to romance then as any man ever gets."

"I wonder," answered Mr. Magee. It came to him suddenly that in each person's definition of this intangible thing might lie exposed something of both character and calling. At the far end of the table Mrs. Norton's lined tired face met his gaze. To her he put his question.

"Well," she answered, and her voice seemed softer than its wont, "I ain't thought much of that word for a good many years now. But when I do—say, I seem to see myself sitting on our porch back home—thirty years ago. I've got on a simple little muslin dress, and I'm slender as Elsie Janis, and the color in my cheeks is—well, it's the sort that Norton likes. And my hair—but—I'm thinking of him, of Norton. He's told me he wants to make me happy for life, and I've about decided I'll let him try. I see him—coming up our front walk. Coming to call on me—have I mentioned I've got a figure—a real sweet figure? That's about what romance means to me."

"Youth, dear?" asks Miss Norton gently.

"That's it, dearie," answered the older woman dreamily. "Youth."

For a time those about the table sat in silence, picturing no doubt the slender figure on the steps of that porch long ago. Not without a humorous sort of pity did they glance occasionally toward the woman whom Norton had begged to make happy. The professor of Comparative Literature was the first to break the silence.

"The dictionary," he remarked academically, "would define romance as a species of fictitious writing originally composed in the Romance dialects, and afterward in prose. But—the dictionary is prosaic, it has no soul. Shall I tell you what romance means to me? I will. I see a man toiling in a dim laboratory, where there are strange fires and stranger odors. Night and day he experiments, the love of his kind in his eyes, a desire to help in his heart. And then—the golden moment—the great moment in that quiet dreary cell—the moment of the discovery. A serum, a formula—what not. He gives it to the world and a few of the sick are well again, and a few of the sorrowful are glad. Romance means neither youth nor power to me. It means—service."

He bent his dim old eyes on his food, and Mr. Magee gazed at him with a new wonder. Odd sentiments these from an old man who robbed fireplaces, held up hermits, and engaged in midnight conferences by the annex door. More than ever Magee was baffled, enthralled, amused. Now Mr. Max leered about the table and contributed his unsavory bit.

"Funny, ain't it," he remarked, "the different things the same word means to a bunch of folks. Say romance to me, and I don't see no dim laboratory. I don't see nothing dim. I see the brightest lights in the world, and the best food, and somebody, maybe, dancing the latest freak dance in between the tables. And an orchestra playing in the distance—classy dames all about—a taxi clicking at the door. And me sending word to the chauffeur 'Let her click till the milk carts rumble—I can pay.' Say—that sure is romance to me."

"Mr. Hayden," remarked Magee, "are we to hear from you?"

Hayden hesitated, and looked for a moment into the black eyes of Myra Thornhill.

"My idea has often been contradicted," he said, keeping his gaze on the girl, "it may be again. But to me the greatest romance in the world is the romance of money making—dollar piling on dollar in the vaults of the man who started with a shoe-string, and hope, and nerve. I see him fighting for the first thousand—and then I see his pile growing, slowly at first—faster—faster—faster—until a motor-car brings him to his office, and men speak his name with awe in the streets."

"Money," commented Miss Thornhill contemptuously. "What an idea of romance for a man."

"I did not expect," replied Hayden, "that my definition would pass unchallenged. My past experiences—" he looked meaningly at the girl— "had led me to be prepared for that. But it is my definition—I spoke the truth. You must give me credit for that."

"I ain't one to blame you," sneered Cargan, "for wanting it noticed when you do side-step a lie. Yes, I certainly—"

"See here, Cargan," blazed Hayden.

"Yes, you did speak the truth," put in Miss Thornhill hastily. "You mentioned one word in your definition—it was a desecration to drag it in—hope. For me romance means only—hope. And I'm afraid there are a pitiful number in the world to whom it means the same."

"We ain't heard from the young woman who started all this fuss over a little word," Mr. Cargan reminded them.

"That's right, dearie," said Mrs. Norton. "You got to contribute."

"Yes," agreed the girl with the "locks crisped like golden wire," "I will. But it's hard. One's ideas change so rapidly. A moment ago if you had said romance to me, I might have babbled of shady corners, of whisperings on the stair, of walks down the mountain in the moonlight—or even on the hotel balcony." She smiled gaily at Magee. "Perhaps to-morrow, too, the word might mean such rapturous things to me. But to-night—life is too real and earnest to-night. Service—Professor Bolton was right—service is often romance. It may mean the discovery of a serum—it may mean so cruel a thing as the blighting of another's life romance." She gazed steadily at the stolid Cargan. "It may mean putting an end forever to those picturesque parades past the window of the little room on Main Street— the room where the boys can always find the mayor of Reuton."

Still she gazed steadily into Cargan's eyes. And with an amused smile the mayor gazed back.

"You wouldn't be so cruel as that," he assured her easily; "a nice attractive girl like you."

The dinner was at an end; without a word the sly little professor rose from the table and hurriedly ascended the stairs. Mr. Magee watched him disappear, and resolved to follow quickly on his heels. But first he paused to give his own version of the word under discussion.

"Strange," he remarked, "that none of you gets the picture I do. Romance—it is here—at your feet in Baldpate Inn. A man climbs the mountain to be alone with his thoughts, to forget the melodrama of life, to get away from the swift action of the world, and meditate. He is alone— for very near an hour. Then a telephone bell tinkles, and a youth rises out of the dark to prate of a lost Arabella, and haberdashery. A shot rings out, as the immemorial custom with shots, and in comes a professor of Comparative Literature, with a perforation in his derby hat. A professional hermit arrives to teach the amateur the fine points of the game. A charming maid comes in—too late for breakfast—but in plenty of time for walks on the balcony in the moonlight. The mayor of a municipality condescends to stay for dinner. A battle in the snow ensues. There is a weird talk of—a sum of money. More guests arrive. Dark hints of a seventh key. Why, bless you, you needn't stir from Baldpate Inn in search of your romance."

He crossed the floor hastily, and put one foot on the lower step of Baldpate's grand stairway. He kept it there. For from the shadows of the landing Professor Bolton emerged, his blasted derby once more on his head, his overcoat buttoned tight, his ear-muffs in place, his traveling-bag and green umbrella in tow.

"What, Professor," cried Magee, "you're leaving?"

Now, truly, the end of the drama had come. Mr. Magee felt his heart beat wildly. What was the end to be? What did this calm departure mean? Surely the little man descending the stair was not, Daniel-like, thrusting himself into this lion's den with the precious package in his possession?

"Yes," the old man was saying slowly. "I am about to leave. The decision came suddenly. I am sorry to go. Certainly I have enjoyed these chance meetings."

"See here, Doc," said Mr. Bland, uneasily feeling of his purple tie, "you're not going back and let them reporters have another fling at you?"

"I fear I must," replied the old man. "My duty calls. Yes, they will hound me. I shall hear much of peroxide blondes. I shall be asked again to name the ten greatest in history,—a difficult, not to say dangerous task. But I must face the—er—music, as the vulgar expression goes. I bid you good-by, Mr. Bland. We part friends, I am sure. Again be comforted by the thought that I do not hold the ruined derby against you. Even though, as I have remarked with unpleasant truth, the honorarium of a professor at our university is not large."

He turned to Magee.

"I regret more than I can say," he continued, "parting from you. My eyes fell upon you first on entering this place—we have had exciting times together. My dear Miss Norton—knowing you has refreshed an old man's heart. I might compare you to another with yellow locks—but I leave that to my younger—er—colleagues. Mr. Cargan—good-by. My acquaintance with you I shall always look back on—"

But the mayor of Reuton, Max and Bland closed in on the old man.

"Now look here, Doc," interrupted Cargan. "You're bluffing. Do you get me? You're trying to put something over. I don't want to be rough—I like you—but I got to get a glimpse at the inside of that satchel. And I got to examine your personal make-up a bit."

"Dear, dear," smiled Professor Bolton, "you don't think I would steal? A man in my position? Absurd. Look through my poor luggage if you desire. You will find nothing but the usual appurtenances of travel."

He stood docilely in the middle of the floor, and blinked at the group around him.

Mr. Magee waited to hear no more. It was quite apparent that this wise little man carried no package wildly sought by Baldpate's winter guests. Quietly and quickly Magee disappeared up the broad stair, and tried the professor's door. It was locked. Inside he could hear a window banging back and forth in the storm. He ran through number seven and out upon the snow-covered balcony.

There he bumped full into a shadowy figure hurrying in the opposite direction.

CHAPTER XVI

A MAN FROM THE DARK

For fully five seconds Mr. Magee and the man with whom he had collided stood facing each other on the balcony. The identical moon of the summer romances now hung in the sky, and in its white glare Baldpate Mountain glittered like a Christmas-card. Suddenly the wind broke a small branch from one of the near-by trees and tossed it lightly on the snow beside the two men—as though it were a signal for battle.

"A lucky chance," said Mr. Magee. "You're a man I've been longing to meet. Especially since the professor left his window open this afternoon."

"Indeed," replied the other calmly. "May I ask what you want of me?"

"Certainly." Mr. Magee laughed. "A little package. I think it's in your pocket at this minute. A package no bigger than a man's hand."

The stranger made no reply, but looked quickly about, over his shoulder at the path along which he had come, and then past Mr. Magee at the road that led to freedom.

"I think it's in your pocket," repeated Mr. Magee, "and I'm going to find out."

"I haven't time to argue with you," said the holder of the seventh key. His voice was cold, calculating, harsh. "Get out of my way and let me pass. Or—"

"Or what?" asked Billy Magee.

He watched the man lunge toward him in the moonlight. He saw the fist that had the night before been the Waterloo of Mr. Max and the mayor start on a swift true course for his head. Quickly he dodged to one side and closed with his opponent.

Back and forth through the snow they ploughed, panting, grappling, straining. Mr. Magee soon realized that his adversary was no weakling. He was forced to call into play muscles he had not used in what seemed ages— not since he sported of an afternoon in a rather odorous college gymnasium. In moonlight and shadow, up and down, they reeled, staggered, stumbled, the sole jarring notes in that picture of Baldpate on a quiet winter's night.

"You queered the game last time," muttered the stranger. "But you'll never queer it again."

Mr. Magee saved his breath. Together they crashed against the side of the inn. Together they squirmed away, across the balcony to the railing. Still back and forth, now in the moonlight, now in shadow, wildly they fought. Once Mr. Magee felt his feet slip from beneath him, but caught himself in time. His strength was going—surely—quickly. Then suddenly his opponent seemed to weaken in his grip. With a supreme effort Magee forced him down upon the balcony floor, and tumbled on top of him. He felt the chill of the snow under his knees, and its wetness in his cuffs.

"Now," he cried to himself.

The other still struggled desperately. But his struggle was without success. For deftly Billy Magee drew from his pocket the precious package about which there had been so much debate on Baldpate Mountain. He clasped it close, rose and ran. In another second he was inside number seven, and had lighted a candle at the blazing logs.

Once more he examined that closely packed little bundle; once more he found it rich in greenbacks. Assuredly it was the greatly desired thing he had fought for the night before. He had it again. And this time, he told himself, he would not lose sight of it until he had placed it in the hands of the girl of the station.

The dark shadow of the man he had just robbed was hovering at his windows. Magee turned hastily to the door. As he did so it opened, and Hayden entered. He carried a pistol in his hand; his face was hard, cruel, determined; his usually expressionless eyes lighted with pleasure as they fell on the package in Mr. Magee's possession.

"It seems I'm just in time," he said, "to prevent highway robbery."

"You think so?" asked Magee.

"See here, young man," remarked Hayden, glancing nervously over his shoulder, "I can't waste any time in talk. Does that money belong to you? No. Well, it does belong to me. I'm going to have it. Don't think I'm afraid to shoot to get it. The law permits a man to fire on the thief who tries to fleece him."

"The law, did you say?" laughed Billy Magee. "I wouldn't drag the law into this if I were you, Mr. Hayden. I'm sure it has no connection with events on Baldpate Mountain. You would be the last to want its attention to be directed here. I've got this money, and I'm going to keep it."

Hayden considered a brief moment, and then swore under his breath.

"You're right," he said. "I'm not going to shoot. But there are other ways, you whipper-snapper—" He dropped the revolver into his pocket and sprang forward. For the second time within ten minutes Mr. Magee steadied himself for conflict.

But Hayden stopped. Some one had entered the room through the window behind Magee. In the dim light of the single candle Magee saw Hayden's face go white, his lip twitch, his eyes glaze with horrible surprise. His arms fell limply to his sides.

"Good God! Kendrick!" he cried.

The voice of the man with whom Billy Magee had but a moment before struggled on the balcony answered:

"Yes, Hayden. I'm back."

Hayden wet his lips with his tongue.

"What—what brought you?" he asked, his voice trailing off weakly on the last word.

"What brought me?" Suddenly, as from a volcano that had long been cold, fire blazed up in Kendrick's eyes. "If a man knew the road from hell back home, what would it need to bring him back?"

Hayden stood with his mouth partly open; almost a grotesque picture of terror he looked in that dim light. Then he spoke, in an odd strained tone, more to himself than to any one else.

"I thought you were dead," he said. "I told myself you'd never come back. Over and over—in the night—I told myself that. But all the time—I knew—I knew you'd come."

A cry—a woman's cry—sounded from just outside the door of number seven. Into the room came Myra Thornhill; quickly she crossed and took Kendrick's hands in hers.

"David," she sobbed. "Oh, David—is it a dream—a wonderful dream?"

Kendrick looked into her eyes, sheepishly at first, then gladly as he saw what was in them. For the light there, under the tears, was such as no man could mistake. Magee saw it. Hayden saw it too, and his voice was even more lifeless when he spoke.

"Forgive me, David," he said. "I didn't mean—"

And then, as he saw that Kendrick did not listen, he turned and walked quietly into the bedroom of number seven, taking no notice of Cargan and Bland, who, with the other winter guests of Baldpate, now crowded the doorway leading to the hall. Hayden closed the bedroom door. Mr. Magee and the others stood silent, wondering. Their answer came quickly—the sharp cry of a revolver behind that closed door.

It was Mr. Magee who went into the bedroom. The moonlight streamed in through the low windows, and fell brightly on the bed. Across this Hayden lay. Mr. Magee made sure. It was not a pleasant thing to make sure of. Then he took the revolver from the hand that still clasped it, covered the quiet figure on the bed, and stepped back into the outer room.

"He—he has killed himself," he said in a low voice, closing the bedroom door behind him.

There was a moment's frightened hush; then the voice of Kendrick rang out:

"Killed himself? I don't understand. Why should he do that? Surely not because—no—" He looked questioningly into the white face of the girl at his side; she only shook her head. "Killed himself," he repeated, like a man wakened from sleep. "I don't understand."

On tiptoe the amateur hermits of Baldpate descended to the hotel office. Mr. Magee saw the eyes of the girl of the station upon him, wide with doubt and alarm. While the others gathered in little groups and talked, he took her to one side.

"When does the next train leave for Reuton?" he asked her.

"In two hours—at ten-thirty," she replied.

"You must be on it," he told her. "With you will go the two-hundred-thousand-dollar package. I have it in my pocket now."

She took the news stolidly, and made no reply.

"Are you afraid?" asked Magee gently. "You mustn't be. No harm can touch you. I shall stay here and see that no one follows."

"I'm not afraid," she replied. "Just startled, that's all. Did he—did he do it because you took this money—because he was afraid of what would happen?"

"You mean Hayden?" Magee said. "No. This money was not concerned in—his death. That is an affair between Kendrick and him."

"I see," answered the girl slowly. "I'm so glad it wasn't—the money. I couldn't bear it if it were."

"May I call your attention," remarked Magee, "to the fact that the long reign of 'I'm going to' is ended, and the rule of 'I've done it' has begun? I've actually got the money. Somehow, it doesn't seem to thrill you the way I thought it would."

"But it does—oh, it does!" cried the girl. "I was upset—for a moment. It's glorious news And with you on guard here, I'm not afraid to carry it away—down the mountain—and to Reuton. I'll be with you in a moment, ready for the journey."

She called Mrs. Norton and the two went rather timidly up-stairs together. Mr. Magee turned to his companions in the room, and mentally called their roll. They were all there, the professor, the mayor, Max, Bland, Peters, Miss Thornhill, and the newcomer Kendrick, a man prematurely old, grayed at the temples, and with a face yellowed by fever. He and the professor were talking earnestly together, and now the old man came and stood before Magee.

"Mr. Magee," he said seriously, "I learn from Kendrick that you have in your possession a certain package of money that has been much buffeted about here at Baldpate Inn. Now I suggest—no, I demand—"

"Pardon me, Professor," Mr. Magee interrupted. "I have something to suggest—even to demand. It is that you, and every one else present, select a chair and sit down. I suggest, though I do not demand, that you pick comfortable chairs. For the vigil that you are about to begin will prove a long one."

"What d'you mean?" asked the mayor of Reuton, coming militantly to Professor Bolton's side.

Magee did not reply. Miss Norton and her mother came down the stair, the former wrapped in a great coat. She stood on the bottom step, her cheeks flushed, her eyes ablaze. Mr. Magee, going to her side, reflected that she looked charming and wonderful, and wished he had time to admire. But he hadn't. He took from one pocket the pistol he had removed from the hand of Hayden; from the other the celebrated package of money.

"I warn you all," he said, "I will shoot any one who makes a move for this bundle. Miss Norton is going to take it away with her—she is to catch the ten-thirty train for Reuton. The train arrives at its destination at twelve. Much as it pains me to say it, no one will leave this room before twelve-fifteen."

"You—crook!" roared Cargan.

Mr. Magee smiled as he put the package in the girl's hand.

"Possibly," he said. "But, Mr. Cargan, the blackness of the kettle always has annoyed the pot. Do not be afraid," he added to the girl. "Every gentleman in this room is to spend the evening with me. You will not be annoyed in any way." He looked around the menacing circle. "Go," he said, "and may the gods of the mountain take care of you."

The little professor of Comparative Literature stepped forward and stood pompously before Magee.

"One moment," he remarked. "Before you steal this money in front of our very eyes, I want to inform you who I am, and who I represent here."

"This is no time," replied Magee, "for light talk on the subject of blondes."

"This is the time," said the professor warmly, "for me to tell you that Mr. Kendrick here and myself represent at Baldpate Inn the prosecuting attorney of Reuton county. We—"

Cargan, big, red, volcanic, interrupted.

"Drayton," he bellowed. "Drayton sent you here? The rat! The pup! Why, I made that kid. I put him where he is. He won't dare touch me."

"Won't he?" returned Professor Bolton. "My dear sir, you are mistaken. Drayton fully intends to prosecute you on the ground that you arranged to pass Ordinance Number 45, granting the Suburban Railway the privilege of merging with the Civic, in exchange for this bribe of two hundred thousand dollars."

"He won't dare," cried Cargan. "I made him."

"Before election," said the professor, "I believe he often insisted to you that he would do his duty as he saw it."

"Of course he did," replied Cargan. "But that's what they all say."

"He intends to keep his word."

The mayor of Reuton slid into the shadows.

"To think he'd do this thing to me," he whined. "After all I've done for him."

"As I was saying, Mr. Magee," continued the professor, "Mr. Kendrick and I came up here to secure this package of money as evidence against Cargan and—the man above. I speak with the voice of the law when I say you must turn this money over to me."

For answer Magee smiled at the girl.

"You'd better go now," he said. "It's a long walk down the mountain."

"You refuse?" cried the professor.

"Absolutely—don't we, Miss Norton?" said Magee.

"Absolutely," she repeated bravely.

"Then, sir," announced the old man crushingly, "you are little better than a thief, and this girl is your accomplice."

"So it must look, on the face of it," assented Magee. The girl moved to the big front door, and Magee, with his eyes still on the room, backed away until he stood beside her. He handed her his key.

"I give you," he said, "to the gods of the mountain. But it's only a loan—I shall surely want you back. I can't follow ten feet behind, as I threatened—it will be ten hours instead. Good night, and good luck."

She turned the key in the lock.

"Billy Magee," she whispered, "yours is a faith beyond understanding. I shall tell the gods of the mountain that I am to be—returned. Good night, you—dear."

She went out quickly, and Magee, locking the door after her, thrust the key into his pocket. For a moment no one stirred. Then Mr. Max leaped up and ran through the flickering light to the nearest window.

There was a flash, a report, and Max came back into the firelight examining a torn trousers leg.

"I don't mean to kill anybody," explained Mr. Magee. "Just to wing them. But I'm not an expert—I might shoot higher than I intend. So I suggest that no one else try a break for it."

"Mr. Magee," said Miss Thornhill, "I don't believe you have the slightest idea who that girl is, nor what she wants with the money."

"That," he replied, "makes it all the more exciting, don't you think?"

"Do you mean—" the professor, exploded, "you don't know her? Well, you young fool."

"It's rather fine of you," remarked Miss Thornhill.

"It's asinine, if it's true," the professor voiced the other side of it.

"You have said yourself—or at least you claim to have said—" Mr. Magee reminded him, "one girl like that is worth a million suffragettes."

"And can make just as much trouble," complained Professor Bolton. "I shall certainly see to it that the hermit's book has an honored place in our college library."

Out of the big chair into which he had sunk came the wail of the uncomprehending Cargan:

"He's done this thing to me—after all I've done for him."

"I hope every one is quite comfortable," remarked Mr. Magee, selecting a seat facing the crowd. "It's to be a long wait, you know."

There was no answer. The wind roared lustily at the windows. The firelight flickered redly on the faces of Mr. Magee's prisoners.

CHAPTER XVII

THE PROFESSOR SUMS UP

In Upper Asquewan Falls the clock on the old town hall struck nine. Mr. Magee, on guard in Baldpate's dreary office, counted the strokes. She must be half-way down the mountain now—perhaps at this very moment she heard Quimby's ancient gate creaking in the wind. He could almost see her as she tramped along through the snow, the lovely heroine of the most romantic walk of all romantic walks on Baldpate to date. Half-way to the waiting-room where she had wept so bitterly; half-way to the curious station agent with the mop of ginger hair. To-night there would be no need of a troubadour to implore "Weep no more, my lady". William Hallowell Magee had removed the cause for tears.

It was a long vigil he had begun, but there was no boredom in it for Billy Magee. He was too great a lover of contrast for that. As he looked around on the ill-assorted group he guarded, he compared them with the happier people of the inn's summer nights, about whom the girl had told him. Instead of these surly or sad folk sitting glumly under the pistol of romantic youth he saw maids garbed in the magic of muslin flit through the shadows. Lights glowed softly; a waltz came up from the casino on the breath of the summer breeze. Under the red and white awnings youth and joy and love had their day—or their night. The hermit was on hand

216

with his postal-carded romance. The trees gossiped in whispers on the mountain.

And, too, the rocking-chair fleet gossiped in whispers on the veranda, pausing only when the admiral sailed by in his glory. Eagerly it ran down its game. This girl—this Myra Thornhill—he remembered, had herself been a victim. After Kendrick disappeared she had come there no more, for there were ugly rumors of the man who had fled. Mr. Magee saw the girl and her long-absent lover whispering together in the firelight; he wondered if they, too, imagined themselves at Baldpate in the summer; if they heard the waltz in the casino, and the laughter of men in the grill-room.

Ten o'clock, said the town hall pompously. She was at the station now. In the room of her tears she was waiting; perhaps her only companion the jacky of the "See the World" poster, whose garb was but a shade bluer than her eyes. Who was she? What was the bribe money of the Suburban Railway to her? Mr. Magee did not know, but he trusted her, and he was glad she had won through him. He saw Professor Bolton walk through the flickering half-light to join Myra Thornhill and Kendrick.

It must be half past by now. Yes—from far below in the valley came the whistle of a train. Now—she was boarding it. She and the money. Boarding it—for where? For what purpose? Again the train whistled.

"The siege," remarked Mr. Magee, "is more than half over, ladies and gentlemen."

The professor of Comparative Literature approached him and took a chair at his side.

"I want to talk with you, Mr. Magee," he said.

"A welcome diversion," assented Magee, his eyes still on the room.

"I have discussed matters with Miss Thornhill," said the professor in a low voice. "She has convinced me that in this affair you have acted from a wholly disinterested point of view. A mistaken idea of chivalry, perhaps. The infatuation of the moment for a pretty face—a thing to which all men with red blood in their veins are susceptible—a pleasant thing that I would be the last to want banished from the world."

"Miss Thornhill," replied Billy Magee, "has sized up the situation perfectly—except for one rather important detail. It is not the infatuation of the moment, Professor. Say rather that of a lifetime."

"Ah, yes," the old man returned. "Youth—how sure it always is of that. I do not deprecate the feeling. Once, long ago, I, too, had youth and faith. We will not dwell on that, however. Miss Thornhill assures me that Henry Bentley, the son of my friend John Bentley, esteems you highly. She asserts that you are in every respect, as far as her knowledge goes, an admirable young man. I feel sure that after calm contemplation you will see that what you have done is very unfortunate. The package of money which in a giddy moment you have given into a young lady's keeping is much desired by the authorities as evidence against a very corrupt political ring. I am certain that when you know all the details you will be glad to return with me to Reuton and do all in your power to help us regain possession of that package."

And now the town hall informed Mr. Magee that the hour was eleven. He pictured a train flying like a black shadow through the white night. Was she on it—safe?

"Professor Bolton," he said, "there couldn't possibly be any one anywhere more eager than I to learn all the details of this affair—to hear your real reason for coming to Baldpate Inn, and to have the peroxide-blond incident properly classified and given its niche in history. But let me tell you again my action of to-night was no mere madness of the moment. I shall stick to it through thick and thin. Now, about the blondes."

"The blondes," repeated the professor dreamily. "Ah, yes, I must make a small confession of guilt there. I did not come here to escape the results of that indiscreet remark, but I really made it—about a year ago. Shall I ever forget? Hardly—the newspapers and my wife won't let me. I can never again win a new honor, however dignified, without being referred to in print as the peroxide-blond advocate. The thing has made me furious. However, I did not come to Baldpate Inn to avoid the results of a lying newspaper story, though many a time, a year ago, when I started to leave my house and saw the reporters camped on my door-step, I longed for the seclusion of some such spot as this. On the night when Mr. Kendrick and I climbed Baldpate Mountain, I remarked as much to him. And so it occurred to me that if I found any need of explaining my presence here, the blond incident would do very well. It was only—a white lie."

"A blond one," corrected Mr. Magee. "I forgive you, Professor. And I'm mighty glad the incident really happened, despite the pain it caused you. For it in a way condones my own offense—and it makes you human, too."

"If to err is human, it does," agreed Professor Bolton. "To begin with, I am a member of the faculty of the University of Reuton, situated, as you no doubt know, in the city of the same name. For a long time I have taken a quiet interest in our municipal politics. I have been up in arms— linguistic arms—against this odd character Cargan, who came from the slums to rule us with a rod of iron. Every one knows he is corrupt, that he is wealthy through the sale of privilege, that there is actually a fixed schedule of prices for favors in the way of city ordinances. I have often denounced him to my friends. Since I have met him—well, it is remarkable, is it not, the effect of personality on one's opinions? I expected to face a devil, with the usual appurtenances. Instead I have found a human, rather likable man. I can well understand now why it is that the mob follows him like sheep. However, that is neither here nor there. He is a crook, and must be punished—even though I do like him immensely."

Mr. Magee smiled over to where the great bulk of Cargan slouched in a chair.

"He's a bully old scout," he remarked.

"Even so," replied the professor, "his high-handed career of graft in Reuton must come to a speedy close. He is of a type fast vanishing through the awakening public conscience. And his career will end, I assure you, despite the fact that you, Mr. Magee, have seen fit to send our evidence scurrying through the night at the behest of a chit of a girl. I beg your pardon—I shall continue. Young Drayton, the new county prosecutor, was several years back a favorite pupil of mine. After he left law school he fell under the spell of the picturesque mayor of Reuton. Cargan liked him and he rose rapidly. Drayton had no thought of ever turning against his benefactor when he accepted the first favors, but later the open selling of men's souls began to disgust him. When Cargan offered him the place of prosecutor, a few months ago, Drayton assured him that he would keep his oath of office. The mayor laughed. Drayton insisted. Cargan had not yet met the man he could not handle. He gave Drayton the place."

The old man leaned forward, and tapped Magee on the knee.

"It was in me, remember," he went on, "that Drayton confided his resolve to serve the public. I was delighted at the news. A few weeks ago he informed me his first opportunity was at hand. Through one of the men in his office he had learned that Hayden of the Suburban Electric was seeking to consolidate that road, which had fallen into partial disrepute under his management during the illness of Thornhill, the president, with the Civic. The consolidation would raise the value of the Suburban nearly two million dollars—at the public's expense. Hayden had seen Cargan. Cargan had drafted Ordinance Number 45, and informed Hayden that his price for passing it through the council would be the sum you have juggled in your possession on Baldpate Mountain—two hundred thousand dollars."

"A mere trifle," remarked Magee sarcastically.

"So Cargan made Hayden see. Through long experience in these matters the mayor has become careless. He is the thing above the law, if not the law itself. He would have had no fear in accepting this money on Main Street at midday. He had no fear when he came here and found he was being spied on.

"But Hayden—there was the difficulty that began the drama of Baldpate Inn. Hayden had few scruples, but as events to-night have well proved, Mr. Magee, he was a coward at heart. I do not know just why he lies on your bed up-stairs at this moment, a suicide—that is a matter between Kendrick and him, and one which Kendrick himself has not yet fathomed. As I say, Hayden was afraid of being caught. Andy Rutter, manager of Baldpate Inn for the last few summers, is in some way mixed up in the Suburban. It was he who suggested to Hayden that an absolutely secluded spot for passing this large sum of money would be the inn. The idea appealed to Hayden. Cargan tried to laugh him out of it. The mayor did not relish the thought of a visit to Baldpate Mountain in the dead of winter, particularly as he considered such precautions unnecessary. But Hayden was firm; this spot, he pointed out, was ideal, and the mayor at last laughingly gave in. The sum involved was well worth taking a little trouble to gain."

Professor Bolton paused, and blinked his dim old eyes.

"So the matter was arranged," he continued. "Mr. Bland, a clerk in Hayden's employ, was sent up here with the money, which he placed in the safe on the very night of our arrival. The safe had been left open by Rutter; Bland did not have the combination. He put the package inside, swung shut the door, and awaited the arrival of the mayor."

"I was present," smiled Magee, "at the ceremony you mention."

"Yes? All these plans, as I have said, were known to Drayton. A few nights ago he came to me. He wanted to send an emissary to Baldpate—a man whom Cargan had never met—one who could perhaps keep up the pretense of being here for some other reason than a connection with the bribe. He asked me to undertake the mission, to see all I could, and if possible to secure the package of money. This last seemed hardly likely. At any rate, I was to gather all the evidence I could. I hesitated. My library fire never looked so alluring as on that night. Also, I was engaged in some very entertaining researches."

"I beg your pardon?" said Billy Magee.

"Some very entertaining research work."

"Yes," reflected Magee slowly, "I suppose such things do exist. Go on, please."

"I had loudly proclaimed my championship of civic virtue, however, and here was a chance to serve Reuton. I acquiesced. The day I was to start up here, poor Kendrick came back. He, too, had been a student of mine; a friend of both Drayton and Hayden. Seven years ago he and Hayden were running the Suburban together, under Thornhill's direction. The two young men became mixed up in a rather shady business deal, which was more of Hayden's weaving than Kendrick's. Hayden came to Kendrick with the story that they were about to be found out, and suggested that one assume the blame and go away. I am telling you all this in confidence as a friend of my friends, the Bentleys, and a young man whom I like and trust despite your momentary madness in the matter of yellow locks—we are all susceptible.

"Kendrick went. For seven years he stayed away, in an impossible tropic town, believing himself sought by the law, for so Hayden wrote him. Not long ago he discovered that the matter in which he and Hayden had offended had never been disclosed after all. He hurried back to the states. You can imagine his bitterness. He had been engaged to Myra Thornhill, and the fact that Hayden was also in love with her may have had something to do with his treachery to his friend."

Magee's eyes strayed to where the two victims of the dead man's falsehood whispered together in the shadows, and he wondered at the calmness with which Kendrick had greeted Hayden in the room above.

"When Kendrick arrived," Professor Bolton went on, "first of all he consulted his old friend Drayton. Drayton informed him that he had nothing to fear should his misstep be made public, for in reality there was, at this late day, no crime committed in the eyes of the law. He also told Kendrick how matters stood, and of the net he was spreading for Hayden. He had some fears, he said, about sending a man of my years alone to Baldpate Inn. Kendrick begged for the chance to come, too. So, without making his return known in Reuton, three nights ago he accompanied me here. Three nights—it seems years. I had secured keys for us both from John Bentley. As we climbed the mountain, I noticed your light, and we agreed it would be best if only one of us revealed ourselves to the intruders in the inn. So Kendrick let himself in by a side door while I engaged you and Bland in the office. He spent the night on the third floor. In the morning I told the whole affair to Quimby, knowing his interest in both Hayden and Kendrick, and secured for Kendrick the key to the annex. Almost as soon as I arrived—"

"The curtain went up on the melodrama," suggested Mr. Magee.

"You state it vividly and with truth," Professor Bolton replied. "Night before last the ordinance numbered 45 was due to pass the council. It was arranged that when it did, Hayden, through his man Rutter, or personally, would telephone the combination of the safe to the mayor of Reuton. Cargan and Bland sat in the office watching for the flash of light at the telephone switchboard, while you and I were Max's prisoners above. Something went wrong. Hayden heard that the courts would issue an injunction making Ordinance Number 45 worthless. So, although the council obeyed Cargan's instructions and passed the bill, Hayden refused to give the mayor the combination."

The old man paused and shook his head wonderingly.

"Then melodrama began in dead earnest," he continued. "I have always been a man of peace, and the wild scuffle that claimed me for one of its leading actors from that moment will remain in my memory as long as I live. Cargan dynamited the safe. Kendrick held him up; you held up

Kendrick. I peeked through your window and saw you place the package of money under a brick in your fireplace—"

"You—the curtains were down," interrupted Magee.

"I found a half-inch of open space," explained the old man. "Yes, I actually lay on my stomach in the snow and watched you. In the morning, for the first time in my life, I committed robbery. My punishment was swift and sure. Bland swooped down upon me. Again this afternoon, I came upon the precious package, after a long search, in the hands of the Hermit of Baldpate. I thought we were safe at last when I handed the package to Kendrick in my room to-night—but I had not counted on the wild things a youth like you will do for love of a designing maid."

Twelve o'clock! The civic center of Upper Asquewan Falls proclaimed it. Mr. Magee had never been in Reuton. He was sorry he hadn't. He had to construct from imagination alone the great Reuton station through which the girl and the money must now be hurrying—where? The question would not down. Was she—as the professor believed—designing?

"No," said Mr. Magee, answering aloud his own question. "You are wrong, sir. I do not know just what the motives of Miss Norton were in desiring this money, but I will stake my reputation as an honest hold-up man that they were perfectly all right."

"Perhaps," replied the other, quite unconvinced. "But—what honest motive could she have? I am able to assign her no rôle in this little drama. I have tried. I am able to see no connection between her and the other characters. What—"

"Pardon me," broke in Magee. "But would you mind telling me why Miss Thornhill came up to Baldpate to join in the chase for the package?"

"Her motive," replied the professor, "does her great credit. For several years her father, Henry Thornhill, has been forced through illness to leave the management of the railway's affairs to his vice-president, Hayden. Late yesterday the old man heard of this proposed bribe—on his sick bed. He was very nearly insane at the thought of the disgrace it would bring upon him. He tried to rise himself and prevent the passing of the package. His daughter—a brave loyal girl—herself undertook the task."

"Then," said Mr. Magee, "Miss Thornhill is not distressed at the loss of the most important evidence in the case."

"I have explained the matter to her," returned Professor Bolton. "There is no chance whatever that her father's name will be implicated. Both Drayton and myself have the highest regard for his integrity. The whole affair was arranged when he was too ill to dream of it. His good name will be smirched in no way. The only man involved on the giver's side is dead in the room above. The man we are after now is Cargan. Miss Thornhill has agreed that it is best to prosecute. That eliminates her."

"Did Miss Thornhill and Kendrick meet for the first time, after his exile, up-stairs—in number seven?" Mr. Magee wanted to know.

"Yes," answered Professor Bolton. "In one of his letters long ago Hayden told Kendrick he was engaged to the girl. It was the last letter Kendrick received from him."

There was a pause.

"The important point now," the old man went on, "is the identity of this girl to whom you have made your princely gift, out of the goodness of your young heart. I propose to speak to the woman she has introduced as her mother, and elicit what information I can."

He crossed the floor, followed by Mr. Magee, and stood by the woman's chair. She looked up, her eyes heavy with sleep, her appearance more tawdry than ever in that faint light.

"Madam," remarked the professor, with the air of a judge trying a case, "your daughter has to-night made her escape from this place with a large sum of money earnestly desired by the prosecuting attorney of Reuton county. In the name of the law, I command you to tell me her destination, and what she proposes to do with that package of greenbacks."

The woman blinked stupidly in the dusk.

"She ain't my daughter," she replied, and Mr. Magee's heart leaped up. "I can tell you that much. I keep a boarding-house in Reuton and Miss—the girl you speak about—has been my boarder for three years. She brought me up here as a sort of chaperon, though I don't see as I'm old enough for that yet. You don't get nothing else out of me—except that she is a perfectly lovely young woman, and your money couldn't be safer with the president of the United States."

The puzzled professor of Comparative Literature caressed his bald head thoughtfully. "I—er—" he remarked. Mr. Magee could have embraced this faded woman for her news. He looked at his watch. It was twelve-twenty.

"The siege is over," he cried. "I shall not attempt to direct your actions any longer. Mr. Peters, will you please go down to the village and bring back Mr. Quimby and—the coroner?"

"The coroner!" The mayor of Reuton jumped to his feet. "I don't want to be in on any inquest scene. Come on, Max, let's get out of here."

Bland stood up, his face was white and worried, his gay plumage no longer set the tone for his mood.

"I think I'll go, too," he announced, looking hopefully at Magee.

"I'm no longer your jailer," Magee said. "Professor, these gentlemen are your witnesses Do you wish to detain them?"

"See here," cried the mayor angrily, "there ain't no question but that you can find me in Reuton any time you want me. At the little room on Main Street—anybody can tell you my hours—the door's always open to any reformer that has the nerve to climb the stairs. Look me up there. I'll make it interesting for you."

"I certainly shall," the professor replied. "And very soon. Until then you may go when and where you please."

"Thanks," sneered the mayor. "I'll expect you. I'll be ready. I've had to get ready to answer your kind before. You think you got me, eh? Well, you're a fool to think that. As for Drayton, the pup, the yellow-streaked pup—I'll talk to Mister Drayton when I get back to Reuton."

"Before you go, Bland," remarked Magee, smiling, "I want to ask about Arabella. Where did you get her?"

"Some of it happened to a friend of mine," the ex-haberdasher answered, "a friend that keeps a clothing store. I got this suit there. I changed the story, here and there. He didn't write her no note, though he thought seriously of it. And he didn't run away and hide. The last I seen of him he was testing the effect of the heart-balm on sale behind the swinging doors."

Mr. Magee laughed, but over the long lean face of Bland not the ghost of a smile flitted. He was frightened, through and through.

"You're a fine bunch," sneered Mr. Max. "Reformers, eh? Well, you'll get what the rest of 'em always got. We'll tie you up in knots and leave you on the door-step of some orphan asylum before we're through with you."

"Come on, Lou," said Cargan. "Drayton's a smart guy, Doc. Where's his proof? Eloped with the bundle of dry goods this young man's taken a fancy to. And even if he had the money—I've been up against this many a time. You're wasting your talents, Doc. Good night! Come on, boys."

The three stamped out through the dining-room, and from the window Mr. Magee watched them disappear down the road that stretched to Asquewan Falls.

CHAPTER XVIII

A RED CARD

r. Magee turned back from the window to the dim interior of the hotel office. He who had come to Baldpate Inn to court loneliness had never felt so lonely in his life. For he had lost sight of her—in the great Reuton station of his imagination she had slipped from his dreams—to go where he could not follow, even in thought. He felt as he knew this great bare room must feel each fall when the last laugh died away down the mountain, and the gloom of winter descended from drab skies.

Selecting a log of the hermit's cutting from the stock beside the hearth, Mr. Magee tossed it on the fire. There followed a shower of sparks and a flood of red light in the room. Through this light Kendrick advanced to Magee's side, and the first of the Baldpate hermits saw that the man's face was lined by care, that his eyes were tired even under the new light in them, that his mouth was twisted bitterly.

"Poor devil," thought Magee.

Kendrick drew up chairs for himself and Magee, and they sat down. Behind them the bulky Mrs. Norton dozed, dreaming perhaps of her Reuton boarding-house, while Miss Thornhill and the professor talked intermittently in low tones. The ranks at Baldpate were thinning rapidly;

before long the place must settle back with a sigh in the cold, to wait for its first summer girl.

"Mr. Magee," said Kendrick nervously, "you have become involved in an unkind, a tragic story. I do not mean the affair of the bribe—I refer to the matter between Hayden and myself. Before Peters comes back with—the men he went for—I should like to tell you some of the facts of that story."

"If you had rather not—" began Magee.

"No," replied Kendrick, "I prefer that you should know. It was you who took the pistol from—his hand. I do not believe that even I can tell you all that was in Hayden's mind when he went into that other room and closed the door. It seems to me preposterous that a man of his sort should take his life under the circumstances I feel, somehow, that there is a part of the story even I do not know. But let that be."

He bowed his head in his hands.

"Ever since I came into this room," he went on, "the eyes of a pompous little man have been following me about. They have constantly recalled to me the nightmare of my life. You have noticed, no doubt, the pictures of the admiral that decorate these walls?"

"I have," replied Magee. He gazed curiously at the nearest of the portraits. How persistently this almost mythical starched man wove in and out of the melodrama at Baldpate Inn.

"Well," continued Kendrick, "the admiral's eyes haunt me. Perhaps you know that he plays a game—a game of solitaire. I have good reason to remember that game. It is a silly inconsequential game. You would scarcely believe that it once sent a man to hell."

He stopped.

"I am beginning in the middle of my story," he apologized. "Let me go back. Six years ago I was hardly the man you see now—I was at least twenty years younger. Hayden and I worked together in the office of the Suburban Railway. We had been close friends at college—I believed in him and trusted him, although I knew he had certain weaknesses. I was a happy man. I had risen rapidly, I was young, the future was lying golden before me—and I was engaged. The daughter of Henry Thornhill, our employer—the girl you have met here at Baldpate—had promised to be my wife. Hayden had also been a suitor, but when our engagement was announced he came to me like a man, and I thought his words were sincere.

"One day Hayden told me of a chance we might take which would make us rich. It was not—altogether within the law. But it was the sort of thing that other men were doing constantly, and Hayden assured me that as he had arranged matters it was absolutely safe. My great sin is that I agreed we should take the chance—a sin for which I have paid, Mr. Magee, over and over."

Again he paused, and gazed steadily at the fire. Again Magee noted the gray at his temples, the aftermath of fevers in his cheeks.

"We—took the chance," he went on. "For a time everything went well. Then—one blustering March night—Hayden came to me and told me we were certain to be caught. Some of his plans had gone awry. I trusted him fully at the time, you understand—he was the man with whom I had sat on the window-seat of my room at college, settling the question of immortality, and all the other great questions young men settle at such times. I have at this moment no doubt that he was quite truthful when he said we were in danger of arrest. We arranged to meet the next night at the Argots Club and decide on what we should do.

"We met—in the library of the club. Hayden came in to me from the card-room adjoining, where he had been watching the admiral doddering over his eternal game. The old man had become a fixture at the club, like Parker down at the door, or the great chandelier in the hall. No one paid any attention to him; when he tried to talk to the younger men about his game they fled as from a pestilence. Well, as I say, Hayden came to meet me, and just at that moment the admiral finished his game and went out. We were alone in the library.

"Hayden told me he had thought the matter over carefully. There was nothing to do but to clear out of Reuton forever. But why, he argued, should we both go? Why wreck two lives? It would be far better, he told me, for one to assume the guilt of both and go away. I can see him now—how funny and white his face looked in that half-lighted room—how his hands trembled. I was far the calmer of the two.

"I agreed to his plan. Hayden led the way into the room where the admiral had been playing. We went up to the table, over which the green-shaded light still burned. On it lay two decks of cards, face up. Hayden picked up the nearest deck, and shuffled it nervously. His face—God, it was like the snow out there on the mountain."

Kendrick closed his eyes, and Magee gazed at him in silent pity.

"He held out the deck," went on the exile softly, "he told me to draw. He said if the card was black, he'd clear out. 'But if it's red, David,' he said, 'why—you—got to go.' I held my breath, and drew. It was a full minute before I dared look at the card in my hand. Then I turned it over and it was—red—a measly little red two-spot. I don't suppose a man ever realizes all at once what such a moment means. I remember that I was much cooler than Hayden. It was I who had to brace him up. I—I even tried to joke with him. But his face was like death. He hardly spoke at all at first, and then suddenly he became horribly talkative. I left him—talking wildly—I left Reuton. I left the girl to whom I was engaged."

To break the silence that followed, Mr. Magee leaned forward and stirred the logs.

"I don't want to bore you," Kendrick said, trying to smile. "I went to a little town in South America. There was no treaty of extradition there— nor anything else civilized and decent. I smoked cigarettes and drank what passed for rum, on the balcony of an impossible hotel, and otherwise groped about for the path that leads to the devil. After a year, I wrote to Hayden. He answered, urging me to stay away. He intimated that the thing we had done was on my shoulders. I was ashamed, frightfully unhappy. I didn't dare write to—her. I had disgraced her. I asked Hayden about her, and he wrote back that she was shortly to marry him. After that I didn't want to come back to Reuton. I wanted most—to die.

"The years crept by on the balcony of that impossible hotel. Six of them. The first in bitter memories, memories of a red card that danced fiendishly before my eyes when I closed them—the last in a fierce biting desire to come back to the world I had left. At last, a few months ago, I wrote to another college friend of mine, Drayton, and told him the whole story. I did not know that he had been elected prosecutor in Reuton. He answered with a kind pitying letter—and finally I knew the horrible truth. Nothing had ever happened. The thing we had done had never been discovered. Hayden had lied. He had even lied about his engagement to Myra Thornhill. There, he had made a reality out of what was simply his great desire.

"You can imagine my feelings. Six years in a tomb, a comic opera sort of tomb, where a silly surf was forever pounding, and foolish palms kept waving. Six years—for nothing. Six years, while Hayden, guiltier than I, stayed behind to enjoy the good things of life, to plead for the girl whose lover he had banished.

"I lost no time in coming north. Three days ago I entered Drayton's office. I was ready and willing that the wrong Hayden and I had done should be made public. Drayton informed me that legally there had been no crime, that Hayden had straightened things out in time, that we had defrauded no one. And he told me that for whatever sin I had committed he thought I had more than atoned down there in that town that God forgot. I think I had. He explained to me about the trap he had laid for Hayden up here at Baldpate Inn. I begged to help. What happened after, you know as well as I."

"Yes, I think I do," agreed Mr. Magee softly.

"I have told you the whole story," Kendrick replied, "and yet it seems to me that still it is not all told. Why should Hayden have killed himself? He had lied to me, it is true, but life was always sweet to him, and it hardly seems to me that he was the sort to die simply because his falsehood was discovered. Was there some other act of cruelty—some side to the story of which we are none of us aware? I wonder."

He was silent a moment.

"Anyhow, I have told you all I know," he said. "Shall I tell it also to the coroner? Or shall we allow Hayden's suicide to pass as the result of his implication in this attempt at bribery? I ask your advice, Mr. Magee."

"My advice," returned Magee, "is that you befuddle no pompous little village doctor with the complication of this unhappy tale. No, let the story be that Hayden killed himself as the toils closed in on him—the toils of the law that punishes the bribe giver—now and then and occasionally. Mr. Kendrick, you have my deepest sympathy. Is it too much for me to hope"—he glanced across the room to where Myra Thornhill sat beside the professor—"that the best of your life is yet to come—that out of the wreck this man made of it you may yet be happy?"

Kendrick smiled.

"You are very kind," he said. "Twice we have met and battled in the snow, and I do not hold it against you that both times you were the victor. Life in a tropic town, Mr. Magee, is not exactly a muscle-building experience. Once I might have given the whole proceeding a different turn. Yes, Miss Thornhill has waited for me—all these years—waited, believing. It is a loyalty of which I can not speak without—you understand. She knows why I went away—why I stayed away. She is still ready to marry me. I shall go again into the Suburban office and try to lift the road from the muck into which it has fallen. Yes, it is not too much for me to hope—and for you in your kindness—that a great happiness is still for me."

"Believe me, I'm glad," replied Magee with youthful enthusiasm, holding out his hand. "I'm sorry I spoiled your little game up here, but—"

"I understand," smiled Kendrick. "I think none the less of you for what you have done. And who knows? It may turn out to have been the wisest course after all."

Ah, would it? Mr. Magee walked to the window, pondering on the odd tangle of events that had not yet been completely straightened out. Certainly her eyes were an honest blue as well as a beautiful—but who was she? Where was she? The great figure of Mrs. Norton stirred restlessly near at hand; the puffed lids of her eyes opened.

"Mr. Magee," she said, when she had made out his figure by the window, "you've been a true friend, as I might say, to a couple of mad females who ought to have been at home by their own firesides, and I'm going to ask one more favor of you. Find out when the next train goes to Reuton, and see that I'm at the station an hour or two before it pulls out."

"I'll do that, Mrs. Norton," smiled Magee. "By the way, is Norton the name?"

"Yes," answered the woman, "that's my name. Of course, it ain't hers. I can't tell that."

"No matter," said Mr. Magee, "she'll probably change it soon. Can't you tell me something about her—just a tiny bit of information. Just a picture of where she is now, and what she's doing with that small fortune I gave her."

"Where is she now?" repeated Mrs. Norton. "She's home and in bed in my second floor front, unless she's gone clear crazy. And that's where I wish I was this minute—in bed—though it's a question in my mind if I'll ever be able to sleep again, what with the uproar and confusion my house is probably in by this time, leaving it in charge of a scatter-brained girl.

Norton always used to say if you want a thing done right, do it yourself, and though he didn't always live up to the sentiment, letting me do most things he wanted done right, there was a lot of truth in his words. I certainly must get back to Reuton, just as quick as the railroad will take me."

"Why did you come?" prodded Mr. Magee. "Why did you leave your house on this strange mission?"

"The Lord knows," replied the woman. "I certainly never intended to, but she begged and pleaded, and the first thing I knew, I was on a train. She has winning ways, that girl—maybe you've noticed?"

"I have," assented Billy Magee.

"I thought so. No, Mr. Magee, I can't tell you nothing about her. I ain't allowed to—even you that has been so kind. She made me promise. 'He'll know soon enough,' she kept saying. But I will tell you, as I told you before, there's no occasion to worry about her—unless you was to think was she held up and murdered with all that money on her, the brave little dear. If you was considering offering yourself for the job of changing her name, Mr. Magee, I say go in and do it. It sure is time she settled down and gave up this—this—gave it all up before something awful happens to her. You won't forget—the very next train, Mr. Magee?"

"The very next," Magee agreed.

In through the dining-room door stamped Quimby, grave of face, dazed at being roused from sleep, and with him an important little man whose duty it was to investigate at Upper Asquewan Falls such things as had happened that night at Baldpate. Even from his slumber he rose with the air of a judge and the manner of a Sherlock Holmes. For an hour he asked questions, and in the end he prepared to go in a seemingly satisfied state of mind.

Quimby's face was very awed when he came down-stairs after a visit to the room above.

"Poor fellow!" he said to Magee. "I'm sorry—he was so young." For such as Quimby carry no feud beyond the gates. He went over and took Kendrick's hand.

"I never had a chance," he said, "to thank you for all you tried to do for me and my invention."

"And it came to nothing in the end?" Kendrick asked.

"Nothing," Quimby answered. "I—I had to creep back to Baldpate Mountain finally—broke and discouraged. I have been here ever since. All my blue prints, all my models—they're locked away forever in a chest up in the attic."

"Not forever, Quimby," Kendrick replied. "I always did believe in your invention—I believe in it still. When I get back into the harness—I'm sure I can do something for you."

Quimby shook his head. He looked to be half asleep.

"It don't seem possible," he said. "No—it's all been buried so long—all the hope—all the plans—it don't seem possible it could ever come to life again."

"But it can, and it will," cried Kendrick. "I'm going to lay a stretch of track in Reuton with your joints. That's all you need—they'll have to use 'em then. We'll force the Civic into it. We can do it, Quimby—we surely can."

Quimby rubbed his hand across his eyes.

"You'll lay a stretch of track—" he repeated. "That's great news to me, Mr. Kendrick. I—I can't thank you now." His voice was husky. "I'll come back and take care of—him," he said, jerking his head toward the room up-stairs. "I got to go now—this minute—I got to go and tell my wife. I got to tell her what you've said."

CHAPTER XIX

EXEUNT OMNES, AS SHAKESPEARE HAS IT

At four in the morning Baldpate Inn, wrapped in the arms of winter, had all the rare gaiety and charm of a baseball bleechers on Christmas Eve. Looking gloomily out the window, Mr. Magee heard behind him the steps on the stairs and the low cautions of Quimby, and two men he had brought from the village, who were carrying something down to the dark carriage that waited outside. He did not look round. It was a picture he wished to avoid.

So this was the end—the end of his two and a half days of solitude—the end of his light-hearted exile on Baldpate Mountain. He thought of Bland, lean and white of face, gay of garb, fleeing through the night, his Arabella fiction disowned in the real tragedy that had followed. He thought of Cargan and Max, also fleeing, wrathful, sneering, by Bland's side. He thought of Hayden, jolting down the mountain in that black wagon. So it ended.

So it ended—most preposterous end—with William Hallowell Magee madly, desperately, in love. By the gods—in love! In love with a fair gay-hearted girl for whom he had fought, and stolen, and snapped his fingers at the law as it blinked at him in the person of Professor Bolton. Billy Magee, the calm, the unsusceptible, who wrote of a popular cupid but had always steered clear of his shots. In love with a girl whose name he did not know; whose motives were mostly in the fog. And he had come up here—to be alone.

For the first time in many hours he thought of New York, of the fellows at the club, of what they would say when the jocund news came that Billy Magee had gone mad on a mountainside, He thought of Helen Faulkner, haughty, unperturbed, bred to hold herself above the swift catastrophies of the world. He could see the arch of her patrician eyebrows, the shrug of her exquisite shoulders, when young Williams hastened up the avenue and poured into her ear the merry story. Well—so be it. He had never cared for her. In her superiority he had found a challenge, in her icy indifference a trap, that lured him on to try his hand at winning her. But he had never for a moment caught a glimmering of what it was really to care—to care as he cared now for the girl who had gone from him—somewhere—down the mountain.

Quimby dragged into the room, the strain of a rather wild night in Upper Asquewan Falls in his eyes.

"Jake Peters asked me to tell you he ain't coming back," he said. "Mis' Quimby is getting breakfast for you down at our house. You better pack up now and start down, I reckon. Your train goes at half past six."

Mrs. Norton jumped up, proclaiming that she must be aboard that train at any cost. Miss Thornhill, the professor and Kendrick ascended the stairs, and in a moment Magee followed.

He stepped softly into number seven, for the tragedy of the rooms was still in the air. Vague shapes seemed to flit about him as he lighted a candle. They whispered in his ear that this was to have been the scene of achievement; that here he was to have written the book that should make his place secure. Ah, well, fate had decreed it otherwise. It had set plump in his path the melodrama he had come up to Baldpate to avoid. Ironic fate, she must be laughing now in the sleeve of her kimono. Feeling about in the shadows Magee gathered his things together, put them in his bags, and with a last look at number seven, closed the door forever on its many excitements.

A shivering group awaited him at the foot of the stair. Mrs. Norton's hat was on at an angle even the most imaginative milliner could not have approved. The professor looked older than ever; even Miss Thornhill seemed a little less statuesque and handsome in the dusk. Quimby led the way to the door, they passed through it, and Mr. Magee locked it after them with the key Hal Bentley had blithely given him on Forty-fourth Street, New York.

So Baldpate Inn dropped back into the silence to slumber and to wait. To wait for the magic of muslin, the lilt of waltzes, the tinkle of laughter, the rhythm of the rockers of the fleet on its verandas, the formal tread of the admiral's boots across its polished floors, the clink of dimes in the pockets of its bell-boys. For a few brief hours strange figures had replaced the unromantic Quimby in its rooms, they had come to talk of money and of love, to plot and scheme, and as they came in the dark and moved most swiftly in the dark, so in the dark they went away, and Baldpate's startling winter drama took reluctantly its final curtain.

Down the snowy road the five followed Quimby's lead; Mr. Magee picturing in fancy one who had fled along this path but a short time before; the others busy with many thoughts, not the least of which was of Mrs. Quimby's breakfast. At the door of the kitchen she met them, maternal, concerned, eager to pamper and to serve, just as Mr. Magee remembered her on that night that now seemed so long ago. He smiled down into her eyes, and he had an engaging smile, even at four-thirty in the morning.

"Well, Mrs. Quimby," he cried, "here is the prodigal straight from that old husk of an inn. And believe me, he's pretty anxious to sit down to some food that woman, starter of all the trouble since the world began, had a hand in."

"Come right in, all of you," chirruped Mrs. Quimby, ushering them into a pleasant odor of cookery. "Take off your things and sit down. Breakfast's most ready. My land, I guess you must be pretty nigh starved to death. Quimby told me who was cooking for you, and I says to Quimby: 'What,' I says, 'that no account woman-hater messing round at a woman's job, like that,' I says. 'Heaven pity the people at the inn,' I says. 'Mr. Peters may be able to amuse them with stories of how Cleopatra whiled away the quiet Egyptian evenings,' I says, 'and he may be able to throw a little new light on Helen of Troy, who would object to having it thrown if she was alive and the lady I think her, but,' I says, 'when it comes to cooking, I guess he stands about where you do, Quimby.' You see, Quimby's repertory consists of coffee and soup, and sometimes it's hard to tell which he means for which."

"So Mr. Peters has taken you in on the secret of the book he is writing against your sex?" remarked Billy Magee.

"Not exactly that," Mrs. Quimby answered, brushing back a wisp of gray hair, "but he's discussed it in my presence, ignoring me at the time. You see, he comes down here and reads his latest chapters to Quimby o' nights, and I've caught quite a lot of it on my way between the cook-stove and the sink."

"I ain't no judge of books," remarked Mrs. Norton from a comfortable rocking-chair, "but I'll bet that one's the limit."

"You're right, ma'am," Mrs. Quimby told her. "I ain't saying that some of it ain't real pretty worded, but that's just to hide the falsehood underneath. My land, the lies there is in that book! You don't need to know much about history to know that Jake Peters has made it over to fit his argument, and that he ain't made it over so well but what the old seams show here and there, and the place where the braid was is plain as daylight."

After ten more minutes of bustle, Mrs. Quimby announced that they could sit down, and they were not slow to accept the invitation. The breakfast she served them moved Mr. Magee to remark:

"I want to know where I stand as a judge of character. On the first night I saw Mrs. Quimby, without tasting a morsel of food cooked by her, I said she was the best cook in the county."

The professor looked up from his griddle cakes.

"Why limit it to the county?" he asked. "I should say you were too parsimonious in your judgment."

Mrs. Quimby, detecting in the old man's words a compliment, flushed an even deeper red as she bent above the stove. Under the benign influence of the food and the woman's cheery personality, the spirits of the crowd rose. Baldpate Inn was in the past, its doors locked, its seven keys scattered through the dawn. Mrs. Quimby, as she continued to press food upon them, spoke with interest of the events that had come to pass at the inn.

"It's so seldom anything really happens around here," she said, "I just been hungering for news of the strange goings-on up there. And I must say Quimby ain't been none too newsy on the subject. I threatened to come up and join in the proceedings myself, especially when I heard about the book-writing cook Providence had sent you."

"You would have found us on the porch with outstretched arms," Mr. Magee assured her.

It was on Kendrick that Mrs. Quimby showered her attentions, and when the group rose to seek the station, amid a consultation of watches that recalled the commuter who rises at dawn to play tag with a flippant train, Mr. Magee heard her say to the railroad man in a heartfelt aside:

"I don't know as I can ever thank you enough, Mr. Kendrick, for putting new hope into Quimby. You'll never understand what it means, when you've given up, and your life seems all done and wasted, to hear that there's a chance left."

"Won't I?" replied Kendrick warmly. "Mrs. Quimby, it will make me a very happy man to give your husband his chance."

The first streaks of dawn were in the sky when the hermits of Baldpate filed through the gate into the road, waving good-by to Quimby and his wife, who stood in their dooryard for the farewell. Down through sleepy little Asquewan Falls they paraded, meeting here and there a tired man with a lunch basket in his hand, who stepped to one side and frankly stared while the odd procession passed.

In the station Mr. Magee encountered an old friend—he of the mop of ginger-colored hair. The man who had complained of the slowness of the village gazed with wide eyes at Magee.

"I figured," he said, "that you'd come this way again. Well, I must say you've put a little life into this place. If I'd known when I saw you here the other night all the exciting things you had up your sleeve, I'd a-gone right up to Baldpate with you."

"But I hadn't anything up my sleeve," protested Magee.

"Maybe," replied the agent, winking. "There's some pretty giddy stories going round about the carryings-on up at Baldpate. Shots fired, and strange lights flashing—dog-gone it, the only thing that's happened here in years, and I wasn't in on it. I certainly wish you'd put me wise to it."

"By the way," inquired Magee, "did you notice the passengers from here on the ten-thirty train last night?"

"Ten-thirty," repeated the agent. "Say, what sort of hours do you think I keep? A man has to get some sleep, even if he does work for a railroad. I wasn't here at ten-thirty last night. Young Cal Hunt was on duty then. He's home and in bed now."

No help there. Into the night the girl and the two hundred thousand had fled together, and Mr. Magee could only wait, and wonder, as to the meaning of that flight.

Two drooping figures entered the station—the mayor and his faithful lieutenant, Max. The dignity of the former had faded like a flower, and the same withered simile might have been applied with equal force to the accustomed jauntiness of Lou.

"Good morning," said Mr. Magee in greeting. "Taking an early train, too, eh? Have a pleasant night?"

"Young man," replied Cargan, "if you've ever put up at a hotel in a town the size of this, called the Commercial House, you know that last question has just one answer—manslaughter. I heard a minister say once that all drummers are bound for hell. If they are, it'll be a pleasant change for 'em."

Mr. Max delved beneath his overcoat, and brought forth the materials for a cigarette, which he rolled between yellow fingers.

"If I was a drummer," he said dolefully, "one breakfast—was that what they called it, Jim?—one breakfast like we just passed through would drive me into the awful habit of reading one of these here books of *Drummers' Yarns*."

"Sorry," smiled Magee. "We had an excellent breakfast at Mrs. Quimby's. Really, you should have stayed. By the way, where is Bland?"

"Got shaky in the knees," said Cargan. "Afraid of the reformers. Ain't had much experience in these things, or he'd know he might just as well tremble at the approach of a blue-bottle fly. We put him on a train going the other direction from Reuton early this morning. He thinks he'd better seek his fortune elsewhere." He leaned in heavy confidence toward Magee. "Say, young fellow," he whispered, "put me wise. That little sleight of hand game you worked last night had me dizzy. Where's the coin? Where's the girl? What's the game? Take the boodle and welcome—it ain't mine—but put me next to what's doing, so I'll know how my instalment of this serial story ought to read."

"Mr. Cargan," replied Magee, "you know as much about that girl as I do. She asked me to get her the money, and I did."

"But what's your place in the game?"

"A looker-on in Athens," returned Magee. "Translated, a guy who had bumped into a cyclone and was sitting tight waiting for it to blow over. I—I took a fancy to her, as you might put it. She wanted the money. I got it for her."

"A pretty fairy story, my boy," the mayor commented.

"Absolutely true," smiled Magee.

"What do you think of that for an explanation, Lou," inquired Cargan, "she asked him for the money and he gave it to her?"

Mr. Max leered.

"Say, a Broadway chorus would be pleased to meet you, Magee," he commented.

"Don't tell any of your chorus friends about me," replied Magee. "I might not always prove so complacent. Every man has his moments of falling for romance. Even you probably fell once—and what a fall was there."

"Can the romance stuff," pleaded Max. "This chilly railway station wasn't meant for such giddy language."

Wasn't it? Mr. Magee looked around at the dingy walls, at the soiled time-cards, at the disreputable stove. No place for romance? It was here he had seen her first, in the dusk, weeping bitterly over the seemingly hopeless task in which he was destined to serve her. No place for romance—and here had begun his life's romance. The blue blithe sailor still stood at attention in the "See the World" poster. Magee winked at him. He knew about it all, he knew, he knew—he knew how alluring she had looked in the blue corduroy suit, the bit of cambric pressed agonizingly to her face. Verily, even the sailor of the posters saw the world and all its glories.

The agent leaned his face against the bars.

"Your train," he called, "is crossing the Main Street trestle."

They filed out upon the platform, Mr. Magee carrying Mrs. Norton's luggage amid her effusive thanks. On the platform waited a stranger equipped for travel. It was Mr. Max who made the great discovery.

"By the Lord Harry," he cried, "it's the Hermit of Baldpate Mountain."

And so it was, his beard gone, his hair clumsily hacked, his body garbed in the height of an old and ludicrous fashion, his face set bravely toward the cities once more.

"Yes," he said, "I walked the floor, thinking it all over. I knew it would happen, and it has. The winters are hard, and the sight of you—it was too much. The excitement, the talk—it did for me, did for my oath. So I'm going back to her—back to Brooklyn for Christmas."

"A merry one to you," growled Cargan.

"Maybe," replied Mr. Peters. "Very likely, if she's feeling that way. I hope so. I ain't giving up the hermit job altogether—I'll come back in the summers, to my post-card business. There's money in it, if it's handled right. But I've spent my last winter on that lonesome hill."

"As author to author," asked Magee, "how about your book?"

"There won't be any mention of that," the hermit predicted, "in Brooklyn. I've packed it away. Maybe I can work on it summers, if she doesn't come up here with me and insist on running my hermit business for me. I hope she won't, it would sort of put a crimp in it—but if she wants to I won't refuse. And maybe that book'll never get done. Sometimes as I've sat in my shack at night and read, it's come to me that all the greatest works since the world began have been those that never got finished."

The Reuton train roared up to them through the gray morning, and paused impatiently at Upper Asquewan Falls. Aboard it clambered the hermits, amateur and professional. Mr. Magee, from the platform, waved good-by to the agent standing forlorn in the station door. He watched the building until it was only a blur in the dawn. A kindly feeling for it was in his heart. After all, it had been in the waiting-room—

CHAPTER XX

THE ADMIRAL'S GAME

The village of Upper Asquewan Falls gave a correct imitation of snow upon the desert's dusty face, and was no more. Bidding a reluctant good-by to up-state romance, Mr. Magee entered the solitary day coach which, with a smoker, made up the local to Reuton. He spent a few moments adjusting Mrs. Norton to her new environment, and listened to her voluble expressions of joy in the fact that her boarding-house loomed ahead. Then he started for the smoker. On his way he paused at the seat occupied by the ex-hermit of Baldpate, and fixed his eyes on the pale blue necktie Mr. Peters had resurrected for his return to the world of men.

"Pretty, ain't it?" remarked the hermit, seeing whither Mr. Magee's gaze drifted. "She picked it. I didn't exactly like it when she first gave it to me, but I see my mistake now. I'm wearing it home as a sort of a white flag of truce. Or almost white. Do you know, Mr. Magee, I'm somewhat nervous about what I'll say when I come into her presence again—about my inaugural address, you might put it. What would be your conversation on such an occasion? If you'd been away from a wife for five years, what would you say when you drifted back?"

"That would depend," replied Magee, "on the amount of time she allowed me for my speech."

"You've hit the nail on the head," replied Mr. Peters admiringly. "She's quick. She's like lightning. She won't give me any time if she can help it. That's why I'd like to have a wonderful speech all ready—something that would hold her spellbound and tongue-tied until I finished. It would take a literary classic to do that."

"What you want," laughed Magee, "is a speech with the punch."

"Exactly," agreed Mr. Peters. "I guess I won't go over to Brooklyn the minute I hit New York. I guess I'll study the lights along the big street, and brush elbows with the world a bit, before I reveal myself to her. Maybe if I took in a few shows—but don't think I won't go to her. My mind is made up. And I guess she'll be glad to see me, too. In her way. I got to fix it with her, though, to come back to my post-card trade in the summers. I wonder what she'll say to that. Maybe she could stay at the inn under an assumed name while I was hermiting up at the shack."

He laughed softly.

"It'd be funny, wouldn't it," he said. "Her sitting on the veranda watching me sell post-cards to the ladies, and listening to the various stories of how a lost love has blighted my life, and so forth. Yes, it'd be real funny—only Ellen never had much sense of humor. That was always her great trouble. If you ever marry, Mr. Magee, and I suppose you will, take my advice. Marry a sense of humor first, and a woman incidental-like."

Mr. Magee promised to bear this counsel in mind, and went forward into the smoking-car. Long rows of red plush seats, unoccupied save for the mayor and Max, greeted his eye. He strolled to where they sat, about half-way down the car, and lighted an after-breakfast cigar.

Max slouched in the unresponsive company of a cigarette on one side of the car; across the aisle the mayor of Reuton leaned heavily above a card-table placed between two seats. He was playing solitaire. Mr. Magee wondered whether this was merely a display of bravado against scheming reformers, or whether Mr. Cargan found in it real diversion. Curious, he slid into the place across the table from the mayor.

"Napoleon," he remarked lightly, "whiled away many a dull hour with cards, I believe."

Clumsily the mayor shuffled the cards. He flung them down one by one on the polished surface of the table rudely, as though they were reform votes he was counting. His thick lips were tightly closed, his big hands hovered with unaccustomed uncertainty over the pasteboards.

"Quit your kidding," he replied. "I don't believe cards was invented in Nap's day. Was they? It's a shame a fellow can't have a little admiration for a great leader like Nap without all you funny boys jollying him about it. That boy sure knew how to handle the voters. I've read a lot about him, and I like his style."

"You let history alone," snarled Mr. Max, across the aisle, "or it'll repeat itself and another guy I know'll go to the island."

"If you mean me," returned Cargan, "forget it. There ain't no St. Helena in my future." He winked at Magee. "Lou's a little peevish this morning," he said. "Had a bad night."

He busied himself with the cards. Mr. Magee looked on, only half interested. Then, suddenly, his interest grew. He watched the mayor build, in two piles; he saw that the deck from which he built was thick. A weird suspicion shot across his mind.

"Tell me," he asked, "is this the admiral's game of solitaire?"

"Exactly what I was going to ask," said a voice. Magee looked up. Kendrick had come in, and stood now above the table. His tired eyes were upon it, fascinated; his lips twitched strangely.

"Yes," answered the mayor, "this is the admiral's game. You'd hardly expect me to know it, would you? I don't hang out at the swell clubs where the admiral does. They won't have me there. But once I took the admiral on a public service board with me—one time when I wanted a lot of dignity and no brains pretty bad—and he sort of come back by teaching me his game in the long dull hours when we had nothing to do but serve the public. The thing gets a hold on you, somehow. Let's see—now the spade—now the heart."

Kendrick leaned closer. His breath came with a noisy quickness that brought the fact of his breathing insistently to Magee's mind.

"I never knew—how it was played," he said.

Something told Mr. Magee that he ought to rise and drag Kendrick away from that table. Why? He did not know. Still, it ought to be done. But the look in Kendrick's eyes showed clearly that the proverbial wild horses could not do it then.

"Tell me how it's played," went on Kendrick, trying to be calm.

"You must be getting old," replied the mayor. "The admiral told me the young men at his club never took any interest in his game. 'Solitaire,' he says to me, 'is an old man's trade.' It's a great game, Mr. Kendrick."

"A great game," repeated Kendrick, "yes, it's a great game." His tone was dull. "I want to know how it's played," he said again.

"The six of clubs," reflected the mayor, throwing down another card. "Say, she's going fine now. There ain't much to it. You use two decks, exactly alike—shuffle 'em together—the eight of hearts—the jack of—say, that's great—you lay the cards down here, just as they come—like this—"

He paused. His huge hand held a giddy pasteboard. A troubled look was on his face. Then he smiled happily, and went on in triumph.

"And then you build, Mr. Kendrick," he said. "The reds and the blacks. You build the blacks on the left, and the reds on the right—do you get me? Then—say, what's the matter?"

For Kendrick had swayed and almost fallen on the admiral's game— the game that had once sent a man to hell.

"Go on," he said, bracing. "Nothing's the matter. Go on. Build, damn it, build!"

The mayor looked at him a moment in surprise, then continued.

"Now the king," he muttered, "now the ace. We're on the home stretch, going strong. There, it's finished. It's come out right. A great game, I tell you."

He leaned back. Kendrick's fever-yellowed face was like a bronze mask. His eyes were fiercely on the table and the two decks of cards that lay there.

"And when you've finished," he pointed. "When you've finished—"

Mr. Cargan picked up the deck on the left.

"All black," he said, "when the game comes out right."

"And the other?" Kendrick persisted softly. He pointed to the remaining deck. A terrible smile of understanding drew his thin lips taut. "And the other, Mr. Cargan?"

"Red," replied Cargan. "What else could it be? All red."

He picked it up and shuffled through it to prove his point. Kendrick turned like a drunken man and staggered back down the aisle. Magee rose and hurried after him. At the door he turned, and the look on his face caused Magee to shudder.

"You heard?" he said helplessly. "My God! It's funny, isn't it?" He laughed hysterically, and drawing out his handkerchief, passed it across his forehead. "A pleasant thing to think about—a pleasant thing to remember."

Professor Bolton pushed open the smoker door.

"I thought I'd join you," he began. "Why, David, what is it? What's the matter?"

"Nothing," replied Kendrick wildly. "There's nothing the matter. Let me—by—please." He crossed the swaying platform and disappeared into the other car.

For a moment the professor and Magee gazed after him, and then without a word moved down the car to join Cargan and Max. Magee's mind was dazed by the tragedy he had witnessed. "A pleasant thing to think about—" He did not envy Kendrick his thoughts.

The mayor of Reuton had pushed aside the cards and lighted a huge cigar.

"Well, Doc," he remarked jocosely, "how's trade? Sold any new schemes for renovating the world to the up-state rubes? I should think this would be sort of an off-season for the reform business. Peace on earth, good will toward men—that ain't exactly a good advertisement for the reformers, is it?"

"It's an excellent one," replied Professor Bolton. "The first essential of good will toward men is not to rob and debauch them."

"Oh, well, Doc, don't let's argue the matter," replied Cargan easily. "I ain't in the humor for it, anyhow. You got your beliefs, and I got my beliefs. And that ain't no reason why we should not smoke a couple of good cigars together. Have one?"

"Thanks. I—" reluctantly the old man took a gay-banded Havana from the mayor's huge fist. "You're very kind."

"I suppose it's sort of a blow to you," the mayor went on, "that your plans up there on the mountain went all to smash. It ought to teach you a lesson, Doc. There ain't nothing to the reform gag."

The train slowed down at a small yellow station. Mr. Magee peered out the window. "Hooperstown," he read, "Reuton—10 miles." He saw Mr. Max get up and leave the car.

"Not a thing to it, Doc," Cargan repeated, "Your bunch has tried to get me before. You've shouted from the housetops that you had the goods on me. What's always happened?"

"Your own creatures have acquitted you," replied the professor, from a cloud of Cargan cigar smoke.

"Fair-minded men decided that I hadn't done wrong. I tell you, Doc, there's dishonest graft, and I'm against that always. And there's honest graft—the rightful perquisites of a high office. That's the trouble with you church politicians. You can't see the difference between the two."

"I'm not a church politician," protested the professor. "I'm bitterly opposed to the lily-white crowd who continually rant against the thing they don't understand. I'm practical, as practical as you, and when—"

Noiselessly Mr. Max slid up to the group, and stood silent, his eyes wide, his yellow face pitiful, the fear of a dog about to be whipped in his every feature.

"Jim," he cried, "Jim! You got to get me out of this. You got to stand by me."

"Why, what's the matter, Lou?" asked the mayor in surprise.

"Matter enough," whined Max. "Do you know what's happened? Well, I'll tell—"

Mr. Max was thrust aside, and replaced by a train newsboy. Mr. Magee felt that he should always remember that boy, his straw colored hair, his freckled beaming face, his lips with their fresh perpetual smile.

"All the morning papers, gents," proclaimed the boy. "Get the *Reuton Star*. All about the bribery."

He held up the paper. It's huge black head-lines looked dull and old and soggy. But the story they told was new and live and startling.

"The Mayor Trapped," shrilled the head-lines. "Attempt to Pass Big Bribe at Baldpate Inn Foiled by Star Reporter. Hayden of the Suburban Commits Suicide to Avoid Disgrace."

"Give me a paper, boy," said the mayor. "Yes—a *Star*." His voice was even, his face unmoved. He took the sheet and studied it, with an easy smile. Clinging in fear to his side, Max read, too. At length Mr. Cargan spoke, looking up at Magee.

"So," he remarked. "So—reporters, eh? You and your lady friend? Reporters for this lying sheet—the *Star*?"

Mr. Magee smiled up from his own copy of the paper.

"Not I," he answered. "But my lady friend—yes. It seems she was just that. A *Star* reporter you can call her, and tell no lie, Mr. Mayor."

CHAPTER XXI

THE MAYOR IS WELCOMED HOME

It was a good story—the story which the mayor, Max, the professor and Magee read with varying emotions there in the smoking-car. The girl had served her employers well, and Mr. Magee, as he read, felt a thrill of pride in her. Evidently the employers had felt that same thrill. For in the captions under the pictures, in the head-lines, and in a first-page editorial, none of which the girl had written, the *Star* spoke admiringly of its woman reporter who had done a man's work—who had gone to Baldpate Inn and had brought back a gigantic bribe fund "alone and unaided".

"Indeed?" smiled Mr. Magee to himself.

In the editorial on that first page the triumphant cry of the *Star* arose to shatter its fellows in the heavens. At last, said the editor, the long campaign which his paper alone of all the Reuton papers had waged against a corrupt city administration was brought to a successful close. The victory was won. How had this been accomplished? Into the *Star* office had come rumors, a few days back, of the proposed payment of a big bribe at the inn on Baldpate Mountain. The paper had decided that one of its representatives must be on the ground. It had debated long whom to send. Miss Evelyn Rhodes, its well-known special writer, had got the tip in question; she had pleaded to go to the inn. The editor, considering her sex, had sternly refused. Then gradually he had been brought to see the wisdom of sending a girl rather than a man. The sex of the former would put the guilty parties under surveillance off guard. So Miss Rhodes was despatched to the inn. Here was her story. It convicted Cargan beyond a doubt. The very money offered as a bribe was now in the hands of the *Star* editor, and would be turned over to Prosecutor Drayton at his request. All this under the disquieting title "Prison Stripes for the Mayor".

The girl's story told how, with one companion, she had gone to Upper Asquewan Falls. There was no mention of the station waiting-room, nor of the tears shed therein on a certain evening, Mr. Magee noted. She had reached the inn on the morning of the day when the combination was to be phoned. Bland was already there, shortly after came the mayor and Max.

"You got to get me out of this," Magee heard Max pleading over Cargan's shoulder.

"Keep still!" replied the mayor roughly. He was reading his copy of the *Star* with keen interest now.

"I've done your dirty work for years," whined Max. "Who puts on the rubber shoes and sneaks up dark alleys hunting votes among the garbage, while you do the Old Glory stunt on Main Street? I do. You got to get me out of this. It may mean jail. I couldn't stand that. I'd die."

A horrible parody of a man's real fear was in his face. The mayor shook himself as though he would be rid forever of the coward hanging on his arm.

"Hush up, can't you?" he said. "I'll see you through."

"You got to," Lou Max wailed.

Miss Rhodes' story went on to tell how Hayden refused to phone the combination; how the mayor and Max dynamited the safe and secured the precious package, only to lose it in another moment to a still different contingent at the inn; how Hayden had come, of his suicide when he found that his actions were in danger of exposure—"a bitter smile for Kendrick in that" reflected Magee—and how finally, through a strange series of accidents, the money came into the hands of the writer for the *Star*. These accidents were not given in detail.

"An amusing feature of the whole affair," said Miss Evelyn Rhodes, "was the presence at the inn of Mr. William Hallowell Magee, the New York writer of light fiction, who had come there to escape the distractions of a great city, and to work in the solitude, and who immediately on his arrival became involved in the surprising drama of Baldpate."

"I'm an amusing feature," reflected Magee.

"Mr. Magee," continued Miss Rhodes, "will doubtless be one of the state's chief witnesses when the case against Cargan comes to trial, as will also Professor Thaddeus Bolton, holder of the Crandall Chair of Comparative Literature at Reuton University, and Mr. David Kendrick, formerly of the Suburban, but who retired six years ago to take up his residence abroad. The latter two went to the inn to represent Prosecutor Drayton, and made every effort in their power to secure the package of money from the reporter for the *Star*, not knowing her connection with the affair."

"Well, Mr. Magee?" asked Professor Bolton, laying down the paper which he had been perusing at a distance of about an inch from his nose.

"Once again, Professor," laughed Magee, "reporters have entered your life."

The old man sighed.

"It was very kind of her," he said, "not to mention that I was the person who compared blondes of the peroxide variety with suffragettes. Others will not be so kind. The matter will be resurrected and used against me at the trial, I'm sure. A plucky girl, Mr. Magee—a very plucky girl. How times do change. When I was young, girls of her age would scarcely have thought of venturing forth into the highways on such perilous missions. I congratulate you. You showed unusual perception. You deserve a great reward—the young lady's favor, let us say."

"You got to get me out of this," Max was still telling the mayor.

"For God's sake," cried Cargan, "shut up and let me think." He sat for a moment staring at one place, his face still lacking all emotion, but his eyes a trifle narrower than before. "You haven't got me yet," he cried, standing up. "By the eternal, I'll fight to the last ditch, and I'll win. I'll show Drayton he can't play this game on me. I'll show the *Star*. That dirty sheet has hounded me for years. I'll put it out of business. And I'll send the reformers howling into the alleys, sick of the fuss they started themselves."

"Perhaps," said Professor Bolton. "But only after the fight of your life, Cargan."

"I'm ready for it," cried Cargan. "I ain't down and out yet. But to think—a woman—a little bit of a girl I could have put in my pocket—it's all a big joke. I'll beat them—I'll show them—the game's far from played out—I'll win—and—if—I—don't—"

He crumbled suddenly into his seat, his eyes on that unpleasant line about "Prison Stripes for the Mayor". For an instant it seemed as though his fight was irrevocably lost, and he knew it. Lines of age appeared to creep from out the fat folds of his face, and stand mockingly there. He looked a beaten man.

"If I don't," he stammered pitifully, "well, they sent him to an island at the end. The reformers got Napoleon at the last. I won't be alone in that."

At this unexpected sight of weakness in his hero, Mr. Max set up a renewed babble of fear at his side. The train was in the Reuton suburbs now. At a neat little station it slowed down to a stop, and a florid policeman entered the smoking-car. Cargan looked up.

"Hello, Dan," he said. His voice was lifeless; the old-time ring was gone.

The policeman removed his helmet and shifted it nervously.

"I thought I'd tell you, Mr. Cargan," he said "I thought I'd warn you. You'd better get off here. There's a big crowd in the station at Reuton. They're waiting for you, sir; they've heard you're on this train. This lying newspaper, Mr. Cargan, it's been telling tales—I guess you know about that. There's a big mob. You better get off here, sir, and go down-town on a car."

If the mighty Cargan had looked limp and beaten for a moment he looked that way no more. He stood up, and his head seemed almost to touch the roof of the car. Over that big patrolman he towered; his eyes were cold and hard again; his lips curved in the smile of the master.

"And why," he bellowed, "should I get off here? Tell me that, Dan."

"Well, sir," replied the embarrassed copper, "they're ugly. There's no telling what they might do. It's a bad mob—this newspaper has stirred 'em up."

"Ugly, are they?" sneered Cargan. "Ever seen the bunch I would go out of my way for, Dan?"

"I meant it all right, sir," said Dan. "As a friend to a man who's been a friend to me. No, I never saw you afraid of any bunch yet, but this—"

"This," replied Cargan, "is the same old bunch. The same lily-livered crowd that I've seen in the streets since I laid the first paving stone under 'em myself in '91. Afraid of them? Hell! I'd walk through an ant hill as scared as I would through that mob. Thanks for telling me, Dan, but Jim Cargan won't be in the mollycoddle class for a century or two yet."

"Yes, sir," said the patrolman admiringly. He hurried out of the car, and the mayor turned to find Lou Max pale and fearful by his side.

"What ails you now?" he asked.

"I'm afraid," cried Max. "Did you hear what he said? A mob. I saw a mob once. Never again for me." He tried to smile, to pass it off as a pleasant jest, but he had to wet his lips with his tongue before he could go on. "Come on, Jim. Get off here. Don't be a fool."

The train began to move.

"Get off yourself, you coward," sneered Cargan. "Oh, I know you. It doesn't take much to make your stomach shrink. Get off."

Max eagerly seized his hat and bag.

"I will, if you don't mind," he said. "See you later at Charlie's." And in a flash of tawdry attire, he was gone.

The mayor of Reuton no longer sat limp in his seat. That brief moment of seeming surrender was put behind forever. He walked the aisle of the car, fire in his eyes, battle in his heart.

"So they're waiting for me, eh?" he said aloud. "Waiting for Jim Cargan. Now ain't it nice of them to come and meet their mayor?"

Mr. Magee and the professor went into the day coach for their baggage. Mrs. Norton motioned to the former.

"Well," she said, "you know now, I suppose. And it didn't do you no harm to wait. I sure am glad this to-do is all over, and that child is safe. And I hope you'll remember what I said. It ain't no work for a woman, no how, what with the shooting and the late hours."

"Your words," said Mr. Magee, "are engraven on my heart." He proceeded to gather her baggage with his own, and was thus engaged when Kendrick came up. The shadow of his discovery in the smoking-car an hour before still haunted his sunken eyes, but his lips were half smiling with the new joy of living that had come to him.

"Mr. Magee," he began, "I hardly need mention that the terrible thing which happened—in there—is between you and me—and the man who's dead. No one must know. Least of all, the girl who is to become my wife—it would embitter her whole life—as it has mine."

"Don't say that," Magee pleaded. "You will forget in time, I'm sure. And you may trust me—I had forgotten already." And indeed he had, on the instant when his eyes fell upon the *Reuton Star*.

Miss Thornhill approached, her dark smiling eyes on Magee. Kendrick looked at her proudly, and spoke suddenly, determinedly:

"You're right, I will forget. She shall help me."

"Mr. Magee," said the girl, "I'm so pleased at the splendid end to your impulsive philanthropy. I just knew the adventure couldn't have anything but a happy ending—it was so full of youth and faith and—and charity or its synonym. This mustn't be good-by. You must come and see me—come and see us—all."

"I shall be happy to," answered Magee sincerely. "It will always be a matter of regret to me that I was not able to serve you—also—on Baldpate Mountain. But out of it you come with something more precious than fine gold, and that shall be my consolation."

"Let it be," smiled Myra Thornhill, "as it is surely mine. Good-by."

"And good luck," whispered Magee, as he took Kendrick's hand.

Over his shoulder, as he passed to the platform, he saw them look into each other's eyes, and he felt that the memory of the admiral's game would in time cease to haunt David Kendrick.

A shadow had fallen upon the train—the shadow of the huge Reuton station. In the half-light on the platform Mr. Magee encountered the mayor of Reuton. Above the lessening roar of the train there sounded ahead of them the voices of men in turmoil and riot. Mr. Cargan turned upon Magee a face as placid and dispassionate as that of one who enters an apple orchard in May.

"The boys," he smiled grimly, "welcoming me home."

Then the train came to a stop, and Mr. Magee looked down into a great array of faces, and heard for the first time the low unceasing rumble of an angry mob. Afterward he marveled at that constant guttural roar, how it went on and on, humming like a tune, never stopping, disconnected quite from the occasional shrill or heavy voices that rang out in distinguishable words. The mayor looked coolly down into those upturned faces, he listened a moment to the rumble of a thousand throats, then he took off his derby with satiric politeness.

"Glad to see one and all!" he cried.

And now above the mutterings angry words could be heard, "That's him," "That's two-hundred-thousand-dollar Cargan," "How's the weather on Baldpate?" and other sarcastic flings. Then a fashion of derisive cat-calls came and went. After which, here and there, voices spoke of ropes, of tar and feathers. And still the mayor smiled as one for whom the orchard gate swung open in May.

A squad of policemen, who had entered the car from the rear, forced their way out on to the platform.

"Want us to see you through the crowd, Mr. Cargan?" the lieutenant asked.

New hoots and cries ascended to the station rafters. "Who pays the police?" "We do." "Who owns 'em?" "Cargan." Thus question and answer were bandied back and forth. Again a voice demanded in strident tones the ignominious tar and feathers.

Jim Cargan had not risen from the slums to be master of his town without a keen sense of the theatric. He ordered the police back into the car. "And stay there," he demanded. The lieutenant demurred. One look from the mayor sent him scurrying. Mr. Cargan took from his pocket a big cigar, and calmly lighted it.

"Some of them guys out there," he remarked to Magee, "belong to the Sunday-school crowd. Pretty actions for them—pillars of the church howling like beasts."

And still, like that of beasts, the mutter of the mob went on, now in an undertone, now louder, and still that voice that first had plead for tar and feathers plead still—for feathers and tar. And here a group preferred the rope.

And toward them, with the bland smile of a child on his great face, his cigar tilted at one angle, his derby at another, the mayor of Reuton walked unflinchingly.

The roar became mad, defiant. But Cargan stepped forward boldly. Now he reached the leaders of the mob. He pushed his way in among them, smiling but determined. They closed in on him. A little man got firmly in his path. He took the little man by the shoulders and stood him aside with some friendly word. And now he was past ten rows or more of them on his way through, and the crowd began to scurry away. They scampered like ants, clawing at one another's backs to make a path.

And so finally, between two rows of them, the mayor of Reuton went his way triumphantly. Somewhere, on the edge of the crowd, an admiring voice spoke. "Hello, Jim!" The mayor waved his hand. The rumble of their voices ceased at last. Jim Cargan was still master of the city.

"Say what you will," remarked Mr. Magee to the professor as they stood together on the platform of the car, "there goes a man."

He did not wait to hear the professor's answer. For he saw the girl of the Upper Asquewan station, standing on a baggage truck far to the left of the mob, wave to him over their heads. Eagerly he fought his way to her side. It was a hard fight, the crowd would not part for him as it had parted for the man who owned the city.

CHAPTER XXII

THE USUAL THING

"**H**ello, Mr. Hold-up Man!" The girl seized Mr. Magee's proffered hand and leaped down from the truck to his side.

"Bless the gods of the mountain," said Magee; "they have given me back my accomplice, safe and sound."

"They were black lonesome gods," she replied, "and they kept whispering fearful things in my ear I couldn't understand. I'm glad they didn't keep me."

"So am I." The crowd surged about them; many in it smiled and spoke admiringly to the girl. "It's great to be acquainted with the heroine of the hour," Mr. Magee continued. "I congratulate you. You have overthrown an empire of graft, it seems."

"Alone and unaided," she quoted, smiling mockingly up into his face.

"Absolutely alone and entirely unaided," said Billy Magee. "I'll swear to that in court."

Mrs. Norton panted up to them.

"Hello, dearie!" she cried. "Thank heaven you're safe. Have you been up to the house? How's Sadie getting along? I just know everything is topsyturvy."

"Not at all," replied Miss Rhodes. "Breakfast passed off like clockwork at seven, and even Mr. Golden had no complaints to offer. Dear, I must thank you for all you've done for me. It was splendid—"

"Not now," objected Mrs. Norton. "I got to get up to the house now. What with Christmas only two days away, and a lot of shopping to be done, I can't linger in this drafty station for thanks. I want you to bring Mr. Magee right up to the house for lunch. I'll have a meal ready that'll show him what suffering must have been going on inside me while I sat still watching that hermit man burlesquing the cook business."

"Delighted," said Magee. "I'll find you a cab." He led the way to a row of such vehicles, Mrs. Norton and the girl following.

"Seems like you're always putting me in a cab," remarked the older woman as she climbed inside. "I don't know what Mary and me would have done if it hadn't been for you. You're a mighty handy person to have around, Mr. Magee. Ain't he, dearie?" She winked openly at Magee.

"And a delightful one," agreed the girl, in a matter-of-fact tone.

Mrs. Norton was driven away up the snowy street. As Mr. Magee and the girl turned, they beheld the Hermit of Baldpate staring with undisguised exultation at the tall buildings of Reuton.

"Why, it's Mr. Peters!" the girl cried.

"Yes," replied Magee. "His prediction has come true. We and our excitement proved too much for him. He's going back to Brooklyn and to her."

"I'm so glad," she cried. She stretched out her hand to the hermit. He took it, somewhat embarrassed.

"Glad to see you," he said. "You certainly appear to have stirred things up, miss. But women are good at that. I've always said—"

"Mr. Magee tells me you're going back, after all?" she broke in.

"Yes," returned Peters. "I knew it. I told you so. It was all right in the summer, when the bands played, and the warm wind was hermiting on the mountain, too. But in the fall, it's always been hard, and I've heard the white lights calling, calling—why, I've even heard her—heard Ellen. This fall you came, and there was something doing on Baldpate—and I knew that when you went, I'd just naturally have to go, too. So—I'm going."

"Splendid," commented the girl.

"It'll be somewhat delicate," continued the hermit, "bursting in on Ellen after all these years. As I told Mr. Magee, I wish I had an inaugural address, or something like that."

"I have it," responded Evelyn Rhodes. "I'll write a story about you for to-morrow morning's paper. All about how the Christmas spirit has overcome the Hermit of Baldpate, and how he's going back to his wife, with his heart filled with love for her—it is filled, isn't it?"

"Well, yes," agreed Mr. Peters. "I reckon you might call it that."

"And then you can send her a copy of the paper, and follow it up in person."

"A good idea," commented Billy Magee.

"At first glance, yes," studied Peters. "But, on the other hand, it would be the death knell of my post-card business, and I'm calculating to go back to Baldpate next summer and take it up again. No, I'm afraid I can't let it be generally known that I've quit living in a shack on the mountain for love of somebody or other."

"Once more," smiled Magee, "big business muzzles the press."

"Not that I ain't obliged to you for the offer," added the hermit.

"Of course," said the girl, "I understand. And I wish you the best of luck—along with a merry Christmas."

"The same to you," replied the hermit heartily.

"Miss—er—Miss Rhodes and I will see you again," predicted Mr. Magee, "next summer at Baldpate Inn."

The hermit looked at the girl, who turned her face away.

"I hope it'll turn out that way, I'm sure," he said. "I'll let you have a reduction on all post-cards, just for old times' sake. Now I must find out about the New York trains."

He melted into the crowd, an odd figure still, his garb in a fashion long forgotten, his clumsily hacked hair brushing the collar of his ancient coat. Magee and the girl found the check room, and after he had been relieved of the burden of his baggage, set out up the main street of Reuton. It was a typical up-state town, deep in the throes of the holiday season. The windows of the stores were green with holly; the faces of the passers-by reflected the excitements of Christmas and of the upheaval in civic politics which were upon them almost together.

"Tell me," said the girl, "are you glad—at the way it has turned out? Are you glad I was no lady Captain Kidd?"

"It has all turned out—or is about to turn out—beautifully," Mr. Magee answered. "You may remember that on the veranda of Baldpate Inn I spoke of one summer hotel flirtation that was going to prove more than that. Let me—"

Her laugh interrupted.

"You don't even know my name."

"What's the matter with Evelyn Rhodes?" suggested Magee.

"Nothing. It's a perfectly good name. But it isn't mine. I just write under it."

"I prefer Mary, anyhow," smiled Billy Magee. "She called you that. It's Mary."

"Mary what?"

"You have no idea," said he, "how immaterial that is."

They came upon a throng blocking the sidewalk in front of a tall building of stone. The eyes of the throng were on bulletins; it muttered much as they had muttered who gathered in the station.

"The office of the *Star*," explained the girl. "The crowd is looking for new excitement. Do you know, for two whole hours this morning we had on exhibition in the window a certain package—a package of money!"

"I think," smiled Magee, "I've seen it somewhere."

"I think you have. Drayton came and took it from us as soon as he heard. But it was the very best proof we could have offered the people. They like to see for themselves. It's a passion with them. We've done for Cargan forever."

"Cargan says he will fight."

"Of course he will," she replied. "But this will prove Napoleon's Waterloo. Whether or not he is sent to prison—and perhaps he can escape that, he's very clever—his power in Reuton is broken. He can't possibly win at the next election—it comes very soon. I'm so glad. For years our editor has been fighting corruption, in the face of terrible odds and temptations. I'm so glad it's over now—and the *Star* has won."

"Through you," said Magee softly.

"With—some one—to help," she smiled. "I must go up-stairs now and find out what new task is set for me."

Mr. Magee postponed the protest on the tip of his tongue, and, climbing the gloomy stairs that newspapers always affect, they came into the city room of the *Star*. Though the paper had been long on the street, the excitement of the greatest coup of years still lingered in the place. Magee saw the deferential smiles that greeted the girl, and watched her as she made her way to the city editor's desk. In a moment she was back at his side.

"I've got my assignment," she smiled ruefully. They descended to the street. "It's wonderful," she went on, "how curt a city editor can be with any one who pulls off a good story. The job I've got now reminds me of the experience of an old New York reporter who used to work on the *Star*."

With difficulty they threaded their way through the crowd, and moved along beside the green-decked windows.

"He was the first man sent out by his paper on Park Row on the Spanish War assignment," she went on, "and he behaved rather brilliantly, I believe. Well, he came back after the fight was over, all puffed up and important, and they told him the city editor wanted him. 'They're going to send me to the Philippines,' he told me he thought as he went into the presence. When the city editor ordered him to rush down to a two-alarm fire in Houston Street he nearly collapsed. I know how he felt. I feel that way now."

"What was it—a one-alarm fire?" asked Magee.

"No," she replied, "a sweet little story about the Christmas toys. I've done it to death every Christmas for—three years. Oh, well, I can do it again. But it'll have to wait until after Mrs. Norton's lunch."

She led him into a street where every house was like its neighbor, even to the "Rooms" sign in the windows, and up the steps of one she could have recognized only by counting from the corner. They entered the murky and stereotyped atmosphere of a boarding-house hallway, with its inevitable hat-rack and the uncollected letters of the homeless on a table. Mrs. Norton came breezily forth to meet them.

"Well, Mr. Magee," she said, "I certainly am glad you've came. I'm busy on that lunch now. Dearie, show him into the parlor to wait."

Mr. Magee was shown in. That rooming-house parlor seemed to moan dismally as it received him. He strolled about and gazed at the objects of art which had at various times accrued to Mrs. Norton's personality: a steel engraving called *Too Late*, which depicted an angry father arriving at a church door to find his eloping daughter in the arms of stalwart youth, with the clergy looking on approvingly; another of Mr. John Drew assuming a commanding posture as Petruchio in *The Taming of the Shrew*; some ennuied flabby angels riding on the clouds; a child of unhealthy pink clasping lovingly an inflammable dog; on the mantel a miniature ship, under glass, and some lady statuettes whose toilettes slipped down—down.

And, on an easel, the sad portrait of a gentleman, undoubtedly the late lamented Norton. His uninteresting nose appeared to turn up at the constant odor of cookery in which it dwelt; his hair was plastered down over his forehead in a gorgeous abandoned curve such as some of the least sophisticated of Mr. John T. McCutcheon's gentlemen affect.

Mr. Magee stared round the room and smiled. Was the romance of reality never to resemble the romance of his dreams? Where were the dim lights, where the distant waltz, where the magic of moonlight amid which he was some day to have told a beautiful girl of his love? Hardly in Mrs. Norton's parlor.

She came and stood in the doorway. Hatless, coatless, smiling, she flooded the place with her beauty. Mr. Magee looked at the flabby angels on the wall, expecting them to hide their faces in shame. But no, they still rode brazenly their unstable clouds.

"Come in," he cried. "Don't leave me alone here again, please. And tell me—is this the gentleman who took the contract for making Mrs. Norton happy?"

"I—I can't come in," she said, blushing. She seemed to wish to avoid him. "Yes, that is Mr. Norton." She came nearer the easel, and smiled at the late lamented's tonsorial crown. "I must leave you—just a moment—"

Billy Magee's heart beat wildly. His breath came fast. He seized her by the hand.

"You're never going to leave me again," he cried. "Don't you know that? I thought you knew. You're mine. I love you. I love you. It's all I can say, my dearest. Look at me—look at me, please."

"It has happened so quickly," she murmured. "Things can't be true when they—happen so quickly."

"A woman's logic," said Mr. Magee. "It has happened. My beautiful girl. Look at me."

And then—she looked. Trembling, flushed, half frightened, half exultant, she lifted her eyes to his.

"My little girl!" he cried down at her.

A moment longer she held off, and then limply she surrendered. And Billy Magee held her close in his arms.

"Take care of me," she whispered. "I—I love you so." Her arm went timidly about his shoulders. "Do you want to know my name? It's Mary—"

Mary what? The answer was seemingly of no importance, for Mr. Magee's lips were on hers, crushing the word at its birth.

So they stood, amid Mrs. Norton's gloomy objects of art. And presently she asked:

"How about the book, dear?"

But Mr. Magee had forgot.

"What book?" he asked.

"The novel you went to Baldpate to write Don't you remember, dearest—no melodrama, no wild chase, no—love?"

"Why—" Mr. Magee paused for a moment in the joy of his discovery. Then he came back to the greater joy in his arms.

"Why, darling," he explained gently, "this is it."

THE END

BEHIND THE SCENES BATTLES FOUGHT BY THE BRAVE.

PULP AVENGERS

> "I want to taste and glory in each day, and never be afraid to experience pain."
> **Sylvia Plath**

SUDOKU

(MEDIUM DIFFICULTY; ANSWERS IN BACK OF BOOK)

8	9	2			3		1	4
				6	8		7	
4	5			8				1
		8				2		
1		3	7			5		
	7	1			6		5	
5		9	2				8	
6					7			9

quick

2 out of 3 with someone near.

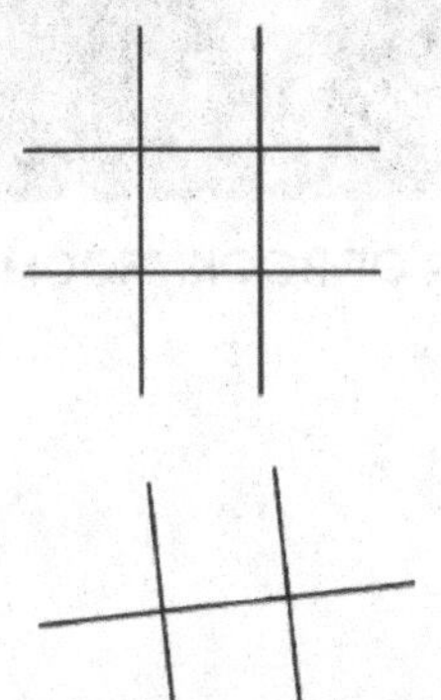

Are you a Bibliotaph?

A Bibliotaph is someone who hoards, hides, or even locks away books.

ARTIST UNKNOWN: FROM COVER OF BOOK, "ROOM AND DAME"

THE DAY TIME STOPPED MOVING

By BRADNER BUCKNER

Dave Miller pushed with all his strength, but the girl was as unmovable as Gibraltar.

All Dave Miller wanted to do was commit suicide in peace. He tried, but the things that happened after he'd pulled the trigger were all wrong. Like everyone standing around like statues. No St. Peter, no pearly gate, no pitchforks or halos. He might just as well have saved the bullet!

DAVE MILLER would never have done it, had he been in his right mind. The Millers were not a melancholy stock, hardly the sort of people you expect to read about in the morning paper who have taken their lives the night before. But Dave Miller was drunk—abominably, roaringly so—and the barrel of the big revolver, as he stood against the sink, made a ring of coldness against his right temple.

CHAPTER I

Dawn was beginning to stain the frosty kitchen windows. In the faint light, the letter lay a gray square against the drain-board tiles. With the melodramatic gesture of the very drunk, Miller had scrawled across the envelope:

"This is why I did it!"

He had found Helen's letter in the envelope when he staggered into their bedroom fifteen minutes ago—at a quarter after five. As had frequently happened during the past year, he'd come home from the store a little late... about twelve hours late, in fact. And this time Helen had done what she had long threatened to do. She had left him.

The letter was brief, containing a world of heartbreak and broken hopes.

"I don't mind having to scrimp, Dave. No woman minds that if she feels she is really helping her husband over a rough spot. When business went bad a year ago, I told you I was ready to help in any way I could. But you haven't let me. You quit fighting when things got difficult, and put in all your money and energy on liquor and horses and cards. I could stand being married to a drunkard, Dave, but not to a coward..."

So she was trying to show him. But Miller told himself he'd show her instead. Coward, eh? Maybe this would teach her a lesson! Hell of a lot of help she'd been! Nag at him every time he took a drink. Holler bloody murder when he put twenty-five bucks on a horse, with a chance to make five hundred. What man wouldn't do those things?

His drug store was on the skids. Could he be blamed for drinking a little too much, if alcohol dissolved the morbid vapors of his mind?

Miller stiffened angrily, and tightened his finger on the trigger. But he had one moment of frank insight just before the hammer dropped and brought the world tumbling about his ears. It brought with it a realization that the whole thing was his fault. Helen was right—he was a coward. There was a poignant ache in his heart. She'd been as loyal as they came, he knew that.

He could have spent his nights thinking up new business tricks, instead of swilling whiskey. Could have gone out of his way to be pleasant to customers, not snap at them when he had a terrific hangover. And even Miller knew nobody ever made any money on the horses—at least, not when he needed it. But horses and whiskey and business had become tragically confused in his mind; so here he was, full of liquor and madness, with a gun to his head.

Then again anger swept his mind clean of reason, and he threw his chin up and gripped the gun tight.

"Run out on me, will she!" he muttered thickly. "Well—this'll show her!"

In the next moment the hammer fell... and Dave Miller had "shown her."

Miller opened his eyes with a start. As plain as black on white, he'd heard a bell ring—the most familiar sound in the world, too. It was the unmistakable tinkle of his cash register.

"Now, how in hell—" The thought began in his mind; and then he saw where he was.

The cash register was right in front of him! It was open, and on the marble slab lay a customer's five-spot. Miller's glance strayed up and around him.

He was behind the drug counter, all right. There were a man and a girl sipping cokes at the fountain, to his right; the magazine racks by the open door; the tobacco counter across from the fountain. And right before him was a customer.

Good Lord! he thought. Was all this a—a dream?

Sweat oozed out on his clammy forehead. That stuff of Herman's that he had drunk during the game—it had had a rank taste, but he wouldn't have thought anything short of marihuana could produce such hallucinations as he had just had. Wild conjectures came boiling up from the bottom of Miller's being.

How did he get behind the counter? Who was the woman he was waiting on? What—

The woman's curious stare was what jarred him completely into the present. Get rid of her! was his one thought. Then sit down behind the scenes and try to figure it all out.

His hand poised over the cash drawer. Then he remembered he didn't know how much he was to take out of the five. Avoiding the woman's glance, he muttered:

"Let's see, now, that was—uh—how much did I say?"

The woman made no answer. Miller cleared his throat, said uncertainly:

"I beg your pardon, ma'am—did I say—seventy-five cents?"

It was just a feeler, but the woman didn't even answer to that. And it was right then that Dave Miller noticed the deep silence that brooded in the store.

Slowly his head came up and he looked straight into the woman's eyes. She returned him a cool, half-smiling glance. But her eyes neither blinked nor moved. Her features were frozen. Lips parted, teeth showing a little, the tip of her tongue was between her even white teeth as though she had started to say "this" and stopped with the syllable unspoken.

Muscles began to rise behind Miller's ears. He could feel his hair stiffen like filings drawn to a magnet. His glance struggled to the soda fountain. What he saw there shook him to the core of his being.

The girl who was drinking a coke had the glass to her lips, but apparently she wasn't sipping the liquid. Her boy friend's glass was on the counter. He had drawn on a cigarette and exhaled the gray smoke. That smoke hung in the air like a large, elongated balloon with the small end disappearing between his lips. While Miller stared, the smoke did not stir in the slightest.

There was something unholy, something supernatural, about this scene!

With apprehension rippling down his spine, Dave Miller reached across the cash register and touched the woman on the cheek. The flesh was warm, but as hard as flint. Tentatively, the young druggist pushed harder; finally, shoved with all his might. For all the result, the woman might have been a two-ton bronze statue. She neither budged nor changed expression.

Panic seized Miller. His voice hit a high hysterical tenor as he called to his soda-jerker.

"Pete! *Pete!*" he shouted. "What in God's name is wrong here!"

The blond youngster, with a towel wadded in a glass, did not stir. Miller rushed from the back of the store, seized the boy by the shoulders, tried to shake him. But Pete was rooted to the spot.

Miller knew, now, that what was wrong was something greater than a hallucination or a hangover. He was in some kind of trap. His first thought was to rush home and see if Helen was there. There was a great sense of relief when he thought of her. Helen, with her grave blue eyes and understanding manner, would listen to him and know what was the matter.

HE LEFT THE HAUNTED DRUG STORE AT A RUN, DARTED AROUND THE CORNER and up the street to his car. But, though he had not locked the car, the door resisted his twisting grasp. Shaking, pounding, swearing, Miller wrestled with each of the doors.

Abruptly he stiffened, as a horrible thought leaped into his being. His gaze left the car and wandered up the street. Past the intersection, past the one beyond that, on up the thoroughfare until the gray haze of the city dimmed everything. And as far as Dave Miller could see, there was no trace of motion.

Cars were poised in the street, some passing other machines, some turning corners. A street car stood at a safety zone; a man who had leaped from the bottom step hung in space a foot above the pavement. Pedestrians paused with one foot up. A bird hovered above a telephone pole, its wings glued to the blue vault of the sky.

With a choked sound, Miller began to run. He did not slacken his pace for fifteen minutes, until around him were the familiar, reassuring trees and shrub-bordered houses of his own street. But yet how strange to him!

The season was autumn, and the air filled with brown and golden leaves that tossed on a frozen wind. Miller ran by two boys lying on a lawn, petrified into a modern counterpart of the sculptor's "The Wrestlers." The sweetish tang of burning leaves brought a thrill of terror to him; for, looking down an alley from whence the smoke drifted, he saw a man tending a fire whose leaping flames were red tongues that did not move.

Sobbing with relief, the young druggist darted up his own walk. He tried the front door, found it locked, and jammed a thumb against the doorbell. But of course the little metal button was as immovable as a mountain. So in the end, after convincing himself that the key could not be inserted into the lock, he sprang toward the back.

The screen door was not latched, but it might as well have been the steel door of a bank vault. Miller began to pound on it, shouting:

"Helen! Helen, are you in there? My God, dear, there's something wrong! You've got to—"

The silence that flowed in again when his voice choked off was the dead stillness of the tomb. He could hear his voice rustling through the empty rooms, and at last it came back to him like a taunt: *"Helen! Helen!"*

CHAPTER II

Time Stands Still

For Dave Miller, the world was now a planet of death on which he alone lived and moved and spoke. Staggered, utterly beaten, he made no attempt to break into his home. But he did stumble around to the kitchen window and try to peer in, anxious to see if there was a body on the floor. The room was in semi-darkness, however, and his straining eyes made out nothing.

He returned to the front of the house, shambling like a somnambulist. Seated on the porch steps, head in hands, he slipped into a hell of regrets. He knew now that his suicide had been no hallucination. He was dead, all right; and this must be hell or purgatory.

Bitterly he cursed his drinking, that had led him to such a mad thing as suicide. Suicide! He—Dave Miller—a coward who had taken his own life! Miller's whole being crawled with revulsion. If he just had the last year to live over again, he thought fervently.

And yet, through it all, some inner strain kept trying to tell him he was not dead. This was his own world, all right, and essentially unchanged. What had happened to it was beyond the pale of mere guesswork. But this one thing began to be clear: This was a world in which change or motion of any kind was a foreigner.

FIRE WOULD NOT BURN AND SMOKE DID NOT RISE. DOORS WOULD NOT OPEN, liquids were solid. Miller's stubbing toe could not move a pebble, and a blade of grass easily supported his weight without bending. In other words, Miller began to understand, change had been stopped as surely as if a master hand had put a finger on the world's balance wheel.

Miller's ramblings were terminated by the consciousness that he had an acute headache. His mouth tasted, as Herman used to say after a big night, as if an army had camped in it. Coffee and a bromo were what he needed.

But it was a great awakening to him when he found a restaurant and learned that he could neither drink the coffee nor get the lid off the bromo bottle. Fragrant coffee-steam hung over the glass percolator, but even this steam was as a brick wall to his probing touch. Miller started gloomily to thread his way through the waiters in back of the counter again.

Moments later he stood in the street and there were tears swimming in his eyes.

"Helen!" His voice was a pleading whisper. "Helen, honey, where are you?"

There was no answer but the pitiful palpitation of utter silence. And then, there was movement at Dave Miller's right!

Something shot from between the parked cars and crashed against him; something brown and hairy and soft. It knocked him down. Before he could get his breath, a red, wet tongue was licking his face and hands, and he was looking up into the face of a police dog!

Frantic with joy at seeing another in this city of death, the dog would scarcely let Miller rise. It stood up to plant big paws on his shoulders and try to lick his face. Miller laughed out loud, a laugh with a throaty catch in it.

"Where'd you come from, boy?" he asked. "Won't they talk to you, either? What's your name, boy?"

There was a heavy, brass-studded collar about the animal's neck, and Dave Miller read on its little nameplate: "Major."

"Well, Major, at least we've got company now," was Miller's sigh of relief.

For a long time he was too busy with the dog to bother about the sobbing noises. Apparently the dog failed to hear them, for he gave no sign. Miller scratched him behind the ear.

"What shall we do now, Major? Walk? Maybe your nose can smell out another friend for us."

They had gone hardly two blocks when it came to him that there was a more useful way of spending their time. The library! Half convinced that the whole trouble stemmed from his suicide shot in the head—which was conspicuously absent now—he decided that a perusal of the surgery books in the public library might yield something he could use.

THAT WAY THEY BENT THEIR STEPS, AND WERE SOON MOUNTING THE BROAD cement stairs of the building. As they went beneath the brass turnstile, the librarian caught Miller's attention with a smiling glance. He smiled back.

"I'm trying to find something on brain surgery," he explained. "I—"

With a shock, then, he realized he had been talking to himself.

In the next instant, Dave Miller whirled. A voice from the bookcases chuckled:

"If you find anything, I wish you'd let me know. I'm stumped myself!"

FROM A CORNER OF THE ROOM CAME AN ELDERLY, HALF-BALD MAN WITH TAN-gled gray brows and a rueful smile. A pencil was balanced over his ear, and a note-book was clutched in his hand.

"You, too!" he said. "I had hoped I was the only one—"

Miller went forward hurriedly to grip his hand.

"I'm afraid I'm not so unselfish," he admitted. "I've been hoping for two hours that I'd run into some other poor soul."

"Quite understandable," the stranger murmured sympathetically. "But in my case it is different. You see—I am responsible for this whole tragic business!"

"You!" Dave Miller gulped the word. "I—I thought—"

The man wagged his head, staring at his note pad, which was littered with jumbled calculations. Miller had a chance to study him. He was tall, heavily built, with wide, sturdy shoulders despite his sixty years. Oddly, he wore a gray-green smock. His eyes, narrowed and intent, looked gimlet-sharp beneath those toothbrush brows of his, as he stared at the pad.

"There's the trouble, right there," he muttered. "I provided only three stages of amplification, whereas four would have been barely enough. No wonder the phase didn't carry through!"

"I guess I don't follow you," Miller faltered. "You mean—something you did—"

"I should think it was something I did!" The baldish stranger scratched his head with the tip of his pencil. "I'm John Erickson—you know, the Wanamaker Institute."

Miller said: "Oh!" in an understanding voice. Erickson was head of Wanamaker Institute, first laboratory of them all when it came to exploding atoms and blazing trails into the wildernesses of science.

ERICKSON'S PIERCING EYES WERE SUDDENLY BORING INTO THE YOUNGER MAN.

"You've been sick, haven't you?" he demanded.

"Well—no—not really sick." The druggist colored. "I'll have to admit to being drunk a few hours ago, though."

"Drunk—" Erickson stuck his tongue in his cheek, shook his head, scowled. "No, that would hardly do it. There must have been something else. The impulsor isn't *that* powerful. I can understand about the dog, poor fellow. He must have been run over, and I caught him just at the instant of passing from life to death."

"Oh!" Dave Miller lifted his head, knowing now what Erickson was driving at. "Well, I may as well be frank. I'm—I committed suicide. That's how drunk I was. There hasn't been a suicide in the Miller family in centuries. It took a skinful of liquor to set the precedent."

Erickson nodded wisely. "Perhaps we will find the precedent hasn't really been set! But no matter—" His lifted hand stopped Miller's eager, wondering exclamation. "The point is, young man, we three are in a tough spot, and it's up to us to get out of it. And not only we, but heaven knows how many others the world over!"

"Would you—maybe you can explain to my lay mind what's happened," Miller suggested.

"Of course. Forgive me. You see, Mr.—"

"Miller. Dave Miller."

"Dave it is. I have a feeling we're going to be pretty well acquainted before this is over. You see, Dave, I'm a nut on so-called 'time theories.' I've seen time compared to everything from an entity to a long, pink worm. But I disagree with them all, because they postulate the idea that time is constantly being manufactured. Such reasoning is fantastic!

"Time exists. Not as an ever-growing chain of links, because such a chain would have to have a tail end, if it has a front end; and who can imagine the period when time did not exist? So I think time is like a circular train-track. Unending. We who live and die merely travel around on it. The future exists simultaneously with the past, for one instant when they meet."

MILLER'S BRAIN WAS HUMMING. ERICKSON SHOT THE WORDS AT HIM STACCA-to-fashion, as if they were things known from Great Primer days. The young druggist scratched his head.

"You've got me licked," he admitted. "I'm a stranger here, myself."

"Naturally you can't be expected to understand things I've been all my life puzzling about. Simplest way I can explain it is that we are on a train following this immense circular railway.

"When the train reaches the point where it started, it is about to plunge into the past; but this is impossible, because the point where it started is simply the caboose of the train! And that point is always ahead—and behind—the time-train.

"Now, my idea was that with the proper stimulus a man could be thrust across the diameter of this circular railway to a point in his past. Because of the nature of time, he could neither go ahead of the train to meet the future nor could he stand still and let the caboose catch up with him. But— he could detour across the circle and land farther back on the train! And that, my dear Dave, is what you and I and Major have done—almost."

"Almost?" Miller said hoarsely.

Erickson pursed his lips. "We are somewhere partway across the space between present and past. We are living in an instant that can move neither forward nor back. You and I, Dave, and Major—and the Lord knows how many others the world over—have been thrust by my time impulsor onto a timeless beach of eternity. We have been caught in time's backwash. Castaways, you might say."

An objection clamored for attention in Miller's mind.

"But if this is so, where are the rest of them? Where is my wife?"

"They are right here," Erickson explained. "No doubt you could see your wife if you could find her. But we see them as statues, because, for us, time no longer exists. But there was something I did not count on. I did not know that it would be possible to live in one small instant of time, as we are doing. And I did not know that only those who are hovering between life and death can deviate from the normal process of time!"

"You mean—we're dead!" Miller's voice was a bitter monotone.

"Obviously not. We're talking and moving, aren't we? But—we are on the fence. When I gave my impulsor the jolt of high power, it went wrong and I think something must have happened to me. At the same instant, you had shot yourself."

"Perhaps, Dave, you are dying. The only way for us to find out is to try to get the machine working and topple ourselves one way or the other. If we fall back, we will all live. If we fall into the present—we may die."

"Either way, it's better than this!" Miller said fervently.

"I came to the library here, hoping to find out the things I must know. My own books are locked in my study. And these—they might be cemented in their places, for all their use to me. I suppose we might as well go back to the lab."

Miller nodded, murmuring: "Maybe you'll get an idea when you look at the machine again."

"Let's hope so," said Erickson grimly. "God knows I've failed so far!"

CHAPTER III

Splendid Sacrifice

It was a solid hour's walk out to West Wilshire, where the laboratory was. The immense bronze and glass doors of Wanamaker Institute were closed, and so barred to the two men. But Erickson led the way down the side.

"We can get in a service door. Then we climb through transoms and ventilators until we get to my lab."

Major frisked along beside them. He was enjoying the action and the companionship. It was less of an adventure to Miller, who knew death might be ahead for the three of them.

Two workmen were moving a heavy cabinet in the side service door. To get in, they climbed up the back of the rear workman, walked across the cabinet, and scaled down the front of the leading man. They went up the stairs to the fifteenth floor. Here they crawled through a transom into the wing marked:

"Experimental. Enter Only By Appointment."

Major was helped through it, then they were crawling along the dark metal tunnel of an air-conditioning ventilator. It was small, and took some wriggling.

In the next room, they were confronted by a stern receptionist on whose desk was a little brass sign, reading:

"Have you an appointment?"

Miller had had his share of experience with receptionists' ways, in his days as a pharmaceutical salesman. He took the greatest pleasure now in lighting his cigarette from a match struck on the girl's nose. Then he blew the smoke in her face and hastened to crawl through the final transom.

John Erickson's laboratory was well lighted by a glass-brick wall and a huge skylight. The sun's rays glinted on the time impulsor.[1] The scientist explained the impulsor in concise terms. When he had finished, Dave Miller knew just as little as before, and the outfit still resembled three transformers in a line, of the type seen on power-poles, connected to a great bronze globe hanging from the ceiling.

"There's the monster that put us in this plight," Erickson grunted. "Too strong to be legal, too weak to do the job right. Take a good look!"

WITH HIS HANDS JAMMED IN HIS POCKETS, HE FROWNED AT THE COMPLEX MA-chinery. Miller stared a few moments; then transferred his interests to other things in the room. He was immediately struck by the resemblance of a transformer in a far corner to the ones linked up with the impulsor.

"What's that?" he asked quickly. "Looks the same as the ones you used over there."

"It is."

"But— Didn't you say all you needed was another stage of power?"

"That's right."

"Maybe I'm crazy!" Miller stared from impulsor to transformer and back again. "Why don't you use it, then?"

"Using what for the connection?" Erickson's eyes gently mocked him.

"Wire, of course!"

The scientist jerked a thumb at a small bale of heavy copper wire.

"Bring it over and we'll try it."

Miller was halfway to it when he brought up short. Then a sheepish grin spread over his features.

"I get it," he chuckled. "That bale of wire might be the Empire State Building, as far as we're concerned. Forgive my stupidity."

Erickson suddenly became serious.

"I'd like to be optimistic, Dave," he muttered, "but in all fairness to you I must tell you I see no way out of this. The machine is, of course, still working, and with that extra stage of power, the uncertainty would be over. But where, in this world of immovable things, will we find a piece of wire twenty-five feet long?"

THERE WAS A WARM, MOIST SENSATION AGAINST MILLER'S HAND, AND WHEN HE looked down Major stared up at him commiseratingly. Miller scratched him behind the ear, and the dog closed his eyes, reassured and happy. The young druggist sighed, wishing there were some giant hand to scratch him behind the ear and smooth *his* troubles over.

"And if we don't get out," he said soberly, "we'll starve, I suppose."

"No, I don't think it will be that quick. I haven't felt any hunger. I don't expect to. After all, our bodies are still living in one instant of time, and a man can't work up a healthy appetite in one second. Of course, this elastic-second business precludes the possibility of disease.

"Our bodies must go on unchanged. The only hope I see is—when we are on the verge of madness, suicide. That means jumping off a bridge, I suppose. Poison, guns, knives—all the usual wherewithal—are denied to us."

Black despair closed down on Dave Miller. He thrust it back, forcing a crooked grin.

"Let's make a bargain," he offered. "When we finish fooling around with this apparatus, we split up. We'll only be at each other's throat if we stick together. I'll be blaming you for my plight, and I don't want to. It's my fault as much as yours. How about it?"

John Erickson gripped his hand. "You're all right, Dave. Let me give you some advice. If ever you do get back to the present... keep away from liquor. Liquor and the Irish never did mix. You'll have that store on its feet again in no time."

"Thanks!" Miller said fervently. "And I think I can promise that nothing less than a whiskey antidote for snake bite will ever make me bend an elbow again!"

FOR THE NEXT COUPLE OF HOURS, DESPONDENCY REIGNED IN THE LABORATO-ry. But it was soon to be deposed again by hope.

Despite all of Erickson's scientific training, it was Dave Miller himself who grasped the down-to-earth idea that started them hoping again. He was walking about the lab, jingling keys in his pocket, when suddenly he stopped short. He jerked the ring of keys into his hand.

"Erickson!" he gasped. "We've been blind. Look at this!"

The scientist looked; but he remained puzzled.

"Well—?" he asked skeptically.

"There's our wire!" Dave Miller exclaimed. "You've got keys; I've got keys. We've got coins, knives, wristwatches. Why can't we lay them all end to end—"

Erickson's features looked as if he had been electrically shocked.

"You've hit it!" he cried. "If we've got enough!"

With one accord, they began emptying their pockets, tearing off wristwatches, searching for pencils. The finds made a little heap in the middle of the floor. Erickson let his long fingers claw through thinning hair.

"God give us enough! We'll only need the one wire. The thing is plugged in already and only the positive pole has to be connected to the globe. Come on!"

Scooping up the assortment of metal articles, they rushed across the room. With his pocket-knife, Dave Miller began breaking up the metal wrist-watch straps, opening the links out so that they could be laid end-to-end for the greatest possible length. They patiently broke the watches to pieces, and of the junk they garnered made a ragged foot and a half of "wire." Their coins stretched the line still further.

They had ten feet covered before the stuff was half used up. Their metal pencils, taken apart, gave them a good two feet. Key chains helped generously. With eighteen feet covered, their progress began to slow down.

Perspiration poured down Miller's face. Desperately, he tore off his lodge ring and cut it in two to pound it flat. From garters and suspenders they won a few inches more. And then—they stopped—feet from their goal.

Miller groaned. He tossed his pocket-knife in his hand.

"We can get a foot out of this," he estimated. "But that still leaves us way short."

Abruptly, Erickson snapped his fingers.

"Shoes!" he gasped. "They're full of nails. Get to work with that knife, Dave. We'll cut out every one of 'em!"

IN TEN MINUTES, THE SHOES WERE REDUCED TO RAGGED PILES OF TATTERED leather. Erickson's deft fingers painstakingly placed the nails, one by one, in the line. The distance left to cover was less than six inches!

He lined up the last few nails. Then both men were sinking back on their heels, as they saw there was a gap of three inches to cover!

"Beaten!" Erickson ground out. "By three inches! Three inches from the present ... and yet it might as well be a million miles!"

Miller's body felt as though it were in a vise. His muscles ached with strain. So taut were his nerves that he leaped as though stung when Major nuzzled a cool nose into his hand again. Automatically, he began to stroke the dog's neck.

"Well, that licks us," he muttered. "There isn't another piece of movable metal in the world."

Major kept whimpering and pushing against him. Annoyed, the druggist shoved him away.

"Go 'way," he muttered. "I don't feel like—"

Suddenly then his eyes widened, as his touch encountered warm metal. He whirled.

"There it is!" he yelled. "The last link. *The nameplate on Major's collar!*"

In a flash, he had torn the little rectangular brass plate from the dog collar. Erickson took it from his grasp. Sweat stood shiny on his skin. He held the bit of metal over the gap between wire and pole.

"This is it!" he smiled brittlely. "We're on our way, Dave. Where, I don't know. To death, or back to life. But—we're going!"

The metal clinked into place. Live, writhing power leaped through the wire, snarling across partial breaks. The transformers began to hum. The humming grew louder. Singing softly, the bronze globe over their heads glowed green. Dave Miller felt a curious lightness. There was a snap in his brain, and Erickson, Major and the laboratory faded from his senses.

Then came an interval when the only sound was the soft sobbing he had been hearing as if in a dream. That, and blackness that enfolded him like soft velvet. Then Miller was opening his eyes, to see the familiar walls of his own kitchen around him!

Someone cried out.

"Dave! Oh, Dave, dear!"

It was Helen's voice, and it was Helen who cradled his head in her lap and bent her face close to his.

"Oh, thank God that you're alive—!"

"Helen!" Miller murmured. "What—are—you—doing here?"

"I couldn't go through with it. I—I just couldn't leave you. I came back and—and I heard the shot and ran in. The doctor should be here. I called him five minutes ago."

"*Five minutes*... How long has it been since I shot myself?"

"Oh, just six or seven minutes. I called the doctor right away."

Miller took a deep breath. Then it *must* have been a dream. All that— to happen in a few minutes— It wasn't possible!

"How—how could I have botched the job?" he muttered. "I wasn't drunk enough to miss myself completely."

Helen looked at the huge revolver lying in the sink.

"Oh, that old forty-five of Grandfather's! It hasn't been loaded since the Civil War. I guess the powder got damp or something. It just sort of sputtered instead of exploding properly. Dave, promise me something! You won't ever do anything like this again, if I promise not to nag you?"

Dave Miller closed his eyes. "There won't be any need to nag, Helen. Some people take a lot of teaching, but I've had my lesson. I've got ideas about the store which I'd been too lazy to try out. You know, I feel more like fighting right now than I have for years! We'll lick 'em, won't we, honey?"

Helen buried her face in the hollow of his shoulder and cried softly. Her words were too muffled to be intelligible. But Dave Miller understood what she meant.

HE HAD THOUGHT THE WHOLE THING A DREAM—JOHN ERICKSON, THE "TIME impulsor" and Major. But that night he read an item in the *Evening Courier* that was to keep him thinking for many days.

POLICE INVESTIGATE DEATH OF SCIENTIST HERE IN LABORATORY

John M. Erickson, director of the Wanamaker Institute, died at his work last night. Erickson was a beloved and valuable figure in the world of science, famous for his recently publicized "time lapse" theory.

Two strange circumstances surrounded his death. One was the presence of a German shepherd dog in the laboratory, its head crushed as if with a sledgehammer. The other was a chain of small metal objects stretching from one corner of the room to the other, as if intended to take the place of wire in a circuit.

Police, however, discount this idea, as there was a roll of wire only a few feet from the body.

THE END

SODUKO ANSWERS

8	9	2	5	7	3	6	1	4
7	4	6	9	2	1	8	3	5
3	1	5	4	6	8	9	7	2
4	5	7	6	8	2	3	9	1
9	6	8	1	3	5	2	4	7
1	2	3	7	4	9	5	6	8
2	7	1	8	9	6	4	5	3
5	3	9	2	1	4	7	8	6
6	8	4	3	5	7	1	2	9

Thanks for Reading...
Catch another new and exciting issue in Winter 2022!

www.ingramcontent.com/pod-product-compliance
Lightning Source LLC
Chambersburg PA
CBHW010842190726
48286CB00012BA/2945